THE STONE OF LIGHT
VOLUME III: PANEB THE ARDENT

The Place of Truth, the exclusive home to the Pharaoh's artisans, is under siege. Inside the ancient Egyptian capital of Pi-Ramses, Amenmessu aspires to the throne, sparking conflict with his ruling family and causing chaos to surround the Place of Truth. Attackers have scaled the village walls; food and drinking water are contaminated; and thievery and treachery run rampant. Only one man is prepared to confront the enemy descending upon the village as well as the unknown traitor lurking within: Paneb the Ardent, whose relentless energy and determination may defend the Place of Truth—and preserve for all time the legendary Stone of Light. . . .

Also by Christian Jacq

The Stone of Light

Volume I: Nefer the Silent

Volume II: The Wise Woman

Ramses

Volume I: The Son of Light

Volume II: The Eternal Temple

Volume III: The Battle of Kadesh

Volume IV: The Lady of Abu Simbel

Volume V: Under the Western Acacia

For orders other than by individual consumers, Pocket Books grants a discount on the purchase of **10 or more** copies of single titles for special markets or premium use. For further details, please write to the Vice President of Special Markets, Pocket Books, 1230 Avenue of the Americas, 9th Floor, New York, NY 10020-1586.

For information on how individual consumers can place orders, please write to Mail Order Department, Simon & Schuster, Inc., 100 Front Street, Riverside, NJ 08075.

THE STONE OF LIGHT

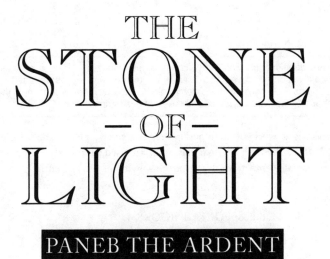

PANEB THE ARDENT

VOLUME III

CHRISTIAN JACQ

POCKET BOOKS

New York   London   Toronto   Sydney   Singapore

This book is a work of fiction. Names, characters, places and incidents are products of the author's imagination or are used fictitiously. Any resemblance to actual events or locales or persons, living or dead, is entirely coincidental.

An *Original* Publication of POCKET BOOKS

POCKET BOOKS, a division of Simon & Schuster, Inc.
1230 Avenue of the Americas, New York, NY 10020

Copyright © 2000 by XO Editions. All Rights Reserved.
English translation copyright © 2000 by Sue Dyson

Published by arrangement with XO S.A.

Originally published in France in 2000 by XO Editions as Paneb l'Ardent

All rights reserved, including the right to reproduce
this book or portions thereof in any form whatsoever.
For information address XO S.A., Tour Maine Montparnasse 33,
avenue du Maine 75755, Paris Cedex 15 BP 143, France

ISBN: 0-7434-0348-7

First Pocket Books trade paperback printing March 2001

10 9 8 7 6 5 4 3 2 1

POCKET and colophon are registered trademarks of
Simon & Schuster, Inc.

Cover design by Rod Hernandez
Front cover illustration by Gary Halsey

Printed in the U.S.A.

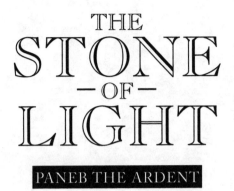

THE STONE OF LIGHT

PANEB THE ARDENT

VOLUME III

The five men had a mission: to break into the temple of the Place of Truth, the secret village on the west bank of Thebes, and steal a priceless treasure. And at last they had made their way through the mountains and succeeded in reaching the forbidden place.

The raiding party's guide smiled, dreaming of the enormous reward he had been promised: no one, not even Sobek, commander of the local guards, could foresee everything; and the risk was all the lower, since the thieves had help from a traitor within the Brotherhood of the Place of Truth, who believed himself safe behind the village's high walls.

▲

The traitor's heart was pounding.

Taking advantage of the unsettled period before the new pharaoh's coronation, he and his coconspirator had decided to try and seize the Stone of Light. This precious treasure was watched over constantly by the craftsmen of the Place of Truth. Like the crew of a ship, the craftsmen were divided into port and starboard crews, and their principal task was to excavate and decorate the pharaohs' tombs in the Valley of the Kings.

In a few hours, the traitor would have left this Brotherhood for good; this Brotherhood in which he had spent long years, learned his trade, and shared so many secrets and exciting moments. He possessed all the qualities required to be crew leader, yet his colleagues had chosen Nefer the Silent instead of him.

Disappointment had been succeeded by resentment and a desire for revenge on this unworthy community. And when destiny had opened up a new avenue, he had not hesitated. By bringing about the Brotherhood's demise, he would at last be able to live in comfort: he would enjoy the benefits of a fine house and a large garden, and have the pleasure of issuing orders to a throng of attentive servants. No more stressful days of toil, during which he must obey the Master; no more unworthy tasks for Pharaoh's benefit. From now on, the traitor was going to enjoy life to the full and would speedily forget his oath and his past.

Fortunately, he had his wife's full support. She was delighted by the prospect of becoming an important, respected lady. For a long time he had kept his plans from her, fearing that she would react unfavorably; but he had been mistaken, for she had proven as determined as he. And she herself had prepared the potion to drug the guard, who was currently in a deep sleep.

This time, success was near—so near that it made the traitor tremble. He had to force himself not to lose his nerve on this peaceful night, which would crown years of patience with success.

He had placed the rope ladder in position. Soon, the men sent by his coconspirator would climb over the wall, and he would lead them to the temple.

▲

A series of raucous cries woke Paneb the Ardent. At thirty-six, the huge dark-eyed man, the adopted son of the Master and the Wise Woman of the Place of Truth, seemed to grow stronger by the day. He slept little and had a horror of being taken unawares when he was asleep.

"What's the matter?" asked his wife, Uabet the Pure, without opening her eyes.

"Go back to sleep. I'll go and see."

Their son, Aapehti, who promised to be as big as his father, was still asleep. But the guilty party was running about in the kitchen where, having devoured some dates, she was attacking the breadbasket.

"I should never have let my son bring you into this house," said Paneb to the fat goose.

She well deserved her name of Bad Girl. She was insolent, aggressive, and apt to steal, and was always hungry. She had a red beak and feet, a yellow neck striped with black, brownish wings, a white belly, and a black tail. She was Aapehti's favorite playmate; she sneaked up on his opponents from behind and attacked them, and was not even afraid of dogs.

"Outside," ordered Paneb, "or I'll roast you!"

In the face of the threat, the goose, protesting loudly, allowed herself to be driven out of the house.

▲

Hidden in a corner by the wall, the traitor saw the first member of the raiding party climb over the wall, using the rope ladder. He decided to wait until they were all over before approaching them.

Suddenly, just as the fifth raider was reaching the ground, one of them cried out in pain. The goose had just pecked him on the legs and was already attacking a fresh victim, who could not help shouting, "We're under attack!"

So quick that she was impossible to catch, the goose kept on pecking them, and she honked more and more loudly.

Rooted to the spot with fear, the traitor remained in his hiding place; his allies tried in vain to catch the bird and shouted to one another, forgetting how important it was to keep silent.

At last, one of them seized the goose by the neck. "I'm going to wring its neck, the filthy beast!"

He was unable to carry out his threat, though, because Paneb knocked him unconscious.

Alerted by Bad Girl's cries, and knowing that she never made a noise without good reason, he had left his house to see what all the noise was about.

While the goose was making herself scarce and the traitor was hurrying back home through the shadows, the four uninjured thieves pounced on the craftsman, confident of dispatching him without difficulty.

Paneb's knee jabbed the first attacker in the belly, his elbow caught the second on the temple, and his forehead struck the third thief on the nose; the fourth managed to hit him on the chest, but Paneb did not even stagger.

Seeing that his allies were out of the game, the fourth man made a dash for the rope ladder. Just as he was seizing it, Paneb hauled him back by his feet, spun him round, and threw him against the wall.

"You're not getting away from me, lad," he said.

The semiconscious thief unsheathed his dagger.

"Drop that weapon," ordered Paneb.

The thief threatened him.

Suddenly, the giant recognized him. "You! You dare attack the Place of Truth!"

With one single, maddened slash of the dagger, the man slit his own throat.

As Bad Girl was still running about the streets, cackling her head off, several villagers had woken up. The first to arrive on the scene, a torch in his hand, was Unesh the Jackal. His curious gaze fixed on the raiders. Three lay unconscious, and another was rolling about in pain.

"They're Libyans," exclaimed Unesh.

"What about the one who's bleeding?"

"No, it can't be!"

Several other craftsmen joined them. One by one, the villagers came out of their houses, and Nefer the Silent, the Master of the Brotherhood, was soon at his adopted son's side.

While Unesh tied up the four Libyans and Bad Girl paraded up and down, as if boasting that she had saved the village, Nefer bent over the corpse of the man with the dagger.

Horrified, he said, "It's one of the guards who are supposed to protect us."

— 2 —

Although seventy years old and a martyr to innumerable ailments, Kenhir was still the scribe of the "Great and Noble Temple of a Million Years to the West of Thebes" (that was the Brotherhood's symbolic name). It was his task to keep the Journal in which, each day, he noted down everything that happened, whether important or trivial. He was also responsible for overseeing deliveries of food, water, and materials, for paying salaries in kind, distributing tools, checking that anyone not at work had a valid reason for his absence, and drawing up the inventory of the Brotherhood's possessions: in other words, ensuring that the Place of Truth was impeccably run and sorting out the thousand and one problems that inevitably arose in a village that housed the married craftsmen and their wives and children, not to mention unmarried people of both sexes.

And the worst possible problem had just arisen: the beer he was drinking was hot and his bed was on fire.

"Wake up, Kenhir!"

The scribe opened his eyes and saw a lean, muscular man of forty-six, with a high domed forehead and gray-green eyes.

"Oh, it's you, Nefer. I forgot to rub my face with cool herbs soaked in a mixture of beer and myrrh, and I had a nightmare. According to the key of dreams, we're going to be victims of thieves, and we'll have to expel someone."

"You're not far wrong. A group of Libyans got into the village with the aid of a guard."

"What are you saying? One of Sobek's men?"

"Yes, I'm afraid so."

Kenhir got to his feet with difficulty, and Nefer supported him.

The scribe's young servant, Niut the Strong, a small, pretty brunette, appeared. She had thought it wise to let the Master wake her employer, whose early-morning ill temper often lasted most of the day.

"Would you like some breakfast?" she asked.

"Warm flat cakes and milk, but be quick," he said.

Kenhir was overweight and rather clumsy, and could only walk with the aid of a stick, though on certain occasions, as if by a miracle, he rediscovered his former mobility. He sat down in a low armchair, beside a sycamore wood table, his old eyes bright with anger.

"How dare they attack the Place of Truth like this! I shall draw up a report for Pharaoh immediately."

"Assuming Seti has been recognized as king," Nefer pointed out. "No one's yet been crowned."

"Those scoundrels chose their moment well. We must summon Commander Sobek."

"I've already done so. He's waiting for us at the main gate."

▲

Sobek was a tall, athletic man with a scar under his left eye, and enormous hands accustomed to wielding a club. An authoritative, straight-talking Nubian, who had spent his entire career in the guards, he permitted no questioning of his orders and was used to taking responsibility himself, not foisting it onto his subordinates.

The great gate of the forbidden village opened a little way. When he saw the Scribe of the Tomb and the Master emerge, he knew he was not going to enjoy the next few minutes. About twenty years ago, one of his men had been murdered, and despite making exhaustive inquiries, Sobek had not succeeded in identifying the killer, although he was convinced it could only be a member of the Brotherhood. Now another of his guards had died in tragic circumstances—but this time, the man had behaved like a criminal.

Kenhir's expression suggested that this was not a good day. "Have you identified the villain who cut his throat?" he asked.

"He was indeed one of my men," replied Sobek. "I engaged him only last year."

"What were his duties?"

"Watching one of the routes through the hills."

"Why, I wonder, did he kill himself?"

"That's simple," replied the Nubian. "When he realized he couldn't escape, he chose death rather than be interrogated by me—and he had good reason."

"Have you questioned the other Libyans?" asked Kenhir.

"The first lost his wits because of the blow he received, the second is dumb, the third has had his tongue cut out, and the fourth doesn't speak a word of Egyptian. I shall have to send them to the central government of the west bank to be identified."

"And the gatekeeper?"

"He was drugged and has only just regained consciousness."

"We know a craftsman is betraying us," Kenhir reminded him irritably, "but we didn't know one of your men was his accomplice. And he was obviously the one who guided the Libyans."

"If you suspect me of having taken any part in this plot," Sobek replied, "don't hesitate to bring a formal charge against me. I shall of course resign immediately."

"You have our trust," cut in Nefer, "and you shall remain in charge of the village's security."

Once before, the Master had taken the Nubian's side. This time, too, Kenhir accepted Nefer's decision, though not in silence.

"How do I know that other guards won't sell out to the enemy?" he grumbled.

"I made a serious mistake," acknowledged Sobek. "That guttersnipe didn't belong to my tribe, so I shouldn't have employed him. I won't make that mistake again, I promise you."

"What are you going to do?"

"I shall have an even closer watch kept over the village, day and night, and until the new pharaoh is crowned I'll suspend all permits to leave the area. It would be as well for none of you to set foot outside the walls of the Place of Truth until the situation is clearer."

▲

The village was in a state of shock.

In order to drive away misfortune, the head sculptor, Userhat the Lion, and his two assistants, Ipuy the Examiner and Renupe the Jovial, were making a small stele depicting seven snakes. Placed near the main gate, within the surrounding wall, the modest monument would help to ward off harmful forces.

But every family was terribly anxious about the village's future. If the new pharaoh did not protect it as his predecessors had done, or if civil war broke out, what would happen to the seventy white houses that made up the village, which their occupants maintained with loving care?

Despite his round, cheery face and his large belly, the painter Pai the Good Bread was so tortured by fear that he had lost his appetite; and his anxious wife had told him to go and see the the Master's wife, Ubekhet, who was Wise Woman, doctor, and spiritual mother to the Brotherhood. Although he was not very proud of himself, Pai felt so depressed that he agreed to do so.

When he knocked on the door of Ubekhet's workshop, there was a volley of barks, then the Wise Woman opened the door, holding a young dog in her arms.

"Ebony's a little overexcited," she explained. "I've just given him some pills made from wormwood to cure his worms."

Already standing tall, with a long muzzle, intelligent hazel eyes, and pendulous ears, Ebony seemed in no danger. His predecessor, also called Ebony, had been mummified and lay in a little tomb, with his favorite cushions, a vase filled with sacred oil, and a succulent meal, which had also been mummified.

Each time he had the good fortune to look upon Ubekhet, Pai was enchanted: at forty, she was still dazzlingly beautiful.

Her finely chiseled features radiated a light that had the power to calm the troubled soul. She had fair hair, blue eyes, slender, supple limbs, and a sweet, melodious voice. She and Nefer had married before being admitted to the Place of Truth, and after long years of training and hard work, the villagers had chosen them as their leaders.

"I don't feel well," confessed Pai sheepishly.

"Have you any specific symptoms?"

"No, I just don't feel well—and I've no appetite. I can't bear this terrible uncertainty. Tomorrow, the village may be destroyed, and we may be scattered, so that our way of life will be no more than a painful memory."

"Lie down on the mat," said Ubekhet.

Ubekhet had been taught by an exceptionally gifted doctor, Neferet, Pharaoh's own doctor, and by the Wise Woman who had preceded her. Day by day, they had passed on more and more knowledge to her, and the previous Wise Woman had bequeathed her the workshop where she prepared remedies for the villagers.

The complexion, bodily odor, and breath were the first useful indicators in making a diagnosis, but above all the pulses must be taken. This was done by laying a hand on the nape of the patient's neck, the crown of his head, his wrists, belly, and legs. This enabled the Wise Woman to hear the voice of the heart, which indicated the condition of the different organs and the channels along which energies flowed.

The longer Ubekhet took, the more anxious Pai became.

"Is it serious?" he asked.

"No, don't worry, but some channels are almost blocked because of your anxiety."

The Wise Woman prescribed a salve made from bull's fat, terebinth resin, wax, juniper berries, and bryony seeds, which Pai was to rub on his chest for four successive days. This would restore the channels to their former flexibility.

The painter stood up. "I feel better already, but my cure won't be complete until the village is out of danger. People say you can read the future, Ubekhet. What do you see for our Brotherhood?"

"I see it following the path of Ma'at and never swerving from the ways of righteousness, for whatever reason. If we do that, no matter what befalls us we have nothing to fear."

3

General Mehy was both governor of the west bank of Thebes and commander in chief of the armed forces of the great city of Upper Egypt. At forty years old, he was thickset with a round face, black hair that lay flat against his head, thick lips, a broad, powerful chest, and pudgy hands and feet. His dark chestnut-colored eyes were full of the arrogance of a self-assured senior official, ambitious and determined, but they also held a spark whose meaning only his wealthy wife, Serketa, understood. A spark that betrayed his ferocious determination to seize the secrets of the Place of Truth, especially the Stone of Light, which would enable him to rule Egypt. To become master of the wealthy Theban region, Mehy had had to kill some inconvenient opponents; since he believed neither in gods nor in demons, he had had no hesitation in basing his career on crime, and he received unconditional support from his wife, sweet Serketa, who derived intense pleasure from killing people.

The irony of fate had decreed that he, the Brotherhood's worst enemy, should be officially appointed by Pharaoh to protect it. He must ensure that the craftsmen had a comfortable existence, so that they could work in the best conditions. So he had been obliged to plot secretly, with the aid of a craftsman who was happy to turn traitor in order to be able to enjoy the possessions he had accumulated outside the village, as payment for services rendered.

But the results had not yet matched up to Mehy's hopes, and his patience had been sorely tried. Fortunately, imminent civil war would make it easy for him to remain in the shadows while dealing death blows to the Brotherhood.

Serketa had just returned from Thebes, leading a veritable procession of servants bearing fabrics, vases, and furniture she had bought in the town. She was wearing an extravagant wig and a flowing pink dress that concealed her opulent curves. Her big pale blue eyes, like those of a little girl, watched Mehy pacing back and forth across the pillared hall of their vast house, which was surrounded by a garden planted with sycamores, acacias, palms, carob, and fig trees.

"You look upset," she commented.

"There's been no news from the Nubian guard we bought."

"Don't be so pessimistic, my sweet love." Serketa put her arms round her husband's neck. He always enjoyed caressing her large breasts roughly, and she enjoyed it, too.

"Shall we drink some palm wine in our bedchamber?" he said.

Feigning ecstasy, as she always did, Serketa thought back over the exciting years with Mehy since he had told her his plans. To win absolute power by using the weapons of learning and new discoveries, to exercise the right of life and death over everyone, to destroy the Place of Truth after stripping it of its treasures: these were the only goals that truly interested Serketa, who was frequently prey to boredom.

If her marvelous husband's commitment had not been genuine, she would have rid herself of him, in the manner of a praying mantis. By becoming his accomplice, and murdering anyone who stood in his way, she had gained a taste for the adventure that united them. And it would be wise for the general not to disappoint her.

She lay down on top of him, as though she wanted to smother him. "Have you heard any news from the capital?"

"Seti will never give up the throne."

"Do you really control Prince Amenmessu?"

"I don't know what he'll do when his father's coronation is announced."

Kept in gilded exile in Thebes on Seti's orders, Amenmessu dreamed of becoming the pharaoh, and Mehy had made sure to encourage him, in the hope of triggering a war that would benefit no one but Mehy himself. But young Amenmessu was not sure which path to take, submission or rebellion.

Gazing into the distance, the general thought back to the first murder he had committed, on the slopes of the Peak of the West. He had killed a guard who caught him spying on members of the Brotherhood as they carried the Stone of Light into the Valley of the Kings.

At that moment, Mehy had realized that the Place of Truth possessed Egypt's most priceless secret, the secret that enabled a pharaoh to reign and to overcome death—that was why the village was so closely guarded and remained inaccessible to outsiders, even officials. To gain possession of the fabulous Stone, he had gone a long way down his chosen path, which was strewn with corpses, acts of violence, lies, and blackmail; but the battle was still far from won. When it was, he would make that accursed Brotherhood rue the day they had rejected his application to join them.

In Serketa he had a ruthless ally whose love of crime was enormously useful. She had even approved of his murdering her father, in order to acquire his fortune. One day, no doubt, she would lapse into madness, and he would have to kill her. For the moment, though . . .

"Are our new weapons ready?" she asked.

"We have enough to fight off an attack from the north, and I haven't told Amenmessu about the new battle chariots I've perfected. Thanks to the good pay and living conditions I've obtained for them over the past years, all the Theban officers and soldiers are devoted to me—even if the prince took command, they'd still obey me, not him. But I'm wary of Seti. He has a strong character, and he'd never be satisfied with ruling only the Delta. So I've sent him secret messages, assuring him of my complete loyalty and outlining the situation . . . in my own way."

"How exciting this is!" exclaimed Serketa, rubbing her breasts against his face.

Weary of his inferior position, Mehy toppled her onto her side. She let out little cries of fright, as though she were afraid he would attack her.

Someone hammered on the bedroom door. "General, come quickly—it's the police!" begged his steward in a frightened voice.

Astonished, Mehy and Serketa stared at each other.

"They'll never arrest me," she declared.

The general stood up. "I am sure it's nothing serious."

"But what if Amenmessu has betrayed you?"

"No," sneered Mehy, "he'd never do that. Without me, he doesn't even exist!" He threw on a tunic and left the bedchamber.

"The doorkeeper did not let anyone in," explained the steward, "but the officer insists on seeing you immediately."

Mehy strode toward the door that led to the garden; several servants had gathered there.

"Back to work," he ordered. "And you, open the door."

They scattered like sparrows while the doorkeeper did as he was bidden. Outside Mehy saw the tall figure of Sobek and, behind him, several Nubian guards surrounding four men whose hands were tied behind their backs.

"Commander Sobek, what's wrong?"

"One of my men tried to get into the craftsmen's village with these four thugs. As you represent the supreme authority on the west bank and are charged with protecting the Place of Truth, I felt I must inform you as soon as possible."

"What happened to your man?"

"He slit his own throat; the vultures will take care of him."

Mehy looked more closely at the prisoners. "These men are Libyans, aren't they?" he said. "Have you questioned them?"

"The only one capable of talking doesn't seem to speak Egyptian."

"I'll have them taken to the main barracks. My men there will know how to loosen his tongue, believe me!"

"The barracks is on the east bank, which is outside my jurisdiction," said Sobek, "and these men are my prisoners."

"As you yourself said, I represent the supreme authority here, and I want to know who these criminals are, what they want, and on whose orders they were acting."

"Allow me to be present at the interrogation, General."

The big Nubian had no liking for Mehy, whom he thought overambitious and quite capable of underhanded scheming to strengthen his position and safeguard his privileges. But so far Sobek had found no solid evidence against him, and he could not attack such a high-ranking official without incontestable proof. But if Mehy kept him away from this inquiry, that would be a revealing error. Sobek would appear to submit, but he would send a report to the capital, highlighting the general's suspicious behavior.

"That's a rather irregular request," remarked Mehy, "but it's understandable. But tell me, what was the Scribe of the Tomb's reaction when he discovered that one of your policemen was a traitor?"

"He and the Master still trust me, and I shan't let them down."

"I've no reason not to do likewise. I'll put my uniform on, and then I'll take you to the barracks."

Mehy did not underestimate the big Nubian. He knew Sobek was stubbornly incorruptible: every attempt to bribe him, make him change sides, or simply unsettle him had failed, for Sobek was deeply attached to the Place of Truth, even though he was only an outsider.

From time to time, the general had the feeling that Sobek was looking at him strangely, even suspiciously. But Mehy had

taken care to leave not a single clue that it was he who had murdered one of Sobek's men all those years ago, and the Nubian's
long quest for the truth was doomed to failure.

Mehy went to put on his uniform. Serketa ran to him, asking to know what was going on.

"Serious problems," he admitted. "The raid failed miserably,
and the Nubian you bought killed himself to avoid being interrogated by Sobek. But those four Libyan imbeciles are still alive.
I'll have to take Sobek to the barracks, and let him watch them
being questioned, so as not to arouse his suspicions. I must think
up a way out of this mess."

"I've only one concern, my sweet love," said Serketa. She
kissed her husband's chest and caressed the hilt of his dagger,
which, in the event of any really serious problem, would soon silence Commander Sobek.

—— 4 ——

The four Libyans were lined up against the wall in a cell. Mehy's
assistant, a senior officer, saluted the general and Commander
Sobek as they entered.

"These bandits attempted to get into the Place of Truth,"
said Mehy. "Thanks to Commander Sobek, they were arrested;
but only one of them can talk, and he speaks nothing but
Libyan." He turned to Sobek. "As my assistant speaks that language well, he will carry out the interrogation. But, first, I have
a question for him: since he engages all the mercenaries employed by our army, does he recognize them?"

The officer understood from Mehy's meaningful look he
was being given a silent order and that Sobek must not learn any
military secrets. But was he to answer yes or no?

The officer examined the prisoners closely, then turned back to Mehy, who was standing behind Sobek, so as to be able to nod without the Nubian noticing.

"Yes, I've seen these fellows before," declared the officer. He pretended to hesitate for a final moment, then continued, "In fact, I have a feeling these are the looters who stole some weapons last month, during an exercise."

"The thieves were indeed Libyan mercenaries, and they've been declared deserters," said Mehy.

"Deserters, thieves, and undoubtedly criminals, General. The sentry they assaulted to get into the armory died of his wounds."

"Proceed with the interrogation."

The officer asked only one question, and the Libyan answered it with short, clipped phrases.

"I asked him if he and his accomplices were guilty, and he confessed everything."

"Why did he try to break into the village, and on whose orders?"

The Libyan spoke again, with equal nervousness.

"He and his band had decided to loot the villages on the west bank, then to return home through the desert with as much booty as possible."

"In that case," said Mehy, "we'll hand them back to Commander Sobek, so that he may bring them to trial."

"I am sorry to contradict you, General," said the officer, "but we can't do that."

Mehy looked disconcerted. "What do you mean?"

"These criminals must be brought immediately before a military court. If you were to decide otherwise, General, you yourself would be found guilty of a serious offense. Given these facts, I must produce a detailed report and imprison them until judgment is passed."

Reluctantly, Mehy had to bow to the law. But as soon as Sobek had left, he ordered that the Libyans be housed secretly and that their trial be held soon—he intended them to be sentenced to imprisonment at Khargeh oasis, from where they would never emerge alive.

"Will you place your seal on the final document?" asked his assistant.

"There's no point," replied Mehy. "I'll hear no more talk of those scum."

"I take it you approve of what I said, General?"

"You were perfect."

"I had to read between the lines—and I could have been mistaken about the answers you wanted."

"But you weren't, and I congratulate you. You and I are striving for the glory of the army, and must never forget that discipline is a soldier's principal virtue."

"I shall always obey you without question, but doesn't this loyal service deserve . . . a reward?"

Mehy smiled. "Since you've served under me, you've come to know me and you know I don't like losing the initiative. If you ever try to make me tell—"

"Of course not, General!" said the officer hastily.

"What if my gratitude were expressed in the form of two milch cows, a splendid bed, and three finely carved chairs? Would you forget those miserable Libyans?"

"What Libyans?" replied the officer.

▲

When Sobek passed the fifth and last of the forts that protected the Place of Truth, and entered the area where the village's lay workers lived, he saw immediately that something was wrong. The blacksmith, the cauldron maker, the potter, the tanner, the weaver, the shoemaker, the laundryman, the woodcutter, the baker, and their assistants had all come out of their workshops and formed a noisy circle.

The guard on duty had armed himself with his club and planted himself in front of the village gate, as though he feared the workers might attack. The other guards kept their distance;

their orders were to bar the way to any intruders, but not to arrest the workers who were paid to ensure the Brotherhood's well-being.

Sobek broke through the circle, in the center of which stood the Scribe of the Tomb, leaning on his stick and arguing with the workers" spokesman, Beken the potter.

"You workers calm down," ordered Sobek, "or I'll tell my men to disperse you."

"But, Commander," protested Beken, "we've had no rations of dried fish for a week, and we're supposed to have enough to eat every day. If this goes on, we'll soon be too weak to work."

"The Brotherhood are no better off," retorted Kenhir, "and all I can do is protest to the governor of the west bank—and he's having to wait for the new tjaty to be appointed."

"So how are we supposed to feed ourselves?"

"The court of the Place of Truth has agreed that the food reserves may be distributed to you. It won't be long until the new pharaoh is crowned, and then the deliveries will begin again." Kenhir wished he could be sure of that; but his firm tone calmed the lay workers, who reluctantly agreed to return to work.

"You were taking a risk, confronting them so directly," said Sobek.

"At my age, I'm not afraid of anybody anymore. Besides, it is my job to sort out these kinds of problem. Did Mehy see you?"

"Yes. He even took me to the main barracks in Thebes, where his assistant interrogated the only Libyan who was in a fit state to speak."

"What did he say?"

"If the officer can be believed, they were a band of thieves who intended to attack all the villages on the west bank and, moreover, were deserters suspected of serious crimes. For that reason, they'll be tried by a military court—I very much doubt we'll ever see them again."

"If the charges against them are that serious, they'll probably be sentenced to hard labor," said Kenhir. "But you don't seem satisfied. Why not?"

"Because the story doesn't stand up. If those thugs had stolen weapons, why didn't they use them to attack the Place of Truth? Besides, this isn't a village like other villages. You're forgetting that they had an accomplice, one of my own men. They're bound to be found guilty, so no other court will hear the evidence, and all we'll know of the truth is what Mehy's officer tells us."

Kenhir leaned heavily on his stick. "What are you getting at?"

"I don't trust that man Mehy. His ambition oozes out of every pore, and I believe he's perfectly capable of manipulating events to his own corrupt advantage."

"Unless I'm much mistaken, you're a rational man who mistrusts mirages. You wouldn't want to commit another error of judgment like the one that once led you to make unjust accusations against Nefer the Silent."

The memories Kenhir called up were painful ones, and the big Nubian was shaken to the core. "Yes," he said eventually, "but this situation is very different."

"Are you sure of that? We must consider the facts, and nothing but the facts. Mehy is the village's official protector, isn't he?"

"And yet the fish deliveries have stopped."

"During the period of mourning between the death of the old pharaoh and the accession of the new one, that is the law imposed by the tjaty. But I've just had a letter from Mehy that will open the central government's reserves to us, if necessary. Since he was appointed governor, have we had a single reason to complain about him?"

"No," said Sobek slowly, "not that I can think of."

"Has he tried to impede your inquiries?"

"No, he hasn't."

"And he took you to the barracks in Thebes, even though it's well outside your jurisdiction and he could quite legally have refused you access, didn't he?"

"Well, yes, he did, but—"

"And let you be present at the Libyans' interrogation?"

"Yes, and he even—" Sobek broke off abruptly.

"He even what?"

The Nubian was annoyed at having to give details, but he owed it to himself to be honest. "He wanted to hand the Libyans over to me, but his assistant reminded him, pretty firmly, that they couldn't be removed from military jurisdiction."

Irritated, Kenhir tapped his stick on the ground. "You dislike Mehy, and you're right to do so—frankly, he irritates me as much as he does you, and I shall continue to be wary of him. But I'm convinced that he sees the Place of Truth as merely a stage in his career, and it's in his interest to protect us so that he won't anger the king."

"And what if the new king decrees that the village is to be closed?"

Suddenly, every one of Kenhir's seventy years showed in his face. "That would be the end of our civilization, Sobek, and the gods would depart this earth."

----- 5 -----

Paneb the Ardent's house was in the southern quarter of the Place of Truth. It was neither the most beautiful nor the largest house in the village, but his slender, pretty wife, Uabet the Pure, had made it both cheerful and comfortable.

The first room was devoted to the cult of the ancestors and contained a ritual bed approached by three steps. The second room had a flat roof supported by a pillar made from a palm tree trunk covered in plaster; this room also had a sacred significance, with its offertory table, its stele depicting a doorway leading to the other world, and another stele set into the wall. The latter stele showed one of the Brotherhood's protectors, "the Effective and Radiant Spirit of Ra," which sailed in the ship of the sun and passed on life to its successors. Nefer the Silent had given this work of art to Paneb.

Next came a bedchamber and bathing room, and then a kitchen with a roof made from tree branches but left partially open to the air. From the kitchen, a staircase led up to the terrace. Two cellars, one for jars of foodstuffs, the other for wine and oil, completed the dwelling.

Uabet was thirty-six, the same age as Paneb, but as she sat putting on her makeup she looked ten years younger. From a pot made from breccia, a hard stone with veins of red and yellowish white, she took a little galenite on the tip of a small stick, and with it drew a thin black line along her eyebrows. Then she poured a little perfumed oil onto her throat from an alabaster shell.

But her thoughts were not on what she was doing: they were on the husband she had to share with Turquoise, his flamboyant mistress. Both women were priestesses of Hathor, and they had never come into conflict, for they respected an unspoken pact. Turquoise had taken a vow to remain unmarried, and Paneb never spent the night at her house; he had no wife but Uabet, who had given him a fine son, Aapehti, and who was meticulous in carrying out her duties as mistress of the house. However, although she tolerated the situation because of her love for him, she was by no means submissive, and her giant of a husband treated her with much respect.

Uabet picked up a necklace of cornelian and red jasper that Paneb had given her, and put it on. It made her feel truly beautiful.

"Still no dried fish this morning," said her husband angrily. "That's Aapehti's favorite food, and I won't put up with him being deprived of it."

"All we can do is wait."

"No, it isn't. We can do more than that."

"Don't argue with the fishermen," said Uabet. "They're only obeying orders—it isn't their fault the deliveries have stopped."

"No, but it'll be my fault if my son goes hungry."

▲

Sitting in a small boat made of papyrus reeds, Paneb lowered into the Nile four large hooks attached to strong lines. After an hour of trying, he at last caught a fine fish, over a cubit long, with a silvery body and red fins. To prevent it suffering, he killed it with a mallet.

Encouraged by his success, he paddled farther out to take advantage of the deeper water. Fortune smiled on him almost immediately: a fierce battle commenced between the fisherman and a Nile perch that was over three cubits long and weighed as much as a large dog. Ordinarily, it would have taken a harpoon and a net to overcome this mighty fish; but, despite the fragility of his boat, Paneb did not give in. He countered each of the perch's leaps and plunges until it tired and seemed to understand that it was not going to escape.

Paneb emerged from the joust victorious, and was careful to hail the soul of the fish, which, when he painted it on the wall of a tomb, would find itself in front of the ship of the sun, warning it of an imminent attack by the demon of darkness.

It took only a few minutes for the current to carry the boat back to the riverbank. Paneb put the first fish in a basket, slung the perch over his left shoulder, and set off through the long grass on his way back to the village. Suddenly, a stick hit him hard behind the knees, making him stumble and fall. A net dropped onto his back, and although he managed to stand up, he was caught fast.

In front of him stood fat, bearded Nia, leader of the fishermen, and his three assistants. They and Paneb had had words before.

"You shouldn't have left your village," declared Nia. "When you live in secrecy, you should stay there."

"You stink like rotting fish," snapped Paneb. "You'd do well to surrender at once."

The fat man laughed heartily. "You're in no position to act proud, my lad. Hasn't anybody told you only I and my men have the right to fish around here?"

"If you want to go on working for the Place of Truth, you'd better restart your deliveries today. Otherwise, I shall take a personal interest in your case."

"Look, I'm trembling already," jeered Nia. "I shall enjoy dining on the superb perch you've caught—but not before I've taught you a good lesson in manners. Come on, lads!"

Four sticks began to hammer down on Paneb. The thick netting cushioned the blows, which were delivered with too much enthusiasm to be precise; and in the meantime, Paneb had managed to bite through one of the strands. He ripped the net apart and let out a furious roar that froze the four fishermen where they stood.

Extricating himself from the net, Paneb caught it up and used it as a weapon, whirling it round his head. Two of the fishermen were mown down and fell to the ground, their faces dripping blood; the third fled.

"Don't touch me!" howled Nia, dropping his stick. "You're a craftsman from the Place of Truth and you have no right to assault a lay worker."

There was such rage in his adversary's eyes that Nia thought his last hour had come. But Paneb flung the net away from him.

"Pick up my fish and come with me to the fishpond," he ordered.

"You . . . you aren't going to throw me into the canal, are you?"

"It would be a sin to dirty the water with a body as foul smelling as yours. But if you bother me again, I'll smash your skull and leave you in the mountains, for the vultures."

Hurriedly, Nia picked up the fish and the two men set off for the fishpond. There, several species of fish were raised for consumption by the villagers, who would never lack for fresh fish, no matter what the season or the weather.

Two guards were grilling a gray mullet, which they were going to share with the man in charge of the fishpond.

"That's a fine catch, Nia," one of them exclaimed. "But where on earth are you off to?"

"He's taking it to the Place of Truth," replied Paneb. "And you're going to fill your baskets with fresh fish and follow us."

The two men snatched up their cudgels.

"You'd better do as he says," advised Nia. "There were four of us, and he still got the upper hand."

The two guards took a step back. "Who are you?" asked one.

"Paneb, a craftsman from the Place of Truth."

"But we've had orders—no one's allowed to take fish from the pond."

"Those orders are stupid," said Paneb, "because the pond belongs to the Brotherhood. Just fill the baskets."

"When all is said and done," cut in Nia, "Paneb has a point."

The two guards exchanged looks. From what Nia had said, it was clear they'd be alone in fighting Paneb, who looked disturbingly big and strong. Even if they managed to knock him down, which seemed highly unlikely, they wouldn't emerge from the fight unscathed—and they weren't paid enough to take that sort of punishment. They lowered their weapons. If the government blamed them, they'd say that they'd been threatened by a group of attackers and forced to obey.

▲

The lay workers and the gatekeeper saw a strange procession arriving, with Paneb at its head.

"Fresh fish!" exclaimed Obed the blacksmith, hands on hips. "Is it for us?"

"You'll get your fair share," replied Paneb.

"Who gave it to you?"

"Nia was very cooperative, and there are lots of good, big fish in our pond."

"Does that mean the deliveries are starting again?"

"Can't you see that they are?"

Two baskets were given to the lay workers, who were in raptures over the mullet with their rounded heads and large scales.

Alerted by all the noise, the womenfolk emerged from the village and were delighted to see that a generous delivery had been made. It would enable them to prepare their favorite dishes.

Paneb took the perch to the Scribe of the Tomb's house and laid it on the doorstep. Kenhir came out and looked at it; he seemed distinctly unimpressed.

"I've seen better ones," admitted Paneb, "but all the same it should be big enough for us to have a feast."

"Where did it come from?"

"I caught it myself. . . . That's not forbidden, is it?"

"Until the new pharaoh's name is proclaimed, no one is permitted to leave the village."

"I acted for the good of the community," said Paneb, "and in the process I reestablished the deliveries of fresh fish. After all, the fishpond belongs to us, so why shouldn't we benefit from it?"

"Rules are rules," said Kenhir sternly. "Breaking them is a serious matter."

"All the villagers will eat fresh fish again—isn't that the main thing? If we had to wait until the people in power settled matters among themselves, we'd all starve to death."

Angrily, Kenhir struck the ground with his stick. "Go home, and don't leave the village again."

"I may belong to the Brotherhood, but I'm still a free man."

"I shall ask the Master to punish you. From this moment on, I forbid you to take part in the work of the starboard crew."

6

Kenhir sent his servant girl, Niut the Strong, to fetch the Master and the Wise Woman; as soon as she showed them into his office, he dismissed her.

The Wise Woman, who had been in the middle of seeing patients when Niut arrived, told Kenhir, "The villagers are very anxious. All I seem to do is prescribe calming remedies."

"And Paneb's behavior isn't making our lives any easier," he grumbled.

"If you are talking about the delivery of fish, we're all happy to eat it."

"Paneb had no right to leave the village, nor to do the job of the head fisherman, who had received strict orders from the government. I shall report this lack of discipline, and ban Paneb from working in the starboard crew for three months."

"In law," Nefer commented, "you're within your rights; but as to the spirit of the matter . . . After all, Paneb's exploits have stirred us. We aren't dependent on any government, and we receive formal orders only from Pharaoh. Why should we go without fish? If we must appoint a team to take our share from the fishpond every day, I'll take responsibility for it."

That was not at all the reaction Kenhir had expected from the Master, and he was speechless for several moments. Then he stuttered, "But . . . but Paneb has committed a serious offense and must be punished."

"He does sometimes tend to forget the rules," admitted Ubekhet, with an irresistibly sweet smile of amusement. "But this time he's done no harm, and he's reminded us that our survival depends on ourselves alone. If we stand together, we'll be the stronger for it."

"All the same . . ."

Niut came back into the room.

"I told you to go away," complained Kenhir.

"Your assistant's here. He wants to talk to you about something very serious: only half the water we're entitled to has been delivered."

Kenhir leaped to his feet as though he were twenty years younger, and marched out like a young man, followed by Nefer and Ubekhet, who were every bit as worried as he was.

The trio hurried to the enormous stone-lined water reservoir near the northern entrance to the village. There they found Kenhir's assistant, the scribe Imuni, a sour, rat-faced little man with a straggly mustache, standing in the middle of a group of housewives who were protesting volubly at the lack of water.

Imuni greeted Kenhir with relief. "We were expecting fifty donkeys," he said, "and they duly arrived—but without any water bags."

"What about the water carriers who came with them?" demanded Kenhir.

"They were empty-handed, too."

"What reason did they give?"

"None," replied Imuni in his honey-sweet voice, "but nevertheless I wrote everything they said on a wooden tablet, so that you can copy it into the Journal of the Tomb."

Imuni prided himself on his knowledge of literature, which had no value in his eyes unless it was particularly difficult to read, and he never went anywhere without his scribe's materials, which he tended with maniacal care, as he did his mustache.

"Have you checked our reserves?" asked Kenhir anxiously.

"The great jar by the southern wall is still half full, and there's enough water in the well of the Temple of Hathor to celebrate the rites for many weeks."

"Has the water delivered today been distributed?" asked Ubekhet.

"No, I forbade it," said Imuni proudly. "None of the street water jars has been filled."

The huge jars, as big as a tall man, were sunk into the ground at intervals around the village streets. They were made of glazed pink terra-cotta, and each bore the name of the sovereign who had given it to the village, such as Amenhotep I, Hatshepsut, Tuthmosis III, or Ramses the Great. They provided housewives with ample quantities of precious water.

Ubekhet headed for the northern gate, accompanied by Nefer.

"The light in your eyes has suddenly disappeared," he told her. "What are you afraid of?"

"The water that's just been delivered may be poisoned."

Sobek himself was guarding the goatskin water bags, which had been set down close to the main gate. The donkeys and carriers had already left for the valley.

"Has anyone been near the water bags?" asked Nefer.

"No one," said the Nubian.

Ubekhet opened them, one by one. "There's no suspicious smell," she said at last. "Have a lay worker bring almonds and balanite fruit. And Sobek, please tell one of your men to bring a heron."

Into each water bag, Ubekhet threw several fruits, which would keep the water clear and free of harmful elements; but this precaution did not satisfy her, and she waited for the arrival of the heron, which two Nubians had caught in a field beside the Nile.

The Wise Woman calmed the beautiful white bird, which was unharmed by its capture, then set it on the ground and gently urged it toward the water bags. If it drank, the water was free from impurities.

The bird took a few more steps, then its beak drew back, and it took flight.

"We must empty these water bags and burn them," Ubekhet declared.

"This," said Kenhir, "is too much! We're being deprived of fish and clean water, and now someone's trying to poison us. A detailed report will be sent to the capital first thing tomorrow."

"I must tell Mehy what's happened," said Nefer, "and find out who's behind this cowardly attempt on our lives."

"I'll come with you," said Kenhir.

"No, you must stay here and take all the necessary measures to defend the village against attack."

"All of them? Really?"

"We no longer have any choice."

"The roads aren't safe," said Kenhir worriedly, "even on the western bank. Take Paneb with you."

▲

Mehy gaped at his wife. "You did *what?*"

"Well, I was bored," said Serketa, "so I poisoned the Place of Truth's water. All I had to do was steal a phial from our friend Daktair and empty the contents into the water bags—there weren't as many as usual, I gather. Isn't it wonderfully amusing? In a few hours, a good many of the villagers will be ill or dead."

The general slapped his wife so hard that she staggered backward.

"You damned little fool! I ordered the water delivery halved to stir up trouble in the Brotherhood, to cause protests and make them think Amenmessu was responsible. If there'd been a water shortage, the craftsmen would have had to leave the village temporarily, and I'd have been able to search it at my leisure! And you may have killed our ally in the village!"

Serketa put on her little girl voice. "Ah, but what if they're all dead?" she lisped.

"You're forgetting that they have a Wise Woman with the skill to care for them. And above all you've forgotten that I, and only I, decide our strategy. Don't ever do anything like that again."

Her cheek burning from his blow, she threw herself at her lord and master's feet.

"Will you forgive me, my sweet love?"

"You don't deserve it."

"Forgive me, I beg you."

Mehy would happily have trampled the madwoman underfoot, but she could still be useful to him. He grabbed her by the hair and dragged her toward him.

Despite the pain, Serketa made no sound. The day her husband showed pity would be the day she killed him.

"If you've failed," he said, "the Brotherhood will react quickly. I could have Daktair accused, but we still need him."

Serketa kissed her husband's broad chest. "I have an idea," she whispered.

▲

Armed with clubs, Nefer the Silent and Paneb the Ardent took the route reserved for craftsmen leaving the Place of Truth. After passing the guard post, which barred the way to anyone trying to reach the village, they passed Ramses the Great's Temple of a Million Years, and headed toward the buildings belonging to the government of the west bank.

The air was heavy. In the fields, no one played the flute or hummed songs anymore; people looked at their neighbors suspiciously and watched passers-by with distrust. Some were whispering that a civil war was inevitable and that the province of Thebes would pay dearly for its loyalty to Prince Amenmessu.

"Are you sure Kenhir won't report me for fetching the fish?" asked Paneb.

"Absolutely sure."

"Why has he changed his mind?"

"Because your lapses of discipline are nothing compared to the attempted murder of the whole village."

"And did you defend me?"

"When a rule becomes stupid," said Nefer, "it is contrary to the harmony of Ma'at."

The area around the government buildings was in a state of unusual upheaval. Soldiers and scribes were running about in all directions, officers were yelling contradictory orders, and there were no guards on duty to screen new arrivals. The two craftsmen walked on until they reached the great courtyard, which rang with the incessant whinnying of horses.

When Nefer crossed the threshold of the building where Mehy had his office, two soldiers rushed out and aimed their spears at his chest.

"We have arrested the guilty party!" they shouted.

—— 7 ——

"All necessary measures," the Master had said. Kenhir had asked him to confirm that decision and had also, being a stickler for legality, and because the orders he would have to give were so unusual, asked the opinions of the Wise Woman and Hay, leader of the port crew. They both supported Nefer, so all that remained was for Kenhir to take action.

He left the village and sought out Sobek.

"Are your men on a war footing, Commander?" he asked.

"No one can get near the village without being seen. My orders are strict: first a challenge, then, if the person challenged doesn't stop, a volley of arrows."

"Let's go and see the blacksmith."

Since King Meneptah's death, Obed the blacksmith, a short, bearded Syrian with muscular arms, had had much less work to do. He took advantage of the fact to sleep and to gorge himself on hotcakes stuffed with goat's cheese. When he saw Kenhir and Sobek entering his forge, he thought he must be dreaming: the Scribe of the Tomb had never come here before, and Obed feared that the roof might collapse about his ears.

"What have I done wrong?"

"Nothing, Obed," said Kenhir. "Don't worry."

"But in that case . . ."

"You make excellent tools, and when repairs are needed you do them as quickly as possible—the crew leaders and I are more than satisfied with your work. But now the whole future of the Place of Truth is at stake. We have enemies in high places, and if we are attacked we must be able to defend ourselves."

"Defending the village is my responsibility," said Sobek in astonishment.

"Indeed it is, but the craftsmen must be able to act as reinforcements if need be."

The blacksmith cracked his fingers, which, according to the village children, looked like crocodiles and smelled worse than fish eggs. "You want me to make . . . weapons?"

"That is what the Master has decided," said Kenhir.

"But that's illegal," protested Sobek. "Only the government is authorized to deliver them to me and—"

"And what has the government delivered to us?" demanded Kenhir. "Poisoned water, that's what! I am the official charged with ensuring the village's well-being, and I consider it vital to strengthen our self-sufficiency in all areas."

The big Nubian realized Kenhir was right. And since he and his men owed obedience to the Scribe of the Tomb, the responsibility was not theirs.

As for Obed, he was rather entertained by this unexpected task. "I'll start work at once," he said, and he set to with a will.

He stoked his fire with wood charcoal and date stones, then took his bellows and plied them until the fire was roaring away. With the steady hand of a seasoned professional, he poured powdered charcoal into several ceramic vases shaped like dogs' teeth. Then he held each vase steady with bronze tongs, enabling the flames from the furnace to enter it through a small, round hole, ignite the powder, and make the vase red-hot. Meanwhile, he inserted into the vases pieces of metal that would be transformed into daggers and short swords.

Kenhir and Sobek watched him for a while, then, satisfied that all was progressing well, left the forge.

The big Nubian was still uneasy. "Surely you aren't intending to arm the craftsmen?" he asked.

"The weapons will be counted and stored in the strong room," replied Kenhir. "I and I alone will decide if and when they should be distributed. And, if necessary, I shall give the Brotherhood the means to defend themselves."

"Don't forget there's a traitor—a shadow-eater—among us. If he's given a weapon he'll use it to murder someone."

"I have an excellent memory," said Kenhir acidly, "and I am well aware of the risks involved. Until I order otherwise, only you and your men will be armed; but if he wants to kill someone, the shadow-eater could use any of our ordinary tools as a weapon."

"He'd be condemning his soul to destruction!"

"Don't you think he's already done that?"

▲

"I am the Master of the Place of Truth, and my companion is a craftsman," Nefer said calmly. "Lower your spear and take us to General Mehy."

The suspect's placid response disconcerted the soldier. His fellow guard eyed Paneb's burly frame suspiciously as the craftsman passed an enormous cudgel from one hand to the other. Spearing the man who claimed to be the Master would be simple enough, but the giant craftsman beside him would massacre them.

"I'm calling for reinforcements," said the first soldier. "You're the guilty parties—I'm sure of it."

"What has happened, soldier?" asked Nefer in a measured voice.

"As if you don't know!"

"The water in one of the pools has been poisoned," said the second soldier, who was reassured by Nefer's attitude. "There are already two dead and several sick. The general has given orders to find everyone who drank from that pool and arrest the suspects."

"Take us to him. I have important information for him."

Won over by the quiet power that emanated from the Master, the soldier agreed.

Mehy's huge office was filled with officers and scribes who were twittering like sparrows; some were there to give their reports, others were begging to be told what to do.

Paneb struck the tiled floor with his stick. Everyone turned to look at the two craftsmen.

"Master, you're safe!" exclaimed Mehy. "I was just about to send a messenger to the village to find out whether you'd used the poisoned water."

"Thanks to the Wise Woman's shrewd insight, we are all safe and well."

"That's excellent news. Unfortunately, I cannot say the same."

"What's happened, General?

"Get back to your posts," Mehy ordered the officers and scribes, "and start calming everyone down. Tell them there's no longer any risk, and that the cause of the incident has been established."

Reassured, they left the office.

Apparently overwhelmed, Mehy collapsed onto a high-backed chair. "Please be seated," he said.

"We prefer to stand, General," said Nefer.

"What an appalling, criminal thing to do. If it hadn't been for the vigilance of a military doctor, there would have been dozens of deaths." He swallowed hard. "Forgive me, my throat's dry. Will you join me in a little date wine?"

"No, thank you."

His face drawn, Mehy drank a cupful in a single gulp. "So

many dreadful things have happened, one after the other, that I'm having difficulty getting my thoughts in order. First of all the capital issued a ban on eating fish during the mourning period, then Prince Amenmessu ordered that deliveries of water to your village be reduced."

"Such violations of the law regarding the Place of Truth are intolerable," said Nefer sternly.

"I know, I know. I immediately sent a note of protest to the provisional authorities, and I explained to the prince that no rationing of any sort could be imposed on your Brotherhood without a direct order from Pharaoh himself. But he sometimes tends to consider himself the new master of the country."

"We have to confess, General," said Nefer, "that we have taken fish from our fishpond."

"A good idea. After all, you've only done what's normally the duty of a few men who've been forbidden to work. No one— least of all me—is going to reproach you for that. As governor, I shall support you wholeheartedly. As regards the water, I couldn't prevent what happened today. But either we shall be back to normal tomorrow or I shall resign, and if I do, a struggle will break out between Amenmessu and those who respect the law of Ma'at."

By throwing all his weight into the balance in this way, Mehy hoped to prove to the Brotherhood that he was their true ally. And, since Amenmessu was young, credulous, and easily manipulated, the general ran no risk of being dismissed from his offices.

"Do you know why the water was poisoned?" asked Nefer.

"For revenge. The brother of one of the Libyans who tried to get into your village worked in the stables. When he learned that the attackers had been tried, and given harsh sentences, the killer stole lethal drugs from the hospital and poured them into the water for the army and the Place of Truth. Fortunately, a doctor noticed that several phials had disappeared and immediately raised the alarm. But by then two grooms, an orderly, and an accounting scribe were already vomiting, and several soldiers were doubled up with pain. We didn't manage to save them all."

Nefer shivered. If the Wise Woman had not sensed the danger, how many villagers would have died?

"How did you identify the criminal?" asked Paneb.

"An officer noticed he was behaving strangely, and had the idea of searching his hut. He found the stolen phials there. The killer tried to run, but the archers shot him down. From his colleagues, we found out who he was, and then it was obvious why he'd done what he did. I've ordered all water and food to be checked each day by doctors, to ensure that nothing like this ever happens again."

He smiled inwardly as he saw the craftsmen accept what he had said. They would never guess it was Serketa who had stolen the drugs, poisoned the water, and then, to make sure the investigation did not center on Daktair's workshop, put the phials in the Libyan's hut.

"I'm sure your checks will be thorough," said the Master, "but we'll carry out our own as well."

Mehy nodded. "Two sets of precautions are better than one."

"And one more thing: if the usual amount of water isn't delivered tomorrow, I fear there may be a revolt among the craftsmen."

The general got to his feet. "I am aware of the gravity of the situation, and I shall do all I can to prevent the worst happening."

—— 8 ——

In accordance with tradition, the Master's house was one of the two finest in the village (the other was the Scribe of the Tomb's). As they did every morning, Nefer and Ubekhet rose before dawn, washed, and prepared themselves to go to the temple to celebrate, in the name of Pharaoh and the queen of Egypt, the rites of the rebirth of the Light.

The Master loved to light the lamps in the bedchamber; he had made them himself. They consisted of bronze cups filled with castor or olive oil, which were placed on small acacia wood columns shaped like papyrus stems and fixed into hemispherical limestone bases. Each time the clear flame leapt up, Nefer thought of the miracle that took place every day in the Place of Truth, where the living tried to communicate with the Invisible and the Divine, to offer Ma'at a place of incarnation. In spite of their faults and their shortcomings, men and women had decided to unite and devote their lives to a work that was greater than themselves.

By means of the Stone of Light, which was handed down from Master to Master, it was possible to transmute matter, to pass from Stone to star and from star to Stone.

The lamps lit up the furnishings the craftsmen had given Nefer when Pharaoh confirmed him in his office as Master: ornate chairs, a folding stool inlaid with ivory and ebony, tables of different shapes and sizes, storage chests: enough to satisfy any leading citizen and make him proud of his success.

But this house had been built in the heart of a unique village, and the leader of the Brotherhood had no ambition other than to pass on the teachings he had received in the House of Gold, so that temples and tombs could be build according to the laws of harmony.

Nefer watched his wife as she put on her jewelery and anointed her skin with a scented ointment to protect it from the sun. He laid his hands gently on her shoulders.

"Who could find words to sing of your beauty?"

Ebony jumped lightly up at Ubekhet and licked her cheek; his long tail wagged briskly, to show how pleased he was to be stroked, which was every bit as important as having a full bowl of food. When the elegant black dog returned to his mat to finish off his night's sleep, Ubekhet opened a round basket and took out a necklace made up of two rows of lotus petals surrounding a row of yellow mandragora flowers, separated by red ribbons.

"Why are you going to wear such a fragile necklace?" he asked.

"It's an offering to the goddess of silence."

"You are going to climb the Peak of the West to meet the cobra again, aren't you?"

"We need her help, Nefer. Her magical power will enable us to withstand fate's blows and to change the course of events."

"But each time you draw her from her lair, you risk your life."

"We must take any risks necessary to protect the village from the doom threatening it."

Nefer kissed his wife's throat.

▲

The countryside looked wonderful under the first rays of the rising sun. The contrast between the ocher of the desert and the green of the fields, which were punctuated at regular intervals by groves of palm trees, was striking. Yet the two worlds complemented each other more than they conflicted, and the austerity of the desert emphasized the warmth of the fields.

Ubekhet climbed steadily toward the Peak of the West. To it she would offer the necklace and a bouquet of papyrus flowers and poppies, with leaves of convolvulus and mandragora; in this way, she would appease the fury of the sacred mountain. The Wise Woman who had initiated Ubekhet into her office as spiritual mother of the Brotherhood had advised her to worship the goddess of silence, Meretseger, who would become Ubekhet's guide, her eyes when the future was dark and unclear.

The pyramid-shaped summit soared skyward above the Temples of a Million Years, which had been arranged in the form of a fan around this most sacred site. The Houses of Eternity in the Valley of the Kings had been placed under the protection of "the Great Peak of the West, Daughter of the Light in its Name of Ma'at."

It was up there, at the summit of the peak, that the divine mother, mistress of births and transformations, queen-regent of those who lived righteously, revealed herself. She helped those who worshipped her and protected those who carried her in their hearts. But this mysterious goddess, who gave untold spiritual sustenance to the Place of Truth, abhorred lies and greed, and her love could take the form of a fearsome fire. Only the Wise Woman could approach the shrine that housed the royal cobra, incarnation of the goddess; in the body of the snake, which was frequently depicted on the walls of royal tombs, the sun's daily regeneration took place. In this way it was both the conqueror of time and the architect of resurrection.

When she reached the summit, Ubekhet laid the bouquet and the necklace on a small altar, and chanted an invocation to the reborn Light, which once again animated all forms of life.

Slowly, the huge cobra came out of her lair, then, with astonishing speed, reared up as if to strike. Like the snake, the Wise Woman swayed from right to left and from left to right, neither stiffly nor jerkily; she gazed into the reptile's eyes, in which burned a red light whose ferocity abated, little by little.

Pacified by Ubekhet's melodious voice, the cobra grew still, as though turned into a granite statue, and listened to the questions asked by the woman who had succeeded in charming it.

▲

As they did every morning, the women had carried out their duty as priestesses of Hathor, placing offerings on the altars of the ancestors, whose protection was more vital than ever. Yet all the villagers were haunted by anxiety, and few of them had slept well. They badly needed drinking water; would the delivery be big enough?

"The authorities are just playing games with us," opined Karo the Impatient, a stocky stonecutter with short, powerful arms, a broken nose, and thick eyebrows. "They won't send us any water—or bread or vegetables."

"Don't be so pessimistic," retorted Renupe the Jovial, a

sculptor with a large belly and the look of a mischievous goblin. "Thanks to Paneb, we've already got fresh fish."

"That was just one of his reckless exploits," commented Nakht the Powerful, another stonecutter, with an athletic build and a heavy step. "No one asked him to do anything, and he'll bring us nothing but trouble."

"Sit down on the stool and stay still," ordered Renupe, who was acting as barber.

"My hair doesn't need cutting," protested Nakht.

"It's your turn today. Don't set a bad example, or life will become impossible."

Nakht didn't want to annoy Renupe, who had sharpened his flint razor and was demonstrating considerable dexterity. No one ever got cut when Renupe shaved them, and afterward he used a lotion that prevented skin irritation.

A tall, slightly flabby figure with an overlong nose and an ugly face was approaching. It was the artist Gau the Precise, who had come to find his colleagues from the starboard crew.

"Any news?" he asked in his gruff voice.

"No," replied Karo. "Userhat has gone to the main gate to see what's happening."

As he spoke, Userhat the Lion, the Brotherhood's head sculptor, whose build was as magnificent as a great wild beast's, rejoined the group. He was accompanied by Casa the Rope, a stonecutter with a square face lit up by small, chestnut-colored eyes.

"Not a donkey to be seen," said Casa.

"You didn't look," scoffed Renupe.

"If you weren't holding a razor, I'd stuff those words down your throat!"

"Calm down," advised Userhat, "and let's not start tearing each other to pieces."

Still half-asleep, the artist Pai the Good Bread emerged hesitantly from his house. "My wife wants water for cooking," he said.

"She'll have to wait like everyone else," said Casa irritably.

"Don't tell me the donkeys haven't arrived—I daren't go back home without some water."

"If need be," promised tall, slow-moving Didia the Generous, a carpenter, "I'll give you shelter."

Thuty the Learned, the fragile, sickly goldsmith, kept silent, as did the artist Unesh the Jackal. Unesh never talked much, but now he was even more withdrawn than usual.

The stonecutter Fened the Nose and the slender, jumpy sculptor Ipuy the Examiner, were playing dice to try and forget their worries.

"Have you nothing better to do than make empty chatter?" demanded the painter Ched the Savior. His straight nose, thin lips, and small, neatly trimmed mustache gave him a disdainful air.

"What do you suggest?" snapped Karo.

"Anything from the upkeep of our tools to working on orders for customers outside the village. There's no shortage of work— and every day we don't try to improve our skills is a day wasted."

"When our whole way of life is in danger," said Pai, "it's impossible to do good work."

"Where has Paneb got to now?" worried Nakht.

"Here he is," said Casa.

Sure enough, he was running toward them. "There are donkeys coming!" he shouted. "At least a hundred of them!"

Quickly joined by their colleagues from the port crew, the starboard crew rushed to the northern gate and went out of the village.

Never had humble donkeys seemed so wonderful, or their loads so marvelous!

Karo seized a goatskin. "I'm dying of thirst," he groaned.

But before he could drink, a strong hand seized his wrist.

"Have you forgotten that the water might be poisoned?" said Nefer.

9

"We must wait until the Wise Woman returns, so that she can check the water's safe to drink," the Master decreed.

"Where has she gone?" asked Nakht the Powerful.

"To the Peak of the West, to draw down its magic and protection upon us."

"But supposing she doesn't come back?" said Fened the Nose worriedly.

The Master turned and looked up at the sacred mountain. "The light is very pure this morning; Ubekhet will have found a way to draw out of the silence the forces whose help we need."

The lay workers unloaded the donkeys and fed them, and the water bags were piled up near the main gate of the village.

An anxious wait began. Some passed the time in more or less pointless tasks, others gazed at the path the Wise Woman must take on her return to the Place of Truth.

When the intensity of the midday sun made dry throats painful, the Scribe of the Tomb ordered the men's water rations to be shared out, after the women and children had received theirs. Hope began to wane, and the pessimists were convinced that they would never see Ubekhet again. Like the Wise Woman who had preceded her, she had vanished into the mountain, to be absorbed by the goddess.

"You must drink a little," Paneb advised the Master.

"She's coming back," murmured Nefer.

The big man turned and scanned the mountainside. He could see nothing, so he turned back to Nefer.

"Drink," he repeated, "and rest awhile."

"Ubekhet is coming back."

Paneb looked again. Straining his eyes, he could just make out a faint shape moving along the pebble-strewn path.

"You're right! It's her, it's really her!"

The good news spread life wildfire, and several children, including Aapehti, were given permission to run and meet Ubekhet.

She was greeted with shouts of joy. Her safe return was a clear sign that the goddess of the peak had granted the Wise Woman's request, and would continue to protect the village.

"Has the water been delivered?" asked Ubekhet.

"Yes," replied Nefer, "but no one has drunk any yet."

Before he could stop her, she opened a water bag and drank a mouthful.

"Ubekhet, you shouldn't have—"

"We have nothing to fear."

The Wise Woman laid her hand on each water bag in turn. "This water may be distributed."

In a few minutes, the village came back to life. Once again its inhabitants could drink, wash, and cook.

"Mehy has done well," commented Kenhir. "By reinstating the water deliveries, he's done us a great service. As long as he supports us, we shall survive."

▲

Prince Amenmessu had changed a lot. He, who had loved nothing more than galloping his horse through the desert, had become progressively flabbier and less fit as he sampled the inexhaustible pleasures of Theban life. Extravagant banquets with unforgettable wines, delicious boat trips on the Nile, swimming in the pool at the luxurious house provided by General Mehy, fleeting liaisons with shameless young beauties, not forgetting the small army of servants who cared for his hair, his hands, and his feet and the masseurs who soothed away the slightest ache . . . What more could he possibly want?

Mehy bowed low. "You wished to see me, Prince?"

"I've just come to my senses, General. Since I've been here,

I've been getting fatter and fatter, and I've no energy left. This dream is enchanting, but it cannot go on. I have decided to return to Pi-Ramses."

"But, my lord, unless you know precisely what is happening there, you might be running into danger."

"When all is said and done, Seti is my father."

"I hope I'm wrong, my lord, but I fear that, in the struggle for power, family ties may not count for very much. If you return to the capital while these troubles continue, who knows what fate will befall you? Here, you're safe."

"Yes, and this safety's suffocating me. Am I to end up as just another fat Theban dignitary who'll die in the arms of a whore?"

"I believe your future is far more promising than that," said Mehy with a smile, "so long as you don't give in to impatience."

"Impatience! I seem to have been bewitched by this magical province for years. And while I've been tasting its charms, my father has been preparing to become Pharaoh."

"That's very likely, but Seti knows very well that he cannot reign without the support of Thebes. And he also knows that your stay here in the city of Amon has made you popular and that you have at your disposal armed forces whose reputation is second to none."

Amenmessu's interest was aroused. "So what do you think will happen, General?"

"Your father may well want to negotiate with you, to secure your loyalty to the throne. Remember, his main concern is to avoid civil war."

Mehy's argument shook the prince but did not convince him.

"My father isn't a conciliatory man. He'll demand my total obedience."

"Then your final decision will be up to you."

▲

As night fell, Fened the Nose guided the craftsmen of the starboard crew to its meeting place, on the far side of the burial ground at the foot of the northern hill.

Gau the Precise asked each craftsman to identify himself before passing through the door, which opened onto a small open-air courtyard where a rectangular purification pool had been created. Pai the Good Bread scooped up a cupful of water and poured it over the outstretched hands of his colleagues as they went one by one into the meeting hall.

They sat down in enclosed stalls, on stone benches arranged along the walls, after the Master had taken his place to the east, on the wooden seat his predecessors had occupied. Behind him, separated from the hall by low walls, was a shrine containing a statuette of the goddess Ma'at and two small side rooms where ritual objects were kept.

Only the Master could enter the sacred shrine, but Paneb remembered having seen light spring forth from it, the light of the Brotherhood's secret Stone, a light so powerful that it had shone through the shrine's wooden doors.

This evening, though, the meeting place was lit only by lamps.

Another craftsman was disappointed by the Stone's absence: the traitor who was searching for its hiding place, in order to exchange the priceless treasure for the huge fortune his allies had amassed for him outside the village. The meeting place was kept locked up except during meetings, but Nefer did not make the mistake of leaving the Stone of Light there.

"Let us pay homage to the ancestors," said the Master. "May they continue to light our way and guide us along the path of righteousness. May the closest stone stall to mine be occupied by the creative power of my predecessor, who has been reborn among the stars and is always present among us."

The dead man's seat would remain empty forever: each crew leader of the Place of Truth was irreplaceable.

"It is still uncertain whether Seti or Amenmessu will soon

govern the Two Lands," continued Nefer, "or what fate the new pharaoh will have in store for our Brotherhood. However, although I do not know the answers to these questions, I would like to consult you now and take some decisions."

"In my opinion," declared Renupe, "some people are worrying about nothing. Without the work done in the Place of Truth, no pharaoh can prepare for the afterlife. As soon as the new king is crowned, he'll put us to work."

"Poison cannot be taken out of a snake or an evil man," objected Gau the Precise. "If the new king is hostile to us, we must prepare for the worst."

"That is very true," said Nakht. "And the blacksmith isn't making weapons for his own amusement. As for me, I'll fight to the death to defend our freedom."

"We're craftsmen, not soldiers," Ipuy the Examiner reminded him. "If the army decides to turn us out of the village, it would be insane to resist."

"Not to resist would be unforgivable cowardice," snarled Paneb. "What good will survival be if we abandon everything we love, and behave like sheep?"

"Don't insult your brother!" protested Casa.

"That's enough," cut in the Master. "You seem to have forgotten that speaking is more difficult than any other work, and that you must do so only if you have solutions to offer."

Paneb could not resist asking the question that burned on his lips. "Will the Stone of Light be moved and hidden outside the village, to prevent it falling into an attacker's hands?"

"Do you think an attack is likely?" asked Didia the Generous tensely.

"The struggle for power will be pitiless," said Thuty the Learned, "and there's certainly a risk that we'll be among its first victims."

"We must take every precaution we can think of to safeguard the Stone," said Pai.

"Where could it possibly be safer than here, inside these

strong walls?" demanded Ched the Savior. "If we're seen leaving the village with it, we'll be spied on, even followed. No, the Stone must be hidden nowhere but here, and in such a way that no thief will ever find it."

A discussion followed, at the end of which the solution proposed by Ched was unanimously approved.

"A perfect word is hidden better than a precious stone," concluded the Master, quoting a saying of the great sage Ptahhotep, "and yet it is found among serving girls who work at the grindstone. If we remember our daily duties and respect our rule of life, our treasures will be safe."

—— 10 ——

Kenhir was having a delightful dream. The desert had vanished, the trees were in blossom, the white-painted village houses shone under a gentle sun, and the old scribe had no incidents to write in the Journal of the Tomb.

"Wake up! Someone's asking for you."

That strident, bossy voice . . . surely it was the voice of his servant, Niut the Strong? His dream broken, Kenhir opened his eyes.

"You again," he grumbled. "What time is it?

"Time to get up and go at once to the great gate."

"I'm too old to hurry."

"Well, I'm just passing on what I was asked to tell you. Now I've got the housework to do."

Rather than have to dodge Niut's infernal broom, Kenhir preferred to get up. And reality hit him in the face: if he was being asked for at the great gate, something must be wrong.

With stiff legs and painful hips, the Scribe of the Tomb trotted along the main street. As he went out through the gate, he bumped into Beken the potter. Beken was renowned for his craftiness, but today he looked badly frightened.

"Hasn't the water been delivered?" asked Kenhir.

"Yes, it has, but we were expecting vegetables, and there isn't a single one. The donkey drivers say the army has commandeered all the gardeners on the west bank, including the ones who work for the Place of Truth. There's a rumor that Prince Amenmessu has decided to fight his father."

Kenhir headed for the Fifth Fort, where he found Sobek giving orders to several of his men, ending with "Get to your posts—on the double!" The big Nubian's voice was harsh and edgy, and his eyes were red rimmed, as if he'd gone too long without sleep.

"Is it true that there's going to be civil war?" asked Kenhir.

"I don't know, but the army's taking your gardeners isn't a good sign. It looks like a general mobilization."

"So you and your men will soon be ordered to—"

"I take my orders from the Scribe of the Tomb and the Master of the Place of Truth, and from no one else."

"That attitude might get you into serious trouble."

"Whatever happens, I shall do my duty."

"If Amenmessu proclaims himself Pharaoh and decides to seize the village, won't you have to obey him?"

"I've thought long and hard about that problem," admitted Sobek, "and I've made my decision: I shall be true to my word. I'm paid to defend this village against its enemies, whoever they are, and that's precisely what I shall do. And I promise you that not one of my men will be disloyal."

▲

In accordance with the will of the goddess of the peak, the inhabitants of the Place of Truth had abandoned their daily tasks to devote a whole day to their sacred duties. They would not need a ritualist from outside the village since, according to the Brotherhood's statutes, the craftsmen were also priests directed by the Master, and the women, led by the Wise Woman, were priestesses of Hathor.

All were purified, anointed with myrrh, dressed in robes of royal linen and white sandals. They processed toward the Temple of Ma'at and Hathor, laden with offerings: loaves in many different shapes, jars of milk, beer, and wine, mirrors, pots of ointment, and wooden models of haunches of bull, antelope, or duck. In this way, they were presenting the whole marvel of creation and energy-giving foods to the great self-born god, who could manifest himself in millions of forms without losing any of his unity, he who ceaselessly re-created the sky, the earth, water, the mountains, and human life.

The Wise Woman and the Master were acting in the name of the king and queen of Egypt, as had been the custom since the time of Menes. After the offerings had been laid upon the altars, they lifted up a figurine of the goddess Ma'at toward Ma'at herself, so that the gift might be total and like unite with like, creating a whole that was both unified and multiple, since Ma'at herself symbolized totality.

"May this celestial dwelling welcome the lady of gold, silver, and precious stones," chanted the Wise Woman. "May she preserve our joy and our unity in the face of adversity."

During the ceremony, the traitor thought only of the Stone of Light. He wondered where the Master had hidden it: in the village's main temple, or in the Brotherhood's meeting place? For a long time, he had been making detailed plans to get inside, and the failure of the Libyan raiding party had not lessened his determination.

But perhaps he was mistaken in his thinking. Nefer and the Wise Woman knew a shadow-eater was on the prowl, and they must have set up defenses. The most effective would surely be to make the thief believe that the Stone of Light was being kept safely in one of the village's sacred places, when in fact it was somewhere else.

They might have been clever enough to choose a hiding

place in full view of everybody, perhaps so clearly visible that nobody paid it any attention. Had Nefer the Silent given himself away by speaking of the perfect word that was hidden better than a precious stone but could be found among the serving girls working at the grindstone?

Grindstones, used for crushing grain to make bread and beer, were made of no ordinary stone. They were pieces of greenish bown dolerite, and exceptionally hard. It was this very stone that replaced the mortal heart of the traveler to the world beyond; equipped with a heart of indestructible stone, he could face the court of the otherworld and its dangers. The lay workers had one mill, and there were several in the village. What if one of them was being used to hide the Stone of Light, a piece of dolerite magically brought to life by rites and endowed with a special energy?

After being on the wrong track for so long, the traitor was sure he had at last found the path that led to the treasure.

▲

"Are you trying to make fools of us?" said Uabet the Pure furiously. "Do you really think that we're going to accept half-washed clothes and sheets with stains still on them?"

The laundrymen hung their heads. However, one of them attempted to do battle with the angry little woman. "We do our best. But our work is exhausting and difficult, and we're badly paid."

"To judge from the results," she said caustically, "you're paid far too much."

Only men were engaged in this unworthy task, which Uabet supervised. Since cleanliness was the basis of good health, she permitted no slackness.

"You've no right to treat us like this," protested the man. "If you do, we may stop working."

"If the idea appeals to you, please do: you will all be dismissed and replaced, first thing tomorrow. I'll have no difficulty in finding better people." She turned, as if to go back into the village.

"Wait," said the man hastily. "We agree our methods could be improved."

"No pay today. And don't behave in this deplorable way again, or I shan't be so lenient."

Heads hanging even lower, the laundrymen returned to the canal with the firm intention of correcting their mistakes and making up for lost time, for they knew Uabet the Pure was not joking. The work might be hard but it was coveted, so it was as well to keep in her good books.

Whatever the rumors might say, the Place of Truth continued to exist, and its demands were the same as ever.

▲

"That ceremony impressed me a lot," Paneb told Nefer. "I hadn't realized how vitally important the offerings are. Suddenly, it seemed to me that the temple was being born, that its hieroglyphs were coming to life, and that its stones took on a golden hue."

"You are a good observer."

"I wasn't the only one involved in the ritual. We were all together, with one heart, and we were thinking not of ourselves but of the secret harmony we serve."

Nefer did not dampen Paneb's enthusiasm, although the latter seemed to have forgotten that there was a traitor among them. The Master had better things in store for his adopted son.

"You have worked hard, many secrets of the craft have been revealed to you, and you have been authorized to paint in a royal tomb. The time has come for you to create your masterwork, if that is what you wish."

Paneb lit up with excitment. "How could I not wish it! Tell me what I must do!"

"It's not that simple. You must take time to reflect and choose the theme of your masterwork, and you must make not one single error in its execution."

"I've got a hundred ideas already."

"That's ninety-nine too many," said Nefer drily. "And don't forget the most important thing."

"Don't keep me waiting!"

"The most important thing is the raw material, the quintessence. Until you can identify it, the masterwork will remain as far from your mind as it is from your hand."

"Must I leave the village to find it?"

"That's up to you."

"Can't you give me a clue?"

"It is so long since I undertook this trial . . . My memory seems to be failing."

If Nefer had not been the Master, Paneb would gladly have shaken him to make him talk.

▲

"The laundrymen tried to cheat us," Uabet confided to her husband, who was stretched out on his bed, "but I soon sorted them out."

Paneb did not answer.

"Are you feeling ill?"

"Have you ever heard tell of the quintessence, Uabet?"

The young woman smiled. "Ah. The Master has asked you to prepare your masterwork, has he?"

Paneb leaped up and seized her by the shoulders. "Then you know about it!"

"I'm only a simple priestess of Hathor, but I hope you will succeed."

—— 11 ——

The Wise Woman confirmed that the water was fit to drink, and Fened the Nose checked the fish. Meanwhile, Kenhir had noted the absence not only of vegetables but also of the lay workers' leader.

"Where's Beken?" he asked Obed the blacksmith.

"No one's seen him this morning. He must have overslept."

"I'll give him 'overslept,'" snapped Kenhir. "Imuni!" His assistant came running up. "Prepare me a fresh tablet. I shall dictate a report to you about Beken, whom I am hereby dismissing."

Imuni was readying his brush when Obed noticed a cloud of dust on the road, and said, "Look, someone's coming, and he's leading some donkeys. Sobek's let him pass, so there's no danger."

The scribes and the lay workers soon recognized the man as Beken, who was leading a train of donkeys bearing heavy baskets.

"Where have you been?" Kenhir asked him in astonishment.

"The Place of Truth has always treated me well, and I've no wish to change my trade. So I made arrangements with some owners of small gardens, and you'll have everything you need until things are back to normal."

In the baskets were lettuces, onions, leeks, lentils, fennel, garlic, cabbages, parsley, and cumin.

"When all is said and done," grumbled Kenhir the Ungracious, "you're the leader of the lay workers and you were only doing your job. What's more, you are in luck: I shall overlook your failure to obey regulations and I'll cancel your letter of dismissal."

Red-haired Turquoise was the most sensual woman in the village. And yet she had taken a vow to remain single, and even her eager lover, Paneb, had not convinced her to marry him. As a free woman and a priestess of Hathor, she had chosen her way of life and decided her own destiny.

Paneb always spent the night with his wife; only passion united Turquoise and the giant, a passion that did not accord well with daily cares or humdrum things. But making love with Paneb remained an incomparable pleasure, and when he entered her house, which he had repainted himself, Turquoise felt delicious shivers run over her skin.

"I've brought you a present," he said, and he handed her a belt made from shells renowned for their erotic power.

Turquoise smiled. "Do you think we need this?"

"I'd love to see you wearing this belt . . . and nothing else."

At thirty-five, Turquoise was magnificent. She knew that many eyes lingered on her splendid body, but no one dared to compete with Paneb.

Eyes fixed on her lover, she took off her dress very slowly, then, with matchless elegance, slipped the belt of shells about her hips. Naked, she slowly turned in a full circle.

Paneb said, "I told you time would never diminish your beauty, and that it would make your charms even more magical. I was right."

With a dancer's grace, Turquoise raised her left leg and rested her foot on his shoulder. "How long are you going to be satisfied with just talking?"

Sated, they lay side by side.

"It's almost time for dinner," murmured Turquoise. "Your wife and son will be waiting for you."

"I wish I could stay."

"You know very well that you can't. If you don't fulfill your duties as a husband and father, I'll close my door to you."

Paneb did not take this warning lightly, so he changed the subject. "You're a more senior priestess than Uabet, aren't you?"

"What's that to you?"

"She claims not to know what the quintessence is."

"So you've been asked to create a masterwork, have you?"

Paneb propped himself up on one elbow to look at her. "You know, too!"

"It's a daunting test—very few craftsmen have succeeded in passing it. Perhaps you should give up, rather than risk the pain of failure."

He drew Turquoise closer. "Tell me about the quintessence."

"A priestess's path is not the same as a craftsman's."

"Why won't you answer me?"

"How can I possibly tell you what I don't know myself?"

▲

In the meeting place, the atmosphere was tense. After calling upon the ancestors, the Master described the situation in detail.

"We have enough provisions for several days," he concluded, "and I hope they'll last us until the new pharaoh is crowned, whoever he may be. The king is supreme Master of the Brotherhood, and he will decide our fate."

"Must we accept his decision, even if it's unfavorable?" asked Karo the Impatient.

"You know very well that we must," retorted Casa the Rope drily.

"And what if there are two pharaohs?" asked Thuty the Learned. "Which one should we obey?"

"We are the crew of a boat whose rudder is Ma'at," Gau the Precise reminded him. "If disorder reigns outside, it's the Master's role to maintain harmony in the Place of Truth."

"He may not be given time to do so," ventured Unesh the Jackal.

"Let's concentrate on the present," said Nefer firmly. "If the uncertainty lasts a long time, we're likely to run short of certain domestic items, so it would be sensible to make our own. That way we can be self-sufficient for as long as necessary."

"Let's use tamarisk," suggested Didia the Generous. "It's the ideal wood for our purpose, because it's said to drive away the forces of evil, and Horus chased away his enemies with a stick made of tamarisk wood."

"I shall need volunteers to cut as much wood as we need and bring it back."

Userhat the Lion was astonished. "Why not tell the lay workers to do it?"

"Because some of them, like the gardeners, have been taken

by the army," said Nefer. "The woodcutters who work for the village will probably be taken soon, too. Besides, they'd be too slow."

"I'll go," said Paneb.

"As the carpenter," said Didia, "I must go with him."

"Three of us won't be too many," added Renupe the Jovial.

▲

"To be frank," Sobek told the Master and his three volunteers, "I'm not at all happy about your doing this. In fact, I must insist that no craftsman leaves the village until the new order is established, for reasons of your collective safety."

"I understand your point of view," conceded Nefer, "but I consider the wood a priority."

"It may be dangerous."

"Give us weapons, then," suggested Paneb.

"That would be even more dangerous," replied Sobek.

"You don't seem to have much confidence in us."

"What would happen if you were armed and you stumbled on a hostile patrol?"

"Then give us an escort of your men," Renupe proposed.

"That would be the best way to attract attention to yourselves," retorted Sobek. "It would be wiser to look like simple peasants."

"Let's be off," urged Paneb impatiently. "We've talked long enough. If we need to defend ourselves, our woodcutters' axes will suffice."

"Be very careful," advised the Nubian.

▲

Didia knew a tamarisk wood that could be reached in three-quarters of an hour if they walked quickly. The roots of the trees sought out water to a depth of up to sixty cubits and extended outward for as much as a hundred cubits. The tamarisks had reddish brown bark, and their intertwined branches provided agreeable shade and acted as windbreaks at the edges of the fields.

Paneb chose the first tree to be cut.

"A good choice," agreed Didia. "It is beginning to interfere with the growth of the others."

Paneb set to work with such energy that his two companions could not keep up with him. After a while Renupe had to slake his thirst with a swig from his water bag, and he asked if they could rest for a moment.

"No," said Paneb. "We mustn't waste time. We must collect enough wood as quickly as possible, and go back."

Selecting the second tamarisk was harder, but to the carpenter's surprise Paneb made another excellent choice. Renupe worked more quickly, and the baskets were soon filled.

"We've got enough to make bowls and spoons for the womenfolk," said Didia. "Whatever task has to be done, the raw material is the most important thing."

Paneb saw the pieces of tamarisk wood in a whole new light. It occurred to him that the Master might have ordered this expedition into the outside world in order to show him that this modest material had a value beyond price. But how could a painter use tamarisk wood as his raw material?

"We have visitors," warned Renupe.

On the path leading to the tamarisk wood stood a party of ten soldiers, commanded by an officer with a brutal face.

12

"What are you doing here?" demanded the officer.

Renupe smiled broadly. "We're cutting a bit of wood—old branches, whose removal will allow the young trees to develop."

"Have you paid the tax?"

"We didn't know there was one. Doesn't this wood belong to everyone?"

"No it does not, peasant. I've brought in a tax to protect the population from looters. In these troubled times, my patrols are essential, but not free."

Paneb pushed Renupe aside. "Does Governor Mehy know what you're doing?"

The officer said aggressively, "Are you trying to make out that you know him? He doesn't mix with scum like you!"

"I'd be careful if I were you. Since he honors me with his friendship, I could quite easily tell him his soldiers are holding the poor to ransom."

The officer drew his dagger.

"Let's not lose our heads," cautioned Renupe. "It's not worth killing each other for a few branches. How much is this tax?"

"Too much for you, peasant! You'll have to pay it through forced labor."

"I warn you," said Paneb, his voice steady and controlled, "there aren't enough of you and you aren't brave enough. In your place, I'd go peacefully on my way."

The officer sneered. "An unarmed man should speak respectfully to soldiers."

"You'd better listen to my friend," put in Didia calmly. "If you make him angry, you won't leave this wood unscathed."

The soldier was impressed by Paneb's huge size, but he did not think even a man that big could defeat a whole squad. He sneered again. "Oh, and he's protected by the gods, I suppose?"

An enormous cat, with a coat of black, white, and russet, leaped down from a branch and landed on the ground between Paneb and the officer. The hairs on its arched back stood erect, and it hissed and bared its teeth, its enraged eyes fixed on the soldier.

"You filthy beast, I'll slit your throat!"

A soldier said quickly, "Don't do that, sir! That's no ordinary cat. I'm sure it's the one that carries a knife to cut off the heads of the serpent of darkness and his allies."

"Yes, it is," confirmed another soldier. "It must be the fearsome cat that embodies the sun. And it's protecting this man. We should get away from here, sir, or terrible misfortune will befall us."

Without waiting for orders, the soldiers fled.

▲

Prince Amenmessu decided to decree a general mobilization, gave up the idea, then considered it again.

Mehy found all this vacillation maddening, but he did not let his feelings show, and even encouraged the prince to ponder a decision that would have dramatic consequences for the country. While Amenmessu was duly pondering, Mehy wrote to Seti that he was attempting to calm the prince's martial enthusiasm, with the firm intention of preserving civil peace.

One of his secretaries brought him reports on agriculture in the Theban province.

"The reports are excellent," announced scribe, "but I'm afraid I have some bad news as well: the mayor of Thebes has died."

"How sad!" lamented Mehy, inwardly delighted by the death of the old ruffian, who had known a little too much about him, but who had been wise enough never to oppose his rise to power.

"For once, a death my gentle wife isn't responsible for," mused the general. He immediately consulted his list of Theban worthies, and from them chose the stupidest and most docile to be the new mayor. The man did not understand the first thing about running a city, so he would defer to Mehy, who would thus continue to rule both town and region without ever emerging from the shadows.

Surrounded by a heady scent of lilies, Serketa appeared on the threshold of her husband's office, preening herself. "How do you like my new green dress with its silver fringing?"

"Superb!"

"I was getting bored without you." Simpering, she sat down

on his knee, and asked, "Has the little prince finally decided to begin hostilities?"

"Not yet, my sweet. And all I am receiving are unimportant instructions, as if no one holds real power in the capital—from which we must assume that Seti dare not seize it."

"The mourning period ends tomorrow. Then things are bound to change, and I know you're ready to face whatever situation arises."

▲

Sobek stared in amazement at the enormous cat perched on Paneb's shoulder. "What on earth is that?" he asked.

"The sun cat, according to those who know about such things," replied Paneb.

"A cat? I'd have said it was a lynx!"

"It seems to want to protect me, so I shall adopt it."

As the big Nubian came closer, the cat hissed angrily and tried to scratch him.

"What a charming creature!" said Sobek. "What are you going to call him?"

"Well . . . why not 'Charmer'?"

Sobek shrugged, and turned his attention to the heavy loads of wood the three craftsmen carrried. "Did you have any problems?"

"Thanks to Charmer, none at all."

When they got back to the village, Paneb, Didia, and Renupe went to see Kenhir, who weighed the wood—something no one but the Scribe of the Tomb was allowed to do—and noted down the amount. He gave Didia the job of working the tamarisk wood, together with two other craftsmen of his own choice.

"I choose my two traveling-companions," decided Didia, "and we'll go to the workshop at once. This little task will make our fingers supple."

As he left Kenhir's office, Paneb met an obstacle he hadn't foreseen. Tail stiff and erect, gaze menacing and teeth bared, Ebony was crouched and ready to spring. He glared at the cat and clearly had no intention of letting it enter the village. As dominant male, he ruled over the domestic animals and didn't accept just anyone.

Paneb and Ebony were good friends, and the dog had not attacked the intruder, but it was clear that negotiations must begin without delay.

"Listen, Ebony," said Paneb, "this cat defended me against some dangerous idiots. By saving their lives, he saved us having to deal with a serious problem. All right, it's a cat, so it will be independent, but I shan't let it intrude on your domain and it won't usurp any of your authority."

The dog listened carefully and, to judge from the glint in his hazel eyes, understood.

"As for you, Charmer," Paneb went on, "don't be haughty, and try to be accepted. In this village, we respect one another, and we observe the order of precedence. In your sphere, Ebony is the leader."

He put the cat down on the ground. It was huge, weighing at least as much as a small dog. The dog growled and Charmer hissed, putting out his claws and fluffing up like a porcupine. Ebony was not used to this kind of monster, but he did not recoil.

"There's to be no fighting here," ordered Paneb. "And the new arrival must behave himself like a proper guest."

Paneb looked deep into the cat's eyes, and it saw clearly the mettle of the man it had decided to live with, so it drew in its claws and crouched down like a sphinx. Ebony did likewise for a few moments, then got up and walked in a circle round the cat, sniffing it from a distance.

When Charmer stood up and rubbed himself against Paneb's leg, the dog confined himself to following them, not without suspicion but without animosity. The village had acquired one more inhabitant.

▲

A peaceful early morning at last! Kenhir had been able to finish his dream without being interrupted by his servant girl. He got slowly out of bed, took his time washing, and reread some ancient poetry while he enjoyed his breakfast.

Suddenly, this beautiful tranquillity was shattered.

"Your office needs a thorough cleaning," declared Niut, with the characteristic impertinence that so infuriated the Scribe of the Tomb.

"Out of the question," he mumbled.

"I have work to do at set times and I must keep to those times," she insisted, "and I will not leave one room in this house to the mercies of the dust."

"Who is the master here?" demanded Kenhir.

"The truth," replied Niut. "And the truth of a house is its cleanliness."

Defeated by that argument, Kenhir confined himself to piling up several papyrus scrolls on a shelf, to protect them from the whirlwind, but he held on to the current section of the Journal of the Tomb. And he watched gloomily as Niut disappeared into his domain with her arms full of brooms, brushes, and dusters.

"Come quickly, Kenhir!" shouted the urgent voice of Userhat the Lion. "The messenger's just arrived from Pi-Ramses, and he wants to see you."

Kenhir hurried out of his house and walked toward the main gate, followed by many craftsmen.

"Have you told the Master that Uputy's arrived?" he asked.

"He's already there," said Userhat.

In the presence of Nefer the Silent, Uputy handed the Scribe of the Tomb a royal decree from the capital.

Uputy's hands were shaking. "I hope this text doesn't bring unwelcome news," he said to Kenhir.

"Let us assemble before the Temple of Ma'at and Hathor," decided the Master.

The villagers gathered quickly, all wondering anxiously what the news would be. Nefer hushed them and, when there was absolute silence, asked the Scribe of the Tomb to read the decree.

It proclaimed the coronation of Seti, the second of that name, who had thus become Pharaoh of Upper and Lower Egypt, and the new supreme Master of the Place of Truth.

—— 13 ——

Seti II was a robust, authoritarian fifty-year-old, well able to direct the armed forces with a firm hand and make senior officials obey him. By choosing to dedicate his reign to the fearsome god Set, master of storms and cosmic disturbances, he hoped to make a decisive mark, in imitation of the great Seti I, father of Ramses the Great.

But Seti II's son was called simply Amenmessu, and he had not been present at his father's coronation to acclaim him and thus recognize him as legitimate ruler.

The new king's *tjaty* was called Bay. Son of a Syrian father and an Egyptian mother, he was small, slightly built, and nervous, with darting black eyes and a small beard. He had succeeded in pushing aside other courtiers to become tjaty, and in doing so had nipped several plots in the bud and broken up more than one dangerous alliance, thus earning Seti's gratitude.

Bay's only rival for the king's favor was Seti's second wife, Queen Tausert, a splendid brunette with the face of a goddess. Aged about thirty and in the full flower of womanhood, she was as formidable a character as her husband. Displeasing her meant falling into disfavor, so Bay never openly opposed her, even if he disagreed with her.

Bay entered the king's office and bowed low before him.

"Have you at last brought me a letter from Amenmessu?" asked Seti.

"Unfortunately not, Majesty, but the news I have gleaned is

not unwelcome. According to rumor—which seems well founded—the most powerful man in Thebes is General Mehy, and his troops are loyal to you."

Just then the queen came in and took her place beside her husband.

Seti said, "I know General Mehy will do everything he can to prevent civil war, but Amenmessu might dismiss him and take command of the Theban troops himself."

"In that case," said the queen, "he would become a rebel and must be fought with every ounce of strength, and without pity."

"Amenmessu is my son, not yours."

"That must not weigh with you, Seti. No one can be allowed to defy the authority of the state without being punished, otherwise the door is open to lawlessness and misery for everyone."

"The queen is right, Majesty," said Bay quietly. "You are ruler of both upper and lower Egypt, and you must maintain the unity of the land."

"If Thebes secedes," said Tausert, "you must act swiftly and with the greatest resolution: a pharaoh's reign cannot be deprived of the protection of the god Amon. And you must create your House of Eternity in the Valley of the Kings and have your Temple of a Million Years built on the west bank of Thebes, not to mention the work you must do to improve the temples at Karnak."

"Tjaty, have you drawn up a report on the Place of Truth?" asked Seti.

"Of course, Majesty. Its Master, Nefer the Silent, enjoys an excellent reputation, and the works he has overseen are flawless. No craftsman has ever made a complaint against him, and I cannot see any reason to replace him. It is felt that the Brotherhood does not bend easily, and that it is better not to go against it."

The queen was astonished. "Is Pharaoh not the supreme Master, then?"

"Indeed he is, Majesty, but it is also felt that these craftsmen are the guardians of great secrets, such as the creation of gold by magic, and that a king must win the Brotherhood's trust in order to benefit from them."

"Is there no representative of the state among them?"

"Yes, the Scribe of the Tomb, whose name is Kenhir. He is about seventy years old and apparently of a somewhat difficult character, but he is scrupulous in the way he runs the village."

"He's much too old," said Tausert, "and should have retired long ago. Draw up a letter of dismissal immediately."

"With whom do you wish to replace him, Majesty?"

"Why not yourself, Bay?"

The tjaty blanched. "I am at your service, but I have no knowledge of Thebes or of this very specialized office, and—"

"We need the tjaty at our side," said Seti firmly. "Without him, I would not have succeeded in defeating my opponents."

"Very well," conceded Tausert, "but he must draw up that letter and appoint a dedicated, obedient scribe to run the Place of Truth and to prepare for our arrival at Thebes. Ah, I was forgetting: we must not let the Master get wind of our decision and support the old man. What we must do is . . ."

▲

Amenmessu was devastated. "He dared to . . ."

"Without wishing to offend you, my lord," said Mehy, "your father's decision was predictable."

"He has dared become pharaoh without consulting me, without summoning me to Pi-Ramses to link me to the throne. He has dared reject me and treat me like a rival of no significance whatever. I hate him! Do you understand me, Mehy? I hate him!"

"I understand your disappointment, my lord, but should you not act as quickly as possible?"

"But to oppose the pharaoh means becoming a rebel, losing one's life and one's soul."

"No one contests that."

"Then what future is there for me? My father will never choose me as his successor—I'll be stuck here until I die."

"Have you forgotten your original plan?"

Amenmessu looked at Mehy in puzzlement. "What do you mean?"

"You did not sanction your father's coronation and you don't recognize him as the true pharaoh. To avoid being considered a rebel and to satisfy your just ambitions, you have only one choice: become pharaoh yourself, with the approval of the priests of Karnak. Then it is your father who will be accused of rebellion and usurpation."

"He'd never yield—and there'll be civil war."

"Who knows, Prince? Seti does not expect such determination on your part. Faced with a foregone conclusion, perhaps he will draw back."

"But the risk is enormous!"

"That is the price of your triumph and your glory, Prince. The decision is yours and yours alone."

▲

As the villagers left the Temple of Ma'at and Hathor, the Master was surprised to find Uputy following him.

"What is it, Uputy?" he asked.

The messenger handed him a sealed papyrus scroll.

Nefer looked at the seal: it was Pharaoh's. "A letter from the palace, addressed to me? But shouldn't official documents be sent to the Scribe of the Tomb?"

"My instructions are precise: I must deliver this message into your hands—your hands, and nobody else's."

Thoughtfully, Nefer carried the scroll home. When he got there, Ubekhet was just about to leave to see some patients. The Master broke the seal and read the document.

"It's incredible," he whispered.

"Bad news?" asked Ubekhet with concern.

"An absolute disaster."

He told her the contents of the letter, and she agreed that "disaster" was not too strong a description. The danger of an armed attack seemed to have receded, now that Seti had been crowned, but there were still plenty of other forms of attack. And none of the craftsmen had foreseen this one.

"What must we do?" asked Ubekhet.

"We shall not yield by so much as the thickness of one of Kenhir's hairs."

"Doesn't that mean breaking the law?"

"Perhaps. But if I accept this order it'll be followed by ten more like it, and soon the Brotherhood will be no more than a group of servile workmen, condemned to extinction."

Ubekhet embraced him. "You're right. We must fight without fear of the consequences."

▲

Kenhir was washing his hair, as he did every morning. It was his favorite pleasure, a moment of perfect happiness when he could forget the weight of his years and his office. After rinsing, he massaged his scalp with castor oil, a miraculous balm that put his thoughts in order and revived his flagging energy. But this morning all that came out of the flask was one miserable drop of oil.

"Niut, bring me another flask of castor oil," he called irritably.

She hurried in. "There aren't any more," she said.

"How is that possible? Haven't you been keeping watch on our stocks?"

"I'm paid to do the cleaning and the cooking, not to run your house."

"That's terrible! How shall I survive without castor oil? Go and find me some in the village."

"With all that's been happening, the stocks are exhausted. You'll have to wait until the deliveries start again."

"I can't wait till then—especially not with all this uncertainty. Go and see Uabet, and ask her to persuade her husband to go and gather some castor-oil plants. And be sure to tell her it's very urgent."

"I'll have to finish cleaning the kitchen first," said Niut. "I can't leave it looking like a pigsty."

Kenhir did not insist, and he rubbed his hair dry. Without

his lotion, he felt defeated. And if that little pest Niut failed, the future looked bleak.

When he emerged from the bathing room, the Scribe of the Tomb found Nefer the Silent waiting for him, a papyrus scroll in his hand. The Master's grave expression did not augur well.

"I've had a letter from the royal palace," said Nefer.

"That's most irregular. All official correspondence is supposed to be sent to me."

"This particular letter couldn't be."

"Why not?"

"Because it asks me to approve the order for your retirement."

— 14 —

After a long silence, Kenhir said, "I may be over seventy, but I have no intention of retiring."

"It seems that you have no option," said Nefer.

"Is the letter signed by King Seti?"

"No, by the new tjaty, Bay."

"Then it's worthless. I don't answer to any officials, and only the king can remove me."

"Bay feels that you're too old to perform such onerous work, and he plans to replace you with a young scribe trained at Pi-Ramses."

"An incompetent who wasn't even born in Thebes! I see: the new regime wants to take control of the Place of Truth and impose its stamp upon it."

"The tjaty is only waiting for my agreement to appoint your successor. In exchange, he is sending me five servants who will relieve me of all material cares, so that I need concern myself with nothing but the king's tomb."

Kenhir's jaw clenched. "What answer are you going to give this man Bay?"

"That I will accept his servants, who will work in the fields and bring me a substantial income."

The old scribe was devastated. "I thought I knew you, Nefer. But I was wrong, wasn't I?"

"And then I shall remind him that there is no age limit for holding the office of Scribe of the Tomb, and say that you're in excellent health, your skills are unrivaled, and the Brotherhood is delighted with the way you run the village."

A thin smile lit up Kenhir's face. "No, I wasn't wrong."

"Lastly, I shall say that both I and the leader of the port crew wish you to remain and that, if you were to leave, we and the Wise Woman would immediately follow suit. The Brotherhood would no longer be in a position to prepare a House of Eternity or a Temple of a Million Years, since no one would be able to use the Stone of Light and give life to the House of Gold."

Kenhir blinked back a tear. "Nefer," he said gruffly, "I—"

"The new government has tried to divide us, thinking that any human society must be based on covetousness, greed, and contention. Bay has simply forgotten that, despite our faults and weaknesses, we live in the Place of Truth, under the Rule of Ma'at."

The two men embraced.

"I feel twenty years younger," declared Kenhir.

His chin resting on his hands, Paneb had spent several hours gazing at a dried branch of tamarisk wood, but he had still not managed to persuade himself that this modest piece of wood could be the raw material for his masterwork. It offered him neither a basis nor a motif; painting on tamarisk or painting tamarisk aroused not the slightest interest in him.

Uabet came quietly up to her husband. "May I disturb you?"

Paneb flung the piece of wood away. "That isn't the quintessence!"

"Of course not," she agreed with a smile. "Would you be willing to go and fetch some castor-oil plants for Kenhir? He's run out of oil, and Niut's afraid he'll be completely impossible if he can't massage his scalp every day. You'll find some plants near the first canal, not far from Ramses' Temple of a Million Years."

"Do I have to?"

"No, but you'd be doing him a kindness."

Uabet was so small and touching that Paneb couldn't refuse her. And after the guards had given him permission to pass, he found himself on the path to the canal.

The castor-oil plants were about the size of a small fig tree, and grew wild at the edge of the marshes or along watercourses; smooth and dark, their leaves sheltered fruits that were dried in the sun until their outer shell split and fell away. By crushing them cold in a mortar, the villagers extracted an inexpensive oil that was used in lamps, and which was said to make the hair grow, cure even the worst headache, and purge the bowels. Paneb began to gather the fruit, which he dropped into a large bag.

Suddenly, his nostrils were filled with the smell of burning. Not far from him, some children were running away, laughing. They had set fire to some dry bushes.

As the flames leapt upward and outward, Paneb mused that they could travel through space and ascend to the heavens. Fire was the archetypal life force. It destroyed old, decayed things and caused new forms to be born. Suddenly, he saw the world as a path leading toward the creative fire; not to follow it meant succumbing to the deathly cold of banality.

He pushed aside the dead branches and banked up the little fire with sand, to prevent it spreading and destroying the row of castor-oil plants. He waited until the flames had completely died down before he walked away, deep in thought.

Fire. That was the quintessence.

▲

Thanks to the castor oil, Kenhir was a new man. The blood flowed more easily around his brain, and he felt ready to dictate to Imuni a long report on the running of the Place of Truth.

Sitting cross-legged on the ground, Imuni had scrupulously prepared his materials, which he never let anyone else use and which he guarded jealously. His brushes were always impeccably clean, as were the pots in which he diluted the cakes of red and black ink, never spilling a single drop.

"Do you feel ready for the fray, Imuni?" asked Kenhir. "This is going to take some time, because I shall omit not one single detail of my working methods."

"Why do you need to do so?"

"Because the central government is thinking of replacing me."

"Why is that?"

"Because I'm 'too old,' " spat Kenhir. "But I've no intention of being forced into retirement."

Imuni displayed no outward reaction, but an unexpected hope had been kindled in his breast. Who was better placed than himself to replace Kenhir? If required to act as a witness, he would inform Pharaoh—respectfully, of course—that the old scribe had indeed come to the end of his working life.

"Will this report be enough to persuade the government to retract its decision?" he asked.

"Of course not, but it isn't my only weapon."

"But aren't we obliged to obey the government?"

"The rule of the Place of Truth forbids us to yield to injustice and arbitrary decisions."

As Kenhir began to dictate, it occurred to Imuni that it might be wise not to reveal his ambitions too quickly. Despite his age, the old Scribe of the Tomb might possess resources Imuni knew nothing about.

▲

It had taken time for the traitor to examine the village mills closely, for he had had to approach them without attracting the attention of the women who worked there, making bread and beer. None of

the grindstones gave off the slightest glimmer of light. All that remained was to look at the large mill the lay workers used. At the
end of their day's work, most went home; and, as it was Beken the
potter's birthday, even Obed the blacksmith had left the modest
hut where he slept, so as not to be too far from his forge.

The coast was therefore clear, but he must be wary of prying
eyes; so the traitor had waited until dusk, and taken care to put
on a tunic he had never worn before, and which his wife had
woven without mentioning it to her neighbors.

Walking with measured steps, he left by the little western
gate and followed the line of the encircling wall, so as not to be
seen by the guard on duty at the main gate. The lay workers' area
was deserted. A great ibis was crossing the orange-tinted sky,
and there was a light northerly wind.

The traitor walked to the mill and crouched down behind it
to observe the lay of the land.

When he stood up again, he had the feeling that he was
being spied on. Someone was hiding behind the sacks of flour
and watching him, someone who was afraid of him and dared
not confront him. Should he retreat without identifying his adversary, or kill him and make it look like an accident? The traitor hesitated.

A cat leapt up, scratched him on the shoulder, and raced off
toward the village.

Charmer, that enormous animal of Paneb's! The monster had
acquired a vast hunting ground, which none of the other cats dis-
puted. Fortunately, however vicious it might be, the damned
creature could not tell anyone that it had seen the traitor near the
lay workers' mill—that most ordinary of objects, which he had
passed so many times without paying it any attention.

Nerves on edge, he went slowly closer. The size of the grindstone was promising, and in the darkness he would know immediately if the dolerite was giving off light.

No, that line of reasoning was stupid. The sacred Stone
could not be exposed to daylight. The Master was an accom-

plished sculptor and would have hidden it under a covering designed to hide its real nature.

With a small, very sharp knife, the traitor made a deep scratch
on the surface of the grindstone, hoping to expose another material underneath, giving off light. But there was nothing but dolerite, which would give useful service for many years to come.

Disappointed, he had to admit that he was wrong again. The
Master had not left the precious stone in the open for all to see,
even well concealed, and the traitor must return to his first the-
ory: the Brotherhood's greatest treasure was kept somewhere se-
cluded, under constant guard.

—— 15 ——

When Tjaty Bay entered Mehy's office, the general knew at
once that King Seti's adviser would be a formidable adversary.

However, he concealed his misgivings and asked, "Did you
have a good journey, Tjaty?"

"To be frank, I hate traveling, but the king and queen insisted that I speak in person with the Master of the Place of
Truth. Have you informed him of my visit?"

"Of course, and you will meet him here first thing tomorrow
morning."

"He is an uncompromising man, it seems."

"Nefer's training has led him to be extremely strict, and he
doesn't easily bend to the demands of government," replied
Mehy ruefully.

"What can you tell me about him?"

"There has been not one single blot upon his career," replied
the general.

Mehy would gladly have blackened the Master's name, but

he was wary of Bay. When he knew the tjaty's intentions more clearly, he would try to manipulate him.

"I suppose Nefer is a thoroughly honest man?" asked Bay anxiously.

"The craftsmen of the Place of Truth make up a unique Brotherhood, Tjaty. They answer directly to the king, and they are absolutely adamant about that."

"I know, General, I know," sighed Bay. "In other words, you cannot help me."

"My official role is to protect the craftsmen's village and spare it any trouble. I do so to the best of my ability, though I'm not permitted to enter the Place of Truth and I have no influence over its leaders. Nevertheless, I am entirely at your service."

"The king values your loyalty, General. He is aware of your authority, and your plea for moderation did much to avert a war that would have been catastrophic for our country. I suppose that you have placed Prince Amenmessu under house arrest?"

"Of course. He is sick, depressed, and will eventually accept the king's sovereignty."

"Indeed, for he has no other choice."

▲

The Master was greeted warmly by Bay, who received him in the garden of the government buildings, under an ivy-covered pergola. Inside, sheltered from the sun, dishes of fruit and cups of beer had been set out on low tables.

"How sweet life must be in Thebes," observed the tjaty. "But I'm not here to discuss leisure pursuits. The pharaoh has received your letter and Kenhir's long report. They surprised us a little, I must confess. We don't dispute that the Scribe of the Tomb's work has been excellent, but is he still young and strong enough to hold such a taxing office? Surely it's time for him to retire—and he has certainly earned it."

"Have you read the whole of my letter?" asked Nefer.

"It bears witness to a magnificent friendship, but would it

not be better to forget that? You are overseeing the building of Seti II's House of Eternity, and I consider it necessary to appoint a new Scribe of the Tomb, a younger man who is more aware of the necessities of the moment. Times are changing, Master, and we all have to adapt. Have I made myself clear?"

"Very clear," said Nefer.

"Then the problem is resolved. I shall send you a scribe trained in the capital. You will approve his appointment, and work together with him." Pleased with himself, Bay took a sweet, juicy fig from the dish in front of him, and bit into it. "I was sure the Master of the Place of Truth must be an intelligent, sensible man, and I am glad I wasn't mistaken."

"I am afraid I must disappoint you, Tjaty."

"Oh no, my dear Nefer, I'm sure you won't. Your skills are well known, and I have no doubt at all that you'll succeed. The king's tomb will be a marvel, I'm sure."

"The Brotherhood will give of its best, that is certain; but in order to do so, it needs a Scribe of the Tomb whose authority is indisputable."

"Be assured, Kenhir's successor will have all the necessary qualifications."

"I doubt it."

The tjaty was confused for a moment, but he quickly understood. "You have your own candidate, have you?"

"Yes, I have," said Nefer.

"Well, nothing could be more natural. You yourself know that old Kenhir is at the end of his career and you have prepared his successor. May I know his name?"

"It is Kenhir himself."

Bay frowned. "Are you mocking me?"

"As I explained in my letter, there could be no better Scribe of the Tomb than Kenhir. It is the will of the Brotherhood that he should continue in the post."

"But I will it otherwise!"

"You," asked Nefer drily, "or the king?"

"We are touching on state secrets, Master, but I can tell you in confidence that Queen Tausert has demanded this change and that it is out of the question to disobey her."

"What are her criticisms of Kenhir?"

"Well, she made no *specific* criticisms."

"So it is a mere whim of hers."

"Be careful what you say, I beg you!"

"We are a Brotherhood of craftsmen," said Nefer, "and we work with materials that tolerate no whims or changes of mood. If the queen has dreamed up a plan to force us to accept a scribe who will be unable to conform with our customs, she must give it up."

"I strongly advise you to submit," said Bay.

"You really have misunderstood me. Without unity, the Brotherhood could not work properly; and that unity requires that Kenhir remain in his post."

"The queen's wishes—"

"Are not above the law of Ma'at, which it is Her Majesty's duty to embody and act upon. Explain to her that Kenhir is not a scribe like any other, and that we need him to run our community. If his health were to decline, he and I would change our views."

"Master, you're putting me in a very delicate situation."

"I count you, Tjaty, to resolve the problem by explaining tactfully to the queen that we must all work to the same end, and that I await the palace's instructions to begin excavating the new pharaoh's House of Eternity."

▲

"This is even worse than I had feared in my nightmares," Bay confided to Mehy. "That man Nefer will never budge—and neither will the queen! If Her Majesty refuses to listen, do you think the Master will resign and render the Brotherhood incapable of working?"

"He is a stubborn man, and he doesn't make promises lightly. If he says he'll do something, he'll do it."

"I had hoped that my warnings would frighten him, but they

haven't even dented his determination. So here I am, forced to return to Thebes without delay, to explain the situation to the royal couple."

"If an agreement can't be reached, what will happen?" asked Mehy.

"Kenhir will be retired, and his replacement will be imposed on the Brotherhood."

"That would be the worst solution possible. The scribe we appointed would be rejected by the craftsmen, and work would be disrupted."

"I dare not even imagine such chaos."

"Then don't provoke it, Tjaty."

"You don't know Queen Tausert! If she's crossed, her anger will be devastating."

"Are her wishes in accordance with the king's?"

"Seti hasn't yet made his views known."

"Don't harm the Place of Truth," said Mehy. "Without it, no reign can be anchored in eternity."

"The pharaoh knows that, and I'm sure that he'll take the measures necessary to avoid a disastrous conflict."

Ignorant of the new regime's real intentions, Mehy had played his role as the village's protector very well. The near future would enlighten him further.

▲

Paneb was painting flames in all their forms. For several days, he had been observing them constantly, watching their dances so as to capture their most intimate movements. Spoiling a great many cakes of color, which he made himself, he used dozens of different shades of red and yellow to conjure up the fire's changes, from the first leaping flame to the slow death of the embers.

Scraps of papyrus and fragments of limestone lay heaped on top of one another. Unhappy with the results, Paneb took no interest in these minor works.

"Have you heard that they want to take Kenhir away from us?" Uabet asked him.

"We shan't let them."

"Wouldn't you like a change?"

"Kenhir never changes. And so much the better."

Uabet sat down beside her husband. "Are you still searching for the quintessence?"

"The fire speaks to me, but I can't understand what it says. And painting it doesn't satisfy me. And yet . . . and yet, I have a feeling that I'm getting close to discovering the secret."

"You're right."

Paneb stared at his wife in astonishment. "Do you mean that fire is the raw material essential to my masterwork?"

"In a way, yes."

"Explain—please, I beg you!"

But she said, "You must find your way alone."

"Why isn't it enough to paint the fire?"

"Ask yourself about the invisible flame that gives life to your hand and the visible one that gives sight to your eyes each morning. Learn to control the degrees of fire, from enthusiasm to the mind's creation. You must advance like an explorer in search of new lands and—if only for a moment—govern the land you have conquered."

"What strange words, Uabet."

"They are not mine but those of the fire whose daughter I am, as are all priestesses of Hathor."

----- 16 -----

Everything had gone wrong. Bay's journey back to Pi-Ramses had been trying because of an adverse wind, then a mast had broken, which meant he had had to switch to another boat, then his secretary had fallen ill, and now this.

Bay had hoped to speak first with the king and to persuade

him to oppose the queen's plan. But he found that Seti was away, inspecting the barracks on the northeastern frontier and, having full confidence in Queen Tausert's abilities, had left her to deal with day-to-day matters. The king often did this, so that he could devote his attention to the army, with a view to preparing for future conflict with Amenmessu. So Bay's plan had been wrecked, and he knew all too well that opposing Tausert would lead only to disaster.

When she received him in the private audience chamber, to which only the most influential state figures were admitted, Bay was once again dazzled by the queen's beauty and elegance. Her perfect curves were displayed to admiration by a light green dress, and her irresistible charm was emphasized by necklaces and bracelets so delicate that they seemed almost unreal. Tausert had enchanted both Seti and the court, and Bay himself was unnerved by her regal presence and formidable intelligence.

She began by asking, "Was your visit to Thebes a success, Bay?"

"More or less, Majesty."

"Tell me the good news first."

"The province is peaceful and General Mehy's troops are loyal to you."

"Did you speak with Amenmessu?"

"No, he is ill and in low spirits. He has probably realized he hasn't the stature to defy his father."

"He may simply be trying to deceive us."

"That's certainly possible, Majesty, but Thebes isn't on a war footing."

"Very well. Now let us move on to the bad news."

The tjaty swallowed. "I met Nefer the Silent, Master of the Place of Truth, to inform him of your intentions and—"

"What do you mean, my 'intentions'?" demanded the queen. "The decision was made and all he had to do was accept it."

Unusually, the tjaty went straight to the point. "The Master refuses, Majesty."

Tausert's beautiful eyes flamed with anger. "Do I understand you correctly, Bay?"

"He confirmed to me what he said in his letter: that he wishes to keep Kenhir as Scribe of the Tomb."

"Has this Master forgotten that he owes obedience to Pharaoh?"

"Of course, Majesty, and in the end he will bow to your will. But my actions did not seem appropriate to him, and he warned me against replacing Kenhir, whose health is excellent."

"Are you taking his side, Tjaty?"

"Indeed no, Majesty," said Bay fervently, "and I am devastated by my failure. But he's a stubborn man, and it will not be easy to make him yield."

"You don't often fail in the missions we entrust to you." The threat was barely veiled.

"Even General Mehy advised me to be careful. Compelling Kenhir to retire would anger the Brotherhood so much that they might not work as eagerly as usual, and might become . . . disorganized."

"Do you mean they would dare to rebel against us?"

"That word is a little too strong, Majesty, but it seems that these craftsmen set great store by their unity."

"In other words, you think I have made a mistake and you hope I will revoke my decision."

The tjaty would have loved to turn himself into one of the tiles on the floor so as not to have to answer. In a few words, he might lose the reward of long years of patient hard work, and he'd end his career at the bottom of the scribes' ladder, in a dismal little settlement somewhere in the provinces.

"I am waiting for an answer, Tjaty," said the queen imperiously.

Since he was damned anyway, perhaps it was better to play the card of sincerity, for once. "In view of my conversation with the Master, I believe, Majesty, that it would be preferable to leave Kenhir in his post. The Brotherhood would thus undergo no upheaval and could respond to Pharaoh's wishes as quickly as possible. Besides, Kenhir is very old. . . ."

"I am surprised at you, Bay."

"I am deeply sorry, Majesty, but I have no choice but to speak the truth. Many think me an opportunist, using lies and flattery to acquire my ends, and there is some truth in that. But today I am adviser to the royal couple who preside over the destiny of the land I love and which I wish to serve. So I must change my ways, no matter what it costs me."

The queen's expression changed from aggressive to almost affectionate. "I think I have misjudged you, Bay. I took you for one of those second-rate courtiers whose sole ambition is personal wealth, but you seem to have chosen the path of honesty."

Tausert was sparing with her compliments, and these relatively benevolent words did not reassure the tjaty. Were they simply a prelude to the fatal blow?

"Tell me more about Nefer the Silent," she said.

"He impressed me greatly, Majesty. He's quiet yet compelling, and he has a truly commanding presence. Face-to-face with him, you feel small, almost powerless. He doesn't raise his voice; he doesn't try to persuade you; he goes straight to his goal as though he isn't afraid of anything at all. Be wary of him, Majesty. He may be only a craftsman, but he has the stature of a true leader and he'll fight unflinchingly to preserve the Brotherhood he leads."

"Even to the point of opposing Pharaoh himself?"

Bay hesitated. "Probably not, but, with the greatest respect, Majesty, I'm not sure that you view the problem correctly."

"What do you mean?"

"Giving orders to a man of that stamp isn't enough. If his obedience is to be not mere submission but true commitment, he must wholeheartedly approve of the proposed plan. Because Prince Amenmessu is in Thebes and we cannot predict what he will do, King Seti's reign is beginning in difficult conditions, and the excavation of his tomb in the Valley of the Kings will be a major undertaking. What would we gain from humiliating Nefer and forcing him to dismiss Kenhir?"

"Respect for our sovereignty, Tjaty," said the queen emphatically.

"Indeed, Majesty, but might it not be preferable to take one small step back?"

Tausert bristled. "Are you advising a queen to humble herself?"

"I am advising her to act in the best interests of Egypt."

"Leave me now, Bay. When the pharaoh returns, we shall make a final decision."

▲

Charmer jumped onto Kenhir's lap as he was enjoying the evening sunshine on the doorstep of his house. Sitting on a three-legged stool, the old scribe was remembering the years he had spent in the Brotherhood's service, with its joys and its sorrows. He regretted nothing, not even the inumerable daily problems and the craftsmen's occasional misfortunes, which even the gods had not succeeded in preventing.

The enormous multicolored cat had retracted its claws, so as not to hurt the old scribe, and was licking his hands attentively.

From nearby, Ebony watched the scene. The black dog had allowed the cat to form bonds of friendship with the Scribe of the Tomb but continued to keep a close eye on it; he had not yet fully accepted it.

"You're cleverer than I am," Kenhir told Charmer, "for you always know how to fall on your feet. I'm not very tactful, and all I've ever thought about is doing my job properly, not pleasing the powers that be—in any case, I'd be very bad at it and I'm too old to change now."

Paneb came over and sat down beside Kenhir. "Charmer likes you, doesn't he, even though he's still wild?"

"We probably have similar personalities."

"You aren't a craftsman, Kenhir, but your long career has enabled you to discover many of the Brotherhood's secrets."

"Don't believe all you hear, my boy."

"Nefer's asked me to create a masterwork."

"That's a decisive step," said Kenhir. "You're very gifted, but, even so, success isn't a foregone conclusion."

"You must know what the quintessence is."

"Human nature. There's nothing more perverse or more ridiculous, but it's the tool the gods have given us, and we must make the best we can of it. Don't reject it. Use it as you'd use a particularly difficult raw material."

"Will I have to change?"

"Don't deceive yourself into thinking you can: as you were born, so will you die. My experience has shown me that no one changes, and that the only man who can become Master is he who was born to hold that office. But, just as the coarse outer layers must be removed from stone and wood, so that their hidden shapes appear, so you, Paneb, must reach into yourself and discover your true heart, the center of your being. You will then discover the quintessence."

The cat was dozing trustingly on Kenhir's knee, but it opened its eyes as Nefer approached.

"Isn't it a delightful evening?" remarked Kenhir, as though he were addressing the setting sun. "It's years since I let myself be idle like this."

"I've just had the final decision about you from the palace," said Nefer.

"Before you tell me the details, let me enjoy the dusk and my last day in the village. My bags are packed, I've sent my servant away, and I shall leave without saying good-bye to anyone. First thing tomorrow, I shall be forgotten, and no one will miss me. That's how life is."

"Perhaps, but sometimes it leads in unexpected directions."

The old scribe looked up in alarm. "Is the king giving me another punishment?"

"That's for you to judge: he's confirmed you in office as Scribe of the Tomb."

—— 17 ——

Nefer and Kenhir went out of the main gate and climbed the slope that led to the village burial ground, where the Master was having his tomb dug. He worked there himself from time to time, with the help of Paneb, who had just finished a painting.

"I want to show you my adopted son's latest work," said Nefer. "I think it's particularly successful."

He led Kenhir down between the tomb's rough-hewn walls and stopped in front of the painting. The light from outside lit up only the lower part of the painting and did not illumine the bright colors—of which the predominant one was ocher yellow—and the scribe could not make out the subject until his eyes had adjusted to the half-light.

The painting was of two men standing face-to-face. One wore the Master's ritual apron, and the other was in a ceremonial robe and carried a scribe's writing materials.

"But that's me!" exclaimed Kenhir.

"I wanted you to be depicted in my House of Eternity, so that we can continue to talk and to take care of the village's happiness when we have left this earth."

"This is a . . . a great honor," stammered Kenhir.

"Most of all, it's a mark of my esteem for a Scribe of the Tomb who puts aside his age and his ailments in order to work for the Brotherhood's well-being."

"This is the most beautiful mark of affection I've ever been privileged to receive, Nefer. How can I thank you?"

"By continuing, Kenhir, simply by continuing, no matter what difficulties you face."

The scribe gazed for a long time at the painting, which showed him in the full vigor of middle age. "Paneb has endowed me with a nobility I don't possess. But it's better to appear that way before the gods."

"Has he spoken to you about his masterwork?"

"He's looking everywhere for his quintessence, and he'll know no peace until he's found it."

"Is he on the right path?"

"I hope so—but many men have failed just when they thought they'd almost reached their goal."

The two men walked together out of the tomb, and stood looking down at the village.

"How lucky we are," said Nefer, "to live here and spend our afterlife with the ancestors, far from the hustle and bustle of the outside world, and under the protection of the Stone of Light. What better destiny could there be?"

Kenhir cleared his throat. "I've been wanting to talk to you about a plan that is close to my heart. You may find it rather surprising."

Nefer listened with interest. The plan was indeed surprising.

Good news must always be celebrated with a feast, so Pai the Good Bread had been quick to organize one to celebrate the fact that Kenhir was staying in his post. Although most people found him difficult to deal with, both crews recognized the old scribe's skill and dedication, and that he was a vital member of the Brotherhood.

The only person who was disappointed was Imuni, who had hoped to take his master's place. Already he felt himself superior to Kenhir, although the latter's fingers had not yet lost their nimbleness. Kenhir kept the Brotherhood's Journal himself, and delegated only lesser tasks to his assistant. Imuni consoled himself with the thought that his master was very old and would soon return to the realm of Osiris.

At the end of the celebration, Kenhir had a visit from Niut the Strong.

"You sent me away," she said, "because you were thinking of leaving the village. As you're staying, are you going to employ me again?"

"Are you aware that you have a dreadful personality?"

"I need one, to put up with yours," she retorted. "What matters is my work. Are you satisfied with it?"

"Apart from the fact that you clean my office far too often, I'm not dissatisfied. As to your cooking, I must admit that it's delicious—though there isn't enough fat in it."

"That would be bad for your health. I spoke to the Wise Woman about it, and she agrees with me. As long as I'm in charge of preparing your meals, I shall use fat sparingly."

"You once told me it wasn't your job to run my house, and that you were supposed to do only the cleaning and cooking."

Niut smiled. "Are you saying you want to give me extra responsibilities?"

"Exactly. I'm facing a period of intensive work, and I'm not as energetic as I was when I was sixty, especially after what I've just been through. So I want to devote myself exclusively to the tomb and its demands. It will be your job to run this house and do everything necessary for its smooth day-to-day running, including seeing to my clothes and the flasks of castor oil for my hair."

"And what about my wages?"

"I've been thinking about that, of course, and I've come up with a solution that you may not like but which would offer many advantages."

"Do you mean you won't increase my wages?"

It was Kenhir's turn to smile. "I don't like waste, but I'm not quite that mean! In order to take on this weighty task, you'll have to live here. So I'm offering to marry you."

Niut was open-mouthed in astonishment. "But . . ."

"But I'm an old man and you're a young woman. Do you think I don't know that? Don't worry. I don't harbor any unhealthy desires toward you, and my only love is that of a grandfather for his granddaughter. I've been watching you, and I've seen that you're honest, hardworking, and worthy of esteem. By marrying you, I'm making you my heir. When I die, you'll be a rich, educated woman, for I shall spend time reading to you and teaching you about the sages' magnificent writings. You can then thank me, choose a man you like, and give him as many children as you wish. Of course, we shall sleep in separate rooms, and you'll have your own bathing room. Announcing our marriage will prevent the rumors that spread so quickly among our imaginative villagers; we shall explain that it's a legal measure, taken to secure your future and for no other reason. I'm counting on your frankness to dispel any misunderstandings."

"Are you . . . serious?"

"Very serious. You aren't like any other servant, Niut. Pleasing me is an achievement that deserves to be rewarded. Becoming my wife will bring you nothing but advantages and will even make the other women respect you. I've already discussed the idea with the Master. He was as astonished as you are, but he understands my reasons. Think about it, young lady, and decide."

"But won't people say"—Niut almost blushed—"that I've seduced you and am behaving like a common slut?"

"I expect they're saying so already," said Kenhir acidly. "Our marriage will put a stop to talk like that, and anyone who fails to show you respect will be punished severely. And I shall explain the true nature of our union to the Brotherhood's court."

"This is so unexpected, so . . ."

"I'm not forcing you into anything, Niut. You're free to choose your own life."

"And you really have no ulterior motive?"

"On the life of the Pharaoh and of the Master, I swear it. I have hidden nothing from you, and you can count on me to behave correctly. There is one risk, though."

Niut's throat tightened. "What is it?"

"That your new status as mistress of the house will go to your head and you won't serve me as well as before. That is the risk, and I'm the one who's taking it."

"You don't know me very well, do you?"

"I know human nature, young lady."

"I promise I shall look after this house as if it were my own."

"That's precisely what it will be, if you marry me."

Niut touched a wall, as if she wanted to be sure she wasn't dreaming. "In that case, how dare you think I'll permit the least untidiness, or that I'll stop doing battle with the dust? There are lots of things I dislike and which I had to keep quiet about if I wanted keep my job. But if I can speak freely, things will be different. The paintings need to be restored, some pieces of furniture aren't worthy of the Scribe of the Tomb, and the bathing rooms must be made more comfortable. We'll see about all the rest later."

Kenhir had foreseen this tornado and he wondered for a moment how long he'd be able to cope with it. But that was the price to pay for offering this remarkable young woman what she deserved.

"Am I to understand," he asked, "that you accept?"

"No, of course not . . . I mean . . . this is so unexpected."

"Have you any requirements I haven't taken into account?"

"No, the terms of the contract are acceptable, but it's so incredible. And why choose me?"

"Because I'm too old for ordinary marriage. Fate has just dealt me a harsh blow to remind me that from now on I must devote all my attention and all my remaining strength to the things that really matter. You have your life to build, and I can offer you a solid base on which to build it. I know myself, and I know I'm neither good nor generous, because the years I've spent running the Brotherhood have made me suspicious and disillusioned. In marrying you, my main aims are my own interest and well-being. You mustn't think I am acting out of charity and generosity of heart."

To calm her nerves, Niut picked up a brush and started dusting a wooden chest. "You may know all about how to file your scrolls, but you don't know how to fold clothes and store them so as to stop them wearing out too soon—and at your age you'll never learn such niceties. And then there's your dreadful habit of wearing a tattered tunic for days on end, for all the village women to see and shake their heads at. Let's be clear about this, Kenhir. Running a house well means taking positive action, and I don't intend to be thwarted in my domain."

"Is there no room for negotiation?"

"None at all."

Kenhir sighed. "Very well, Niut. I accept your conditions."

—— 18 ——

While waiting for orders from Pharaoh, the Master, after consulting Hay, leader of the port crew, shared out tasks between the two crews. They included making repairs to the main temple and the adjoining shrines, laying a new paved floor in the meeting hall, improving their own homes, and reinforcing their granaries.

Paneb and Ched the Savior had put the finishing touches to Kenhir's vast tomb, and the scribe's marriage had been officially recognized by the village court. In the presence of witnesses, he had read out his will, in which he bequeathed all his goods to Niut.

"I'm at peace with myself," Kenhir told Nefer, "for I can die content."

"Are you pleased with your tomb?"

"It's a marvel and I'm not worthy of it—but I shan't let anyone else have it! I'm in no hurry to take up residence in that sumptuous dwelling, but I shall guard it jealously. Many good things await me in the afterworld, Nefer. Thanks to the painters' talent, the peasants will gather in the harvest effortlessly, the wheat will always be ripe, the wind will swell the boats' sails without tearing them, and I shall be eternally young. What more could anyone ask of the Brotherhood? Being forced to leave the village would have broken my heart, and it's thanks to you that I escaped that misery."

"No," said Nefer. "You owe your escape to yourself and your own work."

"In this world of perpetual conflict, true brotherhood is a rare quality. I'm glad I've lived long enough to know its joy."

▲

The sun was shining, the water and food supplies had been delivered, flowers decorated the altars of the ancestors, and the village was buzzing like a happy beehive: but the Master was still worried.

"We're entering a new era," he told Kenhir. "Tjaty Bay will be the intermediary between us and Pharaoh, and I'm not at all sure he'll be a friend to us."

"All a courtier ever wants to do is further his career, which means trying not to displease his superiors. Either he'll think the Place of Truth can be useful to him, or he'll scheme to destroy it."

"He's intelligent, cunning, and, I believe, formidable. The fact that he persuaded the queen to change her mind shows just how much influence he has."

"Did you find out what he really thinks?" asked Kenhir.

"I had the feeling that he hasn't yet made up his mind, and that he's wondering what exactly it is that we do here."

"Fortunately, Mehy's still our official protector, but Amenmessu's presence in Thebes might eventually harm him, and therefore us. If civil war breaks out, we'll inevitably get caught up in it."

"That's why the Stone of Light must remain sheltered from covetous eyes."

"So far, the traitor hasn't even come close to its hiding place, and I'm sure he isn't about to."

"But we must never relax our vigilance," said Nefer. "He's shown how clever he is. We haven't been able to identify him, so he's still there, lurking in the shadows."

"Sobek thinks the shadow-eater's bound to make a mistake sooner or later."

"I'm not so sure. From now on, in everything we do we must take account of his presence."

"And that's not all," said Kenhir. "There's the queen's behavior, too. She didn't take against me solely because of my age. She wanted a spy in the Place of Truth, someone who'd describe all its activities to her, one by one. The new regime wants to take control of us and learn all our secrets."

"But she did change her mind about replacing you."

"I've been wondering why she did, and I'm worried that it's because she has in mind something far worse than forcing me to retire."

"The Wise Woman and the priestesses of Hathor invoke the goddess's protection every day, and we try not to stray from the path of Ma'at. Can you think of any more effective way of ensuring our safety?"

Kenhir felt like saying that he would sometimes have liked a sizeable, well-equipped army at his disposal. He could only hope that the Master was not deceiving himself.

▲

Casa the Rope and Fened the Nose stepped out in front of Paneb, barring his way on the path to the burial ground.

"We want to talk to you," said Casa.

"Don't put yourselves to any trouble."

"Why are you working alone in Nefer's tomb? We don't mind helping you."

"There's no need."

"You aren't acting according to custom," complained Casa.

"I, and I alone, will take care of my adoptive father's last dwelling."

"Aren't you being a bit presumptuous?"

"That's for the Master to judge. If he isn't satisfied with my work, he'll call on others to take over."

"You just want to impress the Master, don't you? And we're left looking like less than nothing. We don't like that, Paneb, we don't like it at all."

"You and the others who agree with you, you've got it all wrong. Now let me pass. I've got work to do."

"Casa's right," insisted Fened. "All right, the Master chose you as his son, but that's no reason for you to treat us as though we're worthless."

"Have you gone mad? I want to do this work well and in my own way, that's all."

"I think there's more to it than that."

"Are you going to let me pass or not?"

Casa and Fened could have called upon other craftsmen from the starboard crew to confront the big man. His calmness bothered them. Usually he was quick to anger, but this time he seemed almost indifferent.

Fened decided it was better keep things calm. "We're not trying to annoy you. Show us what you've painted, and we'll leave it at that."

"I've blocked the tomb entrance with a big boulder. Anybody who touches it will get a taste of my fists."

"You've no right to treat us like this!" protested Casa.

"Be a bit less touchy, and things will sort themselves out."

"You need to be taught a sound lesson, Paneb—you'll be all the better for it."

"Whenever you like."

"Stop it, you two!" demanded Fened the Nose. "This is just a minor disagreement. All Paneb has to do is compromise a little, and the matter will be closed."

Paneb's eyes eyes hardened. "It'll be closed as soon as you get out of my way."

Reluctantly, Fened and Casa stood aside and let him pass.

He climbed up to Nefer's tomb and heaved the boulder aside, unblocking the entrance.

Fire was only one aspect of the quintessence, and Paneb was not satisfied with just that. If the quintessence truly existed, it could not be found except in the heart of the rock, at the place where the young painter was creating his masterwork: the decoration of the House of Eternity dedicated to his adoptive father. He would transform the silent walls into a many-colored song; he would try to make his palette express all forms of life, so that he could offer them to Nefer's soul.

His own quintessence was painting, and he must not stray from it.

For two days, the traitor had had a fever, for the wound on his shoulder where the cat had clawed him had become infected.

How humiliating! After his success in hiding right in the heart of the Brotherhood, moving around in the shadows without making a single mistake, and preparing to steal the Stone of Light, here he was, laid low by a cat!

He couldn't go and see the Wise Woman, because she'd ask him how he'd got the wound. The traitor was afraid of becoming entangled in a lie and attracting suspicion to himself, reducing all his hard work to nothing.

His wife had given him a potion to drink, but it had had no effect and the fever was rising.

"Go and see Ubekhet," she advised him.

"No, it's too dangerous."

"But you might get seriously ill."

"The wound just needs to be cleansed."

"I haven't got the right herbs, and Sobek has forbidden the womenfolk to leave the village, for safety reasons. For the moment, we can't even go to the market."

"There is one solution," said the shadow-eater. "When Obed the blacksmith injures himself, he treats the wound with a copper-based ointment."

"Do you know where he keeps it?"

"In his tool-cupboard, on a shelf."

"Is it easily accessible?"

"Yes, when Obed's busy—and at the moment he's very busy making weapons."

"If I'm caught, I'll be dragged before the village court and I'll have to give my reasons for stealing the ointment. The least that would happen is that we'd be expelled."

"Yes, I know," said the traitor, "but we'll have to risk it. If you're too afraid, I'll go myself."

"You can't. You're shivering, your hands aren't steady, and you're too nervous."

"Aren't you nervous, too?" he asked.

"Not as much as you are. All right, I'll try."

The traitor's wife broke a kitchen pot and threw the pieces into a basket, which she balanced on her head. "I'll go and see Beken to get a new one, and that'll give me an excuse to walk past Obed's tool store."

"I should have strangled that cat!" raged the wounded man.

"From now on, keep well away from it."

When his wife had gone, the traitor remained slumped in the kitchen. His wound was growing increasingly painful. If she failed, he'd flee the village and abandon her to the guards. By the time she talked—and she wouldn't be able to resist intensive questioning—he'd be far from the Place of Truth. What a mess to be in, when he had a fortune within his grasp!

Tired, he dozed off, dreaming of a great estate, fat cows, and attentive servants serving him with a delicious meal. But when he reached out for a leg of roast goose, the Master seized him by the wrist and he cried out.

"Be quiet!" said his wife. "It's me."

The traitor emerged from his nightmare. "Did you get the ointment?"

"Yes."

"And no one saw you steal it?"

"No one at all. And I've brought back a new pot, which, as I said, is my excuse for being in the lay workers' area if anyone wonders. Now, let me see that wound."

Twenty-four hours later, after several applications, the fever had subsided and the wound looked much better. The traitor had been saved.

—— 19 ——

Balancing bundles on their shoulders, the five men trudged toward the Place of Truth. The had asked their way at the landing stage, and they had rested several times to get their breath back, for they were in no great hurry to reach their destination. Barely were they in sight of the First Fort when several Nubian guards surrounded them, threatening them with their short swords.

"Face down on the ground, quickly!" ordered one guard.

Terrified, the travelers obeyed.

"Who are you?" demanded the guard.

"Peasants," replied the youngest.

"What have you got in your bundles?"

"Just a few clothes."

"We shall see."

The guards searched the bundles and found no weapons, only an official-looking wooden tablet.

"On your feet—and no sudden movements," said the first guard.

"Where are you taking us?"

"To see our commander. You can tell him who you are."

The five men were half dragged, half pushed to the fort, where their wrists were tied behind their backs.

The sight of tall, impressive Sobek made them even more scared.

"So you claim to be peasants?" he said.

"We were working on the lands of the temple at Djerty," replied the youngest peasant, "and we received an order to come here."

"An order from whom?"

"From Pharaoh himself."

"To do what, precisely?"

"To cultivate some land the king is giving to Nefer the Silent. Look at the tablet we were given. Apparently, everything is written down there."

The text was written in a rigorously official style, and bore out the peasant's story.

One of Sobek's men hurried in and saluted. "Sir," he said, "one of the lookouts says there's what looks like an army coming this way."

"This time, it's serious. Throw these fellows into a corner and don't untie them. They acted as a decoy to test our defenses. Alert the other forts and the village."

Sobek had trained his men well, and they immediately prepared to resist fiercely, should they be attacked. But who had launched the attack, he wondered, Seti or Amenmessu? Either the newly crowned pharaoh wished to show his authority in a place whose symbolic importance was universal, or else his rival wanted to accomplish his first act of sovereignty. In either case, battle seemed inevitable.

Another guard came in and said, "There are at least a hundred men with donkeys, sir, but there's something very odd: the chariot leading them looks exactly like General Mehy's."

Sobek grimaced. If Mehy had chosen his best troops, the Nubian guards, despite their bravery, would be unlikely to win. So the great offensive had been launched. Sobek knew he ought to surrender, or even join forces with Mehy to destroy the village and drive out its occupants. But he would be true to his mission, through loyalty to himself and to the Brotherhood he so admired.

"And that's not all, sir. Apparently Mehy's soldiers are unarmed."

Sobek hurried out of his office and went to the gate of the fort. Mehy jumped down from his chariot, and the troops came to a halt. Fearing that this was a trick, Sobek's archers prepared to fire.

"What do you want, General?" called Sobek.

"These men bear gifts from Pharaoh Seti II to the Place of Truth. Here is the list, marked with the royal seal."

Astonished and wary, Commander Sobek did not lower his guard. "I must search them, to check that they aren't hiding any weapons."

Pots of green and black makeup, a large quantity of scented and relaxing pomades, jars of castor oil, moringa, linen, sesame and olive oil, lotions for the hair and skin . . . Pharaoh had sent the Brotherhood a veritable fortune, and Assistant Scribe Imuni began to get writer's cramp as he took dictation from Kenhir, who was delighted at how much castor oil there was.

In an accompanying letter, addressed to the Scribe of the Tomb and the Master, the royal couple expressed their trust in the Brotherhood and asked them to choose a site in the Valley of the Kings for the new pharaoh's House of Eternity. Unfortunately, Seti could not come to Thebes immediately, as he was needed in Pi-Ramses, but this setback should not delay the start of the work.

"Things are returning to normal," said Nefer.

"I'm not so sure," said Ubekhet.

"Do you think Pharaoh's word can't be trusted?"

"If he doesn't dare come to Thebes, it's because he's afraid Amenmessu may be going to rebel."

"Seti's busy strengthening our northeastern frontiers, isn't he?"

"You know as well as I do that coming to the Valley of the Kings to worship his ancestors is one of a new pharaoh's first duties. By not doing so, Seti shows that he's weak, and fails to respect the magic of his name."

The Wise Woman's judgment was harsh, but the Master could not argue with it.

"I have something else to worry about," she said, "and resolving it won't be easy."

"Can I help you?"

"I'm afraid not," she replied with a smile. "Many of the king's gifts will be placed in the temple, but the rest of the face lotions, oils, and so on must be shared among the priestesses of Hathor, and they have very definite preferences. . . . So the next few hours are likely to be difficult."

Ubekhet was right. There were heated arguments, and each woman tried to acquire as much as she could. Only Turquoise did not have to wrangle, as if the timeless radiance of her beauty was felt by all the women in the village to be almost a protective force. Uabet the Pure defended herself skillfully, and even young Niut got almost everything she had wanted, including a large jar of castor oil for her old husband.

While the Wise Woman was thus occupied, the Master went to the First Fort, where the five peasants were wondering if they were ever going to emerge from their misadventure alive.

Sobek handed him the wooden tablet the peasants had brought, and Nefer read it attentively. It confirmed that Pharaoh had granted him some land close to Ramses' Temple of a Million Years, and was paying five peasants to cultivate it. The Master could dispose of the harvest however he pleased.

"Please untie them now, Sobek," said Nefer.

"You must understand, I thought them dangerous men who'd been told to create a diversion before the main body of the troops attacked."

"And you were absolutely right to be suspicious. We must be as alert as you."

Sobek looked at him in surprise. "So even this mark of Pharaoh's favor isn't enough for you?"

"The Wise Woman feels that only Pharaoh's presence in Thebes would signify that all risk of civil war is over."

"That's what General Mehy thinks, too," said Sobek. "He says Amenmessu hasn't yet officially recognized his father's sovereignty, and this silence does not bode well."

▲

"As I see it," Karo told Didia, who was making an amulet in the shape of the knot of Isis, "it's all settled. Seti will confine himself to ruling the North and Memphis, while Amenmessu lives a life of pleasure and luxury in Thebes."

"That is contrary to the proper exercise of pharaonic power and the law of Ma'at," objected Didia. "If the Two Lands are set against each other, if North and South are separated, it'll be a recipe for disaster. Seti'd never tolerate seeing his throne destabilized and Egypt sinking into lawlessness."

"Times have changed," cut in Thuty the Learned, who, as usual, looked fragile enough to snap in two. "Seti may content himself with what he already has, so as to prevent irreversible harm."

"I fear the worst," said Unesh the Jackal. "I've a feeling that this is just a brief calm before the storm."

"Then let's make the most of it," advised Pai the Good Bread, handing out cakes to his comrades. "I baked these myself, and they're as light as a feather."

"I'm worried about Paneb," said Didia. "Usually he's larger than life, but now he seems to be getting more and more somber."

"I think I know why," said Unesh.

"Then tell me."

"Haven't you guessed?"

Didia scratched his forehead. "Surely you don't think . . . ?"

"I certainly do."

"You think he's really preparing a masterwork?" asked Pai.

His companions' silence confirmed that that was indeed what they thought.

"Isn't he too young to take on such a challenge?"

"Paneb has no chance of success, and he knows it," said Unesh. "That's why he isn't as cheerful as usual. And when he's failed miserably, he won't be cheerful at all."

"Anyone would think you were happy about that," said Pai.

"I hate pretentious people. Seeing them break themselves on a rock that is too big for them gives me the greatest amusement. More gifted craftsmen than Paneb have had the humility to live for their craft, and nothing but their craft, without claiming to master the quintessence."

▲

In the village burial ground, a muffled sound disturbed the quietness of the evening, as Paneb rolled back into place the boulder that blocked the entrance to Nefer's tomb. He had worked there all day, without giving a thought to the festivities being organized to celebrate the arrival of Pharaoh's lavish gifts.

——— 20 ———

Turquoise had anointed her superb naked body with perfume and taken Paneb even further along the path to ecstasy. Each time they gave themselves to each other, he felt as though he was discovering a new mistress, with an inexhaustible imagination.

Surfacing from their passionate reverie, the lovers gazed at each other as though they had just been reborn.

"You never look any older," said Paneb. "What's your secret?"

"The magic of Hathor."

"Have you searched for the quintessence, too?"

"Our path is different from the craftsmen's."

"But you know what it is, I'm sure you do."

"Hathor is the infinite love that unites all forms of life in the universe," said Turquoise.

"And if the quintessence is that love . . ."

"People say you shut yourself away all day in Nefer's tomb and won't let anyone see your work."

"They're right. Only Kenhir has had the privilege of seeing one scene, which the Master showed him. Since then, I've been blocking the entrance with a boulder, and not even Nefer himself knows all the details of my masterwork."

"But if you don't know what the quintessence is, aren't you bound to fail?"

"I'd fail if I expected to discover it in wood, fire, or I don't know what else! Spending one's time wondering about it is wasting one's life. Either I can create a masterwork or I can't. The quintessence is the union of my heart and my hand, and the only thing that counts is action. And the thing I can do is paint."

Suddenly, they were interrupted by raucous cries outside.

"It's Bad Girl," exclaimed Turquoise. She got up, threw a linen wrap round herself, and went to open the door.

The goose was cackling its head off as it tried to get into Turquoise's house.

"I think Bad Girl wants to speak to you," said Turquoise.

"Yes, but—she's right! I'm going to be late."

▲

Paneb was the last to arrive at the starboard crew's meeting place, and he found the doorway guarded by Karo the Impatient.

"I was just about to close the door," grumbled Karo.

"It is still open—that's all that matters."

Each craftsman sat down in his appointed place, and the Master called upon the ancestors to continue to protect the Brotherhood and show them the way. From the note of seriousness in his voice, everyone could tell that his news was not good.

"Pharaoh has no plans to visit us in the foreseeable future," he told them, "but nevertheless he's ordered us to prepare his House of Eternity. So we shall leave tomorrow for the Valley of the Kings, to choose its site."

"What if he doesn't like it?" asked Fened the Nose anxiously.

"We shall see."

"Why isn't Seti going to visit us?" asked Nakht the Powerful.

"Because Amenmessu's in Thebes."

"Do we know yet what the prince is going to do?"

"Not in detail, no. But he hasn't made an act of allegiance to his father, which means it's possible he's preparing to take power in the city of Amon."

"The South against the North—and us caught in the middle of it all!" said Nakht gloomily.

"For the time being," said Paneb, "we have a royal tomb to excavate, and nothing could be more wonderful."

"What about the port crew?" asked Ipuy the Examiner.

"They'll work in the Valley of the Queens, under Hay's direction. Because of the poor quality of the rock there, several of the ancient tombs need repairs."

"Have you thought about the design of Seti's tomb yet?" inquired Gau the Precise.

"We'll talk about that when we get there."

The Master's reply surprised the craftsmen; he wasn't usually so evasive.

"At dawn tomorrow," he went on, "Kenhir will distribute the tools, and we'll set off for the Valley."

▲

Awoken by his young wife before sunrise, the Scribe of the Tomb nibbled a piece of fresh bread before limping off to the strong room. Making sure that there was no one about, he unlocked it and took out mallets, copper chisels of various sizes, and pickaxes. When the craftsmen arrived, he handed them the allotted tools, and Imuni noted down who had received what. Then the small band set off up the steep path, going at a gentle pace so as not to exhaust Kenhir.

"The old fellow's in a terrible mood," remarked Pai. "He's being really dictatorial and sharp tongued."

"No one will ever change him," replied Renupe, "and he is too old for these expeditions."

Thuty disagreed. "You wait," he said. "In a few minutes he'll be climbing faster than we will. He wouldn't miss a stay in the Valley for anything. Nothing there is like anywhere else. It's almost as if we, the living, have been given permission to enter the world of the dead."

Many shared the goldsmith's opinion. When the crew reached the camp on the pass, and laid down their mats, jars of water, and provisions, they were still discussing family and health problems, but when they began the descent into the Great Meadow where the reborn souls of the pharaohs lived, silence fell. They were not workmen like any others; they were a team whose task was to sail into a sacred, forbidden landscape, where they would explore a new path as they excavated the rock.

Even the traitor felt a certain emotion as he passed through the narrow stone gateway into the Valley of the Kings, which was watched over by Nubian guards. But he had gone too far to turn back, and he had been too humiliated to forgive. If there had been any justice, he, not Nefer, would have led the Brotherhood toward its destiny.

When they entered the Valley, they were all astonished to see the Wise Woman there, dressed in a long golden robe.

The Master bowed before her. "In the absence of the pharaoh, lead us to the place where we will excavate his House of Eternity."

Ubekhet dressed Nefer in the gold apron that denoted his office as master builder, and conferred on him the authority needed to make the first chisel mark in the virgin rock; the knot of Isis protected his throat, and drove away evil forces, so as to free his mind for the task ahead.

Led by the Wise Woman and the Master, the procession made its way past Ramses the Great's House of Eternity, walking on the stones that covered the tomb of Tutankhamon, a secret shrine known to only a few initiates. Then they took a path heading southwest, before forking off to the west and then turning south again, past the tomb of Tuthmosis I. Eventually they came to a halt about fifteen paces farther on, by the rock face.

It was a strange place, almost set apart from the valley. Everyone had a feeling of profound solitude, but without any sadness.

Fened went right up to the rock, sniffed it, kissed it, and

stroked it. He repeated his actions several times, to enter into an intimate relationship with the rock, feel the life flow through its veins, know if it would agree to open itself up.

"The rock accepts," he said at last.

The craftsmen formed a half circle. Nefer stepped forward. By consulting one of the principal state secrets, the plan showing the location of each royal tomb, he had established that at this point the rock face was intact.

He struck the first mallet blow, and the gold chisel sank into the virgin stone, implanting the seed of the coming task.

Hearts raced. Everyone knew that the Brotherhood was once again setting off into the invisible world, to create a new face of eternity on earth. Although barely perceptible, the vibration set off by the tools filled the circle formed by the mountains, as if the entire valley was giving its assent to the crew from the Place of Truth.

The Master stepped aside, and Paneb swung high his heavy stone pickax, which had been marked by heavenly fire with the long snout and ears of the god Set in his animal-head form.

And the fire entered the rock.

▲

Thanks to the crew's sense of unity, the excavations began smoothly.

Only Ched the Savior, who had once almost gone blind, but whose sight had been saved by the Wise Woman's remedies, did not take part in this phase of the work. In the open-air workshop he had set up close to the tomb, he was preparing the decorations for the monumental doorway and the main corridor.

"I may be imagining things," he told Nefer, "but it seems to me that the work is proceeding rather briskly. One might almost think you were in a hurry, which isn't at all like you."

"It is true that we have no time to lose."

"Do you know something confidential that you can't tell us?"

"No," said Nefer. "I'm just trying to adapt to this particular place and time."

"Without wishing to be pessimistic, that's not a good sign."

"I don't know yet." Nefer paused, then asked, "Has Paneb mentioned his masterwork to you?"

"Once or twice. He won't let anyone help him. I thought he'd be unhappy at having to leave the tomb he's preparing for you; but seeing how eagerly he wields his pickax, I'd say he's more than happy to be taking part in the creation of a new royal tomb. That boy has an incredible capacity for work."

"Will it be enough for him to discover the quintessence?"

"I don't know," said Ched. "The number of personal qualities required is unlimited, and nobody will ever be able to work out the recipe for success. But don't you trust the gods anymore?"

"Of course I do."

Under Kenhir's critical gaze the starboard crew made steady progress, their pace set by Paneb and by Nakht, who strove to keep up with him.

The Wise Woman was right: the rock was strong and healthy, and it sang in harmony with the craftsmen's tools.

21

Almost a year had passed since Seti II's coronation, and the situation seemed to have reached a stalemate. The craftsmen of the Place of Truth, though, were hard at work, for the king had accepted their choice of location for his House of Eternity. The starboard and port crews worked alternately on the tomb, dividing their time between it and the Valley of the Queens, where the restoration work was continuing.

Prince Amenmessu had not made any decision, but he had emerged from his lethargy and done a course of military training like that undergone by elite soldiers. The move had won him the sympathy of the Theban army, who were disappointed by the pharaoh's lack of interest. In fact, according to Mehy's informers, Seti never left Pi-Ramses.

There was no contact between Seti and his son, not even a letter; and Amenmessu had still not sworn allegiance to his father. The situation was still tense, and everyone anxiously asked, over and over again, why the king did not show his authority in some way.

True, he had had to spend time reinforcing the northeastern borders and preventing a revolt in Syria and Canaan, but his father, Meneptah, had been a firm ruler, and the results of his firmness were still in evidence; there seemed no immediate danger that Egypt would be invaded. Seti had also to keep a watchful eye on his senior officials, who were forever plotting and scheming, but his tjaty, Bay, kept a firm grip on the government and seemed to have taken the measure of the Pi-Ramses court. In addition, Queen Tausert was becoming a more adept stateswoman with every day that passed—why, people wondered, did she also tolerate Amenmessu's latent sedition?

In this rather unreal climate, Mehy was becoming more and more edgy. The treasures of the Place of Truth were so close and yet they seemed inaccessible, all the more so since the traitor had not yet unearthed the faintest trail leading to the Stone of Light. Also, like the rest of his crew the man was busy excavating and decorating Seti's tomb, and so would be out of contact with Mehy for many months. Several times, Mehy had tried to discuss the problem of the village's peculiar status with Amenmessu, but the prince was not interested. He was far too busy learning how to handle weapons.

Serketa spent many hours in Daktair's workshop, perfecting her knowledge of poisons, which she tried out on small rodents. She found their death agonies—which were swift or lingering, depending on the poison—most entertaining. She would have liked to try the poisons on larger animals, but Daktair had advised against it, for fear of arousing suspicion. He got on very well with his pupil, for she was inventive and dispelled his boredom. Daktair no longer believed it was possible to transform Egypt into a modern country where new discoveries and learning would wipe out the old beliefs, but Serketa's determination gave him hope from time to time. What was needed now was a civil war, which would enable a new power to emerge in the land.

In secret messages, Mehy continued to assure the pharaoh of his absolute loyalty, while also telling him that Amenmessu had not given up his ambitions. Mehy himself was of course, he said, doing everything possible to persuade the prince to remain within the law and not do anything irrevocable.

It was no use: no matter how much Mehy thought about it, he could not understand Seti's waiting game, particularly in view of the name he bore. Being protected by Set, the king ought to have come thundering down on the rebellious son who dared defy him. And Queen Tausert felt no affection for Amenmessu; why didn't she persuade the king to act?

An officer stationed in Pi-Ramses, who had been given permission to visit his grandparents in Thebes, brought Mehy the answer, and was suitably rewarded. The news would soon be official, so Mehy hurried to the house where Amenmessu was staying, near the main barracks, to be the first to tell him. He could already imagine the prince's reaction.

He was disagreeably surprised to find Amenmessu deep in conversation with two highly skilled charioteers; Mehy had told them to keep away from the prince.

"Come and join us, General," said Amenmessu. "Every day I learn more about the quality of Theban weaponry, and I cannot congratulate you enough on perfecting a formidable war machine. But you look concerned. Is there bad news?"

"I must speak with you, alone."

When the two charioteers had left, Amenmessu said, "Your men obey you without question, General—I hope that one day I'll inspire that kind of obedience, too. Now tell me, what is it that's so important and so urgent?"

"I expect you've been wondering why there's been no word from your father."

"I came to the conclusion that he's satisfied with ruling just the North."

"According to information I've just received, that's definitely not so."

The prince looked at him sharply. "What do you mean?"

"Queen Tausert is expecting a child."

"A child! If it's a boy, my father is likely to choose this second son as coregent instead of me, and my claim to the throne will go for nothing. So this is the plan he's devised with that woman Tausert!" He drew his dagger and flung it at a map of Egypt painted on the wall. The blade, of Daktair's newly perfected design, pierced the name of the capital, Pi-Ramses, and sank deep into the plaster. "When is the baby due?"

"In about two months," replied Mehy.

"If my father dares humiliate me, I shan't let him enjoy his throne for long."

▲

When Paneb returned from the Valley of the Kings for his allotted two days' rest, he had several plans in mind. First, he must continue his masterwork, which would take all his talent and skill—and more besides. Next, he would suggest an entirely new decorative scheme for the well room of Seti's House of Eternity. The tomb was very different from Meneptah's, because the atmosphere of the new reign was so different, and the crew from the Place of Truth could not simply produce an imitation. But Paneb's idea was so unusual that the Master might reject it.

Paneb hoped that Uabet had prepared him one of her delicious meals, but the moment he stepped through the door of his house, she ran into his arms, weeping.

"What's wrong?" he asked.

"Come and see the kitchen," she said between sobs.

The place was devastated. Dishes had been broken, the

cooking pot overturned, the sack of charcoal ripped, and there were vegetables all over the place. For Uabet, it was a disaster.

"Who did this?" asked Paneb.

"Your son and his green monkey. Instead of behaving themselves until I got back from the temple, they turned my kitchen into a playground, and this is the result! And Aapehti was in such a hurry to leave for school that he didn't even listen to me when I scolded him."

"Why didn't you make him stay at home?"

"He may be only eleven, but he's already stronger than some adults."

Paneb remained strangely calm. "I'll go and find him."

"Please, don't be too angry with him. He's only a little boy—and even though he's been very naughty, he doesn't deserve a harsh punishment."

Paneb gently kissed his wife on the forehead.

In fact, Aapehti had not gone to school, where a craftsman from the port crew was giving a lesson in mathematics. His father asked around and was told he had gone to see Gau the Precise. When Paneb reached the painter's house, the door was opened by Gau's wife.

"Is my son here?" he asked.

"Yes, he's asking my husband about a complicated sum."

"Tell him to come here."

"Don't you want to come in?"

"No, Uabet's waiting for us."

When Aapehti appeared, he didn't seem in the least embarrassed.

"Why didn't you go to school?" demanded Paneb.

"I don't like the teacher. I prefer Gau—he told me the answer to the problem."

"In other words, you cheated."

Gau cut in. "It isn't all that serious. The boy now understands the principles of division, and surely that's the most important thing?"

"I'm glad about that. Thank you. Come, Aapehti."

The boy ran in front of Paneb as though he wished to escape. But a few steps from their home, a powerful hand lifted him off the ground, and he found himself gazing into his father's angry face.

"Why did you wreck the kitchen?"

"I was playing with the monkey."

"You are less than a monkey, Aapehti, because you failed to show respect for your mother."

"I have a right to—"

Paneb's resounding slap almost took his son's head off. "You have no rights, only duties, and the first of those is to respect your mother, who gave you life. For more than three years she suckled you, and wiped your backside. She taught you to speak, read, and write, and she cares for your health. Go in and grovel to her, Aapehti, and if you ever behave like that again I'll break every bone in your body and kick you out of the village."

22

While working on Seti's tomb, Paneb used two vital things to help him check measurements and proportions: a folding cubit, and the eye of Horus that Ched the Savior had given him.

Ched had devised the symbolic design for the three passage-ways leading to the well room, whose walls had been carefully smoothed and covered with white plaster. On the plaster, the artists had inscribed extracts from the *Invocation to Ra* and the *Book of the Hidden Chamber*, which provided the royal soul with the secret names of the Light and the regions of the afterworld that must be crossed in order to attain rebirth.

The sculptors had created a fine, idealized portrait of the king, eternally young and likened to Osiris, lord of the dead and the underworld. Like the god, Seti would remain forever the incarnation of the sun, which defeated darkness.

The day's work was coming to an end, and the light from the lamps was dwindling. The little chamber had been carved into the rock, but had yet to be brought to life.

"When are we going to excavate the well of souls?" Paneb asked the Master.

"Never."

The painter was astonished. "But it's essential! When the sarcophagus passes above the well, the energy the well contains will drive death away."

"What is that energy called?"

"The Nun, after the great god who brought himself to life, father of creative forces and the source of all life."

"You remember the hieroglyphs you've painted, but do you understand their meaning and importance? Whether the well is actually dug or not is secondary. If we create it in the spirit, in the same way as we think about our ancestors, the hieroglyphs and ritual scenes will make it entirely real. The important thing is the Nun itself. As soon as your mind crosses the boundaries of the visible world, you enter it."

"Does that mean that the Valley of the Kings is one of its expressions?"

"Yes," said Nefer. "It is situated in the Nun, as is our earth, an island that has emerged from it for a limited time. This unlimited energy envelops us and nourishes both our bodies and our minds. We craftsmen from the Place of Truth have the privilege and the responsibility to live within the Nun when we are fashioning a House of Eternity, in which its limitless power is expressed. Without it, our creations would be only tombs, not living shrines."

"Do you mean that the Nun is . . . the quintessence?"

Nefer smiled. "It's late, Paneb, and you wanted to tell me about your plan for decorating this chamber."

▲

"Are you sure?" Pai the Good Bread asked his wife.

"Absolutely."

"This time he's gone too far! I try to be patient, but all he does is make me look a fool."

"What can we do? It's by no means certain the court would decide in our favor, especially if the Scribe of the Tomb was presiding."

"I'm within my rights."

"Then tell him so," said his wife.

Encouraged by her justifiable anger, Pai consulted Unesh and Gau, who were equally indignant and accompanied him to Kenhir's office.

The old scribe was working his way through some official documents that Uputy had just delivered; fortunately, they contained nothing untoward. He looked up at the trio.

"What now?" he said.

"You must listen to us," demanded Pai, flushed with anger.

"Have you anything of importance to say?"

"I certainly have! Why do you refuse me the jars of beer due to me? I haven't a single one in the house, and I won't put up with being treated so badly! When there's hard work to do I'm the first person you think of, but when you're giving out good beer you forget about me."

"It's for your own good," said Kenhir.

"What do you mean, 'for my own good'?"

"You're getting too fat, Pai, and drinking too much beer would only make things worse."

"I don't care if you are the Scribe of the Tomb, it's not your job to tell me how to behave!"

"Yes, it is," retorted Kenhir. "If you make yourself ill, your absence will slow down the crew's work, and the delay will penalize all of us. As we are in the middle of excavating a royal tomb, I must watch over your health. And don't let your friends ply you with drink in secret. If you do, I'll find out about it and have to discipline you."

The three artists retreated, exchanging looks that suggested they thought Kenhir's head as hard as a rock.

▲

The Scribe of the Tomb sat down on his stool, hands resting on the head of his walking stick. He waited until the starboard crew had lit the lamps in Seti's House of Eternity before he addressed the Master.

"Your crew are getting overexcited, Nefer," he said, "and the port crew aren't much calmer—Hay's had to reprimand them twice this week. I've stopped distributing strong beer, so as to prevent the sort of drinking bouts at which the men set the world to rights."

"Their anxiety's understandable," argued Nefer, "and they aren't happy about preparing a tomb that the reigning pharaoh hasn't deigned to visit."

"When people do their work properly, they haven't time to be anxious."

"Everyone knows Amenmessu is likely to react violently if Tausert and Seti's child is a boy."

"If he has any intelligence at all, he won't rebel against his father. Seti will come to present his son to Amon at Karnak. Amenmessu will bow before the rightful king, and everything will return to normal."

"I'm glad you're so optimistic," said Nefer.

"Don't be sarcastic: my optimism is only on the surface. I've learnt that Amenmessu has spoken several times with the high priest of Karnak, and that the regional government is astonished by the change in his behavior. After sampling the pleasures of life, the prince has become a true soldier, capable both of commanding and of fighting in the front line. Such warlike behavior is hardly reassuring."

"Some people are content with vague desires—let's hope he's one of them. Anyway, Mehy's still responsible for our protection, isn't he?"

"All it would take to remove that shield is one royal decree."

"Why would Seti do that to us when we're preparing his House of Eternity?"

"Queen Tausert detests the Place of Truth, don't forget. In trying to replace me with one of her spies, she was hoping to place a worm in the apple."

"Yes, but she changed her mind," Nefer reminded him, "which proves that the royal couple think our work is of prime importance."

Kenhir shook his head. "Recently," he murmured, "I've not been happy with Unesh's behavior. He keeps teaming up with someone or other to protest, but he always stays in the background, as though he wants to damage the Brotherhood without drawing attention to himself."

"Say what you really mean," urged Nefer. "Is he the traitor?"

"I've no proof of his guilt, but I advise you to watch him carefully."

"Nothing more specific?"

"No, nothing. Now, regarding another matter, why are there so many mysteries surrounding the well room?"

"Paneb made a surprising suggestion for its decoration. I accepted it, and he's begun painting."

Kenhir frowned. "I don't approve of surprises in the decoration of a royal tomb."

"This is a very special one, because we're having to work in the absence of the king and without knowing what the future holds. Surely we must take account of these special circumstances?"

"If you don't like what Paneb has done, it must be rubbed out and begun again."

"Come and see for yourself."

Irritated, Kenhir started off along the first corridor, examining the texts, fearing he might discover eccentricities. But he found no faults and even commented that the plasterwork was of exceptionally high quality. As for the offertory scenes, they conformed perfectly to ritual models. But there was still the famous well room to examine. The entrance to it was partly blocked by scaffolding, which Paneb was dismantling. Ten three-wicked lamps filled the room with intense light, picking out every detail of Paneb's surprising paintings.

There were no scenes showing offerings, or gods; instead there were pictures of the sacred objects placed in a pharaoh's tomb during his funeral rites: a falcon, a cobra, a bull, a jackal, an ibis, a crocodile; and statues of the pharaoh in a boat, wielding a scepter, standing on a panther, or shown as a naked child playing the sistrum, and a ritualist carrying a royal offering.

"Thuty will make the statues in gold," explained Nefer, "so long as the Brotherhood isn't swept up in the whirlwind. Even if the worst were to happen the king would lack for nothing, because the paintings, once brought to life by the rites, would become reality."

Kenhir was amazed. Paneb had chosen simple shapes that lacked elegance but which embodied the different powers that would accompany the king during his perpetual journey in the world beyond. A thin red line surrounded some of the figures, and all were painted gold.

"Well, Kenhir," said Nefer, "are you satisfied?"

"No, I'm overwhelmed."

―――― 23 ――――

"Queen Tausert has given birth to a son," Mehy announced solemnly.

Amenmessu turned his back on the general and gazed out of the window, at the main barracks in Thebes. "Do you know what my father intends to do?"

"He wants this child to be linked to the throne, and so does the queen."

A heavy silence fell.

After a few moments, Amenmessu said, "General, you didn't tell me your experts had made a new war chariot, lighter and stronger than the ones used by the armies of the North."

"For the simple reason, Prince, that it hasn't yet been perfected."

"That isn't what the two men I consulted said."

"They are over optimistic."

"I shall check for myself."

"I beg you, my lord, don't take any unnecessary risks and—"

"As of today," interrupted Amenmessu, "I'm taking command of all the troops stationed between Thebes and Elephantine, and those who guard the Nubian fortresses. I shall retain you in the rank of general, provided you carry out my orders to the letter and don't try to hide anything else from me. Make just one mistake, and you'll be dismissed."

Mehy bowed.

"Send in scribes," the prince went on, "so I can dictate a decree."

"A decree, my lord? Do you mean . . . ?"

Amenmessu swung round. Mehy hardly recognized him: his face had lost all trace of flabbiness, and his eyes were piercing, his bearing imperious.

"Didn't I make myself clear?"

Mehy bowed again, lower. "I am at your command, Majesty."

Amenmessu smiled triumphantly. "You're as shrewd as ever, General—which is just as well for you. As soon as I've finished dictating my decree, we shall leave for Karnak."

▲

With the blessing of the high priest of Karnak, Amenmessu, "the Son of Amon," had chosen the coronation name of "He who is Immutable as Ra, the Elect of the Divine Light." He took as his wife a Theban woman of foreign extraction, whom he installed in the royal palace.

The new pharaoh was recognized and acclaimed by the

cheering Theban nobles, and he demanded unswerving loyalty from them. Messengers left immediately for all the provinces in the country, in order to spread the news: Egypt had a true king again, and prosperity would soon return.

To mark his coronation, Amenmessu gave a great banquet for the whole court, and all the guests did their very best to look joyful and relaxed.

All through the feast, Serketa cast alluring looks at the new king. As soon as she got home, she undressed and had a massage. Reinvigorated, she went to look for Mehy; she found him in his office.

"Why are you still working?" she asked. "This is supposed to be a day of celebration."

"I must lose no time in sending Seti a coded letter explaining that I no longer have any freedom of action but that I remain his loyal subject."

Serketa sat down on his knee. "The situation is getting very exciting. Two pharaohs, a father and son who hate each other, imminent civil war—how lucky for us!"

"We must take no chances, my sweet, because young Amenmessu has changed a lot. I'd hoped he'd be a puppet whose strings I could pull, but he's emerged from his trance and taken command of the armed forces."

"Who'll attack first?"

"That's precisely the problem, my sweet little quail. The attacker will be considered a rebel and a troublemaker, and the people will fear that he'll bring down the gods' curse on himself."

"It seems these old superstitions will never die out," said Serketa scornfully. "Well, all we need do is push Amenmessu to the limit and make him lose his nerve. Our army's better than Seti's, isn't it?

"It's hard to be sure. If Seti recalls the regiments he's posted at the borders, he'll have a huge force of experienced soldiers. But there's something more worrying than that: Amenmessu's beginning to be suspicious of me, and he might go his own way, without consulting me."

"That would be very annoying, my sweet love. But surely we aren't going to lose the benefits of all our hard work?"

"No, of course not," said Mehy.

▲

Paneb had spent a day and a night watching the sky, studying the gold of the sun, the silver of the moon, and the lapis lazuli of the starry vault. He feasted his eyes on the metals of the universe, which also formed part of the quintessence. His sight became sharper, and he rejoiced when at last he felt as though he could see through the firmament. His hand caressed the belly of the stars, and he danced like a constellation. The Master's revelation in Seti's tomb had opened up his heart; now Paneb could feel the pulsing and vibrating of the Nun, the ever-present energy.

So he was unafraid as he strode out into the desert, where monsters with lions' bodies and falcons' heads roamed, monsters that even the greatest warrior could not vanquish. He felt a need to cross the boundaries of the visible world and nourish his craft with the intangible substance hidden in the water of a well, in the rain that came from the sky, in the floodwaters that fertilized the lands or in the fire that made the desert uninhabitable.

As Paneb was climbing a sand dune, he suddenly heard hoarse breathing. He turned round slowly and saw an enormous jackal whose black pelt gleamed in the silver moonlight: Anubis, the god charged with guiding the dead to the court of the other world. The animal was so magnificent that Paneb felt no fear. Since it had appeared to him, he would follow it. When the jackal moved off, he did not hesitate to follow it. Walking in his guide's footsteps, he felt as if he were covering immense distances, though in reality the journey brought him back close to the hills of the Place of Truth.

A slope to climb, a crest, a path, and the jackal halted before the entrance to Nefer the Silent's tomb, which was still blocked by the big boulder.

So he was right! This was where his masterwork belonged, where he must create it, using the universal, divine energy hidden in the deepest part of himself, and so prove himself worthy. Paneb lay facedown in submission before the jackal, which, after a few minutes, disappeared into the night. Then he shut himself away in the tomb to continue his work.

▲

The dawn rites had been performed, there were flowers on the altars of the ancestors, and the women had come to collect the water jars the donkeys had brought. They noticed at once that Uabet the Pure, usually so scrupulously punctual, was missing.

"She must be ill," suggested Pai's wife.

"I shall go and see," said Turquoise.

When she reached Uabet's house, the door was opened by Aapehti.

"Is your mother ill?" she asked.

"She won't stop crying."

The magnificent redhead entered. Uabet was lying on her bed, her face buried in a cushion.

"Uabet, it's Turquoise."

Uabet spun round and glared at the intruder. "You! How dare you come here? Why are you being so cruel?"

"I don't understand."

"You've won. Isn't that enough? Why do you have to come here and humiliate me, too?"

"What are you talking about?"

"Paneb spent the night with you, didn't he?"

"No, he didn't," said Turquoise firmly. "A pact is a pact, and I'll never break it."

"Are you telling the truth?"

"Have I ever lied to you?"

Uabet said uncertainly, "I thought Paneb had stayed with you because he wanted to get divorced and remarry."

Turquoise sat down on the edge of the bed. "Don't worry, it was only a nightmare. I shall never marry, and neither Paneb nor any other man will make me change my mind."

"But in that case . . . where is he?"

"I don't know," said Turquoise.

"The stonecutters!" exclaimed Uabet. "They hate Paneb, and they must have attacked him, injured him, and left him for dead outside the village."

The two women ran to Casa the Rope's house. His wife, a small and aggressive brunette, was sweeping the doorstep.

"We want to see Casa," demanded Uabet.

"He's in bed, and he wants to be left to sleep late. With the workload the Master's imposed, the stonecutters need their rest."

"Has he said anything about a quarrel with Paneb?"

"With Paneb? No, nothing. We just have to get used to that sort of thing," and she shut the door.

Uabet and Turquoise went to see Nakht the Powerful, whom they found eating a huge slice of bread spread with cream cheese.

"Paneb?" he said. "Didn't see him last night."

"You didn't have a fight with him?" asked Uabet.

"No, but I wish I had. One of these days I'm going to knock him down and make him beg for mercy."

Neither Karo nor Fened could tell the women anything. They were preparing to question the other villagers, and then alert the Master, when Turquoise thought of Paneb's main preoccupation.

"All he thinks of," she said, "is the quintessence and his masterwork."

"And you think he may have spent the night in the House of Eternity he's preparing?" asked Uabet.

They hurried up the hill to the burial ground. Just as they reached the entrance to Nefer's tomb, the boulder rolled away, and Paneb emerged, blinking in the bright sunlight. There was not a trace of tiredness on his face.

"What are you doing here?" he asked in surprise.

Before they could reply, they heard someone shouting loudly down in the village.

—— 24 ——

Several craftsmen were running toward the main gate.

"Let's go and see what's the matter," said Paneb, and he ran off down the hill, Uabet and Turquoise at his heels.

When they reached the gate, they found the villagers milling around and talking excitedly.

"What's happened?" Paneb asked Thuty the Learned, who was ill at ease in the general scramble.

"A royal decree, apparently. Seti must have announced that he's going to visit us."

"Unless he wants to change the site or the decoration of his tomb," suggested Paneb worriedly.

Everyone gathered around the Master, and the Scribe of the Tomb handed him the papyrus scroll he had received from the royal palace at Thebes.

"Amenmessu has been crowned Pharaoh," Nefer told them, "and he is going to live in the city of Amon."

Few people were surprised at the news, but they were worried all the same, because they had hoped the prince would give up his demands for supreme power.

"Why has he done it?" asked Gau.

"Because he refuses to recognize the legitimacy of Seti or of Tausert's son."

"Is Mehy still in charge of protecting us?" asked Karo anxiously.

"I don't know," admitted Nefer.

"Which pharaoh should we regard as the true one?" asked Renupe.

The Master did not answer.

"We have no alternative but to choose the one who's closer to us," said Kenhir. "Amenmessu has taken command of the Theban troops and he'll crush anyone who doesn't submit."

"But if we side with him and he's defeated, Seti will raze our village to the ground," protested Fened.

"As the Scribe of the Tomb says," pointed out Ipuy, "we haven't much choice."

"Whatever happens," said Nefer, "we have a mission to fulfill: preparing Seti's House of Eternity. I shall therefore lead the starboard crew to the Valley of the Kings, and we shall continue our work."

▲

The craftsmen knew the way to the Great Meadow very well, but it might be dangerous in these troubled times, so at the Master's request, Sobek and several of his men acted as an armed escort.

"What do you think of Amenmessu's decree?" Nefer asked the big Nubian.

"No good will come of it. He should have come to an agreement with his father, not set himself up as his rival."

"What will you do if we're faced by some of his soldiers?"

"My duty is to ensure your safety, no matter where the danger comes from."

"If the situation turns dangerous, you must lay down your arms."

"My men," said Sobek firmly, "aren't afraid of a fight, and they'll obey my orders."

"But fighting soldiers commanded by a pharaoh would be a crime."

"The Place of Truth has become my life. If I didn't fight to save it, I'd despise myself."

▲

The little band reached the Valley of the Kings by midmorning. The guards had had no new instructions and allowed them to pass.

As usual, the Scribe of the Tomb sat down on his stool, and the craftsmen handed him their tools so that he could make his notes. But they all found it hard to concentrate—all, that is, except Paneb, who lit the lamps lining the three passageways to the well room, whose decoration was now complete.

Beyond it, the craftsmen had excavated a chamber with four pillars; its walls were being decorated with scenes and extracts from the *Book of Doors*. Here, too, Paneb had suggested an innovation: painting the figure of a single deity on each side of a pillar and making them converse with each other. After Gau, Unesh, and Pai had drawn the sketches in red ink, Ched had made a few corrections in black, particularly to the curves of the faces; then, using color, Paneb had brought to life Osiris, Ptah, Anubis, Horus, and the other deities who were receiving offerings from the pharaoh.

The stonecutters continued to excavate, and Didia and Thuty prepared the ritual objects that would form Seti's ritual treasure. As they settled once again into the rhythm of the work, the craftsmen forgot their worries and devoted themselves to their tasks.

"Nefer, come quickly!" shouted Kenhir, from the entrance to the tomb.

Followed by Paneb, Nefer hurried up the passageway. When they emerged from the tomb, they found one of the guards waiting with Kenhir.

"Soldiers are coming this way," said the guard. "Commander Sobek awaits your orders."

"What are we to do?" asked Kenhir anxiously.

"The Valley of the Kings must remain sacred and inviolate," said Nefer.

"As Pharaoh, Amenmessu has the right to enter," Kenhir reminded him.

"Stay here with the craftsmen," said Nefer.

"I'm coming with you," declared Paneb.

Arms folded, Sobek was standing with some of his men at the narrow entrance to the valley, gazing at the path along which the soldiers were approaching.

"How many of them are there?" asked the Master.

"About fifty."

"We could beat them easily," said Paneb.

He was the first to see that the man in the chariot at the head of the troops was Mehy himself. The chariot halted twenty paces or so from the little group, and the general stepped down. His archers halted behind him, their bows drawn, ready to fire.

Nefer went toward him.

Mehy said, "I would have preferred to see you again in different circumstances, Master, but destiny's role is to present us with surprises, is it not?"

"What do you want from me," asked Nefer.

"Have you read Pharaoh Amenmessu's decree?"

"All the inhabitants of the Place of Truth have been informed of it. Are you still in charge of protecting us?"

"For the moment, yes, but I don't know what the king's long-term plans are. As his general, I must obey his orders, whatever they may be."

"Even if you think them unjust?"

"Amenmessu has taken power, and all I am doing is my duty. The new king demands his subjects' respect, and I don't think he'll prove very patient with anyone who's slow to give it."

"I must remind you that the Brotherhood is working for Pharaoh Seti II, supreme Master of the Place of Truth."

"It would be better to avoid making that kind of declaration."

"In his decree, Amenmessu did not say that he plans to assume that office."

"As I said, I don't know his long-term plans for you."

"Therefore," said Nefer, "until I hear otherwise, I shall continue to regard Seti II as the ruler of our village, and we shall devote ourselves to finishing his tomb."

"You'd be wise to abandon the project, Master."

"I can't do that. It's my duty to bring it to completion."

"King Amenmessu sent me here to order you to stop on Seti's tomb at once. Whatever I may think, I have no choice: I must have your agreement."

"And if I refuse?"

"I'll deliver your reply to His Majesty," said Mehy, "but as a friend I strongly advise you not to take that attitude. Amenmessu needs to have his sovereignty affirmed, and could not swallow such an insult."

"Given the gravity of the situation, I must consult the Brotherhood."

"I'll try to pacify the king by reminding him of the customs of the Place of Truth, but don't try to win time and don't take Amenmessu's determination lightly."

"Whose side are you on?" asked Nefer.

"I'm caught in a vise, but I'm still on your side, Master, and I will always be, because you embody ancestral values whose disappearance would be catastrophic for Egypt. If Amenmessu goes too far, I'll try to restrain him, but don't make my task any more difficult."

"You'll have my answer tomorrow."

"In the meantime," said Mehy, "grant me a favor: stop work in Seti's tomb and leave the valley. That show of goodwill should calm Amenmessu."

"Very well, on condition that the guards remain at their posts and that you don't try to force your way in."

"Amenmessu hasn't ordered me to do so, and I hope such extreme measures will never be needed."

The general went back to his men, hoping that Nefer's resolution would not weaken. By refusing to obey the new king, the Master would draw down Amenmessu's anger on the whole

Brotherhood, which would be defenseless against it. Mehy would suggest to the king that he place the village under strict military control—with Mehy in command, naturally. That would make it easy to seize the village's hidden treasures.

▲

When the starboard crew arrived back in the village several days early, rumors at once began to circulate. The villagers were close to panic, because they were sure Amenmessu was going to end the craftsmen's sacred mission and destroy the Place of Truth.

Firm statements by Kenhir restored a small measure of calm, but he did not hide the fact that the Brotherhood was in danger and that the decision it was about to take would decide its whole future. With the Wise Woman's agreement, Turquoise immediately led the priestesses of Hathor to a shrine to pray for the goddess's protection.

Even the green monkey stopped playing tricks; as for Bad Girl, she took up a position close to the main gate.

In the presence of the Wise Woman and the Scribe of the Tomb, the two crews assembled in the open-air courtyard of the Temple of Ma'at and Hathor. Their faces were grave, and each man placed his hopes in the wisdom of others.

———— 25 ————

"King Amenmessu is demanding that we stop work on Seti's tomb," announced the Master. "If we refuse, he will send in the army. Whatever his beliefs may be, Mehy will have to obey the king, and I shall ask Commander Sobek to offer no resistance, so as to avoid a bloodbath."

"Has Amenmessu proclaimed himself supreme Master of the Place of Truth?" asked Ipuy.

"Not yet."

"In that case, we should obey Seti."

"That would be signing our death warrant," warned Kenhir. "In the area he controls, Amenmessu permits no one to honor Seti."

"But the Valley of the Kings isn't part of a pharaoh's earthly kingdom," said Hay.

"That's true," said the Wise Woman, "but unfortunately Seti hasn't come here to undertake the magical consecration of his House of Eternity."

"Let's be sensible," urged Thuty. "Mehy can no longer protect us, and the Master refuses to let Sobek's men engage in a battle they couldn't win. It is for us to take up weapons and fight Pharaoh's soldiers."

"What about the women and children?" said Userhat. "What would become of them, if we were arrested and imprisoned for refusing to submit to Amenmessu?"

"We've done our duty," added Karo, "and we're in no position to resist an armed attack. I can't see any reason not to submit."

Each man gave his opinion, and, despite some reluctance, no one wished to defy Amenmessu.

"Very well, we'll submit," said Nefer eventually, "on condition that I myself seal the door of Seti's tomb, and that the soldiers do not enter the Great Meadow."

"I agree with the Master," said the Wise Woman.

▲

Mehy was seething with impatience. To calm his nerves, he had practiced with his bow for more than an hour, but to no avail. Victory was there for the taking. . . . Once he possessed the Place of Truth's treasures, Amenmessu would not resist him much longer. Seti would be a more formidable opponent, but by then Mehy would have better weapons.

"The Scribe of the Tomb, General," announced a junior officer.

"Show him in."

Kenhir walked in slowly and painfully, leaning on his stick, and sat down heavily in an armchair. "The years weigh more and more heavily on my old carcass, General, and we are living in difficult times that do not help matters. May the gods protect us from painful conflicts."

"Indeed, Kenhir, indeed. What is the Place of Truth's answer?"

"It will obey the king, of course, and will hope that His Majesty will proclaim himself protector of the Brotherhood as soon as possible and confirm you in your offices."

The general managed to mask his disappointment.

"There is, however, one small condition," Kenhir went on.

Mehy's hopes soared. "What is it?"

"The Master himself will seal the door of Seti's tomb, and no outsiders will set foot in the Valley of the Kings."

▲

Amenmessu examined the war chariots one by one, and ordered the carpenters to strengthen some of them. Before he attacked the North, all his weapons and equipment must be in perfect condition.

"The Place of Truth has agreed to stop work, Majesty," Mehy informed him.

"Did you doubt that it would?"

"Nefer is a stubborn man, and the craftsmen aren't easy to handle."

"You've just proved otherwise! Leave immediately for the Valley of the Kings, check that there are no craftsmen on the site, and have the entrance to my father's tomb sealed."

"The Master refuses to allow any soldiers into the valley."

"Are you saying he claims he has the right to refuse?"

Mehy nodded. "And he also says, Majesty, that he must seal the tomb's entrance himself, in accordance with the rites of the Brotherhood."

"That would imply trusting him and bending to his will."

Mehy did not have to feed the flames of Amenmessu's anger: it was strong enough to strike down Nefer the Silent.

"Tell the Master I've changed my mind about my father's tomb," said the king.

The general froze: was the Place of Truth's magic so powerful that it could make the king authorize the continuation of the work?

"Sealing the tomb isn't enough. I order the immediate destruction of all the sculptures, texts, and paintings."

▲

Nefer walked slowly down the main street of the village, glancing at each house and thinking about the people who lived there. As the centuries had passed, and the community had worked together, a spirit of unity and a special atmosphere had developed, beyond the faults and meanness inherent in one person or another. Pharaohs had come and gone, as had Masters, and no one had broken the pact that made the Place of Truth the resting place of the Stone of Light, which could transform matter.

And this magnificent adventure was going to end because of a king's vanity, brutality and hatred: the very qualities that proved he was not fit to reign.

Before convening the great assembly once more, Nefer wanted to take time to linger over the well-kept white houses where the villagers lived, with their joys and their pains, their greatness and their pettiness, these people who had experienced the daily miracle of unity and brotherhood.

A damp nose nudged the Master's leg.

"Ebony! Are you out for a walk, too?"

The dog jumped up and put its paws on its master's shoulders. There was anxiety and trust in its hazel eyes.

"Don't worry," said Nefer. "Once someone's word has been given, it cannot be taken back."

▲

"First thing tomorrow," declared the Master, "we must return to the Valley of the Kings."

"So we're starting work again," said Nakht joyfully.

"Quite the contrary, I'm afraid. Amenmessu has ordered us to destroy Seti's tomb."

A gasp of horror ran round the assembled throng.

"Destroy it?" repeated Pai, deeply shocked. "What does that mean?"

"Smashing the sculptures, rubbing out the inscriptions and the paintings, wiping out our work."

"But we don't know how to destroy!" protested Renupe.

"King Amenmessu wants to bring us to heel," explained Kenhir gravely, "and show us that he alone makes the decisions."

"Never has a pharaoh behaved so like a tyrant," said Ipuy. "This order is insane—it's worthless."

"If we don't obey it," warned Thuty, "we're the ones who'll be destroyed."

"Are we going to behave like cowards?" raged Paneb. "We entered the Brotherhood to build and to create. If Amenmessu hates his own father so much, let him send his troops against him, but he cannot make us destroy the valley!"

"Think of the safety of your wife and child," said Gau.

"After sacking a House of Eternity, I wouldn't dare look them in the face."

"And after doing something so terrible," added Unesh, "how could we still use our tools?"

Didia drew himself up to his full height. "When we were admitted to the Brotherhood, we took solemn oaths. To break them would eventually destroy us."

"I agree," said the Master. "And for that very reason, I am refusing to carry out Amenmessu's order."

"Have you thought about the consequences?" asked Fened nervously.

"The best that can happen is that Amenmessu will decree that the village is to be closed, and I'll be accused of high treason. Does anyone disagree?"

No one spoke.

"We cannot do anything else," said the Wise Woman. "If we were to give in to Amenmessu's insane demands, the Place of Truth would lose its soul."

"Those who don't wish to be dragged down with me must leave the village at once, before I give Mehy my answer," said the Master. "In circumstances like these, there's no shame in wanting to save one's life, one's family, and one's possessions."

Ubekhet got to her feet. "The Master and I are withdrawing into the temple until sunset. Every man is free to make his own choice."

▲

Ordinarily, this was the sweetest time of the day, the moment when peace overcame even the green monkey. Tiredness set in, and everyone spontaneously fell silent to admire the setting sun.

In the temple, the Master and the Wise Woman had closed the doors of the shrine. Alone in the darkness of the sacred space, the gold statuette of Ma'at would confront the shadows and rejoin the primordial ocean, from which she would rise again in the morning.

"This is probably my last evening in the village," said Nefer. "As soon as I tell Mehy our decision, he'll have me arrested."

"Will he refuse to understand our reasons?"

"Whether he does or not, his main concern is his own career, so he'll obey Amenmessu without question. I shall plead the village's cause by saying I'm solely responsible and that I forced you all to accept my decision. But will the king believe me?"

"I'll come with you tomorrow," said Ubekhet.

"No," said Nefer. "The Place of Truth needs you. You're the only person who can summon up all our strength, so that the village can confront its enemy."

"You're asking too much of me," she protested. "I've lived my life with you, and I want to die with you."

"You're the Brotherhood's spiritual mother. Without your love, how could it survive?"

They embraced with passion and tenderness, as though they wished to engrave this moment of communion into their flesh, this moment that destiny would never allow them again in this world.

26

Mehy had had a sleepless night. To calm his nerves, he had made love to his wife with his usual brutality, but even that had brought him no release. The cup of too sweet wine Serketa had given him disagreed with him, and he decided to unroll a papyrus containing details of the great wealth of the Theban region—which he would soon govern.

Serketa kneaded his shoulders. "We've almost reached our goal," she purred, "but has that damned Master got another surprise in store for you?"

"That's what I can't stop wondering. And yet Nefer has no way out. How could he ever agree to destroy a royal tomb? Amenmessu has at last found the best way to get rid of him: forcing him to disobey his king. No one will support a rebel."

"Who will take his place?"

"Why not our ally in the village? If he's clever enough about it, he'll get himself appointed."

"Amenmessu would still have to accept his appointment."

"He'll will listen to my advice," said Mehy confidently.

"Don't be offended, my tender love, but I am not so sure. That young man is getting a bit too sure of himself, and he's surrounded himself with military advisers who claim to be your friends but who are scheming to take your place."

Mehy took her warning seriously. "Don't worry. I can control them."

"And if they put a foot wrong," promised Serketa, licking her lips, "I'll take care of them."

He did not dismiss the suggestion. Some senior officers were indeed getting too ambitious. Either they came under Mehy's banner, or their careers would come to an abrupt end.

"You are right, my turtle dove," he said. "I've been too lenient with my subordinates lately. But I hadn't foreseen that our new king would take himself for a warrior chief."

"Would he actually be capable of commanding the Theban troops?"

"Not without me. But I don't mind letting him think he could. Attacking Seti's army will require very detailed planning, which Amenmessu could never manage. And without the Place of Truth's secrets, victory will be at best uncertain."

▲

The day began like any other: waking the gods and goddesses in the temple, paying homage to the ancestors, sharing out the water the donkeys had brought. But the womenfolk did not exchange confidences, as though they bore a burden so heavy that it took away all wish to gossip.

Nefer had bathed in scented water, shaved, and carefully combed his hair, and put on his ceremonial clothes.

"The Scribe of the Tomb wants to see you," Ubekhet told him.

The lines on Kenhir's face had deepened. "I'm an old man and the state's representative in the village," he said. "It's up to me to give our answer to the general."

"You know that wouldn't be enough, and that he'd summon me within the hour."

"Probably, but it's worth trying. You're in such danger!"

"I'm counting on you," said Nefer, "to defend the village with the legal arguments you've mastered so well. Perhaps my downfall won't lead to yours."

"Shouldn't one of us warn Seti? I've written him a letter."

"It's too risky. Mehy's soldiers will search every craftsman who leaves the Place of Truth."

"But Seti's the only one who can save us."

"Amenmessu has decided to act quickly. Seti won't have time to come to Thebes and help us."

Kenhir embraced Nefer. "I'm no flatterer and I'm not skilled in the art of paying people compliments . . . but you're a Master I can be proud of."

▲

Nefer kissed Ubekhet and left his home, wondering what would become of the craftsmen who had fled to refuge in the outside world, where they might be able to escape Amenmessu's vindictive rage.

The main street was deserted. Except for the Scribe of the Tomb, all the inhabitants must have chosen to leave. It was a devastating blow, and the Master felt very much alone as he headed for the great gate, which he would open for the last time. Even Paneb, his adopted son, had preferred to seek safety with his family. Of course, that attitude was understandable, and Paneb had good reason to do what he had. Nefer told himself firmly that he must forget his disappointment and admit that the Brotherhood was dying, even if he still had to defend its spirit to the authorities.

The Master pulled back the bolt and opened the great gate. They were all there—every single one of them—waiting for him: the craftsmen of his own crew and Hay's, the priestesses of Hathor, the children, even Ebony, Charmer, Bad Girl, the green monkey, and all the other domestic animals.

"Nobody's leaving," Hay confirmed.

"And I'm coming with you," said Paneb.

"No, Paneb," said the Master. "Since everyone has chosen to remain united, it's vital that you stay here."

"Very well," said Paneb reluctantly. "I shall finish my masterwork—promise me you'll come back to see it."

Nefer put his hand on Paneb's shoulder and looked into his eyes with an intensity that overwhelmed the big man.

Then, as though setting off on a normal, peaceful journey, the Master walked calmly away. He did not look back.

▲

Mehy felt very elegant in his new and expensive pleated robe, but he could not help being impressed by the Master's bearing and envying his innate authority, even though Mehy was in a position of power and Nefer would soon be less than a slave. He tried in vain to decipher any trace of emotion on Nefer's face. Perhaps, as Serketa feared, Nefer had stored up a new surprise for him, as disagreeable as the previous one.

"What is your answer, Master?" he asked.

"I will not destroy Seti's tomb, and I take the entire responsibility upon myself."

The general could barely contain his joy. The trap had closed on Nefer, and he had no chance whatever of escaping! But it was better that the Master and his Brotherhood should go on believing that Mehy was their friend; their blindness would continue to be to his advantage.

He asked, "Have you thought hard about this?"

"The Brotherhood is sworn to build according to the laws of harmony, and Seti's House of Eternity was born according to those laws. No Master will violate them by ruining the work that has been done."

"Those are noble thoughts, and I admire them. But you must know that King Amenmessu will be angered by them."

"Yes, I know."

"By disobeying him, aren't you condemning the Place of Truth to death?"

"It would cease to exist anyway, at the very moment when it betrayed its vocation."

The general paced up and down. "I don't know how to help you. Amenmessu's orders are precise: either I lead you and your crews to the Valley of the Kings to destroy Seti's tomb, or I take you to the palace to be judged."

"The ancestors of the Place of Truth will bear witness that I have respected my oath. It is better to disobey a tyrant than to commit perjury, even to save one's life."

"If you adopt that tone, you'll be given the maximum sentence! But if you plead your cause reasonably, you might persuade Amenmessu to be lenient."

"You don't believe that yourself."

"I'm pessimistic, it is true, because he's young and warlike. If his father had linked him to the throne, we wouldn't be in this situation. But Seti was suspicious of an overambitious son, and now we are in an impasse, with two kings who are going to make war on each other. The North will fight the South, Egyptians will kill Egyptians. . . . This is a time of appalling misfortune, and we have no idea how to avert it. As for my rebelling against Amenmessu, I no longer have the power to do so, because he's taken command of the Theban troops and gives them orders directly. I'd be dismissed tomorrow, or even arrested, if I showed the slightest hesitation in obeying the king's orders. But taking you like a criminal to the palace to hear an absurd sentence—I'd never have imagined it! You might be able to slip past the guards and escape, Nefer. The king will mount a search for you and your chances of staying free are slim, but there's no other way of escaping the worst. At least save your life so that you can pass on the knowledge you hold. Try to reach the North and place yourself under Seti's protection."

If the Master yielded to temptation, Mehy would allow himself the pleasure of having him arrested on the spot, and handing over this recalcitrant, dangerous prisoner to Amenmessu.

When the general turned back, Nefer was still standing there in silence, his arms folded.

"You're a brave man, Master. You know I hold you in high esteem and that I'll do everything I can to help you. But once we walk out of that door, I can no longer show you any sign of friendship."

"Do what you must, General."

—— 27 ——

Only the first, early-morning delivery of water had arrived. Since then, the road leading to the village had been empty: the villagers had received no fruit, no vegetables, and no fish.

Sobek was in a quandary, so he went to see the Scribe of the Tomb.

"When Amenmessu's soldiers arrive at the First Fort, what should I do?" he asked. "The Master advised me to surrender my weapons, but—"

"He was right," said Kenhir, "Trying to stop the troops entering the village would be futile."

"But it's my duty to stop them!"

"We can't possibly resist the Theban army, and what would be the point of getting ourselves killed? If you obey the pharaoh's orders, you'll be considered loyal and allocated another post. I admire your integrity, Sobek, but sacrificing yourself would be madness."

When the big Nubian had gone back to his post, the Scribe of the Tomb walked wearily across the lay workers' area. Only Obed the blacksmith was still working: all the others had deserted their workshops, preferring to stay in their homes while they waited for Amenmessu to act. In this troubled period, it was better not to be seen close to the village.

"Why are you still here, Obed?" asked Kenhir.

"I've got a pick and some copper chisels to repair."

"The king's soldiers will throw you into prison."

"They'll have to get into my forge first."

"Don't be stubborn. Go home."

The blacksmith stopped stoking up the fire and put down his bellows. "Is it really all over, then?"

"Go home, I said, and forget about the village."

"Can I take a few tools with me?" asked Obed.

"Take as many as you like."

"All right, I'll go. But I shan't forget."

As the Scribe of the Tomb approached the great gate, the guard got to his feet and asked, "May I leave, too?"

"Of course, and take your colleague with you. The two of you must go to the government offices, where you'll be given new jobs."

Kenhir went home, where Niut had prepared an excellent lunch as usual.

"I'm not hungry," he said.

"Try to eat just a little," urged Niut.

"No, all I want is to go to sleep. And I wish I'd never wake up."

"Don't give up hope."

"Is there one single reason why I shouldn't?"

▲

Casa, Fened, and Karo were shaping a block of fine limestone which they were going to use for the entrance chamber of Nefer's tomb. The three stonecutters put all their knowledge and skill into this delicate work, while Nakht finished the base of a pillar to go in the came place. Close by, Userhat, Ipuy, and Renupe were sculpting a naturalistic statue of the Master standing gazing up at the sky.

The three painters, Gau, Unesh, and Pai, were decorating the walls of the entrance chamber under the direction of Ched the Savior, who scrutinized each detail minutely. Didia was carving a piece of acacia wood into an "answerer," in the form of Nefer, so that he could continue to work tirelessly in the otherworld; and Thuty was decorating another such figure with gold leaf.

As for Paneb, he had again shut himself away inside the tomb with his brushes and his cakes of color.

Under Hay's direction, the port crew were carrying out repairs in the Temple of Ma'at and Hathor, to make the building as perfect as possible.

"The Master will come through this," predicted Userhat.

"You're dreaming," scoffed Fened. "Amenmessu won't hesitate to have him executed."

"I'm not even sure they'll return his body to us for burial," lamented Unesh.

▲

Like most of the village women, Uabet was setting her house in order. When the soldiers came to drive her out, they would find her house in a state of perfect tidiness. Household linen had been washed, folded, and laid in wooden chests; baskets containing everyday objects were arranged neatly on shelves. There was not a speck of dust on the chairs or stools, the mats were rolled up, the beds made and scented. As for the kitchen, which Aapehti had put to rights, it was immaculate and not a single pot or dish was missing.

When the people were expelled, they would leave behind them a welcoming, comfortable village, with pretty white houses that looters would sneer at before they began pillaging them.

Turquoise had washed her cosmetics pots and shells, and the horns she kept oil in, and replaced her jewels in their boxes. The proud redhead would take nothing with her. All her happy times had been experienced here; she would go away wearing no jewelery or makeup, and wearing her simplest dress, knowing that her only destination was unhappiness. No place, no matter how beautiful, could bear comparison with this village, where sacred and profane had been happily wedded.

Ubekhet had had no time to tidy her house, for several sick people had needed care, from a young lad with a cold to a port crew craftsman who had toothache. To forget the anguish gnawing at her heart, the Wise Woman had concentrated on her patients, and had succeeded in giving them relief. But as they left, one by one, her loneliness weighed ever more grievously on her.

How enchanting it was, that moment when she and Nefer met after a long day's work; how sweet their loving bond, which the years had only strengthened. Not being at her husband's side when he was in mortal danger caused Ubekhet unbearable pain.

The workshop door opened a fraction and Ebony's nose appeared. The black dog was not allowed in here, and he dared not cross the threshold.

"Come here, Ebony, come here."

Overjoyed to be breaking a rule with his mistress's unexpected permission, the black dog came and lay down at her feet.

▲

"Majesty, I have brought you the Master of the Brotherhood of the Place of Truth," said Mehy, bowing.

Amenmessu was studying a map of the Delta. He asked, "What exactly do you know of my father's army?"

"It contains many experienced soldiers, Majesty, and the garrisons on the northeastern border are formidable."

"In other words, you would not recommend a full-scale attack on Pi-Ramses."

Mehy was taken by surprise. He had not expected such direct questions, and he wondered if Amenmessu was setting a trap for him. He said, "Ramses the Great made his capital a difficult town to capture. If that is what you intend to do, Majesty, thorough preparation would be vital."

"Your opinion is the same as mine," said the pharaoh. "I'm glad to see that your skills are as good as they're said to be. Continue to use them to good purpose and you'll remain an influential member of my court."

"Order and I shall obey."

The general saw that Amenmessu took great pleasure in humiliating him and behaving like a king whose authority was unchallenged. Others had made that mistake, and they had all paid dearly for it. Mehy allowed no one to treat him like some common little runt.

"Did this man Nefer dare defy my decision?"

"He refuses to destroy Seti's tomb."

"Has he given you any reasons worth repeating?"

"No, Majesty. He remains bound to your father, whom he considers the supreme Master of the Place of Truth and the probable victor in the forthcoming war."

"Does he really think Seti will arrive in time to save him? He must be mad!"

All Mehy was waiting for now was the official order. Either the king would summon Nefer before a special court, which would sentence him for the crime of treason, or else he would send him straight to prison, never to come out alive.

"Show me this rebel," commanded Amenmessu.

The game was cruel, but the general would enjoy it. He went to fetch the Master, who was surprisingly calm.

"The pharaoh wishes to see you," said Mehy.

Nefer entered the audience chamber and bowed respectfully.

"So you're the one," said Amenmessu. "The Master of the Place of Truth, who ought to carry out my orders without question."

"May I ask Your Majesty if you consider yourself the supreme Master of the Brotherhood?"

"Of course I do! Do you still not understand that Seti was only a usurper, and that I have assumed all the royal prerogatives?"

"In that case," said Nefer, "you cannot order me to destroy a House of Eternity."

"I exercise supreme power, and I expect to be obeyed by all my subjects, including you. Either you obey me, Master, or you shall be punished with the utmost severity."

Mehy was jubilant at first, but Nefer's long silence began to worry him. Would fear make Nefer change his mind at the last moment?

Eventually, Nefer said, "No Master of the Place of Truth can become a destroyer, Majesty. I am the only person responsible to you, and I beg you to spare the craftsmen's village and the Valley of the Kings. That is where your ancestors' bodies of resurrection lie, and no outside presence must soil it. No pharaoh worthy of the name would violate that most sacred of places."

Nefer's boldness stunned the general. With words like that, he was pronouncing his own death sentence.

"Are you aware what you have just said?" Amenmessu demanded.

"You had to hear it, Majesty, and I hope that you will preserve the heritage of your predecessors."

"That is exactly what I intend to do."

Mehy could not believe his ears.

"I had to put you to the test," continued Amenmessu, "because I couldn't entrust the building of my own House of Eternity to a coward and a perjuror who would agree to destroy my father's. You are indeed the man I took you for, Nefer, and I am happy for our country. As supreme Master of the Place of Truth, I shall visit Seti's tomb, in which he may be buried, if the gods decide so. And then we shall speak of the site that is to be reserved for me."

Mehy bit his lip hard to wake himself out of this nightmare. But the pain did not wipe away the incredible scene at which he was staring in stunned silence: Pharaoh Amenmessu embracing Nefer the Silent.

—— 28 ——

"There are some heavily laden donkeys coming, sir," one of his men informed Sobek.

"And how many soldiers?"

"No soldiers, sir, just donkeys."

"What! Then who's with them?"

"The next report from the lookout will tell us."

There was only one unarmed man—a man dressed in the ceremonial robes of the Master of the Place of Truth.

"What is it, sir?" asked the guard.

"I shall go out to meet him."

"Be careful, sir. It may be a trap."

"I'm not afraid of donkeys."

Sobek hurried out of the First Fort and ran toward the donkey train. It was moving at a brisk pace. Soon the illusion would be dispelled and hope would fade.

An old, experienced gray donkey was in the lead, trotting up the path without hesitation. And the man looked more and more like Nefer the Silent.

▲

"Well, General, what do you think of my way of testing men's souls?" asked Amenmessu.

Mehy tried to put on a brave face. "It is surprising but remarkably effective, Majesty."

"A king must constantly surprise people. So much had been said about the Master's honesty and determination that I no longer believed it. I was sure that he'd bend to my will like any courtier eager to please me, and he astonished me. If he didn't have my House of Eternity to build, I'd gladly call him into my government. Wouldn't that be a good solution?"

"His lack of experience in the management of public affairs would be a handicap," Mehy protested feebly.

"Exactly, General, and I must be careful not to waste skills. But you look tired."

"Oh no, Majesty, simply worried."

"What about?"

"Seti is likely to take violent action, and I fear Thebes is not yet ready to withstand an attack."

"That is my main concern, too, and you are to work ceaselessly to consolidate our defenses, both on land and on the river."

"Since your father is under Set's protection," said Mehy, "he may come thundering down into the region, counting on the effect of surprise and the ferocity of his attack."

"I," said Amenmessu, "am under the protection of both Ra and Amon, in the face of whom Set will be powerless, so long as we stop his devastating charge in its tracks. We must let my father attack first, to show the people who is the aggressor: the follower of Set, who is doomed to failure. I therefore command you, General, to turn Thebes into an impregnable fortress."

"You may rely upon me, Majesty."

"I also confirm you in your role as protector of the Place of Truth. Its work is essential for the greatness of my reign, and nothing must disturb the Brotherhood's peace."

Bitterly disappointed, Mehy bowed before his king.

▲

Scarcely aware of the noise in the village, where everyone was celebrating loudly and happily, Ubekhet and Nefer had made love like exiles banished to lands so far away that they ought never to have returned. Their bodies entwined, they experienced their union as a gift from the gods and rejoiced in it, at the same time knowing that their happiness must be passed on to the Brotherhood.

"I think the voice singing most loudly is Paneb's, isn't it?" murmured Ubekhet as they lay quietly afterward.

"Probably. He's the one who unloaded the jars of old wine from the royal cellars, and he spotted the inscriptions immediately."

"What an honor Amenmessu has bestowed on us!"

"He isn't the only one," said Nefer. "The meat comes from the butcher at the temple of Karnak and the cakes are from its bakery. The king wants to make us forget the ordeal he thought it necessary to make us undergo."

"Do you think he's sincere?"

"Yes—and worried, too. He knows his coronation has turned him into another man, a man suddenly burdened with responsibilities that are much heavier than he realized. The heaviest is the war he's planning to wage against his father and his fellow Egyptians. And then—but aren't you going to grant me any respite on this evening of celebration?"

Ubekhet smiled, and her radiance made Nefer fall even more deeply in love with her.

"I am ready to satisfy your every desire," he said, "but don't forget that we must preside over the banquet."

"Then we mustn't waste any time."

▲

Outside, a deep, strong voice was thundering out a bawdy love song; even the most reserved of the women joined in the chorus.

"The best banquet since I entered the Brotherhood," declared Pai, helping himself to an enormous piece of beef. "Amenmessu may not be too bad a king."

"We'd better make the most of his generosity," advised Gau. "It may not last long."

"Why are you so sceptical?" asked Fened.

"Do you really think there won't be a price to pay for the Master's freedom? Let's eat and drink before he tells us what sauce we're going to be eaten with."

"Well, I'm confident!" shouted Renupe the Jovial. "After a splendid wine like this, the only problem will be going back to our ordinary beer."

"Hush," said Nakht. "Nefer's about to speak."

Everyone stopped talking, and the Master rose to his feet. "King Amenmessu has declared himself supreme Master of the Brotherhood, in accordance with tradition, and we therefore owe him obedience."

"Does that mean we'll have to destroy Seti's tomb?" asked Paneb anxiously.

"Ruling over the Place of Truth requires the king to respect its nature and vocation. I spoke with him at some length, and he and I are in full accord. We in this village are builders and craftsmen, and we shall stay that way. No outsider shall pass through the gates of the village, Commander Sobek stays in his post, and

General Mehy remains our protector. Nothing has changed, and we shall not destroy any part of our work. However, so long as Seti does not come here to consecrate his House of Eternity, work on it is to be suspended. I shall seal the entrance in the presence of the Wise Woman and the Scribe of the Tomb."

"Will soldiers enter the Valley of the Kings?" asked Karo.

"It will remain a sacred place, which only the craftsmen of the Place of Truth may enter to work."

"But in that case," said Thuty in astonishment, "Amenmessu has given way on everything!"

"The king has heard the voices of the ancestors and seen the scope of our Brotherhood's work. He will respect its laws, which are an expression of Ma'at, provided we respect them ourselves. Oh, and our daily deliveries will of course continue."

"What about the lay workers?" asked Casa.

"They'll be back first thing tomorrow morning, and their number hasn't been reduced. In case of need, and on the authority of the Scribe of the Tomb, it can even be increased."

"Will we be free to celebrate our local festivals?"

"Completely free."

"Then nothing's changed," observed Userhat.

"If you weren't so drunk and if you'd been listening to the Master," said Didia, "you'd know that already."

▲

Karo had fallen asleep with his head on Casa's shoulder. The port crew, who had vied with one another in drinking toasts to Nefer the Silent, had fared scarcely any better. Nakht didn't even feel like fighting Paneb any more, and Unesh was staring into space, a beatific smile on his face.

"These young fellows don't know how to hold their wine," commented Kenhir, who—despite Niut's angry looks—had abandoned his diet. "There's one important point you didn't raise, Nefer. Has Amenmessu entrusted us with the construction of his House of Eternity?"

"Indeed he has, and it's to be our first task."

The Scribe of the Tomb relaxed at last. "Until now I couldn't believe you'd succeeded. Give me another drink."

"Let's hope this isn't another ruse," ventured Ched the Savior, who had remained remarkably sober.

"What do you mean?" grumbled Kenhir.

"I mean we should be wary of taking Amenmessu's word at face value. We should wait and see if he sends in his troops when Seti's tomb is sealed, and if he accepts the site for his own when the Master suggests it."

"You're wrong," said Kenhir. "Forget your worries, and eat and drink all these marvelous things he's sent us."

"If the Scribe of the Tomb himself gives me an order, how can I refuse?"

Seeing that people were dozing off, Paneb broke into a lively drinking song. The curious harmonies that rose toward the sky may not altogether have respected the rules of the music of the spheres, but they bore vivid witness to a reborn enjoyment of life.

▲

The Master, the Wise Woman, and the Scribe of the Tomb paused at the guard post at the entrance to the Valley of the Kings, and then, when the guards said everything was quiet and no soldiers had arrived to replace them, walked slowly on toward Seti's tomb.

"Ched's too pessimistic," said Kenhir, who was suffering from a splitting headache, "but can we really trust Amenmessu?"

"Only the facts count," replied Nefer.

Deserted and god haunted, the valley was already shimmering with the heat of the all-conquering sun. In this otherworld, concerned only with eternity, stone was the absolute ruler.

Nefer slid home the bolt that closed the gilded wooden door of Seti's tomb, and Kenhir affixed a clay seal in the name of the Place of Truth.

"Shall we open it again one day?" wondered Kenhir.

"Let's hope so for Seti's sake," replied the Wise Woman. "It is here that the words of resurrection are waiting to allow him to travel into the afterworld."

The trio walked quietly away, awed by the majesty of the place.

"Whatever the future may bring," predicted Ubekhet, "no one will ever succeed in destroying the spirit of this place."

As they left the valley, the guards saluted them.

"That was an important step," said Kenhir. "Ched was wrong: King Amenmessu has kept his word."

—— 29 ——

Tjaty Bay was aghast. For three days, he had tried in vain to speak with Pharaoh Seti about the decree issued by Amenmessu, who had just proclaimed himself King of Upper and Lower Egypt. The new king's messengers had reached no farther than the city of Khmun, in the heart of Middle Egypt, but the information would spread quickly, and the appalling specter of civil war was growing ever more real.

If Seti wanted to save the country from disaster, he must act quickly and decisively, so as to discredit Amenmessu. But the pharaoh spent all his time in the queen's apartments, where doctors were in constant attendance. The baby had a fever and breathing difficulties, and his health was giving rise to increasing concern.

The tjaty was dealing competently with day-to-day affairs, but Amenmessu's actions risked putting the Two Lands to fire and the sword if Seti continued to do nothing. Bay was worried about the queen, too. Her confinement had been long and painful, despite all the doctors' remedies, and she was taking a long time to recover. Drained of her usual energy, she could not advise her husband.

Although alone at the head of the government in such a dangerous period, the tjaty refused to despair. He loved his adopted country too much to abandon it, so he made strenuous efforts to avoid making any mistakes. At least Bay knew one thing for certain: he would never try to become pharaoh! Steering a ship as vast as Egypt was a greater burden than most men could bear. Few people could take it up, and the tjaty was not one of them. No, he would be loyal to his king.

The day was taken up with meetings with notables and ministers; by night, Bay studied official documents. He no longer had a moment to spend with the young orphan he had taken under his wing. Saptah was the son of a priest of Ptah, and had proved exceptionally intelligent during his studies to become a scribe; Bay had hopes that he would one day become a statesman. The road would be a long one, but young Saptah could not take part in the games enjoyed by boys of his age, because he had a slightly clubbed foot, and he spent all his time in the temple library, studying astronomy and mathematics. Happy to learn, he seemed not to suffer because of his infirmity.

The king entered the tjaty's office, his back hunched and his eyes weary.

Bay got to his feet immediately. "Majesty! How is your son?"

"A little better. He's sleeping peacefully, and so is the queen."

"You're exhausted, Majesty. Will you not rest for a little while?"

"Later. You wished to see me, Bay?"

"Something serious has happened. Your son has had himself crowned Pharaoh at Karnak and is ruling the South."

"Has he issued a decree?"

"Unfortunately, yes, Majesty, and he tried to have it proclaimed throughout the land; but our agents intercepted the messengers."

"What have they done with them?"

"They have been imprisoned and will be sentenced for treason."

"Free them," said Seti.

"But, Majesty . . ."

"That is an order, Bay. And have your scribes prepare letters on which I shall place the royal seal. Those men had no choice but to obey their leader, and they aren't guilty of any crime."

"Your leniency will be widely praised, Majesty, but does it," asked Bay delicately, "extend to the person of your son, who has dared to rebel against you?"

"I should have allied him to the throne and appointed him coregent. Now it's too late. Amenmessu has tasted a power that he thinks is absolute and he'll demand my abdication. War, blood, death: that is what lies in store for us. What a sad reign, Bay! Amenmessu should have killed me. Then he'd have succeeded Meneptah, and the country would not have been divided."

"We are living through difficult times, Majesty, but we must think only of Egypt! Although he is your son, Amenmessu must be considered a rebel and fought as such."

"My son Amenmessu. Many people say he's no longer my son, but I cannot. After all, his ambitions are legitimate ones."

The tjaty was deeply alarmed. "Even though it will be painful, war seems inevitable. We must take action, Majesty, and not allow Amenmessu to gain ground."

"What does it matter?" asked Seti wearily. "If he's the stronger man, he will win. Destiny alone will decide."

"But, Majesty, you cannot rule without Thebes. And don't forget that your House of Eternity is in the Valley of the Kings."

"The Great Meadow . . . now inaccessible to me."

"It must be retaken, Majesty, and you must build your Temple of a Million Years on the west bank of Thebes. It will give you the energy necessary to win."

" 'Win' . . . That word has lost its meaning, Bay."

"Majesty, surely you don't intend to yield to Amenmessu?"

"I have thought of it."

"May I implore you to respect your name, Majesty?"

"Seti, the man of the god Set. I ought to behave like fierce thunder and send out my army to reconquer the South. But I have too much love for the queen, for my fragile child, and for the Egyptian people, who want only to live in peace. I chose my name badly, Bay, for I am unworthy of it. And that weakness eats away at my soul."

"Do you mean you are going to do nothing?"

"I certainly have no intention of attacking: he who courts violence rebels against Ma'at. My strategy shall consist of waiting."

"Shall we at least defend Khmun and Middle Egypt?"

"Why not?"

"Majesty, I am not a courtier whose every word oozes flattery. Even if you dismiss me, I cannot hide from you the fact that I do not agree with that policy."

"You may be right, Bay, but it is I who reign, and that policy will be applied. And I have no intention of dismissing you, because you are honest, competent and loyal—I don't think there's another man like you at court."

"Will you permit me to assemble troops at Khmun to prevent Amenmessu's army progressing any farther?"

"On condition that their commander has strict orders not to launch any attacks."

The tjaty's secretary came in, and informed him that a doctor wished to speak with the king.

"Follow my wishes, Bay, and do nothing that goes against them."

"Majesty, we cannot manage without knowing what is happening in Thebes, and I would like to set up a network of informants."

"As you wish, but remember that it is up to Amenmessu to take the initiative. Take care of the state, Tjaty. I am going back to the people who are dear to me," and the king hurried out.

Distraught, Bay almost laid down his brushes, tore up his papyri, and left his office, where he would be forced to apply directives he disagreed with. But such a desertion would only make the situation worse. The king was in low spirits, and this was certainly not the moment to abandon him, in the midst of his troubles.

Since Seti would not address his army generals himself, Bay would have to carry out this delicate task, for which he was thoroughly unprepared. Although an outstanding scribe, and a lover of ancient writings, the tjaty had never had any contact with military men, nor did he feel any affinity with them.

▲

The four generals looked disdainfully at the foreign civilian who had summoned them to the palace. Usually it was Pharaoh who received them and gave them their orders. They had decided that the general of the army of Amon would be their spokesman and that he would swiftly bring Tjaty Bay to heel.

"Where is the pharaoh, Tjaty?" he asked.

"With his wife and son."

"Some courtiers are saying the king is ill. Is that true?"

"His Majesty is merely very tired, which is why he has entrusted me with the task of informing you of his strategy."

"There is only one possible course of action," said the general. "We must attack at once."

"Would you call the Theban army insignificant?" asked Bay.

"Insignificant? Certainly not."

"Didn't your colleague General Mehy make thoroughgoing reforms to improve the quality of his troops? And—who knows?—it's possible their weapons may be better than ours."

"These are only rumors, Tjaty, and in our opinion they are absurd."

"But it might be advisable to check them."

"That would mean losing precious time," protested the general.

"Such is not the king's view."

The officer looked shocked. "You're playing games with us, Tjaty. Seti cannot afford not to attack Amenmessu. He must break him without delay."

"The king is wary, and I agree with his caution. The reports we have had from Thebes have convinced us that Amenmessu's forces are substantial and that we should not take them lightly."

"But—"

"Our best strategy is to mass a large part of our troops at Khmun, whose fortifications have been strengthened. They will be able to repel any attack, and if necessary we can quickly bring up sizeable reinforcements. Amenmessu would be making a mistake if he attacked Khmun."

The four generals exchanged looks.

"We're surprised by what you say," admitted their spokesman, "but if that's Pharaoh's will . . ."

"I assure you it is," said Bay, "so make the necessary arrangements to put it into practice quickly: our safety is at stake. And I should like to talk to you about a plan which I think you'll approve of."

In fact, the generals approved of it wholeheartedly, and they saw the tjaty in a new light. At the end of the day, the king was right to put his trust in him.

As for Bay, he was happy to have succeeded in justifying the monarch's position to the generals, and he hoped his plan would result in success.

—— 30 ——

The Master and the Scribe of the Tomb were shown into the audience chamber of the palace in Thebes. The palace was near the vast temple complex of Karnak, where Amenmessu had celebrated the dawn rites. The brilliant colors on the walls and pillars gave the place a happy, pleasant atmosphere; but the king's two guests barely noticed the delicate paintings of clumps of papyrus filled with birds, for they were nervous about the outcome of the audience; they remembered Ched the Savior's warning.

In accordance with the pharaoh's wishes, they had brought with them a highly secret document, the map of the Valley of the Kings showing the location of each House of Eternity. Up till now the young ruler had kept his promises; but had that been just a clever strategy to seize this treasure?

Amenmessu was surrounded by ministers and courtiers who had come to assure him of their perfect loyalty and beg to be allowed to retain their privileges; the owners of large estates needed to be reassured, and the king was careful to do so. Once he had consolidated his throne, he would act differently.

"Ah, Nefer!" he exclaimed. "Come nearer. And this old man must be the famous Kenhir, the irreplaceable Scribe of the Tomb?"

"At your service, Majesty," said Kenhir.

"You are the state's representative inside the Brotherhood, Kenhir, and I congratulate you on your running of the village. I have taken the time to consult the report you sent me and I was impressed by its clarity and precision. For your part, are you satisfied with the quality and quantity of the goods delivered to you?"

"We have no criticisms at all, Majesty."

"Is the lay workers' work of an acceptable standard?"

"Again, Majesty, we have no complaints."

"Do you wish me to increase the number?"

Kenhir shook his head. "That will not be necessary, Majesty."

"Have you brought me the document I wish to consult?"

"We must speak in private, Majesty," said the Master.

"Are you asking me to send my ministers away?"

"If it please Your Majesty."

"You will not speak before them?"

"That would be contrary to the rules of the Place of Truth."

"You take no chances, Master—and so much the better!" Amenmessu turned to the courtiers. "Leave us, all of you."

Ministers and courtiers left the audience chamber, and the door was closed.

"Well, where is the map?"

Kenhir took a roll of yellowed papyrus out of a leather case and placed it on a low porphyry table. "This is one of the most precious secrets of the Brotherhood and of Egypt, Majesty."

Amenmessu could not conceal his impatience, but Kenhir unrolled the papyrus very slowly. The first artist had drawn the contours of the valley, then each Master had indicated the location of the tomb he had excavated.

"The Tuthmosids, the Amenhoteps, Ramses the Great," murmured the king. "They are all here, brought together in the afterlife. And I shall live close to them, with them, in the Great Meadow. What location do you suggest?"

Nefer indicated a point almost midway between the tombs of Ramses I and Horemheb, to the south of the tomb of Ramses II.

"It's in a part of the valley that hasn't been used yet," noted Amenmessu, "and a long way from my father's House of Eternity."

The Master and the Scribe of the Tomb waited in silence. This was the moment of truth: either Amenmessu would have his own House of Eternity excavated by the Brotherhood, or he would seize the map so as to loot his predecessors' wealth.

"How did you choose the site?" asked the king.

"By experience and intuition," replied Nefer. "It's necessary to judge the feel of the rock and gain the agreement of the Wise Woman."

"What if I preferred somewhere even more isolated, or somewhere closer to an illustrious pharaoh?"

"Suggest one, Majesty, and we will prove to you that you are wrong."

Kenhir held his breath.

"Begin excavating my House of Eternity," ordered Amenmessu, "and let it lack for nothing at all."

▲

To forget his recent disappointments, General Mehy was working furiously. Surrounding Thebes with impregnable walls would have taken too long, so he had taken other defensive measures, lighter but effective.

He had increased the number of lookout posts along the Nile, and prepared barrages of heavy cargo boats that would prevent the enemy's ships from moving south and thus, for a time at least, block the transport of enemy troops. The archers, footsoldiers, and charioteers were undergoing special training, for each section of the army would attack at a particular time, using its detailed knowledge of the terrain to best advantage.

Once in place, these arrangements would safeguard Thebes from invasion, even if Seti's army was much larger. And, besides, there was the superior quality of the Theban soldiers' weapons.

The army's officers were wholly unimpressed by the fact that Amenmessu had taken command. Their true leader, the man on the ground, the one who guaranteed them good living conditions and generous bonuses, was General Mehy. The few senior officers who had tried to escape from his influence by banking on the king had soon realized their error.

Activity eased the bitterness a little, but Mehy would never forgive Amenmessu for abusing and humiliating him. To judge from the evidence, this ambitious young noble did not possess what it took to make a great king. He was a ruthless opportunist who thought he was more skilful than anybody else—Mehy intended to show him he was wrong.

For the time being, what Mehy wanted was precise information on Seti's plans and his army's movements. Thanks to his spies—whom he had not mentioned to Amenmessu—he would soon be better informed than the king, and he was planning a devastating battle in which both father and son would die. It would then seem that there remained only one man strong enough to run the country and reunite it: General Mehy. He must be sure not to use his best men in the battle, and keep in reserve an elite regiment that would fight only for him.

A young officer came in and saluted. "General, a messenger has arrived from the North."

"Send him in."

Mehy greeted the spy, whom he knew well and had used before.

The man said, "This will be my last mission into enemy territory, General. I shan't be able to get past the Khmun blockade to return to the capital."

"A blockade? What sort of blockade?"

"A solid mass of soldiers."

"That's strange. Doesn't Seti intend to attack Thebes?"

"It seems that the king is ill. Tjaty Bay is ruling in his place."

"A civilian? A frightened civilian? What about the queen?"

"She is recovering slowly from a very difficult birth, and her son is sickly. As soon as they are both better, things may change radically."

"This blockade at Khmun may be just a decoy."

"No, General," said the spy. "Bay is hoping that the Theban troops' attack will be halted and then defeated; and that they will be blamed for starting the civil war. Moreover, if Khmun is attacked, it will be able to call on substantial reinforcements."

"The garrisons from the northeastern border?"

"Exactly."

"This tjaty isn't as stupid as he seems. But has Seti forgotten that he is under the protection of Set and that he should be faithful to him and strike like lightning?"

"You are saying openly what is whispered in his army. No one understands the king's behavior. Without Bay, who has managed to justify it on strategic grounds, grave splits would have appeared already."

They could, thought Mehy, simply leave Seti's regime to rot on its feet in Pi-Ramses while they easily plucked the fruits of victory. Unfortunately, though, in that situation the only victor would be Amenmessu. To achieve power, Mehy needed the two kings to go to war. Since the Place of Truth's treasures seemed once more beyond reach, he must use his own weapons, forcing father and son to deal each other such crushing blows that neither of them would recover.

The day would come when Mehy led a squadron of soldiers up the road to the Place of Truth and Sobek's men no longer had the right to intercept him. The great gate would open, and Nefer the Silent would throw himself at the feet of his new master, who would play at being magnanimous before laying everything waste and taking possession of the Stone of Light.

The spy went on, "Getting reliable information will be more and more difficult, General, but not impossible. Some officers are hesitant about serving Seti. If you can enlist some of them as allies, they'll provide you with information of the highest importance."

"Go and rest in the main barracks at Thebes. Later, you'll be appointed to senior rank in the corps of charioteers."

"Thank you, General." The man bowed and went out.

As usual, Mehy ate a greedy breakfast. He ate and drank quickly, in a hurry to get back and direct the maneuvers.

His assistant came in and told him, "A special message has arrived, sir."

"Where from?"

"Pi-Ramses."

Mehy choked. "Say that again?"

"It's from Pi-Ramses—and it bears the seal of Seti II. The messenger was alone and unarmed, and he handed this message to our most distant outpost, to the north of Thebes."

Impatiently, the general broke the seal, which seemed genuine. The papyrus was of excellent quality, the writing elegant and refined. It did not look like a forgery.

And yet, when Mehy read the text, at first he thought it was a joke. It took the signature, "For Seti, King of Upper and Lower Egypt, Tjaty Bay," to make him realize that it was nothing of the kind.

The general rushed outside, leapt into his chariot, and galloped to the palace.

—— 31 ——

King Amenmessu read the message Mehy had brought him.

"This is utter madness, Majesty, isn't it?" said the general.

" 'In the name of Seti II, Tjaty Bay summons you to Pi-Ramses to report on the state of the Theban troops.' What's mad about that, General? Neither I nor my father have officially declared war. He wants to ignore my coronation, and I have not recognized him as Pharaoh, but the country is at peace and we are each keeping to our respective lands. As for you, my dear Mehy, Seti authorized your promition, didn't he?"

"Indeed, Majesty, but the situation—"

"The tjaty wants to know whose side you're really on."

"That's perfectly obvious."

"Who knows, General? Perhaps your obedience is nothing but a sham. You might be pretending to be loyal to me, while at the same time believing my father will win."

Mehy was white with rage.

"In the struggle for power, treason is a weapon like any other, isn't it?"

"Not for a general in your army, Majesty!"

Amenmessu smiled strangely. "I have no grievance against you, Mehy, but I feel it would be appropriate to take advantage of the situation."

"I don't understand how."

"You are to go to Pi-Ramses, where you will meet Tjaty Bay and perhaps my father. You will answer their questions and make them believe that I am a puppet who oppresses the people and thinks of nothing but amassing wealth by sacking the rich cities of the South. Tell them my army is ready to rebel against me, and all it would take to topple me would be an attack from Seti."

"No one will believe me," protested Mehy.

"Be persuasive, General. If you succeed in this mission, we shall win the war."

"If I do manage to convince my audience, will they let me leave?"

"I think so, for you will become their secret correspondent in Thebes, not only their informant but also the person to whom they pass information. Can you imagine the advantage that will give us? The venture is rather dangerous, I grant you, but it's worth trying. Leave immediately, General."

▲

Wearing his ritual golden apron, Nefer struck the gold chisel with a mallet and it sank into the rock. Paneb immediately attacked it with the large pick, which heavenly fire had marked with the muzzle and two ears of Set. Nakht quickly did likewise, still eager to strike harder and for longer than his rival. The other two stonecutters worked more slowly, after Fened had checked that the limestone was of good quality.

"What is the plan of the tomb to be?" asked Ched.

"The one I suggested to the king, which he has accepted: a succession of four passageways, followed by the usual symbolic rooms."

"So his House of Eternity won't be very different from his father's."

"It is true that Amenmessu does not wish to move away from tradition."

"Has he any special requirements as regards the decoration?"

"He wishes his mother to be shown, making offerings to the gods. The rest he entrusts to us."

"That's surprising. I hadn't expected him to follow custom so closely. He really does seem to want to reign, and if he recognizes the importance of this Valley, he may succeed in doing so. I shall therefore consult my crew and choose the texts and figures."

Nefer asked the sculptors to prepare royal statues and to show Amenmessu in relief on the walls of his tomb. Didia and Thuty were already making the burial furniture, from statuettes of "answerers" to shrines made of gilded wood. They would probably need help from their colleagues in the port crew, although the latter were already overloaded with work. Since the new pharaoh had confirmed the role of the Place of Truth, many nobles had renewed orders they had previously canceled, so as not to displease the new regime.

The song of the picks and chisels, the long series of sketches, studying models, the love of the raw material to be transformed into beauty . . . the old enthusiasm was back, after a dark period in which the craftsmen thought they had lost everything. Launching themselves into the creation of a House of Eternity was a new affirmation of the crew's unity.

The traitor felt that unity as true pain. Despite his discreet efforts, he had been unable to create dissent in the village, where no one contested the Master's authority. And all his attempts to discover the Stone of Light's hiding place had failed.

Yet he did not give up hope. In this anxious time of waiting for the inevitable civil war, he might have opportunities to search places that were usually difficult to get into. And when war broke out, the Place of Truth would not be unaffected by the disturbances. It was up to him to make the most of them.

▲

All the way from Khmun to Pi-Ramses, Mehy and his escort were kept under strict guard, although he was treated with the proper respect due a general. Tjaty Bay's official letter acted as a permit and enabled them to pass the military posts that were watching traffic on the Nile.

Mehy was deeply anxious, so much so that dozens of small, painful red spots broke out on his left thigh. Several times a day, he applied an ointment that eased the discomfort a little.

Amenmessu was sending him right into the jackal's mouth,

and it was impossible to disobey—unless Seti had believed Mehy's coded messages assuring him of his fidelity, and demanded that Mehy fight with him against his son. Even if that happened, Seti would certainly not appoint a turncoat to an important position.

Mehy got no pleasure from seeing Pi-Ramses again, magnificent though the capital was. The charming canals, gardens, and orchards held no appeal for him, and he felt defenseless when he was deprived of his escort and asked to go alone into the palace. There, he waited in an empty antechamber until an aged scribe showed him into the tjaty's vast office, which was dominated by a granite statue of Seti.

"Thank you for responding to my invitation, General," said Bay. "I hope you had a good journey?"

"There were many checkpoints, but the boat was comfortable."

"Please, take a seat. Egypt is going through a delicate period, and I think all of us in authority should join forces to try to avert the worst. Don't you agree?"

"Of course, but I'm only a soldier who must obey orders. And at the moment—"

"Don't underestimate your importance, General. King Seti and I know that you have undertaken a thorough reorganization of the Theban troops, and we have been wondering how good their weapons and equipment are."

"I hope you have been receiving my coded messages?"

"I assure you they have reached us, and we appreciate your fidelity to the rightful king, who will no doubt reward you suitably. Did Amenmessu make any difficulty about your coming here?"

"I showed him your letter, and he had no objection to my journey because he believes Egypt is still at peace."

"That is a somewhat optimistic view of reality," said the tjaty. "But you haven't yet answered my question about the Theban troops' weapons."

"As I had not foreseen the crisis that is tearing our country apart, I did my best to give them good weapons and well-maintained chariots."

The tjaty was taking notes. "Has Amenmessu recalled the Nubian garrisons?"

"Not yet."

"When does he intend to begin his offensive?"

"He hasn't yet made up his mind."

"Why not?"

"Because he isn't certain of winning, and he doesn't want to be seen as the aggressor in case the people condemn him."

"Does he really dream of reigning over the whole of Egypt?"

"I think he'll soon realize that that's impossible, and his position will become correspondingly weaker. Nevertheless, he has ordered the Master of the Place of Truth to begin excavating his House of Eternity in the Valley of the Kings."

"What is to become of Seti's?"

"The work has been suspended, and the Master has sealed the entrance."

"I was sure Amenmessu would have had it destroyed, it being a monument to his father. Such moderation is surprising. A sign of weakness, perhaps?"

"Amenmessu really only rules Thebes, and that is thanks to the support of the high priest of Karnak, who approves of the king's devotion to Amon. But the alliance is fragile, and decisive action by Seti would put an end to it."

"In other words, you would advise the pharaoh to launch a major offensive against his son."

"If he wishes to restore unity to the country, what other solution is there? It's tragic, I know, and many soldiers will die, but the ordeal is as inevitable as it is painful."

"There might be a way of avoiding it, General," said Bay.

"What is it?"

"When we attack, your troops must desert and allow ours to advance right to the heart of Thebes and halt the rebel there."

In front of this formidable man, Mehy knew he must not say too much. And the solution Bay proposed was the worst one possible, because it meant there would be no war.

"You seem hesitant, General."

"No, not at all," said Mehy quickly. "I congratulate you on your plan. But there is just one small weak point: my men's absolute obedience."

"Are you sure of them?"

"A few of the senior officers believe the future lies with Amenmessu."

"Could you make them see that they are mistaken?"

"I'll try, but it will require a good deal of tact."

"I have a much better suggestion: you can assure them that Seti will not be ungrateful, and loyalty to the rightful pharaoh will be well rewarded."

"With an assurance like that, I should have no difficulty convincing them. There's just one other important point, Tjaty: when will your offensive begin?"

"As soon as His Majesty has been persuaded that it's necessary. You will receive a coded message giving details of the operation."

---- 32 ----

At the end of a meeting of his most senior ministers, who had praised him in glowing terms, Amenmessu learned that General Mehy had returned from Pi-Ramses. He received him immediately in a small room in the palace, well away from indiscreet ears.

"So," said the king, "my father did not keep you with him. You are very lucky, General."

"It's not a matter of luck, Majesty. It's a plan the enemy have dreamed up—and I'm the principal element of it."

"What do you mean?"

In the dangerous game he was playing, Mehy knew he could not afford to make any mistakes if he was to keep the trust of both enemies and succeed in setting them against each other.

He said, "Seti is massing his troops at Khmun, which he regards as the new border of his kingdom."

"Can we break through?"

"Probably, but only at considerable cost. We would have to face reinforcements sent from the North, notably the formidable northeastern garrisons."

"In other words, we'd be doing exactly what my father wants us to do."

"Exactly, Majesty. He hopes you will attack Khmun and be broken there."

Amenmessu was silent for a moment. Then he said, "Tell me, General, how were you treated by the enemy?"

Mehy sensed that Amenmessu suspected he might be playing a double game. The king must have been amazed at his safe return from Pi-Ramses, and now Mehy must dispel his doubts.

"Very coldly, Majesty, but my rank was respected and I was treated correctly, thanks to the letter from Tjaty Bay. But I was expected to transfer my allegiance to Seti."

Amenmessu turned a piercing gaze on him. "And you refused?"

"Yes, Majesty, I did, because I believe in your eventual victory—in fact, 'believe' is too weak a word."

"Why?"

"Because I know how to destroy the enemy."

The king could not but be affected by the strength of Mehy's belief. "Did you see Seti?" he asked.

"No, only the tjaty, and I have no precise information about your father's health. It's whispered that the queen's confinement was difficult and that her son is sickly, but that could be a lie designed to make us think Seti and Tausert have preoccupations other than making war on you."

"But what if it's true?"

"I learned the truth, Majesty, from Tjaty Bay's own mouth."

"Ah yes, the famous plan," said Amenmessu. "What is it?"

"The idea is simple, but formidably effective. Bay thinks I'm loyal to Seti, that I'm forced to obey you but am looking for a way to betray you. When the army of the North attacks, I'm to order my men not to fight. The soldiers of the two armies will be reconciled, and you'll be left alone and defenseless."

"That . . . that's monstrous! And you agreed?"

"If I'd refused, Majesty, I wouldn't have left the tjaty's office alive. I should add that he asked me to bribe any officers who were reluctant to join me, and he said I'll be told in advance when the attack will be, so as to avoid any mistakes."

Amenmessu seemed lost. "That man Bay is a devil."

"No, Majesty, just a strategist who believes he's found the best way to win a quick and decisive victory."

"If you're telling me his plan in detail," said the king hesitantly, "that means . . . you aren't betraying me?"

"Of course not, Majesty," Mehy assured him with an open smile. "And we're going to turn this plan against its creator. When Seti's troops approach Thebes, they'll expect to be welcomed with open arms. Instead, we shall catch them in a trap I'm in the process of creating. The surprise will work in our favor, I shall unleash several waves of attackers, and the enemy will have to surrender or be wiped out. And you, Majesty, at the head of your army, will win a memorable victory."

Mehy permitted himself an inward smile as he thought of what would really happen. He would keep his best troops back from the battle, and wait for Amenmessu and Seti to kill each other. When the moment came, it was he, Mehy, who would win the true victory. A delicate operation, certainly, but one that would lead to great things.

Amenmessu looked at him closely. "There is still one question troubling me, General: why should I trust you?"

"I realize it isn't enough for me to say I believe more in your ability to reign than in your father's, and rightly so. The real reason is very simple, Majesty, but a decisive one for me: I'm a Theban and I've never accepted the fact that the city of Amon has been supplanted by a capital in the Delta. You came to live here and you have learned to love this town and this region, whereas your father has nothing but contempt for them. Thebes will give you victory, and in return you will give it back the status it should never have lost. Only you can make my dream a reality, and it's a dream shared by most of the senior officers in our army. That is why I shall destroy our enemies."

Mehy saw from Amenmessu's expression that his words had found their mark. Of course, he had other arguments in reserve, but since the first was enough to convince this sensitive, credulous monarch, there was no need to add to it.

▲

Tjaty Bay had examined in detail all the records pertaining to General Mehy; there was a great deal of information there, from his service record to gossip put about by his subordinates. After talking with him, the tjaty had come to the firm conclusion that Mehy was indeed the man he needed.

Skillful, hardworking, energetic, the general had the ear of his men and he knew how to make them obey him. Sufficiently clear-sighted to see that Amenmessu had no future, he would serve Seti out of self-interest, if not out of genuine feeling, and would enable him to rule the entire country once again.

When they entered Bay's office, the pharaoh's four generals were very tense.

Their spokesman, the general of the army of Amon, wasted no time in pleasantries. "Well, Tjaty, what have you learned?"

"Some information on the Theban troops."

"Are they as well equipped as you feared?"

"Unfortunately, yes, if I've understood Mehy correctly."

"Then he agrees to collaborate?"

"Like you, he thinks only of the greatness of his country and of restoring its lost unity."

"And yet," said the general, "he's gone back to the enemy camp."

"The situation is extremely complex, and we should not complain about it."

"Would Amenmessu agree to recognize the error of his ways?"

"It's difficult for me to tell you anything more until I have His Majesty's agreement to the strategy that seems the most effective. Your troops should, however, be kept on a war footing and the fleet must be ready to sail."

The generals were delighted: the tjaty's words meant that a general offensive was imminent.

▲

"I must see the king urgently," Bay told the head steward.

"That's impossible, Tjaty. His Majesty is at his son's bedside and has ordered that no one disturb him, not even you."

"Will the queen see me?"

"Please wait here. I will inquire."

Bay had a chance to give the whole of Egypt back to Seti, and he could not even talk to him and obtain his permission to launch the victorious attack! Yet he could not take such action without the king's agreement.

A doctor approached him. "Her Majesty agrees to see you, Tjaty. She is doing so against my advice, for I consider her too weak to concern herself with affairs of state, so please be brief and don't tire her."

"You may rely on me, Doctor."

A lady of the bedchamber showed Bay into a light-filled room, whose walls were painted blue and whose principal decorations were friezes of lotus blossoms. Tausert was lying on an ebony wood bed, her head resting on embroidered pillows.

The tjaty halted some distance away, and bowed. "Majesty,

your health . . . ," he said with difficulty, his voice breaking with emotion.

"I am much better, Tjaty. Come and sit beside me."

"Permit me to remain standing."

As he came closer, he could see that Queen Tausert was as beautiful as ever. With her face made up, and her hair dressed, she was the very embodiment of distinction, and her direct gaze had lost none of its power.

"Forgive me for inconveniencing you like this, Majesty, but I believe I have found a way out of the impasse, if I can obtain Pharaoh's agreement."

The queen listened intently as he outlined his plan. When he had finished, she said, "If you succeed, Bay, you will have saved Egypt."

"The sooner we launch the attack, Majesty, the greater our chance of victory. If we delay our decision, however, General Mehy's confidence might waver. Could you perhaps speak to the king?"

"Seti is no longer interested in anything but his son's health. He places all his hopes in the child, as if he feels the boy will one day have the strength to accomplish what Seti himself cannot."

"It is imperative that the decision be taken urgently, Majesty. Our troops are ready to attack, but I have not yet told the generals that their true mission will be to capture Amenmessu and achieve peace."

The queen gazed at him in admiration. "You are a remarkable servant of the state, Bay, and a true friend: Egypt will remember your devotion. Help me up. I am going to try and persuade the king to let you act."

The bedchamber door opened. Seti stood on the threshold, his arms hanging slackly by his sides; he stared blankly before him with empty eyes.

"My son is dead," he whispered.

33

Thanks to his lessons with Gau the Precise, Aapehti's mathematics had improved a little, but he remained firmly at the bottom of the class, and Kenhir and Imuni were thinking of excluding him from the school.

Because of his age, Kenhir now taught the village children only literature. The best pupils were studying the subtleties of Ptah-hotep's teachings, or discourses on the need to respect Ma'at and fight injustice. Sour-faced Imuni taught reading, writing, arithmetic, and other basic subjects. Some of the children would remain in the Brotherhood; others would make use of their learning to build careers in the outside world.

"Your son is disrupting my classes," Imuni complained to Paneb. "He talks, distracts his friends, and is rude to me in front of them."

"Why don't you punish him severely?"

"I've threatened to, but he laughs in my face."

"You're afraid of him, aren't you?"

"No, of course not!" said Imuni. "But he's tall and strong for his age, and I—"

"Listen, Imuni, we don't like each other much, you and I, but my son must respect his teacher and work properly. I myself shall set him back on the right path and I insist that you tell me if he commits even the smallest misdemeanor in the future. Do I make myself clear?"

"Perfectly," replied Imuni in a small voice.

▲

A group of about ten children were running around a spiral, drawn on the ground and marked out with squares. Some squares gave the players advantages and allowed them to continue, others carried penalties and meant they had to retrace their steps.

"You cheated, Aapehti!" exclaimed Ipuy's son, a studious, re-served boy.

"All you ever think about is pleasing the teacher," jeered Aapehti.

"You cheated, so you're out of the game."

The others agreed.

"You're all dirty little tattletales," said Aapehti. "I was going to win again, and you didn't like it."

"We don't like it when you cheat."

Aapehti made as if to walk away, then turned back suddenly and hit Ipuy's son on the back with a willow switch.

"You're going to remember this, you little sneak!"

Nearly a cubit taller than his opponent and a good deal heav-ier, Aapehti knocked him over and was preparing to cut his back to ribbons when a formidable kick in the backside lifted him off the ground and threw him against the wall of a nearby house.

"Are you going to hit your father?" Paneb inquired calmly.

Aapehti had nowhere to run to. And there was no escape from two resounding slaps, which turned his cheeks crimson.

"I was a horrible child myself," said Paneb, "but I always wanted to learn and I never cheated. Either you change your ways or I'll throw you straight out of the village and put you to work in the fields with the lay workers—at least you'd be doing something useful."

"Don't do that!"

"Then give me one good reason for letting you stay. You're incredibly lucky to be living in the Place of Truth. You get a bet-ter education here than you would in most temple schools. If you're too stupid to understand that, go and try your luck some-where else."

"I don't like Imuni, I prefer Gau—he's ugly and stern, but I understand what he's saying."

"I don't care what you prefer, boy. What matters is to obey your teacher and to learn."

▲

"King Amenmessu is fortunate," said Nakht. "He'll live for all eternity in the most beautiful part of the Great Meadow."

Karo laid down his pick. "Personally, I prefer the site of Seti's tomb."

"Isolated places didn't work very well for Seti," commented Fened.

"Do you think they'll work for Amenmessu?" asked Karo. "Instead of attacking, he's waiting for the enemy. That isn't how a real leader behaves."

"So you're an expert in military strategy, are you?" said Casa sarcastically.

"We shan't be excavating for long, I'm telling you, and work on this tomb won't get far."

"At the speed the Master is making us work, that would amaze me."

Paneb also stopped working. "Are you complaining about something, Casa?"

"I don't see why Nefer insists that we keep working and working, without ever a break. He even canceled two rest days last month."

"They were only optional ones," Paneb reminded him. "When we're overworked, the Master has the right not to use them."

" 'Overworked' is the right word," grumbled Casa.

"It is easy to understand, though," said Karo, rubbing his arms. "The Master is convinced that Amenmessu's reign will be only brief, and he wants to build him a real House of Eternity in time."

Nakht gulped down some fresh water and passed round the water skin. "Let's hope he's wrong. If Seti enters Thebes as the victor, I wouldn't give much for our hides."

"You shouldn't be so gloomy," disagreed Fened. "Have you forgotten how he defended us and saved the Brotherhood?"

"I'm not criticizing him in any way, but what can he do against the armies of a pharaoh bent on revenge?"

"First of all," replied Paneb, "we haven't reached that stage yet, and for another thing our break is over."

▲

All Pi-Ramses was in mourning. At the palace, courtiers and servants had not shaved; and the women had taken off their wigs and wore their hair loose. The mummification of the baby prince had begun, and was being carried out by the most skillful embalmers.

Tjaty Bay was ensconced in his office, trying to reassure a series of senior dignitaries who were worried that the kingdom was not being governed properly; despite all his efforts, he could not convince them, and a doom-laden atmosphere had taken hold of the capital. While the tjaty was struggling against despondency, demonstrating through his own and his scribes' work that the state was not going to wrack and ruin, a kind of miracle occurred: Queen Tausert summoned the court.

Immediately, despair was replaced by curiosity, and people jostled one another in the rush to get into Ramses' great audience chamber.

Dressed in a long, light-green dress and wearing a crown of gold, a turquoise necklace, and fine gold bracelets, the queen sat down on Pharaoh's throne. In Seti's absence, it fell to the Great Royal Wife to govern the country.

The courtiers closest to the queen tried in vain to discern signs of tiredness on her face, but her bearing was as majestic as ever. Tausert was making her first appearance alone at the summit of state, and many expected her to make a mistake.

"The king is unwell," she explained. "His son's death has affected him profoundly, and his doctors think he will need a long rest and careful nursing before he can once again wield the scepters of state. It falls to me to rule in the meantime. You may be sure that I shall do so with a firm hand, as will Tjaty Bay, who is running affairs of state with a skill we all greatly appreciate."

"When will our army attack Thebes?" asked a courtier aggressively.

"Pharaoh has decided that we must not be the first attackers. However, all necessary measures will be taken to ensure the security of the regions under our control, and any attack by Amenmessu will of course be fiercely resisted."

"Does that mean we are abandoning Thebes and the South?"

"It means that we shall not be the first to spill the blood of thousands of Egyptians, and that for the moment Pharaoh prefers the present state of affairs to carnage. But we are aware that, to survive, the Two Lands must be united. So we shall take other paths to achieve that."

"What paths are those, Majesty?"

"It is not for a second-rate courtier with a sharp tongue to know such important state secrets," replied Tausert calmly. "Let him be content to obey and to serve his country—if he can."

She stood up, signifying that the audience was at an end.

Impresssed and reassured, Bay saw at once that the queen had won the court over.

"Allow me to congratulate you on your action, Majesty," he said to her. "I am sure it will silence mischievous tongues and reassure those who are downcast. But is it really possible to persuade the king to follow my plan and attack Thebes?"

"Seti had invested all his hopes in our son, Bay. The child's death has almost completely robbed him of his will to live, and he fears he may become subject to the influence of Set. That is why he is trying to avoid a war with Amenmessu and does not wish to start one under any circumstances."

"But, Majesty, you know that war is inevitable."

"There's something else, Tjaty."

The queen's serious manner worried Bay.

"Seti demands," she continued, "that his son, who should have succeeded him, be buried in a House of Eternity in the Valley of the Kings."

"But the Theban region is under Amenmessu's control."

"Since the king cannot carry out this task, the burden falls on me."

"Do not accept it, Majesty, I beg of you. It would be madness! Amenmessu hates you. He'll refuse your request and take you hostage. The country needs you. You must not throw yourself into the mouth of a bloodthirsty lion."

"Have a ship made ready, Tjaty," said the queen. "I shall leave tomorrow morning."

"Only one? But you need a sizeable escort, experienced soldiers and—"

"One ship only, and it is to have a funerary shrine for my dead son—and no soldiers."

—— 34 ——

Mehy was on tenterhooks. "Still nothing?" he asked his assistant.

"No, sir, no messages at all today."

The general mounted into his war chariot and set off back to the barracks, where he was directing the archers' practice: equipped with their new arrows, they would cut down the enemy in record time. Thanks to the troops' intensive training, he now had a formidable army, very mobile and able to obey his orders instantly.

He was proud of himself. Long years of hard work had enabled him to create a peerless fighting force, which, so long as he used it wisely, would open up his path to supreme power. In the ancient land of the pharaohs, he could not simply use force to seize and keep power; that would be contrary to the law of Ma'at, and would never obtain the scribes' or priests' assent, still less that of the common people. So Mehy must seem the country's savior, and emerge successful following the struggle to the death between Seti and Amenmessu.

As he drove, he had an amusing thought: he owed his rise to power, at least in part, to the Place of Truth. The hatred he had felt for the Brotherhood, ever since the court of admissions had rejected his application for membership, had led him to equip himself with the means to fight, and he had therefore become stronger and more influential with each day that passed.

Razing the village to the ground after seizing its treasures would give him as much pleasure as being crowned, if not more.

But why was Bay's coded message taking so long to arrive? Mehy was certain he had convinced the tjaty of his good faith, and by all accounts the tjaty believed in the success of his plan. In fact, he had seemed eager to put it into practice and reconquer the South. Seti must still be wavering, but Bay's strategy was so clever that it was bound to win the king over, since it assured him of an easy, bloodless victory.

As Mehy reached the archery ground, an officer ran up. "General, a suspicious ship has been spotted, approaching from the North."

'Do you mean a fleet?"

"No, sir. According to the lookouts, there's only one ship."

Mehy was intrigued but did not want to take any risks. "Have it intercepted and tied up at the main landing stage on the west bank. If the soldiers on board refuse to surrender, kill them, but keep one or two alive for interrogation."

▲

The village was almost smothered by a strong-smelling fog, dominated by the scent of fresh frankincense. It was the day when the houses and public areas were fumigated, and each housewife had thrown gum-resin into oil burners containing hot coals. Insects and disease-bearing germs would be destroyed by this cleansing, which was accompanied by laughing stampedes of children, who were delighted by this collective entertainment.

The traitor approached the starboard crew's meeting place. After sober reflection, he was convinced that the Stone of Light must be hidden there, probably under the innermost shrine. If he made the most of his chance, he could at least be certain.

Unfortunately for him, the Master had already instructed Karo to carry out a task that the stonecutter regarded as forced labor. When it was time for the next cleansing, the traitor would try to take his place, though without actually volunteering, as that would only draw attention to him.

A hand came down on his shoulder, turning his blood to ice.

"So you've escaped from your house, too?" said Paneb.

"Yes, I must admit I have. I don't like those strong smells."

"Neither do I. And Uabet's increased the quantity in order to kill even creatures too small to see, so it's impossible to breathe in there."

By the time Paneb left, the traitor was soaked in sweat. His head swimming, and unsteady on his feet, he went back home. There he found several women were engaged in a lively discussion with his wife.

"Sobek wants to to see Kenhir," said one. "We should go to the main gate."

▲

The fog was drifting away, and the village had been purified, but no one was thinking about the banquet that would celebrate the cleansing, for the Scribe of the Tomb had just returned, and everyone had gathered to hear what he had to say.

"The northern fleet is attacking Thebes," he told them.

"War!" exclaimed Pai's wife, in terror. "It's war!"

"No one is to leave the village," ordered the Master. "Sobek will keep us informed of what's happening."

▲

The enemy ship slowly drew alongside the main landing stage on the west bank, watched by three hundred archers primed to loose their arrows the moment General Mehy raised his hand. But Mehy, like his soldiers, was staring in astonishment at the strange vessel.

It was not a warship but a large funerary ship, the center of which was occupied by a shrine flanked by two statues of the goddesses Isis and Nephthys kneeling, their hands outstretched toward the sarcophagus to protect it with their magnetic energy. The twenty oarsmen were unarmed, and so was the captain.

There were sharp intakes of breath when Tausert, dressed in a long white mourning robe and the Red Crown of the North, stepped onto the gangplank.

Mehy bowed before the queen.

"You are General Mehy?" she asked.

"Yes, Majesty."

"This ship carries the mummy of my son, whom the pharaoh and I wish to be buried in the Valley of the Kings."

Mehy could not believe his ears. "You . . . you are not accompanied by escort boats?"

"I have come alone, General, and these oarsmen are not soldiers."

"Majesty, how can I say—"

"You are the governor of the west bank of Thebes, are you not?"

"Indeed I am, Majesty, but—"

"But we are almost in a state of war and you must obey the orders of Prince Amenmessu. Is that it?"

"The prince has become Pharaoh, and—"

"There is only one pharaoh," said Tausert firmly, "and I am acting in his name."

Mehy had not been expecting an attack like this, but perhaps he could reap some advantage from the queen's insane behavior.

"You will understand, Majesty, that I am obliged to consult King Amenmessu. May I ask you to follow me to the palace of the temple of Ramses, where you will be housed?"

"You could have made a worse choice, General."

▲

"It isn't war," Kenhir told the villagers.

"Wasn't it the northern fleet?" asked Ipuy.

"No, it was a funerary ship bearing Queen Tausert and her son's mummified body."

"Queen Tausert!" exclaimed Nakht. "Has she gone mad?"

"They say she wants her child to be buried in the Valley of the Kings."

"Amenmessu will never agree," said Didia. "He'll put Tausert in prison, and then Seti will order his troops to attack Thebes."

"He wouldn't dare," argued Karo, "in case Amenmessu executed the queen."

"In any case," said Renupe, "it's no business of ours."

"Are you sure about that?" asked Paneb. "Who'll excavate the tomb, if not our Brotherhood?"

"King Amenmessu's bound to have other plans, and fate has bestowed on him a priceless gift."

"Far from being a madwoman," said Ched, "the queen knows exactly what she's doing. By entrusting herself to Amenmessu like this, she's preventing war between father and son."

"All the same, she is taking an enormous risk."

"The queens of Egypt are generally remarkably courageous women. Even if her gesture fails, it shows no lack of grandeur, and that grandeur proves that Egypt still has life left in it."

The Master was gazing in front of him, as though he had glimpsed another reality. And he said not a word.

▲

"Tausert was making a fool of you, General," said Amenmessu furiously.

"No, Majesty. Her son's sarcophagus was indeed inside the shrine."

"This is simply an act of provocation."

"Undoubtedly, but with what aim?"

"Make her talk, General."

"Majesty . . . Tausert is the queen!"

"Nonsense," snapped Amenmessu. "There is only one queen of Egypt, and that is my wife."

"Forgive me, Majesty, but I cannot treat the lady Tausert like a common prisoner."

Enraged, Amenmessu pounded his clenched fist against a pillar. "I hate that scheming woman! She stole my mother's place and turned my father against me."

"I assume she knows your feelings?"

"Of course she does."

"Then, Majesty, her presence in Thebes is all the more astounding."

"Did she give you a message from Seti?"

"No, Majesty."

"She really spoke only of her son's funerary rites?"

"She did."

"It's a trap, General. It can't be anything else."

"I agree, Majesty, but I cannot work out what it is."

"Tausert is an ambitious, calculating woman, capable of using even her son's death to kill me. Whatever you do, don't let her soften your heart. She's a formidable actress, and she'll try to win you over by charm. I take it your lookouts haven't reported the arrival of a war fleet taking advantage of this diversion?"

"All is quiet, Majesty."

"How many times have you questioned her so far?"

"Three times, and each time she has given the same calm answers and has made the same request."

"What trap is the witch trying to lure us into? The best solution would be to have her sentenced to death by an emergency court."

"If you did, Majesty, you would unleash your father's fury," cautioned the general; he fervently hoped that that would happen.

Amenmessu leaned back against the pillar he had punched and raised his eyes to the ceiling. "Bring Tausert to me, General."

—— 35 ——

"Queen—that is to say, the lady Tausert is here, Majesty," announced the palace steward.

"Show her in."

Amenmessu had decided to receive his enemy in the throne room of the palace at Karnak. He was sitting on the gilded wooden throne Meneptah had occupied, and he wore the Blue Crown. No one would be present.

As soon as she appeared, the king lost his composure. In a red dress that highlighted her gold jewelery, Tausert looked more like a goddess than a mere mortal. Amenmessu's throat was so dry that he could not utter the tirade of insults he had planned to hurl at this hated woman.

"Will you not offer me a chair, Amenmessu?" she asked.

He ought to have ordered her to bow before Pharaoh, but he dared not. He said sulkily, "I am not your servant."

"However powerful he may be, a king should know how to behave in front of a queen."

Amenmessu rose. "Follow me."

He led Tausert into a small room where the king rested between audiences. The two enemies sat down simultaneously, on stone benches covered with cushions.

"What do you want," he demanded.

"Did General Mehy not tell you?"

"What he said made no sense."

"Whatever your ambitions may be," said the queen, "will you really be so cruel as to trample on a mother's grief and refuse to grant her legitimate requests?"

"You don't know what feelings are! You married my father not out of love but to gain power."

"I gave Seti a son, a son he hoped would ascend to the throne and whom fate has taken from us. The boy's death has plunged your father into despair, but he has made his wishes known: that his child, who should have been Pharaoh, be buried in the Valley of the Kings alongside his ancestors. That is the sole reason for my journey, and if you think I have other reasons you are wrong."

Her dignity shook him. He had expected her to reproach him for proclaiming himself Pharaoh and refusing to recognize Seti's sovereignty and had thought the discussion would soon become venomous; but the queen expressed herself calmly and without animosity. He even thought he saw real suffering in her beautiful eyes.

"I don't believe you. You came to Thebes to ask me to renounce the throne and recognize my father as sole pharaoh, didn't you?"

Tausert smiled. "Would you do it?"

"Never!"

"Then it would be pointless to ask you. You have gone too far, Amenmessu, and you won't turn back. But you should know that Seti doesn't want civil war, which would cause the deaths of thousands of Egyptian soldiers, spread unhappiness through our land, and weaken it so much that it would become easy prey for invaders."

Amenmessu had one decisive advantage over Tausert: Mehy's plan. But suddenly he had a vision of thousands of corpses, their blood reddening the Nile waters, and that waking nightmare horrified him. Ruling did not mean bringing about death.

"You look troubled," said Tausert.

"Will you tell me why you really came?"

"I have already told you."

"How can I possibly believe you?" he demanded. "You never do anything without an ulterior motive, or without a specific goal in sight."

"Your father and I love each other, and we loved our child. His death has turned our lives upside down, and I would be happy to carry out my husband's wish. I tell you again, that is the only reason for my journey, and I hope that you can understand it."

"It was you, wasn't it, who prevented my father choosing me as coregent and thus making me his heir."

"Yes, it was."

"Why do you hate me?"

"I don't think you're capable of governing."

"You're wrong, and I shall prove it to you! Today, I should have you tried for disrespect to the throne."

"Do as you wish, but first grant your father's request."

Amenmessu hesitated. Tausert seemed sincere and had not tried to evade the issue when she found herself in a position of weakness, as if all that mattered was the fate of her dead son.

"Showing clemency to a dead child would not damage your authority," added the queen.

"I've already proved my magnanimity by not destroying Seti's tomb."

"Could you really have sacked your father's House of Eternity and thus soiled the Great Meadow where the souls of the pharaohs dwell?"

Cut to the quick, Amenmessu lowered his eyes. The woman was a prisoner in his palace, yet she dared defy him!

"Your child was not a king. His mummy should not rest in the Valley."

"People who were not of royal blood have been admitted, under exceptional circumstances. Consult the Master of the Place of Truth: he'll tell you that's so."

"Do you want me to come to the palace with you, Master?" asked Sobek.

"No, there's no need."

"All the same, it might be wise. The people asking for you may be civilians, but they haven't said why Amenmessu has summoned you."

"I've nothing to fear," said Nefer.

The Nubian sighed, close to despair at the Master's lack of caution. He watched Nefer leave, escorted by a delegation of five royal scribes and their assistants, who had come to the First Fort of the Place of Truth, asking Nefer to act. They explained that King Amenmessu said their mission was urgent, so the charioteers bore them at a full gallop to the landing stage, where a fast boat took them across the Nile.

At the main gate of the palace, Nefer was taken in hand by a steward, who took him to the chamber where Amenmessu was waiting. With him was a woman of extraordinarily noble bearing, whose gaze rested with interest on the Master.

"At last!" exclaimed Amenmessu.

"We came as quickly as we could, Majesty."

"Explain to the lady Tausert that her child cannot be buried in the Valley of the Kings, because he was not crowned."

From the way the king spoke, it was evident what he wanted Nefer's answer to be. But what Amenmessu wanted did not correspond with reality, and the Master could not and would not lie.

"In fact, Majesty, there have been some exceptions."

Amenmessu turned purple. "What exceptions?"

"For example, the immense House of Eternity, with its many shrines, which Ramses the Great had excavated for his faithful servants who each bore the title of 'Royal Son.'"

"That is an exception worthy of Ramses, and those sons were, at least symbolically, linked to the throne. That is not the case with Tausert's child. The matter is therefore resolved."

"I don't think so, Majesty, for I must mention the case of re-

markable individuals to whom your predecessors granted unpar-
alleled honor by welcoming them into the valley. I am thinking
of Queen Hatshepsut's nurse, Amenhotep II's tjaty, Tuthmosis
II's fan bearer, or even the parents of Queen Tiyi, Great Royal
Wife of Amenhotep III. And then there are the tombs granted
to other faithful companions such as dogs, cats, monkeys, and
ibis."

The queen was careful not to show her delight; she contented herself with looking long and hard at Amenmessu. The
Master had made it clear that a pharaoh was free to welcome in
the Valley of the Kings any person on whom he wished to be-
stow high honor. But that person was a child who had been
destined to take Amenessu's place, a child he hated as much as
he hated Tausert.

Amenmessu still had one argument left, and he was sure it
would leave the Master lost for words. He said, "The
Brotherhood of the Place of Truth is busy excavating my own
tomb, and it has neither the time nor the men to undertake the
construction and decoration of another such monument. It is
therefore impossible to grant the lady Tausert's request."

"In fact, Majesty, it is not impossible," Nefer corrected him.
"The tombs of people who are not of royal blood are simple, un-
decorated caverns—sculpture, paintings, and texts are reserved
for pharaohs. If you wish to proceed, I will ask two stonecutters
to excavate a well and then a single chamber where the sarcophagus will be placed."

"But he will have no funerary furniture!"

"I have brought all that is needed," said the queen.

Amenmessu could not bring himself to give in to his prisoner. And he found it intolerable that the Master, instead of
helping him, was supporting her.

Tausert rose to her feet. "In your father's name and in my
own," she declared, with a solemnity that made Amenmessu
shiver, "I thank you for your generosity. Thanks to you, this little
boy, your half-brother, will know eternal happiness."

36

"I am extremely displeased, Nefer," said Amenmessu angrily. "Didn't you understand what I expected of you?"

"Indeed I did, Majesty."

"In that case, why did you tell Tausert what you did?"

"Because you were obviously asking me for the truth, Majesty."

Amenmessu ought to have dismissed this insolent Master, but where would he find another man of comparable quality, courageous enough to hide nothing of what he thought, even when faced with his king?

He asked, "Is your proposal a serious one?"

"Of course, Majesty."

"I want a modest vault, such as you described, with no decorations."

"That is the rule, Majesty, and we shall respect it."

"Where do you intend locating it?"

"Have you a scrap of papyrus?"

Amenmessu handed him one, and on it Nefer drew a map of the Valley of the Kings.

"Here, Majesty, not far from the tomb of Horemheb."

The king frowned. "But that's very close to my own House of Eternity."

"On one hand, that will make our task easier by enabling us to concentrate our efforts in a small area. On the other, you could not have let the vault be built next to Seti's tomb, for you are the child's official protector."

▲

The craftsmen of the starboard crew listened attentively to the Master. Some were seated, some standing with their arms folded.

"Excavate a vault quickly," echoed Karo. "What does that mean?"

"Giving up our rest days until the work is finished," replied Fened.

"Is that a stupid joke?"

Nefer was silent.

"You mean it's true?" asked Karo. "We're already breaking our backs on Amenmessu's tomb, and now we have to find the extra strength to build another one?"

"The Master said it's to be only a simple vault," Casa reminded him.

"Won't doing this for Tausert's child get us into trouble?" asked Ipuy worriedly.

"I persuaded Amenmessu to grant the queen's request," explained Nefer, "but he might change his mind if we delay too long. That's why I need two stonecutters to do the work as quickly as possible."

"Fortunately I'm not involved," commented Ched, "as it isn't customary to decorate this kind of tomb."

"Since the stonecutters can think of nothing but their rest days, I'll do it," said Paneb. "Thanks to my stone pickax, I shan't need any help."

"If there are two of us, we'll work more quickly," said Nakht, "and I'm a proper specialist." He cared more about his duel with Paneb than about having time off and didn't want to miss such a fine opportunity to prove his superiority.

"When the rest of the crew return to the village, we'll sleep at the pass and I'll work with you in the valley," said Nefer.

▲

Serketa was amusing herself by crushing grapes between her fingers and watching the juice drip down onto Mehy's bare chest. He was lying on his back, dozing in the shade of a vine-covered pavilion. He was finding it more and more difficult to sleep at night, and was less and less able to bear the heat. A nap after lunch restored his strength, so long as he was not disturbed by the sun.

"Wouldn't you like to caress me, my tender love?" cooed Serketa.

The sugary juice had stuck the general's chest hairs together, and he awoke in a foul mood. "That's enough, Serketa! I need at least an hour's sleep."

"I know nicer ways of relaxing you," she purred, rubbing herself against him. "And you seem wide awake to me."

Although she did not love her husband, Serketa once again enjoyed his brutal lovemaking; one day, he might even manage to satisfy her.

While she tidied her clothing, Mehy smoothed down his black hair onto his round skull with a pomade containing essence of lilies. Then Serketa called her serving woman and told her to bring them some cool white wine.

When it came, she poured Mehy a cup, and asked him, "Why have you stopped your troops' intensive training?"

"Because Seti isn't going to attack."

"Are you sure?"

"His son's death has grieved him deeply, and he doesn't want to be the aggressor."

"Doesn't he listen to his tjaty?"

"Fortunately not."

"The situation might change."

"I don't think so," said Mehy. "Seti wants to avoid civil war, and Amenmessu is afraid of starting one. Father and son are watching each other like two wild beasts, each waiting for the other to show a sign of weakness. And perhaps the sign will never come."

"We could make it come," suggested Serketa, running her fingertip round the rim of her wine cup.

"Whatever have you dreamed up now?"

"While the craftsmen of the Place of Truth are excavating her son's vault, Queen Tausert is living in Thebes. If some misfortune were to befall her, and Amenmessu were blamed for her death, Seti would have no choice but to attack."

Mehy sat up and seized his wife by the shoulders. "I forbid you to kill her! Tausert has been housed in the palace of Ramses' temple, and that is under my responsibility. If anything happens to Tausert, I'm the one who'll be blamed."

"What a pity. I've honed my poisoning skills to perfection, and I'd so have loved to try them out on a queen."

"Don't despair, my tender gazelle. Go on working with our friend Daktair, but, whatever you do, don't rush things."

"Would it be impossible to have Queen Tausert transferred to the eastern bank?"

"Amenmessu would be suspicious, and what reason could I give him? No, let him go on thinking about what fate he should reserve for the queen—I still hope he'll commit an error of judgment."

"Can't you influence him in the right direction?"

"If I insist too stongly on the need to get rid of Tausert, he'll do just the opposite. He's a strange character, sometimes assertive, sometimes indecisive. I'd never have thought the queen would get what she wanted, but she succeeded in charming her worst enemy."

"You make her sound a formidable woman."

"If no one blocks her path, Tausert will end up taking power."

Like a little girl delighted to have played a good trick on a friend, Serketa jumped up and down and clapped her hands.

"I see it now," she cried. "You hope she'll go back to Pi-Ramses, get rid of her old husband, and declare war on Amenmessu!"

"If she heeds Bay's advice, she'll send her army in the certainty that my soldiers will not fight and that they will capture Amenmessu without meeting any resistance."

Serketa stretched out at her husband's feet. "You're so far-sighted, my insatiable cheetah, and I want to relish the future with you."

▲

While Paneb dug, Nakht tidied up. Then they swapped roles while Nefer gave the walls a rough polish. Working at top speed, Paneb and Nakht had hollowed out a room measuring about six paces by nine—much larger than the vaults normally created for people who were not royal—and hollowed out some alcoves.

"Will Amenmessu be angry?" wondered Nakht.

"He probably won't come to the funeral ceremony and won't know anything about it," Nefer reassured him.

"In any case," said Paneb, "I worked twice as fast as you did, Nakht. Your muscles are getting soft, and if they go on like that you'll have to change your job."

"That's not true!" said Nakht hotly. "I worked just as fast as you. The Master's my witness."

"What matters is the result," said Nefer, dragging the last baskets of earth and limestone fragments out of the vault.

"Let me do that," said Paneb. "It isn't your job."

"We're a team, aren't we? I only hope Queen Tausert will be satisfied."

"Is she still locked up in the palace of Ramses' temple?" asked Nakht.

"According to what Kenhir's heard, she's won the hearts of everyone there, even the soldiers ordered to guard her."

"Tausert is doomed," said Nakht. "After showing mercy to the child, who no longer threatens him, he'll have to make an example of her. And that means war, with all its attendant horrors."

Paneb laid down his pick, sat down beside Nefer, and gazed up at the cliffs that surrounded the Valley of the Kings, cutting it off from the outside world.

"How lucky we are to work here," murmured Nefer, "to feel the tiniest pulses of the rock and to understand its language. We think we transform it, but in fact the rock dictates its law to us. In this Great Meadow, where nothing mortal grows, the gods speak words of stone, words it is our duty to draw, to sculpt, and to paint. And that is our only way of opposing war and mankind's madness."

—— *37* ——

Paneb and Nakht carried the little sarcophagus down into the vault, then the Master added the treasure that Queen Tausert had brought from Pi-Ramses. This consisted of rings, bracelets, and necklaces bearing the names of Seti II and the Great Royal Wife, together with silver sandals and gloves.

Nefer spoke the words of resurrection from the *Book of What Is in the Heart of the Stars,* then the well was blocked with stones and the tomb covered with sand.

"The king will find peace now," said Tausert. "Our son rests far from the tumult that will besmirch the coming years. Thank you for your help, Master. I must confess to you that I used to feel no affection for the Place of Truth and that I demanded the departure of Kenhir, your Scribe of the Tomb, in order to replace him with an official from Pi-Ramses. It was your determination that made that plan fail."

"Kenhir's experience is essential to us, and I shall always fight against injustice."

"Is Seti's tomb really unharmed?"

"Amenmessu has not damaged it in any way, Majesty. Its three passageways, its well room, and its four-pillared chamber are all just as we created them, and I myself sealed the entrance."

"Your work is not yet finished," said Tausert, "and you will reopen that door when the legitimate pharaoh rules once again over Thebes. Be sure that you choose the right side, Master."

"There is only one side for me: the Place of Truth."

"Which is directly dependent upon Pharaoh."

"Indeed, Majesty, but when the Brotherhood are confronted by two pharaohs, what can we do but excavate two Houses of Eternity?"

"I can see that bringing you to heel won't be easy," said Tausert with a smile.

"We have already submitted to the Rule of Ma'at, which rules over our village. As soon as we stray from it, misfortune strikes."

"Are you trying to give me a lesson in politics, Master?"

"No, Majesty, for here, in this valley where eternity reigns, worldly preoccupations have no place."

The queen was beginning to think this man capable of running a country. No event, happy or sad, would ever weaken his resolve or make him deviate from the path the gods had shown him. But, after all, the craftsmen's village was a miniature state, whose work was essential for the survival of Egypt.

"Legend has it," she said, "that the Place of Truth contains fabulous treasures. Have the storytellers exaggerated in their tales?"

"Since Your Majesty is the Great Royal Wife, you will know of the role and duties of the House of Gold. And you know that, without the Stone of Light, the Houses of Resurrection would be nothing but tombs."

"Does Amenmessu also know this?"

"I don't know. He hasn't yet honored the village with his presence."

"Nor has Seti. That's why you don't recognize either of them as Pharaoh, isn't it?"

"I have not that power, Majesty. My role is only to preserve the Brotherhood and make the Place of Truth live so that the work may be accomplished."

"Would you have the audacity to disobey a king?"

"When Amenmessu gave me orders contrary to the practice of Ma'at, I refused to carry them out."

"He could have dismissed you from your offices!"

"Certainly he could, Majesty. But a ruler who flaunts destruction condemns himself to be destroyed."

The queen said drily, "If you speak with Seti, I would advise you not to say things like that."

"Silencing my thoughts so as not to annoy the Lord of the Two Lands would be an unpardonable sin."

Tausert decided she had tested Nefer enough: he was as solid as the rock he worked.

"I should like to walk for a while in the valley," she said.

As she walked, she savored these brief moments of peace and solitude, and hoped she might perceive the radiant energy of this incomparable place, where quarrels over worldly power became incongruous, almost ridiculous. Ambition and vanity had no place here, where one should think only of the supreme trial of death and the transmutation of earthly into eternal life.

The secret of that transmutation resided with the Place of Truth and its Master. Nourished by so much power, they would have the strength to resist the worst torments.

When the setting sun began to turn the stones to gold, the queen realized that her wanderings in this oasis of the after-world had lasted several hours, during which she had forgotten even Amenmessu. Reluctantly tearing herself away from the magic of the Great Meadow, from which her child's soul would fly up to the celestial paradise, she went back toward the Master.

"I lost all sense of time," she said.

"The valley was not made for humans, Majesty, for they carry too much death within them. Each time I enter it, I wonder if it will accept the craftsmen's presence."

"May the gods protect you, Master."

"Have you thought about your own safety, Majesty?"

"Not while I was walking in the valley—but reality has unfortunately not disappeared. I must return to my gilded prison, before being transferred to the east bank, where Amenmessu will have me killed."

"Do you think he is so cruel?" asked Nefer.

"My son has been buried, so the time of generosity is past.

Amenmessu knows that reconciliation between us is impossible. Officially, I shall no doubt die of sickness or be the victim of an accident."

"If you believe he has such a terrible fate in store for you, why did you come to Thebes?"

"Because I love Seti and I wanted to carry out his wish. Not only do I not regret it, but I also thank destiny for allowing me to know the Valley of Eternity."

"Giving up the struggle is not like you, Majesty."

"I am at Amenmessu's mercy and I have no illusions about his intentions."

"There might be a solution," said Nefer thoughtfully.

"To escape? It would be impossible."

"I'm thinking of another possibility."

▲

Amenmessu had to be absolutely sure of the loyalty of the man to whom he had entrusted overall command of the Theban troops and, through them, the future of his throne. He had therefore asked several courtiers to spy on the general, to establish whether his deeds matched his words. The spies' reports all confirmed that Mehy was a general of great worth, highly esteemed by his senior officers, and he had created an army that was both well trained and well equipped. He devoted much time to training his soldiers, was unstinting in his efforts on the parade ground, and managed the west bank with a thoroughness that safeguarded its wealth. None of the spies accused him of any failings, and they were unanimous in saying that he was above suspicion of disloyalty.

Amenmessu now knew he could utterly rely on the general who had invited him to Thebes, never suspecting for a moment that in so doing he was also opening the gates of royalty to him. And, thanks to Mehy's advice, he would succeed in establishing himself as the sole master of Egypt. He called for the map of Middle Egypt and ordered his steward to summon Mehy.

When the general arrived, Amenmessu was studying the map, which showed clearly that Khmun formed an effective barrier; it would have to be removed before his armies could march north. When he saw this, Mehy feared that the young king had decided to attack, thereby ruining his plan.

"The border at Khmun," said Amenmessu, "will it delay us for long, General?"

"We need as much information as possible before attacking such a well-fortified city. To attack in haste would be dangerous."

"You are right. However, there's a more urgent matter: we must decide what to do about Tausert."

"Your magnanimity to her son has proved very popular, Majesty."

"But my magnanimity is not inexhaustible, and Tausert isn't a child—she's our greatest enemy. His son's death seems to have broken Seti, and only this woman can give him back his courage. Well, she's in our hands, and by getting rid of her we'd strike a death blow at my father. In the depths of despair, he'd feel that destiny itself was against him and would eventually abdicate in favor of me. What do you think, General?"

By asking Mehy such a serious question, the king was making him his special adviser; and the general knew he must not disappoint him.

"You're right, of course, Majesty, but may I suggest that you act discreetly."

"What do you mean?"

"If you are to avoid being accused of having her killed, she must not die on Theban soil."

"But if I let her leave for Pi-Ramses, she'll be out of reach."

"Not while she's aboard her ship."

Amenmessu was puzzled.

"We could introduce a trusted man into the crew," explained Mehy. "He would kill the queen and then escape. The official

records would show that the abominable crime had been committed by one of her own sailors."

"Excellent, General! But I don't wish to know any more—in
fact, I've already forgotten what it was you just said."

As Mehy was leaving the king's office, he bumped into the
officer in charge of guarding Tausert.

"What are you doing here?" he asked.

"We have a problem, General, a serious problem."

"Tell me!"

"Queen Tausert has disappeared."

"Are you playing games with me?"

"She escaped from our guards, General, but I'd never have
expected her to do what she's done."

"You had better find her at once, or your career is finished."

"From what one witness said, I think I know where she
has taken refuge: in the craftsmen's village of the Place of
Truth."

38

"This time, sir, it really is the army!" shouted a Nubian guard,
hurtling into Sobek's office.

"How many men?"

"More than a hundred, sir."

Sobek ran to the First Fort, and he saw the troops approaching.

"Every man to his post," he ordered.

At the head of the detachment was General Mehy. He halted
fifty paces or so from the fort, and Sobek went toward him.

"I have come for the lady Tausert," declared Mehy.

"Your request is outside my authority, General."

"I wish to see the Master immediately."

"I shall inform him of your wish."

To Mehy's surprise, it was not Nefer who emerged from the protected area to explain his actions; it was the Wise Woman, dressed in a simple white robe and wearing a short black wig of the type worn in the time of the pyramids.

"Where is your husband?" asked Mehy. "Is he afraid to appear before me?"

"It was I who, as the High Priestess of Hathor in the Place of Truth, granted Queen Tausert's request for sanctuary in the temple of the goddess."

"King Amenmessu has ordered me to take her back to the palace," said the general, less confidently now.

"Are you no longer the village's official protector?"

"Yes, but I'm also a soldier and I must obey the king's orders."

"You know very well that the Place of Truth is forbidden to outsiders, whether they are soldiers or not."

"But Tausert is not a member of your Brotherhood."

"As queen and as head of all the priestesses of Hathor in the entire country, she has a right to belong to it. Who would dare violate the right of sanctuary granted by a temple?"

Mehy knew the Wise Woman was right. If he committed such an atrocity, Amenmessu would disown him. There was only one thing he could do."

"Will you come with me," he asked, "and explain the situation to the king?"

"Of course."

Nefer did not know that his wife had decided to take such a risk, and if he had, he would have strongly opposed it; but Ubekhet knew that Amenmessu would not allow himself to be defied in this way, and that it was essential to negotiate.

She climbed up into Mehy's chariot. He fastened her in by one wrist, using a leather safety strap, and asked her to hold on to the shell. Impressed by her serenity, he set off at an easy pace.

He had always despised women; yet now he had the curious feeling that light was shining forth from his passenger; and its gentleness made him ill at ease. During the journey, he did not speak one word to her, as though they were total strangers and did not even speak the same language. He realized she would never trust him and that he must consider her an implacable enemy.

▲

King Amenmessu avoided looking at the Wise Woman.

"The right of sanctuary granted by a temple is sacred," he said, "and no one is contesting that. But this is an affair of state, and the village has no right to stand against its supreme Master, the Pharaoh of Egypt."

"Neither the Master nor the village is involved, Majesty," said Ubekhet calmly, "and they have no intention of standing against you. Queen Tausert is under sacred protection."

"I should have you arrested for treason!"

"You are the king."

Amenmessu continued to avoid Ubekhet's eyes; she was like no other woman he had ever met, and she seemed not to know the meaning of fear.

"Has Tausert said why she sought refuge with you?"

"The queen is afraid that she will not be allowed to return freely to Pi-Ramses."

"What dark scheme does she suspect me of?"

"I cannot tell, Majesty."

"Tausert deserves to end her days as a recluse in your temple, but I'm sure my father would hold me responsible and declare war in order to free her. You are called 'the Wise Woman.' How would you act in my place?"

"In order to avoid bloodshed, I would allow the queen to return to the capital."

"Clemency, always clemency! I've already allowed her to bury her son in the Valley of the Kings, and now I'm supposed to grant her her freedom, even though all she wants is to destroy me."

"I don't think that's true, Majesty," said Ubekhet.

"Has Tausert taken you into her confidence?"

"Surely her first concern is to avert a civil war, which would ruin Egypt."

Amenmessu pretended to consider this. "Very well. I may be making a mistake, but I agree to allow Tausert her freedom. But she must leave Thebes at once."

"Have I your word that you will not try to harm her in any way?"

"You ask a great deal!"

"There is nothing more solid and more precious than a king's word, Majesty."

"I promise you that Tausert may return to her ship and leave for Pi-Ramses in peace. But she must never return to mock me, or I shall show her no mercy."

▲

Square-Head had been an oarsman in the trading fleet for twenty years. He enjoyed the work, and it was not too badly paid. Moreover, the sturdy fellow liked to see some of the country and meet girls while his boat was being unloaded at the quayside. Discovering this, his wife had succeeded in making his colleagues testify before a court and obtained a food allowance that was bleeding him dry.

He was sitting on the riverbank, eating an onion, when a woman approached him. She wore a heavy wig, whose locks hid her face. At first, Square-Head thought she had been attracted by his virile body. He even tried to stroke her breasts but stopped abruptly when the point of a blade pricked him in the navel.

"No touching, friend! But tell me, do you want to become very rich?"

"Me?"

"You're the one I'm talking to."

Square-Head burst out laughing. "An oarsman's job is to row, not get rich!"

"But what if fortune were to smile on you?"

Square-Head took another bite of his onion. "Go and say that to someone else, my pretty one. If you want to pay me to sleep with you, that's fine. But keep your stories for idiots."

"Your wife's food allowance will be paid, you'll have a house in the country, a wheat field, five milch cows, two donkeys, and a funerary priest to look after your tomb on the west bank."

Convinced that he was dreaming, the oarsman rubbed his eyes. When he opened them again, the woman was still there.

"It's not nice to poke fun at a decent fellow," he grumbled.

"My proposition is a serious one."

"Don't make me laugh! And what do you want in return?"

"The death of a woman who has many crimes on her conscience."

"A murder . . . ? Who is this woman?"

"Queen Tausert," replied Serketa.

"A queen? Is that all? No thanks, I don't fancy risking my neck."

"You won't have to risk it. You will be taken on in the crew of oarsmen who are taking her back to Pi-Ramses. On the fifth night of the voyage, the captain will call you and show you into the queen's cabin. You will kill her and and escape."

"And supposing the captain denounces me?" said Square-Head.

"He's a friend of ours."

"Why doesn't he do it himself?"

"Because he must go on to Pi-Ramses, where he will continue to serve us. He will also explain that an oarsman whose name he does not even know committed the crime and then somehow escaped."

If the prospective victim had been his wife, Square-Head would not have hesitated for a moment. But . . . "I don't know who you are," he said suspiciously.

"And you never will—for your own safety."

"How do I know I'll be paid?"

Serketa placed a gold ingot on the oarsman's knees. "Here's an advance."

Square-Head was struck dumb for a long moment. All marks had been removed from the ingot, which was only the result of a quite cheap alloy, perfected by Daktair.

"You see, friend," said Serketa, "you're already rich. And that's only the beginning, if you do your work properly."

"I'd like a boat, too. A boat that belongs just to me, with a square sail and oarsmen who are always at my beck and call."

"You're expensive! Very well, but nothing more."

"I am not very good with a dagger. Would a leather thong be all right? I'll pull it so tight that she won't even have time to cry out."

"Use whatever method you like best, but don't fail."

"Where shall we meet afterward?"

"Here, and then I'll take you to your house in the Theban countryside."

Square-Head stroked the ingot. He had decided to bury it beneath the earth floor of the riverside cabin where he lived between voyages.

"All right," he said eventually, "I accept."

"Tomorrow morning, go to the queen's ship and the captain will take you on. Above all, remember: the fifth night."

"Understood."

"You're a very lucky man," said Serketa.

—— 39 ——

Queen Tausert was so captivated by the life of the village that she did not feel, even for a moment, as if she had shut herself away to escape Amenmessu's enmity.

Far from the cares and intrigues of the court, she carried out the rites of opening the innermost shrine in the Temple of Hathor and Ma'at, so that the divine presence could emerge from the darkness and light up the Place of Truth. Then, with Turquoise, she went to each house in turn, to place offerings of flowers and food on the ancestors' altars. After that, she and the priestesses played music and danced in honor of Hathor, and seven of them, including the queen, shook sistra to drive away negative forces and drawn down the goddess's generosity upon the Brotherhood.

Everyone was astonished by the queen's simplicity. She was interested in the most mundane aspects of village life, from the deliveries of fresh water to how cereal crops were stored, or how the school was run by the Scribe of the Tomb. Delighted to be able to approach the Queen of Egypt, the children tried harder than ever to show that they could read and write hieroglyphs with ease. Even the abominable Aapehti behaved himself, while Ebony kept a close eye on the green monkey, for fear that he might annoy Her Majesty.

These were wonderful times, which passed too swiftly; but the queen's happiness was shattered when she learned that soldiers had taken the Wise Woman away to Thebes. Immediately, Tausert received Nefer in the vaulted hall of the little palace Ramses had built in the village, where she was staying.

"I'm the one who should confront Amenmessu," lamented the Master, visibly upset. "Ubekhet shouldn't have run such a risk."

"If Amenmessu takes her hostage," said Tausert, "I shall set her free by taking her place. Don't be anxious about your wife. I'm the one he wants to harm, and he'll use every means at his disposal to make me leave the village, because he knows he cannot violate the sacred refuge of the Temple of Hathor and Ma'at."

"I don't know if Ubekhet will manage to escape from this hornet's nest on her own, but I won't abandon you to the vengeance of Amenmessu, Majesty."

"If he threatens the Wise Woman, you must."

"Would the pharaoh behave in such a cowardly manner?"

"He believes I'm his main enemy, and he won't waste such a fine opportunity to silence me."

"But what danger could you be to him if you lived here?"

Tausert gave a sad smile. "I may dream for a few hours, Nefer, but it couldn't last. If I were to remain among you, it would be such an insult to Amenmessu that his fury would be transformed into madness and would threaten the very existence of the village. And for my part, I have a battle to fight, to restore Seti's full authority."

Nefer did not admit to the queen that he considered her hopes unrealistic; to save her life would be a remarkable result in itself.

He said, "The Place of Truth cannot continue to live without the Wise Woman. So I shall go to the palace first thing tomorrow."

"That would be most unwise!" exclaimed Tausert.

"I have no choice, Majesty."

Tausert realized she would never change his mind. If Ubekhet didn't return before nightfall, the queen decided, she would leave the village, so as not to bring misfortune upon it.

▲

"We can't just sit here and wait," stormed Paneb, pacing up and down in Nefer's house. "And it's out of the question for you to go and throw yourself into the jackal's mouth as well!"

"I must bring Ubekhet back," said Nefer.

"Let me get my pickax and tell this tyrant what I think of him!"

"Do you really think that's the best way to free her?"

Paneb wanted to smash down the walls of the house. "It's not for us to interfere in these power struggles. We should get rid of the queen."

"The right of sanctuary is sacred," Nefer reminded him. "Handing Tausert over to her mortal enemy would be an act of unspeakable cowardice."

"We shouldn't have taken her in in the first place."

"I don't regret granting her the protection of the Place of Truth. She now loves the village she once wanted to destroy."

They heard people running along the street outside.

"I'm going to the main gate!" exclaimed Paneb.

People were already shouting. Paneb thought they sounded like shouts of enthusiasm, but he wanted to make sure.

She was there, surrounded by children and priestesses of Hathor. Calm and radiant, Ubekhet looked as if she had just returned from a simple walk outside. Overcome with emotion, Paneb kissed her on both cheeks, taking care not to suffocate her.

Nefer was next. He held his wife in his arms for a long time.

"Amenmessu has given me his word," she said. "He will allow the queen free passage. But he will show no mercy if she returns to Thebes."

▲

In a few hours, Pai the Good Bread had managed to organize a banquet worthy of Queen Tausert. She was deeply sad to leave this place, which was both outside the world and vibrantly alive, a place where she had experienced unforgettable moments.

Gathered together for this impromptu celebration, the villagers invoked Hathor to protect peace and destroy the specter of civil war.

The queen praised the cooking of Pai and Renupe, who had been assisted by several of the women. The roast duck was as delicious as it was at the palace in Pi-Ramses, and the baked vegetable dish would not have been out of place on the royal table.

Toward the end of the feast Tausert had an opportunity to talk quietly with Ubekhet, and asked her, "Did Amenmessu seem sincere?"

"He gave me his word, Majesty. If he did not keep it, I would bear witness, and the liar's reign would be at an end."

The queen knew that a solemn oath, given in the name of Pharaoh, carried a sacred value. "You are a good diplomat," she said, smiling. "I believe Amenmessu feels respect for your person and that he has the intelligence not to yield to blind violence. And yet . . ."

"And yet, you're still worried."

"I must advise you to be extremely cautious, Majesty. I myself shall accompany you to your ship."

"Are you afraid Amenmessu might be abject enough to have lied?"

"No, but you are the main obstacle to the extension of his sovereignty, and I find his goodness somewhat surprising."

"You have obtained the best possible guarantee, Ubekhet, and I must leave the village hoping that it will not suffer reprisals. I don't know what the future holds for me, but I can assure you that Pharaoh Seti and I will always support you."

"The Place of Truth is currently under Amenmessu's control, Majesty."

"You are building his House of Eternity, and he needs you. If I return safe and sound to Pi-Ramses, I shall not be idle. But who would be mad enough to unleash a civil war? May Hathor come to our aid, for without her we shall sink into the darkness."

▲

The dawn rites had been carried out and the ancestors honored, and Tausert gazed sadly out over the craftsmen's village, which she might never see again. Sheltered by its high walls, she had tasted a serenity she had believed impossible and which would melt away the moment she stepped out through the main gate.

The reborn sun was awaking the colors of the desert and turning the fronts of the houses to shining white. How sweet it would be to remain here, with the priestesses of Hathor, and to forget the demands of power! But the Wise Woman was here, and that meant it was time to leave.

"I have only touched the surface of the secrets of the Place of Truth," said the queen, "and I have realized that it's necessary to live and work with you to understand them properly. But will you tell me if the Stone of Light is legend or reality?"

"It is real, Majesty. Without it, the Valley of the Kings would not have seen the light of day and it would not be anchored in eternity."

"In that case, keep the Stone safe, whatever happens."

"You can rely on the Master and myself, Majesty."

Accompanied by the priestesses of Hathor, the two women left the village. Sobek and Paneb were waiting for them, Paneb with his huge pickax on his shoulder.

"It's out of the question to leave the Queen of Egypt and the mother of the Brotherhood defenseless," he decreed. He took the lead, followed by Tausert and Ubekhet, with Sobek bringing up the rear.

When they reached Ramses' Temple of a Million Years, at the border with the outside world, they saw that fifty soldiers had replaced the usual few guards.

"I have the feeling Amenmessu hasn't kept his word," ventured Paneb.

40

The Wise Woman stepped away from the little group to speak to the soldiers. An officer came to meet her.

"Will you not let us pass?" she asked.

"I have had strict orders. Is the lady Tausert with you?"

"We are accompanying her to her ship."

"I shall inform my senior officer. Wait here."

The wait was a short one. A cloud of dust announced the arrival of General Mehy's chariot, and the general jumped down to speak to the Wise Woman.

"I have orders to escort Queen Tausert to the landing stage," he said.

"I shall stay with her until she sails."

"That isn't allowed."

"I insist, General, otherwise the queen will remain in the village."

"King Amenmessu would be furious!"

"Then don't displease him. Just grant my request."

Mehy seemed embarrassed.

"If Queen Tausert and I have nothing to fear, why do you hesitate?"

"Very well. But only you may accompany her."

Ubekhet had to persuade Sobek and Paneb to accept the general's guarantee of the two women's safety.

"If anything happens to you," promised Paneb, "I'll sink my pick into his skull. And I shan't move from here until you return."

Even when the chariot had disappeared into the distance, his anger did not abate.

▲

The journey passed without incident. When they reached the landing stage, Tausert's ship was at the quayside, and the sailors were making ready to cast off the mooring ropes. The queen walked apprehensively toward the gangplank, aware that as she crossed this space a final attack might be unleashed against her.

But nothing happened, and the queen turned back to embrace the Wise Woman.

"My brief stay in the Place of Truth has transformed me into a different person," she said. "My thanks go out to you, Ubekhet."

"May your journey be a happy one, Majesty."

Tausert stepped on board. The anchor was raised immediately, and the oarsmen began steering the boat into a favorable current. If the wind agreed to blow from the south, the sails would be used.

A tall, bearded fellow bowed before Tausert. "I am the captain of this boat, Majesty, and I have taken measures to ensure your comfort. General Mehy has ordered me to serve you to the best of my ability, and I hope to give satisfaction."

"What has happened to the captain who brought me?"

The man cleared his throat awkwardly. "It's a rather delicate matter, Majesty."

"I want the truth."

"He has chosen to remain in Thebes and join Amenmessu's war fleet."

The queen entered her luxuriously appointed cabin. The coolness of the early morning had quickly vanished, but she felt as cold as ice. Amenmessu had kept his word: no one had attacked her on Theban soil, and she had left for Pi-Ramses a free woman.

The murder would take place on the boat and would probably be made to look like an accident. Tausert was defenseless and would have no chance of escape.

Amenmessu was condemning her to terrible anguish as she awaited her execution, which would necessarily take place before they reached Khmun, in Seti's jurisdiction. There was a long way to go before then, six to eight days' sailing if the conditions were favorable and the crew skillful.

When would the assassin strike? That question would haunt the queen from now on.

▲

When Ubekhet returned to the guard post at the Temple of a Million Years, she found it now occupied by only a dozen or so soldiers. The others had followed Mehy, whose chariot was returning at a steady pace.

Ubekhet untied the safety strap, climbed down from the chariot, and crossed into the realm of the Place of Truth.

Paneb was waiting for her, still holding his pickax. "Has the queen left?" he asked.

"Her ship is sailing north."

"I am not entirely happy. A ship can sink!"

"Two Theban warships are escorting it."

"So, you think Tausert is going to escape from Amenmessu?"

"I'd like to think so," said Ubekhet somberly.

"Have you seen . . . a sign?"

"When the boat cast off, a black shadow was hovering above the mast. But perhaps it was just a bad water sprite, a spirit born in the mist that dissolves in the morning light."

▲

Heavily drugged, King Seti was undergoing a sleep cure at the Temple of Hathor. The doctors here treated difficult illnesses by first putting the patient to sleep, particularly when the patient was suffering from depression. Since the palace doctors had not succeeded in relieving the king's sufferings, and he was locked away in a silent world, Tjaty Bay had resorted to this final solution to restore the monarch's health.

Despite his anxiety, the tjaty held meetings with senior ministers each day and worked in close contact with them. The news about the country's finances was reassuring; thanks to a good flood the previous year, the harvests were excellent; and the temples were conscientiously sharing out the riches.

The man Bay was waiting impatiently for entered his office at last. He was an officer in a footsoldiers' regiment, and he had volunteered to travel to the South and gather information about Amenmessu's intentions towards Queen Tausert. Up to that moment, the tjaty had feared that his spy had been arrested; but he was even more afraid of what the man might be about to say.

"Is the queen alive?"

"Yes, Tjaty."

"Where is she?"

"If all has gone well, she is sailing toward Khmun where she will be welcomed by our army."

"Amenmessu freed her?"

"According to a courtier who claims to be well informed, the queen has achieved all she asked for. Her son has been buried in the Valley of the Kings and she escaped from Amenmessu's grasp after seeking sanctuary in the Place of Truth."

"The craftsmen may pay dearly for their courage," commented Bay, "but how can we defend them?"

"Amenmessu has not punished them in any way, and Nefer the

Silent is still leading the Brotherhood, which has been officially instructed to excavate and decorate the king's House of Eternity."

"Amenmessu, a king!" said Bay. "He's nothing but a puppet, drunk on his own vanity! Why did you return to Pi-Ramses before the queen left?"

"I'd been asking a lot of questions, and was beginning to draw attention to myself. General Mehy's soldiers are rather suspicious."

"Do you think any of his troops will desert?"

"The Thebans are proud of their army and they have confidence in it; but it is possible to buy informants."

"Is the atmosphere warlike?"

"To be frank, no. The region is wealthy, its inhabitants seek only happiness and peace, and everyone is hoping that the current conflict will be resolved without any harm coming to the population."

If Bay had obeyed his heart, he would immediately have left the capital and rushed to the queen's rescue; but his absence, in the current circumstances, would have caused such turmoil that he must remain in charge of the government. Instead, he contented himself with going to the Temple of Hathor, to inquire after the king's health.

The senior doctor had good news. "His Majesty's health is improving."

"Is he able to talk with me yet?"

"Not yet, Tjaty. The periods of deep sleep are becoming shorter, but His Majesty remains very tired. Nevertheless, I am quite optimistic, so long as he is spared any overwork before he is completely cured."

"Will you tell him that his son is resting in the Valley of the Kings, as he wished?"

"That news will be an excellent remedy. And is there any news of the queen?"

"I hope that she will soon return, but it is too early to be certain."

As he left the temple, the tjaty was convinced that he would never see Tausert again. If she had succeeded in setting sail, her boat would not reach Khmun. However inexperienced Amenmessu might be, he would act like a statesman and not allow his principal opponent to escape.

—— 41 ——

Square-Head had counted the nights carefully. The journey had been slower than expected, because of weak currents, but at last the fifth night had begun.

In a few hours, he would be rich. Murdering a queen daunted him a little, but he was not going to miss an easy opportunity to achieve a comfortable life, the like of which he had never dared dream. During the voyage, he had talked with his fellow oarsmen, who were resigned to their lot, and he had to bite his tongue so as not to blurt out his bit of good fortune. But Square-Head knew that silence was part of the contract and crucial to his own safety.

The captain moored the ship at sunset, for sailing by night was too dangerous. The oarsmen took advantage of the halt to step onto dry land, light a fire on the riverbank, and grill some fish. They gave scarcely a thought to the queen, whom they hardly ever saw—she emerged from her cabin only once a day and spoke to no one.

This evening, Square-Head did not join his comrades, for the captain had ordered him to stay on board and guard the ship. He had to make do with beer, a hunk of bread, dried fish, and a string of onions, but he had permission to sleep late the following morning.

The following morning . . . Square-Head would already be far away! Sitting down on the bridge, he checked the strength of the leather garrotte with which he would strangle his victim. Her death would be painful, but quick.

The bread was not very good, and neither were the onions. . . . A second-rate meal, but the last of its kind. The oarsman promised himself that in the future he'd eat meals worthy of Theban nobles, meals so big that his belly would bulge. He'd eat only the best meat—and spicy sauces. A cook . . . Yes, he'd employ a wonderfully talented cook.

Night had fallen. The captain left the prow and headed for the oarsman, who stood up slowly.

"Are you ready?" asked the captain.

"Whenever you like."

"What weapon have you chosen?"

"A strong leather strap."

"You're sure you can do it?"

"Trust me, Captain."

"And you're sure you won't hesitate?"

"Absolutely."

The captain handed Square-Head an ax.

The oarsman shook his head and said, "I prefer my garrotte."

"You'll need it to smash the bolt, which the queen will probably have drawn. Hit hard and go straight into the cabin. She'll have no chance of escape."

"Can I do it now?"

The captain scanned the riverbank. Most of the sailors were asleep, and no one was taking any interest in what was happening on the boat.

"Yes, now."

▲

Queen Tausert awoke suddenly from a light sleep. She had left three oil lamps burning, and by their light she could see that someone was forcing the cabin door.

Calling for help would be no use, and she had no weapon with which to defend herself. How many would there be? Three? Four? Perhaps more? The fifth night . . . Amenmessu had waited until the ship had nearly reached Khmun so that, right up to the last moment, Tausert would think there was a small chance of escape.

The queen did not cry out. She rose from her bed and went to stand in front of the door, just as its wooden bolt was broken by an ax.

A man entered. He was stocky, unshaven, and had a square head.

"Who are you?" asked the queen coolly.

The oarsman had expected to surprise a sleeping woman, and was disconcerted to find himself face-to-face with a queen whose dignity made him weak at the knees.

"Don't resist—otherwise, it'll take longer."

"Answer my question: who are you?"

"The man ordered to kill you, Majesty. Don't make it more difficult." He raised his garrotte.

Tausert stood her ground. "At least tell me who's paying you."

"That doesn't matter. Now, turn your back to me. That way it won't hurt so much."

"Get out of my cabin."

Squre-Head moved closer. "Sorry, Majesty."

He raised the leather strap and leapt toward the queen. At that instant, the captain rushed into the cabin and plunged a dagger into his back. His eyes bulging, his open mouth emitting a cry of pain that tailed off into a death rattle, Square-Head reached out toward Tausert, as though he was still trying to fulfill his contract. The captain stabbed him again, and Square-Head collapsed onto the floor.

"I saw the door open, Majesty," explained the captain, "and I was worried. General Mehy asked me to be especially watchful, because he was afraid you might still be in danger."

A final spasm shook Square-Head's body and he died, still clutching his garrotte.

"Who was this wretch? asked Tausert.

"One of the oarsmen we took on at Thebes, Majesty."

Tausert turned away from the corpse. "Remove him, Captain."

"I shall stand guard outside your door until we reach Khmun, Majesty. You may sleep safely."

▲

"Come quickly, Tjaty," exclaimed Bay's assistant.

"What's so urgent?"

"The queen's ship has just entered the great canal."

Bay abandoned the army statistics he had been working on and ran to a window that looked out over the landing stage. Its sails furled, the ship was gliding over the water, to the gentle rhythm of the oars.

At the risk of breaking his neck, Bay rushed down the enormous staircase and pushed his way past the dignitaries who were beginning to assemble on the quay, alerted by the rumor that was already spreading like wildfire through the capital: Tausert had escaped from the rebel Amenmessu!

Bay still feared the worst. It might be the queen's ship, but was it carrying a living queen or a corpse? Infuriated by the time it was taking to maneuver the ship alongside, Bay hopped from one foot to the other.

And then there she was, at the prow of the ship, wearing the Red Crown, which was decorated with a spiral, symbolizing the permanent regeneration of life and its formation among the stars.

On the quay, people stopped rushing about and silence fell.

As soon as the ship had moored up, the sailors knelt to worship the water and the wind, which had allowed them to reach port safely. The queen burned incense on an altar beside the mast and sang a hymn to Hathor, goddess of the stars and protector of navigators. Then she walked across the gangplank, and Bay was the first to bow before her.

"Majesty . . . ," he managed.

"You feared you would never see me alive again, Bay, and your fears were well grounded. Just before we arrived in Khmun, an oarsman tried to murder me, but the captain, one of Mehy's soldiers, saved me."

Bay was not only overjoyed to see Tausert safe and sound, but also deeply satisfied that Mehy's loyalty had been proven. Mehy was already proving a vital ally to the rightful pharaoh. The plan devised by Bay and the general would perhaps not remain untried.

The queen asked, "How is Seti? Is there any improvement in his condition?"

"The news that his son is resting in the Valley of the Kings brought the king out of his trance, Majesty. His sleep cure is finished, and he has just returned to the palace. Your return will mark his complete recovery, I am sure."

"I learned a great deal during my time in Thebes."

"Did you meet Amenmessu, Majesty?"

"I did indeed. He has not the bearing of a pharaoh, but we mustn't underestimate his ambition."

"He doesn't yet realize that there's nothing he can do."

"I hope that's true, Bay, but he controls the west bank of Thebes and also the Place of Truth. If he succeeds in laying hold of the village's hidden treasures, our defeat will be inevitable."

—— 42 ——

Nefer was astonished to discover the strong room locked. Kenhir should have been handing out new copper chisels ready for the starboard crew's departure for the Valley of Kings, where they were to continue work on Amenmessu's tomb.

He went to Kenhir's house, where he was greeted by Niut, armed with a new broom.

"Is Kenhir ill?" he asked.

"No, he's expecting you. Wash your feet before you come in."

The house smelled clean and had never been so spruce. Kenhir was seated on the ground, writing the day's page for the Journal of the Tomb.

"Surely you haven't forgotten that we're leaving for the valley today?" said Nefer.

"There's been a change of plan."

"Am I no longer Master, then?"

"You most certainly are! And don't hope that your duties will be lightened, particularly in view of what's happening in the village."

Anxiety followed surprise. "Could you be a bit more explicit?"

"Don't worry. The Wise Woman knows all abut it."

Kenhir rolled up the papyrus, stood up with difficulty, and seized his walking stick. "We haven't far to go, but it's a bit of a climb."

As they went out, Niut called to her husband, "Don't come back too late. My roast beef must be eaten as soon as it is ready."

Kenhir took the path leading to the western burial ground, where Nefer's own House of Eternity was being built, high above the whole site. The craftsmen had built a long ramp ending in a forecourt from which a doorway led to an open-air courtyard. There all the members of the starboard crew had gathered, with the exception of Paneb. They stepped aside to reveal, standing on either side of the entrance to the shrine, two statues depicting Nefer as eternally young.

"They are the sculptors' and stonecutters' offering to your *ka*," explained Kenhir.

Nefer was very moved. "But . . . they never told me anything about it."

"Your decisions have sometimes surprised them, and they're delighted to give you a surprise for a change."

Userhat the Lion stepped forward. "We have completed our Master's House of Eternity," he said in a low voice tinged with emotion. "It is the largest and most beautiful tomb in our sacred meadow. The well is wide, the chamber of resurrection is vaulted and hollowed out of the rock. When the day of his final voyage comes, we shall install the stele, the statues, and the offertory tables we have prepared in our workshops. Nefer the Silent, you shall look down forever upon your village and nourish it with your power."

Nefer was overwhelmed. "You've treated me like a king!"

"You are the pilot of our ship, the one who enables the Brotherhood to sail upon the ocean of strength-giving energy," said Ched. "As such, you deserve this dwelling; but what would it be without the painter's work?"

Paneb stepped onto the threshold of the shrine in which, after Nefer's death, the craftsmen would celebrate banquets in his honor.

"Master," he said, "may I have your permission to show you what I believe is my masterwork?"

Nefer had never before seen Paneb so unsure of himself.

"Very well."

Paneb went into the shrine and lit the lamps. The Master followed him and was the first to see the pictures of Ramses the Great and Nefer, standing before the ship of Amon. Others depicted the trinity of Thebes comprising Amon the Father, Mut the Mother, and Khonsu the Son, and a procession of priests bearing royal statues. Then there were scenes depicting Nefer and Ubekhet making offerings, ritualists worshipping the divine powers of the First Cataract of the Nile, a banqueting scene, and Ubekhet worshipping the Divine Light.

The Master lingered over each detail, then summoned the other members of the crew.

Ched was almost speechless. "What has he done here, the little . . . ?" He soon recovered his natural meticulousness and began to search for crooked lines or errors in composition; but he searched in vain.

The craftsmen stood in silent, awed admiration, dazzled by the bright, unchanging shapes and by the colors, which were protected by a special varnish. Then they followed Paneb and Nefer into the second shrine. Here, Paneb had painted his adoptive parents sitting down, their voyage to Abydos to live the immortal life of Osiris, and the moment of grace where they drank the water of eternity from a pool hollowed out at the foot of a palm tree. In one of the paintings Kenhir was shown, making him part of Nefer's afterlife.

"Paneb has forgotten nothing," said Gau, who knew by heart every one of the necessary symbolic scenes.

"He has conjured up the Brotherhood of yesterday, today, and tomorrow," said Didia, gazing at a painting showing the brothers accompanying Nefer's sarcophagus to his tomb. "We're all with Nefer, and we'll continue to work with him in the afterlife."

In the alcove at the far end of the shrine, Paneb had painted Horus the celestial, Hathor the lady of gold, Anubis the guide in the world beyond, Osiris the conqueror of death, and Min the fertility giver. Perhaps the most remarkable scene showed Isis and Nephthys giving magic energy to a scarab, the symbol of resurrection, placed above a "stability" pillar, the incarnation of the reborn, living Osiris. On the ceiling, the sky goddess was beating her wings to bring the pictures to life.

Nefer gazed at the painting in silence for a long time. At last, he asked, "Have you also finished the sarcophagus chamber?"

"I applied the varnish last night," said Paneb.

The two men went down into the chamber. Paneb had depicted his adoptive parents in a boat where they were worshipping the solar disk, together with the baboons who made it rise up each morning with their shouts of joy. They were also accompanied by a falcon, a cat who stabbed the serpent of darkness, and even Amon's sacred goose, whose first cry had accompanied the birth of the world.

The sacred texts would enable the Master to pass through the afterlife's gates, whose guards were armed with knives, and receive the energy radiating from the hands of the goddesses of the West and the East; finally, Ubekhet and Nefer were shown drinking the heavenly water given to them by the sky goddess.

Again the Master contemplated the images for a long time; then he put out the lamps and went back to the first shrine.

"How did Paneb manage to do this all on his own?" wondered Pai.

"It's unbelievable," agreed Casa.

"A masterwork is a masterwork," said Nakht solemnly, "and it must exceed what is possible."

"Let that be an example to you," advised Unesh.

"Each man has his own talents," objected Fened. "This doesn't mean Paneb can discover the good vein in a bed of stone, or know where a tomb entrance should be dug in the cliff."

An unexpected visitor arrived in the forecourt.

"Look!" cried Karo, and he pointed at an enormous scarab beetle, shimmering gold in the sunshine.

The beetle crawled toward the shrines and the craftsmen watched its progress. The presence of the insect, which was the incarnation of Khepri, god of the rising sun and of metamorphoses, was the very best of omens.

But it did not make Paneb feel any less tense as he awaited Nefer's judgment.

The Master's face remained inscrutable. He asked, "Are you pleased with yourself, Paneb?"

"I haven't asked myself that question and I don't have to answer it."

"Do you think you've made any mistakes?"

"As regards technique, I tried to be beyond reproach; as for the choice of themes, I tried to draw a path of symbols, governed by the love of the work."

The craftsmen had moved away; the Master and the painter were left facing each other.

"Upon what did you base your work?" asked Nefer.

"Upon my painting and my desire to create."

"That isn't enough."

Paneb clenched his fists. "So I've failed."

"I have no criticism of your work. It lacks nothing but the quintessence."

"But I searched the very depths of my being!"

"That wasn't far enough."

"Must I wipe it all out?" asked Paneb miserably.

"Certainly not," said Nefer.

"But this tomb will be abandoned, won't it?"

"I must consult the Wise Woman. Stay here until sunset."

—— 43 ——

The craftsmen of the starboard crew realized that Paneb's masterwork had not been recognized as such, and they had waited for him in the main courtyard to try and console him.

"Don't make a fuss," advised Renupe. "No one's questioning your talent."

"I give up," said Karo. "Why set yourself goals you know you can't achieve?"

Seeing that Paneb was annoyed by what they'd said, the two men went and sat down, leaving their colleagues admiring the paintings.

"Don't be bitter," whispered Ched.

"Why not? I put all my energy into this work and I was sure I'd succeeded."

"You'll find another way."

"I don't think so," said Paneb.

"It's not like you to give up—surely you won't let one moment's discouragement put out Paneb the Ardent's fire? Forget your resentment and go on working. Your pride's hurt, and this won't be the last time; but you must build on this ordeal and go further. Don't forget, a disappointed person is often disappointing."

Paneb would have rather been beaten by a crazy prizefighter than criticized by Ched; but perhaps Ched was living up to his nickname of Savior, by pointing out Paneb's weaknesses and trampling on his feelings?

"I'm getting old, and I'm no longer strong enough to paint a whole tomb," lamented Ched, "which is why I chose the least untalented of my artists to succeed me. If you step back into the ranks, and make do with your gifts as they are, I'll have to train someone else. Spare me that labor, Paneb. I detest teaching."

"Show me what I've done wrong."

"Who said you've done anything wrong? I wouldn't have let someone incompetent decorate a Master's tomb. I don't care for your intense colors, but they are in such harmony that I bow before the flame that dwells within them."

"But that's not enough to create a masterwork."

"We'd better wait until the end of the day, when we'll find out more."

▲

The warm rays of the setting sun cast a golden light on the court-yard and shrines of Nefer's tomb. Softer than usual, the light was so peaceful that the craftsmen fell silent to savor this moment of grace.

Paneb was the first to see Nefer, Hay, Ubekeht, and Kenhir climbing the ramp. Ubekhet was in the lead, and the Master was carrying an object covered with a cloth which, although thick, did not prevent a light shining through.

"The Stone!" thought the traitor, suddenly jolted out of his thoughts. "But why have they brought it here? And I didn't see where they got it from! When they leave, I must follow them."

Kenhir and Hay's crew stood like statues on the threshold that separated the forecourt from the courtyard while the Wise Woman and the Master entered the first shrine.

"Come, Paneb," said Nefer.

The trio walked in farther, and the Master laid the Stone in the last alcove.

"Did Ched point out any serious faults?" he asked.

"He didn't find any," answered Paneb.

"Yet your masterwork isn't finished," said the Wise Woman,

"because no man can discover the quintessence alone. You drew from within yourself the energy you needed to complete your task, but only the Stone will transform it into a true work, imbued with Light. Your own quintessence will join with that of the Place of Truth, which brings its buildings to life. It is in this communion between the individual and the Brotherhood that the masterwork is born."

Nefer removed the cloth, and the light from the Stone gave life to each painted figure, each color, each hieroglyph.

"Your masterwork is accepted," said Nefer. "Do you wish to proceed further along the path?"

"It is my most passionate desire."

▲

The man was young and strong, but he had surrendered without resistance to a Theban patrol. They took him immediately to headquarters, where Mehy was organizing maneuvers for the different divisions of his army.

Mehy was in his tent, giving out orders to his officers. At last the messenger had arrived from Bay, at last the civil war was beginning—the war that would open up his route to power.

Mehy saw at once that the man was a soldier. "What's your name?" he asked.

"Mecha, captain of archers in the army of Set."

"Give me the message."

"I don't understand."

"Don't worry, you are indeed in the presence of General Mehy. So, the message?"

"I haven't any message, General."

"In that case, what are you doing here?"

"I've left an army that refuses to fight and I want to join Pharaoh Amenmessu and serve in the Theban forces. I should add that I'm probably the first officer to leave Pi-Ramses, but certainly not the last."

"The army of Set? That's Seti's best army, isn't it?"

"Not for much longer, General. It no longer deserves that

name—any more than does Pharaoh Seti, who betrays the god who protects him. Set will soon turn against him, and that's why I want to belong to the winning side."

"Seti's forces are much bigger than Amenmessu's, even without the garrisons from the northeastern frontier. Aren't you afraid you may have made a mistake?"

"Sir, a soldier knows that victory depends not on numbers but on the quality of the leaders. Seti's no leader. Pharaoh Amenmessu and yourself will crush the enemy."

"Who's in charge of the government in Pi-Ramses now?"

"Seti has undergone a long sleep cure and he's resting in his palace, unable to make any decisions. Bay deals with day-to-day matters, but he's just an official, of no great stature. But there's always Queen Tausert, whose return seemed almost like a miracle. With respect, General, you should have killed her."

"King Amenmessu preferred to show mercy. Surely that's a mark of his greatness?"

"Yes, sir, but the queen is dangerous."

"Does she have the ear of the high command?"

"Not yet, sir. Some of the generals hope Seti will recover, because they don't want to have to take orders from a woman, but that's wishful thinking. The king is a broken man, and the capital is sinking deeper and deeper into inertia."

"You're forgetting the Khmun blockade, which will prevent our troops from heading north."

"General, a massive attack, from the Nile and the desert simultaneously, would smash the blockade, which isn't nearly as effective as it looks. I'm sure a lot of soldiers will change sides and join you. Why die for a man like Seti, who behaves like a frightened rabbit? Even my superiors are beginning to utter thinly veiled criticisms. If the queen hadn't come back, several generals would have recognized the sovereignty of Amenmessu. It's all well and good for Tausert to show how able she is, but that isn't enough to make up for the shortcomings of a pharaoh who can't exercise command."

Another path was opening up before Mehy: the rapid disintegration of Pi-Ramses and the disappearance of Seti. But that meant putting too much trust in the future and forgetting that a strong man, from the northern army, might impose military rule and reconquer the South.

The plan that Bay had accepted must be carried out, and no other. As for this man Mecha, was he a spy, whose mission was to enlist in the Theban army and act as an informant for Tausert?

"Would you like to see how I train my elite troops?"

"That would be a great honor, General."

Mehy led his guest to his chariot. Since Mecha was unarmed and had tied himself to the shell so as not to fall out, the general had no fear that he'd attack.

When he galloped between two rows of infantrymen who were practicing hand-to-hand combat, many thought that the general had chosen a new assistant. The charioteers working on their horses' endurance thought the same, though they were surprised not to recognize the lucky man.

"Your chariots are impressively fast, sir," said Mecha.

"My specialists have found a new way of building wheels, which are much lighter and stronger than the ones Seti has."

"That gives you an enormous advantage."

"Our short swords, spears, and shields are also of better quality, not to mention our bows and arrows—the northern armies have nothing like them."

"Then I was right, sir. Victory will indeed be yours."

"There are, however, still a few problems to resolve, such as the one I'm about to put to you."

Mehy drew up close to the archers' training ground and called the instructor over.

"Mecha, look carefully at this man," he said. "He's a vile traitor."

The instructor froze in terror.

"He comes from the North, too," continued Mehy. "I discovered that he's the nephew of a senior officer in the army of Ptah, and that he was sent here as a spy. He was to inform the enemy how many archers we have and what strategy they'll adopt in battle. Take my sword and kill him."

Mecha gazed in horror at the weapon the general held out to him. The instructor dared not speak or move.

"General . . . ," stammered Mecha.

"What are you waiting for? If you meant what you said, you should be glad to kill a traitor."

"I'm a soldier, not an assassin!"

"You refuse to execute your accomplice. That's it, isn't it?"

"Arrest him and put him on trial," said Mecha desperately.

"We don't try spies," declared Mehy, slashing Mecha's throat with his dagger.

Under the general's cold gaze, the unfortunate man died in a pool of blood.

The instructor was shaking from head to foot. "General, you know I'm not a traitor!"

"Of course I do."

"But then . . ."

"I set a trap for a snake that was preparing to bite me."

"He . . . he might have killed me."

"Those are the risks of your trade," said Mehy. "Get rid of this corpse and get back to work."

—— 44 ——

Like his fellow craftsmen, the traitor saw the Stone of Light bring Paneb's paintings to life. Then the Master covered it with its thick cloth again, ready to take it back to its hiding place.

The rest of the starboard crew were gathered round Ardent, so the traitor had a chance to follow Nefer and the Wise Woman—or, at least, to set off in the same direction.

But two unexpected guards appeared at the top of the ramp and prevented him from going any farther: Bad Girl and Ebony. The dog bared its teeth and the goose snapped its beak at him. So the traitor had to turn back and rejoin the crew.

As soon as they saw the Stone, everyone had realized that Paneb had succeeded in creating his masterwork and that a new door would be opened to him. Pai was already dreaming up a small banquet, with a more lavish one to follow when Paneb was promoted to a higher rank.

The last to offer his congratulations was Ched the Savior.

"You knew what the Master had decided, didn't you?" asked Paneb.

"All I did was give him my opinion as a painter; the rest was for him to judge. At least I won't have wasted my time with you. But don't imagine for a moment that you've reached the end of your path—in fact, I'm sure the most difficult part begins here and and now."

▲

Work on Amenmessu's tomb was continuing steadily, and the sculptors had begun to create statues of the pharaoh. On a large block of stone, Userhat had traced the outline of the planned work in red ink. Ipuy was in charge of rough-shaping the rock by chipping away at it, after which Renupe would undertake the first polishing with an abrasive, quartz-based paste. Userhat would then remove any excess stone with a copper-bladed saw before separating the statue from the rock.

"Have you checked the copper tube?" he asked Ipuy.

"It turns wonderfully well between my fingers and I'll remove the stone between the statue's legs exactly as you wish me to."

"And the flint drill, Renupe?"

"I shall drill perfect nostrils and shape the best lips you've ever seen. At last Amenmessu's having some good luck. His is going to be one of the most beautiful portraits of the whole dynasty."

It was no idle boast. The Master watched as a face as noble

as that of Tuthmosis III or Amenhotep III appeared; and he felt bounless admiration for his three brothers, whose hands had the same genius as their ancestors'.

Didia and Thuty had already produced a good many of the funerary objects that would be placed in the tomb. The mummy's gold jewelery was of marvelous quality, as were the wooden statuettes representing benevolent spirits, like the frog of metamorphoses.

Paneb had hoped that the Master would soon announce the date of his initiation into his new rank; but Nefer didn't mention it, speaking to him only about decorating Amenmessu's tomb. Paneb managed to contain his impatience and concentrated on his paintings.

▲

Ubekhet and Nefer were enjoying an unheard-of luxury, a morning's rest after the dawn ritual. The Master was not going to visit the workshops, and the Wise Woman was not going to see any patients. They had stretched out on mats, on the terrace of their house, and were gazing up at the sky as they shared happy memories.

But this stolen happiness was much briefer than they had hoped: from the street below came Kenhir's voice, demanding to see Nefer as soon as possible. Ubekhet did not try to stop her husband going down. Duty had won again, and no one, not even she, could oppose it.

When Nefer opened the door, he saw that Kenhir was shaking with anger.

"A requisition," spat the old scribe. "Our head sculptor is to go immediately to the palace, and the document bears Amenmessu's royal seal! Nothing like this has ever happened before in the entire history of the Place of Truth!"

The Master saw that Kenhir had put on his finest clothes, obviously with a view to a royal audience. He must do likewise.

▲

Nefer and Kenhir both thought King Amenmessu looked much older. His youth was vanishing surprisingly quickly, as if defeated by the heavy cares that weighed on him.

"I don't understand why you're protesting," he told them. "After all, I'm the supreme Master of the Place of Truth, and you must obey me without question."

"The law is quite clear, Majesty," said Kenhir, not hiding his anger. "No craftsman belonging to the Place of Truth can be conscripted, for any reason whatsoever."

"Are you daring to tell me that my orders are against the law?"

"They are indeed, Majesty. And no one, in this country, can place himself above Ma'at."

"Don't bother me with fine phrases."

"What do you want our sculptor to do?" asked the Master.

"Several of my senior officials want to have their statues made, to be placed in the temple at Karnak so that their *ka*s may live with the gods. I have decided to grant them this favor, and I need an exceptional sculptor so that no time is lost. As the best belongs to the Brotherhood, I am calling upon him."

"That's utterly impossible," interrupted Kenhir, "because the Master is authorized to assign work to members of the Brotherhood. However, sculptures can be made for the outside world—so long as their creation doesn't interfere with our current work."

"And you're going to tell me," said Amenmessu, "that your current work is my own House of Eternity."

"Exactly, Majesty."

"That is unacceptable! I'm in a hurry and I require your head sculptor."

"I repeat, it's impossible."

"If you go on defying me, Kenhir, I shall transfer you to a village in the farthest corner of the country."

"That is your right, Majesty."

Amenmessu turned to the Master. "Are you going to be more reasonable than this cantankerous old scribe?"

"I'm afraid not, Majesty."

"Be careful, Nefer! What I want, I get. It is the king of Egypt who is talking to you, and you must heed what he says."

"A pharaoh who abuses his power is unworthy of his office," said Nefer quietly. "It's the voice of Ma'at that we must heed, at every moment and in all circumstances. And it's precisely because we cannot do so that we must continually build her temple within us, and fight against our natural tendency to injustice and greed."

"So you, too, want to teach your sovereign a lesson in morality! Will you obey my order—yes or no?"

"No, Majesty."

"Are you aware of the fate reserved for those who rebel against Pharaoh?"

"We have painted such rebels on the walls of tombs in the Valley of Kings: they have their heads cut off, are turned upside down, or burn in cauldrons."

Amenmessu was impressed by the Master's calm. He said, "What alternative is there, Nefer?"

"We aren't rebels, Majesty, and if we yield to injustice the Place of Truth will never recover."

"Ruling involves making choices."

"Don't indulge your courtiers' whims to the detriment of our Brotherhood, Majesty. You'd win a small victory today, but suffer a heavy defeat tomorrow. People who flatter you will betray you; it's in their nature, just as it's in a wild beast's nature to devour its prey."

"No matter what I threaten you with, you aren't afraid, are you?"

"No member of the Brotherhood will be made to work by force."

"Are you aware what you're asking, Nefer? I have made my decision, and you're asking me to go back on it."

"It is you who reign, Majesty, not your courtiers."

"It seems there's no limit to the Place of Truth's independence!"

"It was born to serve the souls of the pharaohs, to tame matter and to overcome time. By weakening it, you would weaken yourself."

Amenmessu walked away from his visitors, deep in thought. Then he came back to them and said in a clear voice, "Go back to the village and complete my House of Eternity."

The Scribe of the Tomb and the Master bowed and turned toward the door of the audience chamber.

"One moment, Nefer. I'd like to speak with you alone."

Kenhir bowed again, and went out.

The king looked the Master straight in the eyes. "I need a first minister of your stamp, Nefer. I know it would be no use ordering you to take the post, so I am asking you: will you take it?"

"No, Majesty."

"Is that your final answer?"

"It is."

"Is the Place of Truth so important?"

"Yes, Majesty."

45

A little girl had been badly scalded on the legs, two boys had cut each other while fighting with sticks, Karo had a stomachache, and Gau's wife was suffering from severe fatigue. To complete the morning's series of accidents, Aapehti had broken his forearm trying to prove that he could break a block of limestone with a single blow.

It was the first time the Wise Woman had had to confront so many serious cases in such a short time, and she had had to use up almost all her reserves of honey. It was used to seal and heal wounds, it reduced internal and external inflammation without side effects, and it restored vitality. Kept in carefully sealed and labeled pots, the honey was a vital and very valuable remedy, and so it was used only sparingly in baking. Through centuries of experimentation, Egyptian doctors had also found it was sometimes useful in treating eye problems, and even in problems relating to childbirth.

When she had seen all her patients, the Wise Woman went to see Imuni, who was responsible for maintaining stocks of all the products that the Place of Truth used. He was busy in his office, copying out a list of copper chisels, but as soon as he saw her he jumped up and stood very stiffly, like a soldier on parade.

Imuni had always been nervous of the Wise Woman, fearing that she could read his thoughts and detect his ambitions, legitimate though they were, to take old Kenhir's place and get revenge, one way or another, on Paneb, who was forever making fun of him.

"I need more honey urgently," said Ubekhet.

"How many pots would you like?"

"One today, and several next week—assuming that the current rush of injuries calms down!"

"I'll see to it straight away."

He hurried off, but when he returned he was empty-handed. "I'm afraid there's been a mistake in our record keeping. We have plenty of ointments, but not a single pot of honey."

"It's a very serious mistake, Imuni. I've barely enough to treat emergencies for one week."

"I am sorry, really sorry. We'd better tell Kenhir—he'll know the answer."

Kenhir's anger would go down in the village's history. He had accused his assistant of every failing under the sun, and a few more besides, and told him that if he ever made a mistake again the village court would banish him.

"Of course, you'll have no wages and no days off this month!" thundered the Scribe of the Tomb. "You seem to have forgotten that you're a state official, who moreover serves the Place of Truth, and that you must be even more alert than Bad Girl."

Imuni hung his head and didn't even try to make an excuse. He thought himself fortunate to have survived such a storm.

"And now, in order to sort everything out, I shall have to go myself to the central government, even though I've got a bad back! We shall speak of this again, Imuni. In the meantime, check the stocks and make good your other mistakes."

The assistant scribe left, thoroughly downcast.

"You weren't exactly kind to him," commented Niut, who had paused in her housework so as to observe the scene.

"A village doesn't run on kindness! Give me my walking stick and a warm cloak."

▲

Escorted by two of Sobek's men, who acted as bodyguards, Kenhir went to Mehy's office.

"The general is directing military exercises on the east bank," said his assistant.

"When will I be able to see him?" asked Kenhir.

"Not for a fortnight at the earliest."

"Much too late! Who is in charge here while the general is away?"

"Perhaps I can help you?"

"It is a serious matter: the Place of Truth is running short of honey. We need a delivery urgently."

"You've come at a bad time," answered the assistant with regret. "All available stocks have been sent to the palace, the main hospital, and the barracks. I have left only a very small amount, which we need for treating our own sick and injured."

Such arrangements suggested that war was imminent. Many soldiers would be wounded, and the army doctors would use honey to dress the wounds.

"The village takes priority," the Scribe of the Tomb pointed out.

"Please put your request in writing, and I'll have it sent by special messenger to the palace. But you must be patient. At the moment, all government departments are overwhelmed with work."

▲

"I've done what I can," Kenhir told the Wise Woman and the Master, "but the preparations for war are taking precedence over everything else. Only Mehy can solve the problem, and he can't be contacted at the moment. I shall write a detailed report, complaining about this unacceptable state of affairs."

"I must have honey," said Ubekhet. "Without it I shan't be able to treat my patients."

"There is one possible solution, though it would be risky. We could go and get some from old Boti, in the desert."

"Why would it be risky?"

"Because there are bands of marauders out there, not to mention the guards who patrol the area. What's more, Boti is a strange fellow. He's obliged to sell all his harvest to the state, but he sometimes keeps some for himself. We can't send a large group, because it would be spotted almost at once."

"Then I shall go alone," decided Ubekhet.

"You are not even to think of doing so," declared Nefer.

"I must check the quality of the honey for myself, and persuade the beekeeper to sell me some."

"Then I'll go with you."

"I cannot permit that," said Kenhir. "In the present circumstances, the Master's presence in the village is vital. If the Wise Woman insists on going, let's ask Paneb to go with her. We can trust him completely, and he'll conscientiously carry out all the duties of an adopted son."

"We must arm him with some of the weapons Obed has made."

Kenhir looked dubious. "An armed craftsman? If the guards stopped him, Paneb would run a terrible risk."

"He must be able to protect Ubekhet," insisted Nefer.

"The weapons we've had made remain within the village walls," decreed Kenhir.

▲

The archers were becoming more and more skillful and the chariots were remarkably maneuverable. The intensive training was beginning to bear fruit, and the soldiers would soon be able to defeat any opponent.

When he entered his tent after a trying day, Mehy looked at the letters sent to him through the military messenger service. Among them was a report from his assistant in Thebes, regarding the Scribe of the Tomb's unexpected request.

The general at once told one of his junior officers, "Bring me a fast, well-rested horse. I'm going to the city, and I'll be back tomorrow morning."

▲

Mehy galloped into the center of Thebes, where Serketa lived whenever major military exercises were held. She made the most of the opportunity to receive the great ladies of the city of Amon, and to wax lyrical about her husband, whose courage and skill were vital to both province and country. Little by little, her campaign had reinforced his high reputation. Many people were doubtful about King Amenmessu's future, and Mehy seemed the man of the hour, who would protect Thebes from adversity, no matter what.

When he entered his house, the mayor's wife and her best friends were congratulating Serketa on her hospitality. They had all so much enjoyed the exquisite pastries, and they all looked forward to seeing her again. The ladies were delighted to see the general, who, with his usual force of conviction, promised them that their safety was guaranteed.

The pleasantries over, Mehy led his wife into their private apartments.

"It seems," he said, "that the Place of Truth is running out of honey."

"Is that important?"

"It means the Wise Woman will have difficulty caring for the sick. I've blocked their deliveries of honey, and the Scribe of the Tomb has submitted a request for more. The government will have to grant his request—but not for a long time. That means the craftsmen will have to try to obtain some by other means. Whoever the Master entrusts with this task will have to leave the village, and they might stray into danger . . ."

"Who but the Wise Woman can check the honey to see if it can be used for healing? She'll have to be part of anything they do, and I have an inkling of a delightful plan, my darling. Raiders might ambush her and kill her, and without her the Brotherhood would be considerably weakened and would lose most of its magical protection. While she's inside the village walls we can't reach her, but on the trail of honey . . . the opportunity is more than tempting."

The general kissed her roughly. "Your farsightedness delights me, my tender quail; but I can't use my soldiers for this type of mission."

"So you want me to find some strong men who have no links with us."

"Our old friend Tran-Bel will give us valuable assistance. You may have to push him a little to make him collaborate without ulterior motives, but I have every faith in your ability to do so."

—— 46 ——

Tran-Bel was a Libyan; he had a moon face and black hair plastered to his scalp. He ate and drank too much, but he needed to build up his strength to carry on his trade as a furniture seller and secret intermediary for all sorts of more or less unsavoury transactions.

During a period of unbelievably good trade, Tran-Bel had used the services of one of the craftsmen from the Place of Truth, who had made luxury furniture for him and produced designs that the Libyan had used to manufacture beautiful objects for sale at a high price—not everything was declared to the tax collectors. In the current tense situation, the craftsman could no longer leave the village, so Tran-Bel would have to wait for better times to restore his profits to their former levels. Fortunately, his wealthy customers had remained faithful to him, and he had done them some small but highly lucrative services.

When a woman entered his secret workshop, a heavy wig masking much of her face, Tran-Bel recognized her at once and his optimism dwindled a little. This formidable creature held him in the palm of her hand, and she never put herself to any inconvenience without good reason. On the brink of a civil war, such a visit did not augur well.

"Are we alone?" she asked, her voice sharp.

"I'll close the workshop." Nervously, he did so. Then he asked, "How may I be of service to you, my dear protector?"

"I need a band of killers."

"Killers! I'm just a simple shopkeeper, and—"

"I shan't repeat myself," she snapped. "Time is pressing."

"But where am I supposed to find them?"

"I'm sure you know some Libyans who'd do anything to earn a fortune."

"Perhaps, but my commission . . ."

"I shall fix the amount. Don't forget that you're in the service of a very powerful man, and you must obey him without question unless you want problems with the tax collectors."

Tran-Bel knew that resistance was futile. "I know three former prisoners who have served out their sentences and are now employed as laundry workers in the port. They aren't bothered by scruples, and they'll do whatever you want if you offer them enough money."

"Contact them at once and tell them to go to a place I'll show you."

Happy to play only a minor role, Tran-Bel promised Serketa to do so straightaway.

▲

The honey route was a closely guarded secret, which even the Scribe of the Tomb had been able to learn only a part. He knew that old Boti tended many hives in the western desert, but he did not know exactly where.

"All the same, we must try," said the Wise Woman as she and Paneb examined the rough map Kenhir had brought them.

"From the last guard post, at the far end of this wadi, to the hives," said Kenhir, "it must be at least a day's walk; but in which direction?"

"The desert is my friend," said Paneb. "It will show us the answer."

"There's no shortage of water sources," said Kenhir, "and there must be one on Boti's land. But you may run into serious trouble."

"Then give me a weapon," demanded Paneb.

"I am sorry, but that's impossible. If the guards stop you, try to talk your way out of trouble—at the worst, they'll bring you back here. But if you were armed with a sword or a spear, you'd be considered dangerous."

"I shall take my pickax."

"I forbid it," said Kenhir. "It belongs to the Place of Truth, and it will not pass outside the village walls."

"What food should we take?"

"I'll provide you with dried fish, onions, figs, and jars for transporting water. The load will be heavy, but you have strong shoulders."

▲

Adafi the Tall and his two brothers, Adafi the Lesser and Adafi the Short, were three Libyans who had entered Egypt illegally. They committed small thefts on behalf of Tran-Bel, who had promised them something much better as soon as the opportunity arose. And it had just arisen: all they had to do was kill a troublemaker or two.

This prospect immediately raised the Libyans' spirits. They were tired of working as laundrymen and washing women's soiled linen. In their country, they had robbed and murdered a few travelers, and they could slit a man's throat as easily as if he were a pig.

The woman was dressed in peasant garb, with a scarf covering her head. When she headed toward the thicket of thornbushes where they had been hiding since the previous evening, Adafi the Short felt an unstoppable desire mounting inside him. In Egypt rape was punishable by death; but he and his brothers had spent far too long in forced abstinence, for the girls they had met had all been married or betrothed, and were faithful.

"Get moving," ordered Serketa. "Your quarry has just set off along the path into the western desert."

"How many are there?" asked Adafi the Lesser.

"Two."

Adafi the Tall burst out laughing. "It'll be child's play!"

"As it's going to be so easy," commented Adafi the Short, "perhaps we could enjoy ourselves a little with you before we go to work."

"Come here," said the woman.

"You agree? With all three of us?" he said, astonished and a bit disappointed.

The moment the Libyan laid a hand on her hip, Serketa slashed open his forearm with a short dagger. He leapt backward.

Serketa brandished her weapon in the brothers' faces. "Next time," she promised, "I'll cut off your testicles."

They believed her.

"Your two victims won't be easy to capture," she went on. "One of them is a sort of sorceress who may well sense you approaching, and the other is a huge man, almost a giant, whom no one has yet beaten in a fight."

"Does he have a knife, too?"

"I don't know, but it's unlikely."

"This sorceress, is she old and ugly?" inquired Adafi the Short.

"She's an attractive forty-year-old."

"Can we rape her before we slit her throat?"

"If you like. I shall return in three days and I trust that you will have succeeded."

"Don't worry, my beauty," Adafi the Lesser reassured her.

"Your word won't be enough. I want proof."

"The giant's penis and the sorceress's head—will they do?"

Delightfully impressed by the Libyans' cruelty, Serketa nodded.

"Will it be you who pays us?"

"You won't be disappointed. And we may even have a little fun together."

Adafi the Short salivated. Two women in prospect: what luck!

Serketa had not made up her mind. Should she use these three brutes again, after they'd killed Paneb and Ubekhet, or would it be better to have them killed by archers searching for three dangerous escaped criminals? She decided to discuss it with Mehy.

▲

"I don't think the hives are very far from the last guard-post on our map," said the Wise Woman. "There is still quite a lot of vegetation in this area, notably rare flowers and acacias, which enable the bees to make excellent honey. Farther into the desert, they would not be able to find the nectar they need."

Paneb was carrying a heavy sack of provisions, and two jars of fresh water.

"Why has Boti set himself up so far from the fields?" he asked.

"Because he has worked out how far the bees will have to fly to gather nectar from the maximum number of flowers, and because the desert is the ideal place for the hives. When Ra wept, his tears fell onto the sand and were transformed into bees who, by their work, give us back the sun's gold, which they need to create honey. The desert's fire gives them its full power, and they can control it.

"That's why Pharaoh is both 'the Man of the Reed' and 'the Man of the Bee.' Within his being, he unites moist and dry, the humble reed linked to the earth and the tireless bee who travels through the sky to transform the subtle energy of flowers into a food and a remedy. Pharoah is the most useful of all beings, and it's the goal of our Brotherhood to create useful works, filled with light."

"And," said Paneb excitedly, "that's the very word, *akh*, which means 'useful being,' 'light-filled being,' 'light-filled ancestor,' that we worship and 'the Light of the Spirit' that we seek to attain. And it's the quintessence, the light that springs forth from the Stone! But in that case . . . Were this search for honey and this meeting with the bees designed to make me truly understand what I already knew?"

Ubekhet smiled. "The village needs this vital remedy, Paneb, but sometimes destiny is also filled with the Light."

Paneb no longer felt the weight of the sack of food and the jars; the pathway seemed wonderfully soft and the sun as refreshing as an evening breeze. The words had been made flesh and the Light of the work was becoming reality—a reality as tangible as the Stone itself.

"We must leave the path," said Ubekhet, "because we're getting near a guard post."

They climbed up a flint-strewn hillside and lay down on their bellies to peer over the brow of the hill.

"We're being followed," she whispered.

— 47 —

Paneb gazed around. Far to the west, an adobe hut stood in the shade of a tall palm tree.

"That's the guard post marked on the map," he said quietly. "We shall pass it at a distance. Are you sure we're being followed?"

"There's a hostile presence behind us."

"Could it be a hyena or some other predator?"

"Let's go on."

They went back down the hill and walked on, parallel to the path, Paneb turning round frequently. The sun was blazing down, but the two travelers walked at a steady pace and drank only occasionally, to avoid feeling the pain of thirst.

"It's strange," said Paneb, "that Kenhir was so intransigent and refused to let me bring a weapon. He's the one who recommended this route, so he knows the dangers."

"Our Scribe of the Tomb likes everything to be in accordance with the rules."

"I hope you're right. What if he's the traitor, hiding in the shadows and sending us to our deaths?"

"That's impossible."

"How can you be sure?"

"Because Kenhir knows where the Stone of Light is hidden. If he was the traitor, he would have stolen it long ago."

The argument impressed Paneb but did not wholly reassure him. What if Kenhir was playing an even subtler game, consisting of first getting rid of the Wise Woman and then running off with the Stone? Kenhir might have appointed Paneb to protect Ubekhet because he knew Paneb would have objected fiercely if someone else had been chosen. The only problem was that it would take several men to kill Paneb, so there must be more than one person following them.

The two travelers reached the end of the route marked on the Scribe of the Tomb's map. The last guard post was to the east, hidden by a sand dune.

"Which direction do we take?" asked Paneb.

"Let's wait for a sign," replied Ubekhet.

"The people following us will get closer. It's you they want to kill, I am sure. What will become of the village without the Wise Woman? We've fallen into a trap."

"The sign will come, and we shall reach the hives."

"Not if we don't survive! I have an idea, but it won't work if there are too many attackers."

Paneb explained his strategy, and Ubekhet agreed with it.

"They're coming," she whispered.

▲

There being no wind to blow sand over the tracks, the brothers Adafi had no difficulty at all following their quarry. The man was obviously heavily laden, because he had sometimes sunk into the soft sand before finding harder ground again.

"Are they going far?" asked Adafi the Short, who hated the desert.

"We are gaining on them fast," replied Adafi the Tall, "and they'll put up less of a fight if they're tired."

"That's true. We should attack right away and go back to the valley."

"Listen to your brother, imbecile," retorted Adafi the Lesser.

"I can think too! The sooner we kill them, the sooner we make our fortunes."

The three Libyans halted. A few hundred paces farther on, at the foot of a dune, someone was standing.

"Shall we go on?" asked Short.

Adafi the Tall gripped the handle of his sickle, and his brothers brandished their butchers' knives. Cautiously, they glanced around. They saw nothing unusual.

"Come on," said Tall.

"It's the woman!" exclaimed Lesser greedily.

"Me first!" protested Short.

"Don't get excited," said Tall. "Don't forget, the most important thing is that we slit her throat."

"Oh no, we're going to have fun first! She looks very appetizing."

Ubekhet stood motionless, as if she had not noticed the three brothers.

Her behavior puzzled Tall. "She's got a bodyguard, remember. Where's he got to?"

"Behind you," replied Paneb, leaping up out of the sand; he

had buried himself in the hope that the attackers, attracted by the Wise Woman, would remain grouped together.

Adafi the Short had no time to realize what was happening, for a large stone thrown by Paneb smashed his temple.

With a bellow of rage, Lesser rushed at the giant, who dodged aside at the last moment and twisted his arm back; losing his balance, the Libyan made the mistake of clutching on to his weapon, and was impaled on it.

Heavier than his brothers, Adafi the Tall also rushed forward and swung his sickle through the air, thinking that he could cut his opponent's throat. But Paneb promptly bent down and butted the Libyan hard in the stomach, winding him, then dealt him a mighty blow on the back.

Terrified, Tall tried to run, but Paneb's fist caught him on the nape of the neck, and the last of the Adafis collapsed, not far from his brothers.

"I only meant to knock them out," Paneb said when Ubekhet joined him, "but Libyans seem to have fragile bones. No one will miss those three, and at least the jackals and vultures will have a feast."

The Wise Woman looked up at the sky. "Look! There's the sign!"

A bird with a yellow breast, gray back, and long tail was flying southward.

"It's showing us the right direction," she explained.

▲

Old Boti was finishing smoking out a hive with candles fixed into a pot when he spotted Paneb and Ubekhet on the path leading to his hives, which were made out of interwoven reeds formed into cylinders and placed on a plinth. Ordinarily, he had no fear of being stung, for he loved his charges and they responded well to him; but since midmorning they had been very nervous, and he had thought it wise to take the precaution of removing the honeycombs.

He now understood the reason for their agitation.

If the man had been alone, Boti would have offered up his last prayers to Amon, protector of unfortunates; but the woman's presence and her radiant face reassured him a little.

The beekeeper snuffed out the candles. Surrounded by anxious bees, he stood in front of his hives, like a final rampart.

"Who are you?" he asked.

"I am the Wise Woman of the Place of Truth, and my companion is a craftsman."

"So you really exist?" Boti took a step back. Rumor had it that she was a formidable sorceress, who could drive any demon back underground. "Don't come any closer, or my bees will attack you."

"We mean you no harm," said the Wise Woman.

"The man with you, what's that he's carrying on his shoulders?"

"A sack of food and jars of water, which we are happy to share with you."

"I have all I need," said Boti.

"But the Place of Truth hasn't. We are short of honey, and I need it to care for the sick and injured."

"Everything I produce goes to the state. I can't let you have a single drop."

Paneb lowered the sack and the jars to the ground. "Do you never make exceptions?" he asked.

"Never—except in an emergency."

"This is an emergency," said the Wise Woman gently.

"All the same, it's not legal."

From a pocket of her dress Ubekhet took a small ingot, which glinted in the sunshine. "Our Brotherhood's gold for your bees."

"Can I . . . touch it?" Boti's doubts melted away: it was indeed gold. "Will ten large pots be enough?" he asked.

"Twelve," said Paneb.

The beekeeper gave in.

"And I must check the quality," added Ubekhet.

"Do you doubt it?" asked Boti indignantly.

"I need honey, royal jelly, pollen, and propolis, which cures a number of infections and inflammations. Have you all those things?"

"What do you take me for? No one knows the bees' treasures better than I do!"

The beekeeper was not boasting; none of the riches of the hive had escaped him, and he proudly showed them to the Wise Woman, all in carefully sealed and labeled pots.

"Why doesn't the state send more honey to the Place of Truth?" he asked.

"Because there may be war," explained Ubekhet. "King Amenmessu cares first and foremost about his soldiers."

"This ingot you are paying me with, does it really come from the village?"

"We're sworn to secrecy," the Wise Woman reminded him.

"I have the joy of gathering the gold dust that my dear bees bring back to me and I live happily here, alone with them, far from wars and strife. The only people I see are the guards who come to collect my harvests, and we exchange no more than a few words. I've never talked so much."

Boti opened a disused hive and took out a small, long-necked pot.

"This is my masterpiece," he said. "I hadn't meant to show it to anyone, but as you are the Wise Woman of the Place of Truth . . . It'll be very useful, you'll see. With it, you'll be able to cure many serious or difficult ailments."

"How can I thank you for such a gift?"

"You've given me gold from the Place of Truth, and I've had the good fortune to meet you and see the light that radiates from you. What more could I want?"

For a few moments, Boti wanted to become one of the village's lay workers and set up his hives close to the village. But it was here, in the burning solitude of the desert, that he had learned his craft and the language of the bees. And it was here that his charges made the best honey in Egypt.

—— 48 ——

Seti was recovering slowly, but he still had no taste for the affairs of state, which were managed by Tausert and Bay. He remained pharaoh however, and neither the Great Royal Wife nor the tjaty could make a decision affecting the future of the country without the formal agreement of the Lord of the Two Lands.

After his long stay in the Temple of Hathor, Seti had retained a taste for contemplation, so he stayed in the shrine of Amon for a long time after celebrating the morning ritual. He joined the priests when they came to fetch the food that had been made sacred by the divine energy. A portion of it was eaten, and the rest distributed to the members of the many trades who worked in the capital's temple.

The king often ate his midday meal with the high priest of Ptah, and they discussed the divine Word, whose power entered the hearts and hands of craftsmen, enabling them to create dwellings for the gods. Seti granted no audiences to ministers or courtiers, and it was the queen who received foreign delegations and confirmed that trade relations would continue unchanged. In the middle of the afternoon, Seti spent an hour or two in his office, consulting the documents prepared by Bay, the only official he would converse with from time to time.

Today, the first papyrus was a detailed plan for general mobilization of the northern armies.

"Will you listen to me, Majesty?" asked Bay.

"Are you going to talk about the war again?"

Majesty, it is your duty to reconquer Thebes and Upper Egypt."

"Each day, I worship Amon in the peace of his shrine at Pi-Ramses, and he does not inspire me with warlike thoughts."

"The thought of civil war horrifies me just as much, Majesty, and the plan I'm suggesting to you offers the immense advantage of avoiding it, as well as enabling the country to be reunited, as all Egyptians wish it to be."

"A plan that depends entirely on General Mehy, it seems to me."

"That's true, Majesty, but I don't doubt his fidelity to our cause—he has proved it several times."

"If we assume that you're right, Bay . . . But aren't you overlooking the possibility that the general is being manipulated by Amenmessu?"

"In what way, Majesty?"

"Suppose Amenmessu has realized Mehy is only pretending to support him? He would let your plan unfold, kill the general, and order the Theban troops to wipe out our unsuspecting armies. Slaughter and disaster—is that the destiny you want for our country?"

"Of course not, Majesty, but would Amenmessu be so devious?"

"Underestimating one's opponent is an unforgivable sin. If my son has embarked upon this adventure, it's because he feels he has the makings of a leader; and if he's right, he knows how to fight us. Your plan, Bay, might lead us into a deadly trap."

The king's clear-sightedness undercut Bay's whole argument.

"Thank you for enlightening me, Majesty," he said, "but must we give up all thoughts of military action?"

"Yes."

"So you will allow Amenmessu to believe that he has triumphed and that Upper Egypt belongs to him."

"By becoming too sure of himself, he will become the aggressor and draw down the anger of the gods. They will punish his rebellion better than I ever could."

▲

As soon as she reached the village again, the Wise Woman examined her patients. Fortunately, their condition was no worse, and thanks to Boti's honey she was able to treat them; she was sure they would all be completely cured.

Paneb had been summoned by the Scribe of the Tomb.

"Any trouble?" asked Kenhir.

"Do you really want to know?"

Kenhir frowned. "I hope you didn't break poor Boti's head to get the honey?"

"Oh no, nothing like that, at least not with Boti—he was very cooperative."

"Then who was uncooperative?"

"Can't you guess?"

The old scribe put down his brush and looked Paneb in the eye. "There are certain attitudes that annoy me, beginning with hypocrisy. If you want to criticize me, tell me to my face, not in a roundabout way."

Paneb turned purple with anger. "We were attacked by three brigands, probably Libyans."

"I warned you that the honey road was dangerous."

"They followed us, as if they knew where we were going."

The scribe's face darkened. "Are you accusing me of sending you and the Wise Woman into an ambush? How dare you accuse me of even thinking about such a crime, even for a moment!" The old man's vehemence made him look twenty years younger.

"I suspected you, it's true, and I had my reasons."

"What reasons?"

"For one, your refusal to let me have a weapon to defend us with."

"Don't you realize that it was in your interest and that of the Place of Truth? I'm an old man but I could still knock you out with my stick!" Kenhir rose to his feet, threateningly.

"I warn you, if you attack me, I shall defend myself."

"Unless you're a coward, take your logic to its conclusion and kill the criminal standing before you."

Paneb clenched his fists.

"Go on, hit me," commanded the scribe. "If I'm the vilest of traitors, why do you hesitate?"

Paneb went closer to Kenhir, who did not lower his gaze.

"All right," said Paneb, "you're innocent. But I had to check."

"What made you change your mind?"

"The way you looked at me. Your eyes aren't those of a man who'd have sent the Wise Woman to her death. But if you've deceived me, Kenhir, you'll find me on your trail again, and I shan't give you even the ghost of a chance."

▲

Serketa took off her peasant clothes, removed her coarse wig and shook out her hair, then hurried into the bathing room, where two serving women washed and scented her body.

While she was still only half-clad—she was choosing between two clinging dresses—Mehy burst into her bedchamber.

"Out of here," he ordered her servants.

Serketa coyly covered her breasts with a shawl. "Unfortunately," she said, "I still haven't any good news, darling. This is the third time I've been to the meeting place, and still nobody!"

"Those Libyan imbeciles aren't coming. A guard patrol has just found their corpses, a little way from a path in the desert."

"All three of them?" gasped Serketa. "But they were such strong fellows! Did they do at least part of what they were supposed to?"

"Both the Wise Woman and Paneb have returned safe and sound to the village—and Paneb was carrying something heavy."

"So, single-handed, he defeated three attackers," murmured Serketa greedily. "What a pity he isn't in our service. But we mustn't give up hope."

"I'm afraid the Wise Woman may have used her magic to add to Paneb's strength. Those three imbeciles overestimated their own abilities."

Serketa stroked her husband's cheek. "This small setback is annoying, but you have more serious worries, haven't you?"

"Exactly, my sweet."

"Is Amenmessu suspicious of you?"

"No, but I no longer have the slightest confidence in that vacillating fool."

"I did warn you he has no backbone. Is he going to give in and beg his father's forgiveness?"

"If he goes on isolating himself like this, he may well yield to temptation. He's just sent away his last advisers, and even I now have to request an audience. Amenmessu wants to make his decisions alone and rule alone! If he's mad enough to send the Theban troops out to attack the North, how am I going to stop him?"

"Refusing to obey him would be fatal. But I shan't let anyone, not even Amenmessu, block your rise to power."

"Would you even dare attack a pharaoh, my sweet?"

"Everyone will soon have to acknowledge that Seti is the only rightful pharaoh, my tender darling."

▲

As the sun was setting, Paneb went to find his son. Aapehti had organized a wrestling competition near the large grain store and was sure to win it.

When they saw Paneb, the children ran off home, and Aapehti set off as fast as his legs would carry him, in the hope that his mother's indulgence would once again protect him from his father's wrath. Paneb had, however, made up his mind to administer punishment.

He had almost caught up with Aapehti when his attention was drawn to a strange light, at the summit of the highest hill to the west of the village: fire.

Paneb crossed the burial ground and climbed up toward the place where the flames were leaping toward the lapis lazuli sky. No one was allowed to light a fire in that place, and he expected to lay his hands on a few more scamps and take them home.

Out of the shadows sprang a short, bearded man, wearing a lion mask with thick eyebrows and a mass of curly hair.

"I am Bes the Initiator," he announced, sticking out an enormous tongue before bursting out laughing. "Are you brave enough to follow me?"

Bes set off fast along the path to the pass. Paneb hesitated for only the briefest of moments, then fell into step alongside him.

——— 49 ———

Bes reached the pass and descended toward the Valley of the Kings. Although astonished, Paneb followed him, and they reached the entrance to the Great Meadow, which was guarded by a ritualist wearing the mask of Anubis.

He gestured to Paneb to cross the threshold.

Torch held aloft, Bes passed Ramses the Great's House of Eternity and headed for the tomb of Amenmessu, but he did not stop there. Without turning round, he followed a winding path that led down to the floor of the valley.

Paneb thought his guide was leading him into a blind passageway, for the edges of the valley narrowed to a bottleneck toward the cliff face.

Bes disappeared, but the painter could still see the light from the torch, twenty or so cubits above him. As he approached the rock face, he made out a rope ladder. He climbed it, and reached the entrance to a cavern, in front of which burned four torches.

Here and there were guards with the heads of a vulture, a crocodile, a lion, and a scorpion. When Paneb made to go forward, they brandished knives.

"I am the master of fear," declared the vulture, "and you stand before the secret door of the hidden chamber. If you dare enter, you will discover a new life, as long as you hear the call of the Light. But beware, Paneb: let your heart not be deaf."

"Stand aside."

Neither the guards' faces nor their weapons frightened him. If they refused, he would force his way past them.

"Like the sun, which dies in the evening," said the lion, "you must cross the night, confront fearsome trials, and attempt to be reborn in the morning. Have you the strength and the courage to see the Light in the darkness?"

Paneb showed the eye of Horus and the heart that he wore in the form of amulets, and the guards lowered their knives.

Inside the cave, a torch had been lit and a path appeared in the darkness. Paneb passed through a narrow door and entered a passageway about ten paces long, which led down into the rock and grew gradually narrower. He halted on the first step of a very steep staircase, which led to a second passageway interrupted by a vast well, lit by a torch. On the ceiling of this cavern of Nun, the primordial energy, stars were painted.

Paneb crossed the well by means of a wooden sledge laid across it, and entered a small, two-pillared chamber whose walls were decorated with 775 strange figures, expressing the many ways in which Light could act. He forgot the passage of time and lingered over these shapes, hidden in "the Secret Chamber of Reunited Wholeness," trying to assemble them into a view of the world; but he sensed that he lacked keys, and he was drawn by a new light, shining in the northwestern corner of the room.

Another staircase led down into a second, larger chamber with two rectangular pillars.

When Ched the Savior and Turquoise lit the torches, the light was dazzling. Paneb found himself inside a book, whose words were written on the walls. Hieroglyphs and symbolic scenes revealed the entire contents of "That which Dwells in the Heart of Creation," the place where the stars were ceaselessly born. Close to the red sandstone sarcophagus, which was painted and resting upon an alabaster plinth, stood the Master and the Wise Woman.

Ched took his pupil by the hand and led him to the start of the voyage that the ship of the sun undertook through the underworld each night. The first hour corresponded with the first door drawn on the wall, the door of the West.

"What do you see, Paneb?"

"I see a fearsome serpent that I must avoid and the sun's ship whose flesh never decays."

"May your spirit strike out into this universe."

Paneb felt as though he was traveling through a vast, peaceful region before entering the second hour, in which he crossed luxuriant countryside, bathed in sweet music. Emerging from these fields of happiness, he entered the third hour, which was refreshed by a breeze.

"Here the union of Ra, the Light of the sky, and Osiris, the Light of the underworld, takes place," intoned Ched. "Because of it, evil shadows are imprisoned and nothingness is destroyed."

Up till then, Paneb had experienced matchless peace; but the confrontation with the fourth hour shook him out of his well-being. The paintings on the wall showed the descent of the sarcophagus and the ship of the sun being hauled through a barren, waterless, desert landscape; he felt as though his muscles were straining so that the ship would not have to stop.

"Enter the cavern of birth, which fertilizes the sun of the fifth hour," commanded Ched. "It is here that the egg of Light is kept; this contains the many forms of life."

At the sixth hour, Paneb's spirit garnered its meager energies, the better to confront Apophis in the seventh hour. The terrifying god attempted to drink the river waters in order to stop the ship continuing its journey. But knives pinned him to the ground and prevented him from doing harm.

Then another, undulating snake appeared. This was the incarnation of the life running through all things; and after gazing at the stars of the zodiac, in their twelve masculine and twelve feminine forms, Paneb passed through the eighth hour, where he heard the voices of the beings from the world beyond: the cry of a falcon, the cheep of a fledgling, the mew of a cat, and the buzzing of bees.

"At the ninth hour," intoned Ched, "the mummy is raised up, Osiris vanquishes the darkness, and the soul-bird is born."

At the tenth hour, Paneb discovered the scarab beetle, which rolled before it the ball of the fetal sun; then he swam in the waters of the celestial ocean and felt that he was breathing as he had never breathed before.

And what joy, at the eleventh hour, to be present at the defeat of the enemies of Light, their heads cut off and thrown into braziers. Then the celestial serpent appeared, with the two complete eyes that gave greater powers of sight.

"At the twelfth hour, observe the new sun, strengthened at the head of the stars, and your own birth. You have thus crossed the twelve regions of the secret space where the boat sails, from West to East, from death to resurrection."

The twelve hours had passed like a second. The door of the shrine where Paneb had experienced the radiant night of the soul had been locked once more, and he sat before it, gazing at the sun's disk, enthroned in a blue sky.

Now he knew it from the inside because he had taken part in its formation, stage by stage. From now on, whenever the sun set, he would pass with it through the western door and undertake the perilous voyage toward the East.

Paneb thought of the difficult moments he had undergone when he passionately wished to become a painter and enter the Place of Truth, but without hope of succeeding; refusing to give in to discouragement, he had followed his instincts, which told him that his destiny would be played out there, and nowhere else.

The Master, the Wise Woman, and the ritualists had gone back to the village; only Ched the Savior had remained at the foot of the cliff face, waiting for his pupil.

"I would happily stay here for the rest of my life," confessed Paneb.

"Your discoveries aren't yet at an end."

"What more could I hope for?"

"That your hand may translate what your spirit has perceived. Do you think such secrets have been revealed to you so that you can indulge in adolescent dreaming?"

"I'm going to destroy my paintings and begin again."

"You most certainly are not, you impetuous ram! As I see it, your are not yet free of pride. How can you possibly think I'd have let you carry out a work unworthy of the Brotherhood? Because you always wanted to learn, in spite of your rebellious character, your hand knew what your spirit did not. Thanks to this initiation, you are becoming a little more aware of the great scope of our work; but the path that you have yet to walk is certainly no easier than that of the ship of the sun."

"We were in the tomb of Tuthmosis III, weren't we?" asked Paneb.

"It was he who compiled the *Book of Resurrection*. It is drawn on the walls of that oval room, in the form of a cartouche with his name in it. And you have traveled through its pages."

"His sarcophagus itself is the same shape," added Paneb.

"You have traveled inside the being of Pharaoh, who is himself identified with the sun. Few have had that good fortune; do try to show yourself worthy of it."

"Why do you think I won't?" demanded Paneb.

"Because life sets us trials that make us fall from a great height. And for you, the fall will be even more severe than for others; when misfortune comes, remember your victory over the dragon of darkness."

—— 50 ——

The moment Paneb stepped through his front door, he realized that the whole house had been cleaned from top to bottom, and smelled delightfully sweet.

Uabet was standing in the doorway of the second room, where the stele dedicated to the ancestors stood. She was wearing elaborate makeup, her white priestess's robe, and the necklace of cornelians and red jasper that her husband had given her. Her dignity impressed him, and he was astonished when she bowed before him.

"I know that you have completed the sun's night voyage," she said, "and that you are no longer the same man. Very few of the village's inhabitants have had access to that mystery, and that is why I am paying you homage."

Paneb took his wife gently in his arms. She was trembling.

"Your spirit has crossed regions I don't know," she said, "and, unlike Turquoise, I shall never know them; but I'm not bitter or jealous. Ched chose you as his pupil, the Master as his adopted son, and it is normal that you should continue on your way to becoming the head painter of the Brotherhood. As for me, I am just a simple housewife, but I love you with all my heart. And you, of course, will leave."

Paneb lifted her gently and carried her into their bedchamber, which was as spick-and-span as the rest of the house. Even the simple hooks on the walls looked brand-new.

With her arms round her husband's neck and her head resting on his chest, Uabet dared to let herself go and admit, "I'm afraid, Paneb, so afraid of being unworthy of you!"

He laid her on the bed, sat down next to her, and took her hands.

"I've taken a step forward, it's true, but I'm still a craftsman like the others, and I've no reason at all to abandon you. Without you, I'd have lived in a chaotic hovel, and the Scribe of the Tomb would have ended up expelling me. No one has done more than you to enable me to work free from cares."

"So . . . I've been useful?"

"How can you doubt that for a single second?"

"Do you accept me the way I am?"

"Don't you dare change!"

"Will you stay here, with me?"

"On one condition, Uabet: that you never ever bow before me again. Only the gods, Pharaoh, the Master, and the Wise Woman are worthy of that homage."

Slowly, Paneb took off her necklace and slid down the straps of her white dress.

"I love you in my own way," he said, "and it certainly isn't the best way. It's more likely to be a question of you leaving me, to find a better husband."

Naked and abandoned, Uabet smiled. "I've a better idea. Shall we have a second child?"

"Are you strong enough to carry it?"

"I've consulted the Wise Woman. She has no fears."

"Give me a little girl who looks like you."

"I shall pray to the ancestors, that they may carry out our wish."

Uabet, so small and so determined . . . Paneb loved her with an immense tenderness.

▲

Ched the Savior had thrown a banquet in Paneb's honor. Already the craftsmen of the port crew, as well as those of the starboard, were beginning to see Paneb in a new light. Even Nakht and Fened had to admit that he had good qualities and understood why the Master and the Wise Woman had adopted him. In addition to a controlled technique, he had a breadth of vision that adapted itself to every type of work and place to be decorated. The three artists, Gau, Unesh, and Pai, did not contest their colleague's talent, even though he was younger than they were, and they already considered him the future head of their workshop.

"Someone's asking for you at the main gate," Nefer told Paneb.

"For me? Are you sure?"

"Certain."

"Who is it?"

"The gatekeeper doesn't know him."

"What does he want?"

"You won't know that until you meet him."

"Won't you tell me any more?"

"If Sobek has allowed him to pass, he can't be dangerous."

Intrigued, Paneb followed Nefer to the main gate.

A donkey was standing just outside the gate. It had a white muzzle and belly, a light gray coat, big black eyes, long, slender ears, and large nostrils. And it was enormous, weighing as much as a small horse. On its back sat an empty saddle, attached by a buckle.

"Was someone riding it?" asked Paneb.

"One of the five peasants who work for me," explained Nefer. "But I did warn him when we bought North Wind that the animal won't tolerate having anyone on his back. As you can see, he already knows the way to the Place of Truth."

Proud and skittish, the beast eyed Paneb.

"Here is my gift, to mark your rising to your new rank," said the Master. "North Wind belongs to a line of illustrious donkeys, whose strength and intelligence are beyond reproach. His personality is scarcely better than yours, but I hope that you will reach an understanding."

"He's magnificent!"

"The head of a family must think about owning a few possessions, especially when his wife is expecting a second child."

"Uabet has told you?"

"Ubekhet will keep a close watch on her, and the pregnancy will go well. North Wind will go to my estate and bring you back what you need, as well as the provisions delivered by the state. All you have to do is explain carefully to him what you expect of him."

North Wind explored the giant's hands with the tip of his moist muzzle, sniffed him for a long time, then began to bray so loudly that a large number of villagers ran up to see what was happening.

"Do you think he accepts me?" asked Paneb.

"Stroke his head."

The attempt met with success. Well pleased with this sign of affection, North Wind rubbed himself vigorously against his new master.

▲

After a long wait, General Mehy finally received permission to enter the great audience chamber in the palace at Karnak. King Amenmessu was seated on a gilded wooden throne, gazing unseeingly in front of him.

He had not summoned any advisers for more than two months. His most senior minister, a tired old official, dealt with day-to-day matters and with complaints from the courtiers, who were as irritated as they were worried by the king's attitude.

As he bowed low, Mehy saw that Amenmessu had grown thinner and that his cheeks had grown alarmingly hollow. Nothing remained of the triumphant young man who loved to go for long horseback rides in the desert and dreamed of becoming a great pharaoh.

"Be brief, General. I can spare you only a little time."

"It is my duty to inform you of my anxieties, Majesty."

"War and blood, that's all you think about, General, and you're wrong! Violence leads nowhere. My father hasn't attacked the South, and I shan't attack the North, even if my decision displeases soldiers who are eager for blood."

"My only wish is to ensure your safety."

"Stop taking me for an idiot, Mehy! By cutting myself off in this palace, I have lost not a single second. On the contrary, I have at last succeeded in escaping from the whirlpool I was caught in for several years, and I have taken a necessary step back. Around me circle the vultures, thinking only of stripping my carcass so as to enjoy a share of power—and you are one of them."

"No, Majesty, I am not, and I don't deserve such a harsh

judgment. I'm a soldier and a governor, and it's not for me to take the initiative. That you order me to put the Theban troops into the service of peace fills me with joy, but I must tell you that their morale is low because their wages are several days late. That hasn't happened for a very long time, and the men are afraid they won't be paid at all."

Amenmessu's anger abated. "Why has it happened?"

"I complained to the first minister, who explained that it costs a great deal to remain in readiness for war, and that Thebes's finances are threatened. If you wish to avert a grave crisis, it might be wise to send back to their fields most of the peasants who have been mobilized."

"Are you in favor of doing that?"

"Our defenses would be much weakened. In the event of an attack by the northern armies, I'm not sure that I could be able to hold out with smaller forces."

Amenmessu stood up and leaned against a column, as if the contact with the stone renewed his strength. "Perhaps my father is taking time to prepare for a great offensive. If he learns that Thebes is weakening and that our defenses are less effective, he won't hesitate."

"Why not acquire riches that are a bit more liquid, Majesty?"

"What do you mean?"

"It may be only a legend, but people say that the Master of the Place of Truth can create gold. He'd be useful in solving our current problems."

Amenmessu closed his eyes for a moment. "Will you see to the matter yourself, General?"

"It should by rights be dealt with by the first minister, Majesty."

—— 51 ——

One of Sobek's men ran up to him and saluted. "Sir, a hundred soldiers have been sighted!"

"Every man to his post," ordered Sobek.

The guards had practiced the maneuver often, and they carried it out with impressive speed. Their leader, meanwhile, left the Fifth Fort to go out and confront the soldiers. They halted about ten paces from him, and a young officer stepped down from the leading chariot.

He saluted and said, "I am in command of the first minister's escort."

"You are forbidden to enter the Place of Truth," said Sobek.

"I may be, but the minister appointed by Pharaoh isn't." He showed Sobek the papyrus on which Amenmessu had set his seal.

"Wait here," said Sobek. "I must consult the Scribe of the Tomb."

"The minister isn't a very patient man."

"And my archers are rather jumpy," retorted Sobek. "If you come any farther, they'll fire."

▲

When Sobek reached Kenhir's house, he found the old scribe finishing his breakfast and daydreaming before writing up the Journal of the Tomb.

Since their marriage, Niut had made him eat grilled cereals and honey sweet figs, as well as round cakes stuffed with dates. Thanks to this diet, complemented by remarkably fine meals, the old scribe had recovered much of his youthful vigor. Nevertheless, he had to fight every day to be allowed a reasonable amount of light beer and a cup of wine at least every three days, watched carefully by Niut who would not tolerate drunkenness.

"We may have a serious problem," said Sobek. "The first minister is demanding entry to the village."

"What's the fellow doing here?" grumbled Kenhir. "Until now he's been less in evidence than a ghost!"

"He has a hundred soldiers with him, and he seems to be in a hurry. May I turn him away?"

"Unfortunately not, if he's here on the king's business."

Taking his time, and leaning on his stick, Kenhir trudged off to the Fifth Fort. The minister was as old as he was, and was standing in the shade of a large parasol held over him by a soldier.

"Are you the Scribe of the Tomb?" asked the minister.

"Why was I not informed that you were coming?"

"Because it's an emergency—King Amenmessu says so."

"Why are you here?"

"To see the Master."

"He's about to leave for the Valley of the Kings, to work on the king's House of Eternity. Come back in eight days' time."

"Amenmessu wants an immediate answer. Unless you do as I say, I shall order the troops to force their way in and seize the Master."

Asserting that Seti II was the only legitimate pharaoh, and that the document signed by Amenmessu was worthless, would provoke a bloody confrontation; so Kenhir tried to play for time.

"What do you want with the Master?"

"That's strictly confidential."

"I am the Scribe of the Tomb and the state's representative in the village. As such, I must be kept fully informed about everything that happens."

"I shall speak to no one but the Master."

Kenhir sensed that he was not going to win the argument. "You have permission to enter, but I shall not allow any soldiers to accompany you."

"Very well."

The two men headed for the main gate of the village. The gatekeeper got to his feet, anxious at seeing a stranger at the scribe's side.

"You may open the gate," Kenhir told him.

As he entered the forbidden village, the minister had a curious feeling. What was he going to discover in this forbidden world, where the pharaohs' eternity was planned and created?

A giant of a man, armed with a pickax, stepped out in front of him, while a black dog bared its teeth and a fat goose threatened to peck his legs.

"Wait here," said Kenhir. "I'll inform the Master."

Niut had warned the villagers that an intruder had arrived, and everyone had gone home and shut their doors. The Place of Truth lay silent, apparently deserted.

The minister did not dare move. "Who are you?" he asked Paneb.

"We're sworn to secrecy and we don't like people who talk too much. Or pointless questions."

The minister gave up and waited in silence until the Scribe of the Tomb returned.

"Follow me," said Kenhir.

Paneb, the dog, and the goose escorted Amenmessu's envoy to Ramses' little palace, whose door stood open, revealing a paved passageway.

"You are to enter, alone," said Kenhir.

The minister found himself in a hall whose paintings depicted the king making offerings to Hathor, surrounded by vines and bunches of grapes. He walked through it and entered a room with a vaulted ceiling, where Nefer was sitting on the ground.

"Are you the Master of the Brotherhood?" asked the minister.

"Was it indeed the king who sent you?"

"Yes, it was. My mission is particularly delicate, but it is official. I am speaking in the name of Amenmessu, and I remind you that you owe him obedience."

"I have not forgotten that Pharaoh is the supreme Master of the Brotherhood, and that he is first to conform to the Rule of Ma'at, of which he and his first minister are guarantors."

"Yes, yes," said the minister. "Is it true that you have a great deal of gold?"

"It is destined for sacred buildings."

"But there really is a House of Gold, where you make it?"

Nefer smiled. "Surely a pharaoh's first minister doesn't listen to legends?"

"Pharaoh Amenmessu demands the wealth that belongs to him."

"Even supposing that this gold exists, it would be impossible to remove it from the Place of Truth."

"I repeat: the gold belongs to the king."

"Then let him come here and gaze upon it," suggested Nefer, "in the secrecy of the work that is being done."

"That is completely unacceptable! You are to collect all the gold you have and bring it to the Fifth Fort."

"I cannot do that."

"I remind you that I am the first minister and that I am giving you an order from the king."

"It is no more than an aberrant decision, taken in ignorance of the nature and duties of the Place of Truth."

"Are you aware of the implications of what you are saying?"

"The Brotherhood's treasures are not designed for the outside world, where they would only be squandered. If you, the first minister, don't understand that, you're heading for serious trouble."

"For the good of the state, I will forget what I've just heard, but be aware that my patience has run out. Either you obey immediately, or—"

"Or what?"

Struck by the tranquil power emanating from Nefer, the minister searched for the right words.

"I shall advise the king to take serious measures against you. Such disobedience cannot be allowed."

"What you call disobedience is only respect for the rule of the Brotherhood established by Pharaoh himself at its creation. And I must ensure that it is respected."

"You're risking your life."

"It's better to die than to betray one's solemn oath."

"Is that your final word?"

"Go back to your king, and try to convince him that he's wrong."

"You're making a fatal mistake, Master."

When the minister left the palace, he found Paneb, the goose, and the dog still waiting outside.

"Don't harm the Brotherhood," Paneb warned him, "or you'll rue the day."

"Are you daring to threaten me?"

"With respect, I don't trust you, and I'm sure you haven't understood anything of the spirit that gives this village its life. Just accept that it's a sacred place, and don't try to harm any aspect of its life."

▲

The furious minister gave Amenmessu a detailed report, stressing the Master's disobedience, Paneb's insolence, and the Scribe of the Tomb's unwillingness to cooperate. Mehy, who had been summoned to the meeting, listened with delight.

The minister ended by saying, "Because of Nefer's scandalous behavior, and the insults aimed at you, Majesty, I recommend that he be arrested immediately and brought before my court."

"Are you sure the village has a lot of gold?"

"Absolutely sure, Majesty. The Master admitted as much, but he flatly refused to hand it over to you."

Mehy's delight grew: Nefer had reacted just as he had hoped, and had signed his own death warrant. Deprived of its leader, the Brotherhood would fall apart and become easy prey.

"What is your opinion, General?" asked the king.

"Without in the least doubting the minister's words, I confess I'm surprised by the Master's attitude. When I met him, he seemed a responsible, deep-thinking man. And I must remind you that I am the official protector of the Place of Truth, whose cause I must plead."

"Isn't it rather late for that?"

"I believe in the virtues of negotiation, Majesty, and I'm sure we can make Nefer see reason."

"You don't know him," said the minister. "He's a stubborn man who refuses to recognize our king's authority."

"That attitude is incomprehensible."

"Go to the village, General," ordered Amenmessu, "and bring Nefer here to me."

—— 52 ——

Kenhir was having a short nap near Amenmessu's tomb, in which the Master and the starboard crew were working, when Penbu, one of the Nubian guards on duty in the Valley of the Kings, tapped him on the shoulder.

"I'm sorry to wake you," said Penbu, "but General Mehy is at the entrance to the Valley and he wants to see you urgently."

The old scribe got up with difficulty and walked slowly in the noonday sun. The general had come alone; frothing with sweat, his superb black horse seemed exhausted by its exertions.

"Is the Master here?" Mehy asked anxiously.

"I don't have to answer that."

"King Amenmessu has ordered me to arrest him and take him to the palace."

"You cannot enter the Valley of the Kings, or the craftsmen's village."

"You must believe that I am very worried, Kenhir. I'm charged with protecting you, and I have boundless admiration for Nefer the Silent. Amenmessu's first minister is a dangerous schemer: his advice leads the king to make bad decisions, but I can't countermand it."

"What is the Master accused of?"

"Disobedience and insulting the royal person."

Kenhir was shaken. "Has the minister decided to bring him before his court?"

"I'm afraid so."

"Nefer might be sentenced to death!"

Mehy's silence spoke volumes.

"I refuse to hand the Master over to you."

"In your place, I'd do the same, but resistance would be use-less—Amenmessu would send in the army and take him by force."

"How could a pharaoh violate the Rule of Ma'at like that?"

"Amenmessu rules only over Thebes, and he wants to rein-force his faltering authority by whatever means he can. He thinks that, by making an example of the Master, he'll be able to impose his authority on officials who criticize his way of ruling. Unless Nefer comes with me now, tomorrow, I'll be compelled to bring armed troops and force the gates of the village."

"As state representative, I consider such action illegal and I shall write to the minister to demand that he prevent it."

"He won't even answer you," said Mehy sadly. "The only thing I can do is resign, but the king will appoint in my place a brutish soldier, someone who'd do anything to please him."

Kenhir seemed defeated. "I must talk to Nefer."

▲

"We mustn't give in," said Kenhir. "If you go with Mehy, you'll never come back."

"We must think above all of the village's survival," replied Nefer. "If Amenmessu is mad enough to do this, he's mad enough to do anything."

"But you're the Master of the Place of Truth! Without you, what will become of it?"

"You, Hay, and the Wise Woman will choose another Master, who will be recognized as such by the whole Brotherhood."

"Are you aware that the charges you face carry the death penalty?"

"It is the Place of Truth, not me, that must be saved."

"But what makes you think Amenmessu will spare your successor?"

"If he commits this crime his reputation will be soiled forever, and he'll be reluctant to act like a tyrant."

"I am coming with you, Nefer," declared Kenhir.

"No, you can't. The Brotherhood needs you here."

"I shall write a report on this whole affair and send it to Seti and to all the leading citizens of Thebes. If Amenmessu really is mad enough to attack the Master of the Place of Truth, I'll see that all the world knows about it."

"Ask Ubekhet to help me, and tell her I shall think of her constantly."

The two men embraced.

Just as Nefer was leaving the site, Paneb came out of Amenmessu's tomb.

"I can tell something unusual is happening," he said.

"Kenhir will explain," said Nefer.

▲

"My men are waiting for me with the chariots, a little farther on," Mehy told Nefer. "I take it the Scribe of the Tomb has told you how serious the situation is?"

"I shall be arrested, taken before the minister's court, and condemned to death. That's the fate I can expect, isn't it?"

Mehy looked apologetic. "I'd have preferred to see you again in different circumstances, but no one can oppose the will of Amenmessu. He listens to no one but his minister, who has sworn to have you killed."

"Why?"

"I don't know, but he's a touchy old man, and he resents your independence and doesn't understand the importance of your work."

The general led his horse by its bridle, and the two men walked along the path between the rocky hills.

"Once you enter the palace," said Mehy, "your fate will be sealed. It's not a very honorable suggestion, but you could run away. Where we are at the moment, my soldiers can't see us."

The general turned away. If Nefer gave in to temptation, Mehy would draw his dagger and stab Nefer in the back. No one would reproach him for killing a criminal who was trying to escape.

"I prefer to come with you, General. If I disappeared, the king's anger would be unleashed on the village."

Mehy was not particularly disappointed. He had not thought the Master a coward, and even though his hand would have been steady, he preferred to strike down his enemy with at least the appearance of legality.

"I admire your courage," he said. "Whatever happens to you, I promise to do my best for the village. And if I'm called as a witness at your trial, I shall speak in your favor."

Nefer entered the royal palace at Thebes as a free man, for the general had refused to bind his wrists in wooden shackles.

Mehy was amazed by the Master's calm. Although there was no hope for him, he showed no fear and behaved like a visitor who was happy to be received by the king.

At the entrance to the audience chamber, the minister greeted Nefer with the words: "Your behavior is intolerable, but I shall grant you one last chance: will you accede to the demands I made in the king's name?"

"I have not changed my mind."

"You deserve your fate, Nefer! Justice shall be implacable."

"Are you sure you're using that word wisely?"

Enraged, the minister said no more but escorted the Master to Amenmessu, who was sitting on the stone sill of a wide window, gazing out at the holy city of Karnak.

"Here is the prisoner, Majesty."

"Leave us."

"I must remind you of the charges, Majesty, and—"

"Leave us, Minister."

Reluctantly, the old man obeyed.

"My predecessors turned Karnak into a spendid sacred city where the gods are happy to dwell," said the king. "Like them, I want to make it more beautiful, to build new temples, erect great carved pillars, cover the floors with silver and the monumental gateways with gold. But before undertaking such work, I must consolidate my power by ensuring the obedience of all my subjects. Do you understand that?"

Nefer nodded.

"I'm surrounded by cowards and hypocrites. Only General Mehy has dared tell me the truth. There is muttering in Thebes, the soldiers are pawing the ground in impatience—their pay is late, and there will be more and more desertions. To save my throne, I must convince the waverers, reassure the timid, and prove that I can increase the wealth of the city of Amon, the god of victories. Do you understand that, too?"

"It is your duty as king."

"The Place of Truth possesses much gold, does it not?"

"Only what is necessary for our goldsmith to carry out his work. The gold is given to us by the palace, and the Scribe of the Tomb notes down the amounts."

Amenmessu turned toward the Master. "But, Nefer, you know how to make gold!"

Nefer did not answer.

"I am the supreme Master of the Place of Truth, and I must have that secret!"

"Any gold we might make would have no value beyond the walls of the village."

"You are my subject and you must obey my orders."

"Not when they are contrary to the Rule of Ma'at, which rules the village. You are its principal servant, and it is thanks to you that the weak are protected from the strong."

"Enough talking! I demand that you use your powers and give me the wealth I need."

"The House of Gold is inside the Place of Truth, Majesty, and what is done there is not of this world."

"Take care, Master! My patience is at an end. If you persist in this stubbornness, I shall hand you over to my minister."

"You know very well that no genuine charge can be brought against me."

"You are a rebel who refuses to obey his king!"

"On the contrary, I am faithful to him—and I can prove it."

"Prove it?" repeated Amenmessu in astonishment. "How?"

"By consulting the oracle of the Place of Truth."

—— 53 ——

Although Nefer had been placed under guard in one of the palace rooms, Mehy and the first minister were none too happy after hearing what Amenmessu said.

"The Master is completely within his rights, Majesty," said the minister.

"What does this oracle consist of?"

"One or several questions are addressed to the founder of the Place of Truth, Amenhotep I. The craftsmen will carry his statue, and it will answer by, for example, tilting forward if the answer is yes."

"And obviously the answer will be the one he wants," sneered Amenmessu. "He must be refused permission."

"That would gravely offend your ancestors, Majesty," said the minister, "and discredit you utterly in the eyes of the Theban population."

"So that's why Nefer was so sure of himself. With the dead pharaohs' support, and the immense prestige that goes with it, he knows he'll win. Can we at least choose the questions?"

"Indeed yes, Majesty. It's the accusers who have to ask them."

"There shall be only one: is Nefer the Silent faithful to Pharaoh, the supreme Master of the Place of Truth? But what good will that do us? The craftsmen will tilt the statue forward to make it say yes."

"I have an idea which should prevent that," said Mehy with a meaningful smile.

▲

"Sir, it's the first minister, and he's wearing his panther skin over his white robe, and has twelve shaven-headed priests with him."

"No soldiers?" asked Sobek.

"None—oh, the Master's there, too."

"Is he free?"

"He is walking in the middle of the procession."

Sobek left the Fifth Fort. Ignoring the minister he pushed aside two priests and headed straight for the Master.

"Welcome," he said with emotion. "I hope no one has tried to shackle you?"

"Nefer the Silent is still accused," said the minister. "I am here to consult the oracle, which will confirm his guilt."

The procession halted before the great gate. Ubekhet came out of the village, and she and Nefer embraced for a long time.

"The priestesses of Hathor have prayed for you constantly," she whispered.

The minister called to them, "Bring forth the statues of Amenhotep I and his mother, Ahmose Nefertari. I wish to question the worshipful protector of the Place of Truth immediately."

Six members of the starboard crew and six from the port crew brought the statues of the royal couple, which had been placed on a wooden boat with two long crosspieces made from Lebanese cedar wood.

The craftsmen had stopped work in order to be present, and

the whole village gathered round to wait for the royal soul judgment.

"Let the accuser ask his question," said the Wise Woman.

"Not until the boat bearers have been changed."

Paneb spoke up immediately. "Only the craftsmen of the Place of Truth are permitted to carry this boat."

"In order to ensure the objectivity of this consultation, the priests of Amon will replace them. That way, no one can contest the answer."

"That's against tradition!" thundered Paneb.

"Let the minister do as he wishes," decreed the Wise Woman.

Everyone was amazed at her words. Paneb was furious. He swore silently that he would allow no trickery by the priests and would force a new consultation of the oracle if necessary.

The craftsmen put down the boat, and it was lifted up by the priests of Amon, temporary priests who spent only a few days in the temple each year and who had been promised a sizeable reward if they gave the right answer.

The minister looked at Amenhotep's limestone statue, which sat on a colored throne and whose eyes were extraordinarily intense.

"Venerable ancestor," he said, "we are gathered here to learn the truth. Nefer the Silent, leader of your Brotherhood, is accused of rebellion against King Amenmessu. If he is judged guilty, he will undergo the supreme punishment.

"Venerable ancestor, answer this question: Is Nefer the Silent loyal to Pharaoh, supreme Master of the Place of Truth?"

For a long time, the boat did not move. The priests were trying to step back, so as to make the statue give a negative reply; but a mysterious force rooted them to the spot and, little by little, forced them to move forward.

"The oracle has spoken!" boomed Paneb. "Our Master is loyal to Pharaoh and has done nothing wrong."

"Glory to Amenhotep!" shouted Nakht, and all the villagers began to cheer.

Petrified, the minister thought about the consequences of his failure; and Paneb's ironic expression added to his alarm.

When the enthusiasm had died down, he made a final attempt.

"The question is so serious that I also require the opinion of Queen Ahmose Nefertari. If she approves of the Master's actions, let her show herself."

Paneb was ready to hurl this worthless old man out of the village. But, before he could move, the statue's black-painted face lit up with a broad smile that rooted Amenmessu's flabbergasted envoy to the spot.

▲

The minister could not prevent Kenhir accompanying him to the royal palace, where King Amenmessu received them immediately.

"Why have you not brought back Nefer the Silent?"

"The oracle answered in his favor, Majesty, but—"

"Not only," interrupted Kenhir, "did venerable Amenhotep I recognize the Master's righteousness, but his mother unmistakably confirmed the judgment."

Amenmessu's face grew still more hollow cheeked, as if he were ill.

"Nevertheless, Nefer must be arrested," insisted the minister. "You cannot allow such disobedience to go unpunished."

"I have another suggestion," said Kenhir, leaning on his walking stick.

The minister felt a surge of unexpected hope: perhaps this old scribe could show him a way of ending the career of this Master, whom he himself had been unable to defeat? In exchange for this small treason, Kenhir would be given a well-paid, undemanding post.

"In the consultation," Kenhir went on, "there were two unacceptable irregularities, both attributable to the first minister."

"What are you saying!" protested the minister.

"First, you insisted that the oracle's boat be carried by priests of Amon, strangers to the Place of Truth, when only the craftsmen are fit to fullfil this office. Second, you refused to accept the sacred judgment, in order to continue your vindictive pursuit of an innocent man. Such behavior is unworthy of a minister whose task is to apply the Rule of Ma'at in all circumstances. I therefore ask the king to dismiss you at once. If he refuses, I shall make a complaint to the court of Amon—and I shall win my case. The higher the office, the more impeccable the behavior it demands; that is how Egypt was built and that is how it will survive."

The minister turned to Amenmessu. "Majesty, don't listen to this vengeful old scribe!"

"Because of you," replied the king, "I have committed a serious error. Leave this palace, and never come back."

▲

Once again out hunting among the tall grasses where a myriad birds had their nests, Mehy still felt just as edgy. True, he had had the pleasure of killing many birds with his throwing stick, but although he had worked off his energy he had not calmed his anxieties.

On the bank, Serketa was reclining in the shade of a vast parasol set up by her servants, who had piled up several mats covered with fabric, so that their mistress would enjoy the greatest comfort.

"This grape juice isn't cool enough," she scolded them. "Go and fetch me some more."

Mehy sat down beside her.

"You are magnificent, my darling," she said, "but you look so worried!"

"Amenmessu has dismissed his first minister, a stupid old man who was made to look ridiculous by the Master and the Scribe of the Tomb. I told him how to make the oracle rule in his favor, but he still failed."

"Who has the king appointed in his place?"

"Another fool—and one who doesn't much like me."

CHRISTIAN JACQ

— 54 —

Nefer stroked Ubekhet's hair as she savored the early-morning sun on the terrace of their house, where they had spent a delightful night under the stars. Each day strengthened the loving magic that had united them since their first meeting, and they both thanked the gods for granting them such happiness.

He asked, "Weren't you afraid of trickery by the minister and the priests of Amon?"

"No," she said, "not on village ground and under the protection of our founding ancestors."

For the starboard crew, it was a rest day; but there was no rest for the Master. He had to supervise the installation of a new grain store designed by Gau and built by Didia with the help of Karo and Renupe. After that, he must check the grain that had just been delivered, before going to see Kenhir and listening to his complaints.

"Are you up there?" called Paneb's powerful voice.

Nefer stood up and looked down into the street.

"We have a notable visitor," said Paneb.

"Not the new minister already?"

"Much better: King Amenmessu in person. Sobek is worried that he may be an imposter and has asked the Scribe of the Tomb to come and identify him. If it really is indeed him, perhaps you ought to come down."

Nefer looked out across the village. The hustle and bustle around the main gate confirmed that something unusual was going on. He put on his kilt and sculptor's apron, and went down into the street.

There he bumped into Unesh, who said, "It's Amenmessu!"

"Who's with him?"

"Only a charioteer."

Kenhir pushed the villagers aside with his stick, to allow the king to make his way down the main street and reach the Master.

When the two men's eyes met, a heavy silence fell.

Then, "I am happy to welcome you to our village, Majesty," said Nefer, bowing low.

Amenmessu was thinner, very pale, and seemed bewildered. "I want to follow the path you take to the Valley of the Kings and see my House of Eternity."

"Immediately?"

"Time is pressing, Master."

Nefer asked Paneb to accompany them. Halfway to the pass, Paneb had to support the king, who was short of breath, his legs giving way beneath him, Amenmessu seemed at the end of his strength.

"Do you wish to return to the village, Majesty?" asked Nefer.

"We shall go on."

Paneb slowed down. At the camp on the pass, Amenmessu rested for a while, gazing out at the sun-scorched hills and the peregrine falcons soaring above them.

"The bird of Horus, protector of royalty," he murmured. "Does he still think of me? Instead of raising myself toward the sky, I have become mired in a bog. You, Master, have followed the path of righteousness, which leads to the other life, and I regret not having realized the importance of your role until so late. But today I have the chance to walk through this domain, whose master I should have become."

Amenmessu explored the stone huts where the craftsmen lived when they slept at the pass and was amused by the inscriptions engraved by Kenhir, who was concerned about preserving his own comfort after choosing the best place.

"We shall descend into the Valley," he said at last.

He walked hesitantly, and Paneb watched him continually for fear that he might fall. But they reached the end of the journey without incident and entered the Great Meadow, whose silence was peopled by the memory of illustrious reigns.

"This place is more alive than my palace," said Amenmessu. "There, there is nothing but intrigues and ambitions; here, I find at last the peace that has always eluded me."

When he inspected his House of Eternity, Amenmessu was dazzled by the quality of the sculpture and the beauty of the scenes showing him in the company of the gods. He walked very slowly along the passageways, read the texts revealing the transformations of Light, and halted before the figure of his mother making offerings to the creator and to Isis.

"I should have come here long ago, but I was afraid of meeting my death. How wrong I was! Nothing on these walls speaks of death. You have given me much more than those who claim to be my friends and my allies, you whom I have distrusted and fought against."

Nefer and Paneb left Amenmessu alone, to commune with the gods. When he emerged, the sun was beginning to set.

"It's late," he said to the Master, "so late . . . But I have lived long enough to know the marvels you have created for me."

▲

Daktair was short, fat, and bearded. He was, he said, proud to be the son of a Greek mathematician and a Persian alchemist. Little by little, he had been seduced by the comfort of the workshop he ran, thanks to Mehy. He had long since ceased believing in the possibility of a revolution that would force Egypt to abandon the old ways and enter a new era dominated by discoveries and new learning. The general had tried hard to shake up the old land of the pharaohs, but circumstances had defeated him.

Daktair drank only water, but he was eating more and more. Naturally he was putting on weight, which made him angry; he vented his anger by being hateful to his employees. No Egyptian woman wanted him, so from time to time he resorted to the

Libyan girls who sold their charms in an ale house on the out-skirts of Thebes.

And yet, what a clever man he was! He still felt capable of inventing new machines and using substances such as stone oil to change the basis of the country's economy. But Egypt was mired in its respect for the law of Ma'at, an illusory harmony, and could not understand that material success, at whatever price, was preferable to righteous living. As he took his nap after the midday meal, Daktair dreamed of the wealth he was amassing.

"Have you prepared what I asked you for?" demanded a woman's voice.

Daktair started awake and looked wildly around. "Serketa! Forgive me, I was having a little rest."

He was afraid of this curvaceous woman who played at being an adolescent, with her sugary voice, fluttering eyelashes, and simpering smile.

"I am in a hurry," she said.

"I've been overwhelmed with work recently, and—"

"Thanks to you," acknowledged Serketa, "I've learned a great deal about preparing poisons, but I know much less than you do about sleeping draughts made from lotus flowers. I mustn't make a mistake, but I must act soon, because the situation is becoming dangerous for my husband—who is also, I remind you, your protector."

"I don't want to know anything!"

"Oh, but an ally like you must know all about my plans. As soon as you have given me the sleeping draught, I shall use it to drug the soldiers guarding King Amenmessu's bedchamber. Then I shall enter and administer to him a poison I've devised myself."

"Be quiet, I beg you!"

"I tested the poison on a bullock: its death was lightning fast. In this way, we shall be rid of that stupid princeling. He's thinking of appointing a new commander in chief for the

Theban armies. What a ridiculous idea! It fully deserves the severest punishment."

"But Amenmessu is a pharaoh!" quavered Daktair.

"The only rightful pharaoh is Seti, and we have always been faithful to him. Remember that, my fine friend, and obtain that sleeping draught for me without a moment's delay."

▲

Amenmessu had spent the night in Ramses the Great's palace, inside the Place of Truth. Like the villagers, he had paid homage to the ancestors at dawn; then he ate his morning meal with the Master and the Wise Woman.

The king looked less haggard, and he had regained a little of his appetite. "Is there anything you need, Master?"

"Nothing, Majesty, when the state keeps its promises."

"Wouldn't you like to enlarge the village?"

"Absolutely not! It functions like a ship, with a port crew and a starboard crew, and each man strives for excellence in his speciality, while also being part of the community effort. Increasing the number of craftsmen would be futile, even harmful, for all that matters is the unity of the Brotherhood. It takes many years to train a true servant of the Place of Truth to exercise his art unfailingly and put into practice what he has seen and experienced."

"My minister lied about you," said the king, "and only General Mehy defended you. Be careful, Nefer. Your position and the secrets you hold have aroused formidable jealousy."

"So long as Pharaoh watches over the Place of Truth, we have nothing to fear."

"I shall make it inviolable," promised Amenmessu.

"Forgive me, Majesty," put in Ubekhet, "but should you not take better care of your health?"

"I have just signed a decree appointing a certain Daktair my head doctor—I've been told great things about his skill. But would the Wise Woman agree to care for me, as she does for the other members of the Brotherhood?"

"I am at your service, Majesty."

"I have lost all the energy I had as a young man, and have worn myself out preparing for an absurd war that never happened. After seeing my House of Eternity and taking a small part in village life, I want to put an end to the disorder I've caused. First thing tomorrow, I shall begin negotiations with my father, the rightful pharaoh, and beg him to forgive me—the only favor I shall ask of him is that he permits me to rest in the Valley of the Kings when I die. When harmony is reestablished, I shall come back to see you, Ubekhet, and you will give me back my health."

—— 55 ——

"It's much too risky, Serketa. And it'll never work," said Mehy.

"Yes it will, my tender love, because it's a very simple plan. A serving woman will take drugged food to some of the palace guards, and as soon as they have fallen asleep they'll be replaced by some of your men. Then I shall enter Amenmessu's bedchamber and persuade him to drink a charming potion of my own devising. A deadly potion: he won't suffer and will leave this world for a better one."

"But you might be caught!"

"That is not my style," she purred. "Tell me you'll let me do it."

"No," said Mehy firmly.

There was a knock at the door and the head steward came in. "Your assistant wishes to see you, General. He says it's very urgent."

The officer was in a highly emotional state. "Alarming news from the palace, General! According to the rumors—which I think may well be true—Amenmessu has decided to recognize

Seti as sole Lord of the Two Lands. To prove his sincerity, he will disband the Theban armies and in your place he will appoint a government official. I should add that the new first minister, a scribe from the granaries, is hostile to you. What is more, our men are very anxious about their future."

"Tell them not to worry. I shall plead their cause to the king."

When the officer had left, Serketa kissed the general's knees. "Will you let me do it, sweet love?"

▲

Imuni's ratlike face was even crosser than usual. "Thirty-six, thirty-seven," he counted. "There's definitely a jar of beer missing."

"Count again," ordered Kenhir.

"I've already done so! Thirty-eight jars were delivered to us this morning, and I have put only thirty-seven in the store room. The only answer is that someone has stolen one."

"Don't get flustered, Imuni. A good scribe must keep a cool head."

"We must find the thief."

"Do you suspect anyone in particular?"

"I've already made some inquiries. This morning, only three craftsmen from the starboard crew were present at the unloading: Pai, Didia, and Paneb."

"And of course you're accusing Paneb."

"According to two of the women, he was the last person seen at the scene of the crime. He's so strong that he can carry more jars than the other two, and he probably didn't hesitate to steal one."

"Have you any proof?"

"All the indications are that that's what happened, and you're obliged to inform the Master."

Imuni was right, but his shrill voice set Kenhir's nerves on edge. "Very well, I'll tell him."

"As the accuser," insisted Imuni, "I shall also be present."

"Come on, then," growled Kenhir.

▲

Nefer was working in the sculptors' workshop, where he was finishing a statue of Amenmessu. The king was depicted sitting down, and his peaceful face was that of a young king at the height of his strength and vigor.

Imuni was about to open his mouth when Kenhir put a hand over his mouth. "Be quiet."

Imuni was so taken aback that for a moment he forgot the war he was waging against Paneb. His eyes followed the Master's hand, which was shaping the pharaoh's smile, in which the divine and human came together in an impossible harmony. The fine chisel danced on the stone without hurting it and transformed the seemingly inert material into a bearer of life.

Nefer laid down the chisel and wiped his brow with a linen handkerchief. Emerging from a world apart, in which he conversed with the statue, he saw the Scribe of the Tomb and his assistant.

"There is a thief in the Brotherhood," declared Imuni.

"Who is it, and what has he done?" asked Nefer.

"Paneb has stolen a jar of beer. I demand that the court be convened and his house searched."

"Have you questioned him?"

"He might react violently."

"He won't if I'm there."

Nefer left the workshop with the two men, and they went to see Paneb, who at his wife's request was giving the front of his house a fresh coat of white paint.

"An impressive delegation," he commented. "I'll wager Imuni has another grievance against me."

"This time it's serious," asserted Imuni, "and you must confess immediately."

"I confess that I find you more and more unbearable and that my paintbrush might well wander onto your face."

"Did you steal one of the jars of beer that were delivered this morning?" asked Kenhir.

Paneb's look became threatening. "I bet it was that runt Imuni who dreamed up that story."

"A jar has indeed been stolen, and you were there at the time," said Imuni defensively.

"Not alone, so far as I know. You might have stolen the jar yourself, to cause trouble for me."

Sensing that Paneb was about to strangle Imuni, Kenhir hastily stepped between them.

"It's a serious matter, Paneb," he said. "Are you willing to be questioned, together with Pai and Didia?"

"First, you'd better look in my cellar."

"Let's take him at his word," suggested Imuni.

Paneb opened the door of his house. "Go in and check."

"This doesn't exactly gladden my heart," said Kenhir. "And I'm grateful to you for being so cooperative."

He followed Imuni into the house, but the Master remained outside with Paneb.

"One day," promised Paneb, "I shall squash that bug Imuni's head between two rocks."

"Try to resist the temptation, because otherwise at the very least you'd be thrown out of the Brotherhood."

"You at least know I'm innocent, don't you?"

"Do you really need to ask?"

When the two scribes emerged from the house, Imuni looked thoroughly dejected, while Kenhir looked well satisfied.

"No suspicious jars at all," announced Kenhir.

"The problem's still unsolved, though," his assistant reminded him bitterly. "Let's confront Paneb with the two other suspects."

"Well do it quickly, then," said Paneb. "I hate wasting time."

▲

They found both Didia and Pai at the latter's house, where Pai was busy cooking some kidneys according to a secret recipe of his own.

"Paneb is accused of stealing a jar of beer," said Imuni. "Did you witness this crime?"

"Don't talk rubbish," cut in Didia. "I was so thirsty that I took a jar from this morning's delivery to drink there and then. Take the price out of my wages, and let's have done with it."

"All the same—"

"Go back to your office," commanded Kenhir.

Seduced by the delicious smell, Paneb bent over the cooking pot.

"Why did you take that jar?" he whispered in Pai's ear.

"I needed it to make the sauce for the kidneys—and my wife would have complained about the expense."

"Don't do it again. And thank Didia."

"We colleagues stick together," said the carpenter, "but I think Pai ought to invite us to lunch, don't you?"

▲

The Theban court was buzzing. Rumor had been piled upon rumor, and everyone thought they knew that King Amenmessu was on the point of giving up the throne. Some people felt relief, others were afraid of losing all or some of their privileges; and everyone wondered what fate lay in store for General Mehy, whose silence was becoming deafening.

At dusk, Serketa arrived at the palace with the serving women who worked at night. Modestly dressed, she passed through the first two checkpoints without difficulty. But at the third, one of the guards was more suspicious.

"I don't know you," he said.

"I'm here to replace a laundry woman who's ill."

"Go and see the lady of the bedchamber. She'll tell you what to do."

Serketa set off down the corridor that led to the laundry, but once out of sight of the guards she turned into the passageway that led to the royal apartments. Mehy had drawn her a map of the palace and she had memorized it throughly; she ran no risk of getting lost.

In the inside pocket of her coarse robe were a dagger and a phial of poison. The first would enable her to kill anyone who got in her way; the second was for Amenmessu.

The guards outside the king's rooms had just been changed. In less than half an hour, the sleeping draughts would have plunged Amenmessu's bodyguards into deep sleep and the way would lie open. No one would stop her entering the king's bedchamber.

Serketa slipped into in a small room where vases were stored. She waited there until complete silence fell over the palace.

Suddenly, she heard hurried footsteps on the flagstones. She knew that she had been right to be wary. Someone had betrayed her and the guards were looking for her. If she had hurried, she would have been caught.

How could she get out of the room without being spotted? There was a small window that looked out onto the garden, but it was blocked by stone bars. There was no way out, and nowhere to hide. When the door was opened, she'd have no chance of escape. She decided she'd plunge her dagger into the belly of the first guard who tried to stop her, then try to slip between the others by clawing at their eyes as she ran past.

Men's voices, panic-stricken. Then the voices of women, lamenting and weeping.

Intrigued, Serketa opened the door a fraction. Soldiers, officials, and serving women were running along the corridor.

Serketa seized one of the women by the wrist. "What's happened?"

"King Amenmessu is dead!"

—— 56 ——

Soaked with sweat, Kenhir woke with a start and let out a cry of terror that roused his young wife. Niut got up and knocked at the door of his bedchamber.

"May I come in?" she asked.

The sound of coughing answered her, and she opened the door. Kenhir was sitting on his bed, trying to get his breath back.

"I had a terrible nightmare," he explained. "I saw a follower of Set coming, violent, quarrelsome, aggressive, stronger than any athlete, with bloodshot eyes, and so powerful that even the desert didn't frighten him."

"Getting yourself into such a state, at your age! Get up and wash. I'll change the sheets and clean the room from top to bottom."

Niut was setting to work when she heard a disturbance in the street outside, even though it was still dark. She peered out of the window.

A torch in his hand, Unesh was running down the street, shouting, "Wake up, everyone! King Amenmessu is dead!"

Nefer ran out of his house, caught Unesh's arm, and asked how he knew.

"From the messenger, Uputy," said Unesh. "When he heard the news, he knew he must tell us at once."

While the Wise Woman was calming the villagers, the Master talked with Sobek, who had put his guards on full alert.

"Now," said the big Nubian, "everything depends on General Mehy, who is the only strong man in the region. Either he'll submit to Seti, who'll punish Thebes for its rebellion, or he'll succeed Amenmessu himself, which will mean civil war."

▲

The first minister, other ministers, senior officials, and courtiers who served Amenmessu had been led into the great courtyard of the principal barracks in Thebes, where General Mehy was giving instructions to his senior officers. Evidently, thought the courtiers, the general had decided to seize power and appoint his own soldiers to key posts.

"Prince Amenmessu died last night," announced Mehy, "and I have ordered the embalmers to begin their work. Messengers have left for Pi-Ramses to inform Seti as soon as possible. Seti is the legitimate pharaoh, and I have always served him faithfully."

Faces registered stunned disbelief. Many had thought he wouldn't hesitate to follow Amenmessu's example, but they did not know that Mehy had detailed knowledge of the balance between the forces of North and South, which was not in his favor. In the event of war, his superior weaponry would not be enough to overcome such a handicap; only trickery and the element of surprise could have given Mehy victory—but he must not think of that anymore.

"We are also the loyal servants of Seti," claimed the treasurer appointed by Amenmessu, "but the usurper left us no choice. We shall nevertheless prove to the pharaoh that we did our best to safeguard Thebes."

"And we mustn't decree a period of official mourning," advised the mayor, "because that would be an insult to Seti. All things considered, this is just the death of a prince of royal blood. Let's forget the titles Amenmessu gave us and take up our old offices again. When Pharaoh enters Thebes, he will be acclaimed by a loyal, obedient city."

"As long as we have wiped away all traces of the usurpation," said the former minister of agriculture. "Didn't Amenmessu have a tomb built in the Valley of the Kings? Imagine Seti's rage when he finds out! In his capacity as governor of the west bank, General Mehy should order the craftsmen of the Place of Truth to destroy this infamous monument. If not, the Brotherhood will be severely punished and Seti will take revenge on us, too."

▲

"Majesty," said Tjaty Bay, bowing low before Seti and Tausert, "I have just had a letter from General Mehy. I have to inform you that he says Prince Amenmessu is dead."

"How? What happened?" asked Seti.

"According to the palace doctors, he died in his sleep; his body was that of an old man, thin and worn out. The general is having him embalmed, and is doing everything necessary to prevent unrest in the Theban region."

"Could the letter be a forgery?" asked the queen, "intended to deceive the king as to the real situation in the South?"

"This is certainly the general's seal, Majesty, and the writing matches that in his previous messages."

"But suppose he was forced to write it? Amenmessu has been unable to win by using force, so perhaps he has decided to resort to trickery."

"I believe that my son is dead," declared Seti sadly, "and that he has paid dearly for his refusal to submit."

"Let us send observers into the region to gather reliable information," suggested the queen. "If we send only a few lightly armed troops into the area, they might suffer heavy losses."

"There are much more urgent matters," replied the king, and he proceeded to outline his wishes to the Great Royal Wife and Tjaty Bay.

▲

"I didn't even have to poison Amenmessu," lamented Serketa. "That poor young man died all on his own. Thirty-three and his reign not even three years old—a sorry state of affairs! Unfortunately, the fool didn't even enable us to destroy Seti."

She curled up at Mehy's feet. He had taken to his bed because of a severe skin rash and a high fever. The doctor had offered reassuring words, but said the patient must remain in his room for a week or risk complications, an inconvenience that infuriated the general, who thoroughly distrusted the Theban courtiers.

Officially, Mehy was studying documents; each day, his assistant passed on his orders to the army who—like everyone else—were impatient to know what Seti would do. Some hoped for clemency, others feared that he would break the back of proud Thebes.

"No messages from Pi-Ramses this morning?" asked Mehy.

"No, my sweet love."

"I feel much better, and I've wasted enough time. Tomorrow I shall deal with the Place of Truth."

"Aren't you forgetting that the Master refused to destroy Seti's tomb?"

"The situation has changed. Nefer isn't stupid. He knows that removing all traces of that mayfly Amenmessu will win him the rightful pharaoh's gratitude."

"And what if he refuses?"

"That is my secret hope, my turtledove. If he refuses, I shall have him arrested."

▲

The entire village had gathered in the open-air courtyard of the Temple of Hathor and Ma'at.

"Amenmessu's mummification has begun," said the Scribe of the Tomb, "but the official mourning period has not yet been proclaimed. This proves that Thebes is bowing down before Seti, Pharaoh of Upper and Lower Egypt. The unity of the country has been reestablished, and we rejoice. But it is certain that Amenmessu's will be removed from all royal lists."

"What will become of his House of Eternity?" asked Paneb.

"That is precisely why I'm asking everyone their opinion: the village's future depends on it."

"Fortunately," said Renupe, "the Master safeguarded Seti's own tomb."

"To prove our absolute loyalty, we ought to destroy his son's," suggested Ched.

"I think so, too," agreed Kenhir. "We can be sure that General Mehy, supported by all the Theban courtiers, will demand that we drive the usurper from the Valley of the Kings."

All eyes were turned on the Master.

"The Scribe of the Tomb is right to put us on our guard," said Nefer. "What does the leader of the port crew think?"

"Whatever the Master thinks," replied Hay.

"And the Wise Woman?"

"Whatever the circumstances, our only concern is to respect Ma'at."

"It's all perfectly simple!" exclaimed Paneb. "We can't destroy a House of Eternity, and its paintings and sculptures, which we created with love. Amenmessu wasn't a great king, but he didn't harm the Brotherhood. We mustn't behave like barbarians because of sordid maneuverings by the authorities. Time will wipe out minor events; eternity will preserve only the ritual scenes where Amenmessu appears as a pharaoh who knows the words of resurrection. Everything about the man will be forgotten, but people will remember the symbols we drew for a king."

"Yes, but we're living today, not in eternity," objected Casa. "Your fine words will have no effect on the general, and Seti will raze the village to the ground if it shows the slightest sign of loyalty to Amenmessu."

"By preserving the work we have done, we shall be showing our loyalty to ourselves and to the Place of Truth."

"Well, I agree with Casa," put in Karo, "but don't ask me to demolish anything."

"Is any of you prepared to destroy Amenmessu's tomb?" asked the Master.

Some gazed up at the sky, others down at their feet, and some at the priestesses of Hathor.

"Be fully aware of what you are doing," advised Kenhir. "Seti will not forgive you for it."

"Amenmessu's House of Eternity is almost finished," said Paneb, "and it's good that no one in this Brotherhood wants to spoil it. If the pharaoh is angry with us, let him find other people to finish his own tomb."

Kenhir recognized that the argument was not without its good points, but what weight would the Brotherhood really carry with a king who was determined to wipe out every trace of a rebellious son?

"We have work to do," said Paneb. "Instead of talking, we

should start preparing Amenmessu's funerary chamber to receive the royal mummy."

"The prince will never be allowed to rest in the Valley of the
Kings," objected Nakht.

"That's for the men of power to decide—it's nothing to do
with us. Let's keep to the Master's plan, and all will be well."

Paneb's infectious enthusiasm removed the craftsmen's last
doubts, and they prepared to leave for the valley.

Nefer had not even had to take the final decision. The
Brotherhood had taken it themselves, and with all their hearts.

—— 57 ——

Mehy had fully recovered and was preparing to leave for the
Place of Truth with fifty footsoldiers, when his assistant brought
him an urgent message.

"There are ships approaching from the North, General."

"How many?"

"Five, sir, and one of them's a royal barge."

"Seti himself, already! Where are the ships?"

"They'll soon be in sight of Thebes."

Mehy assembled as many soldiers as possible on the western
bank, so that they could greet the king and the king could appreciate the Theban army's unfailing loyalty. Relegated to the
back, the courtiers would be lost in the crowd.

Already the news was circulating in the great city, and
fear mixed with curiosity: upon whom would the king's anger
fall?

To the general's surprise, the flotilla headed for the landing
stage on the west bank. He immediately commandeered a light,
fast boat to cross the Nile and welcome the pharaoh.

But the man who stepped out onto the gangplank was not Seti but Tjaty Bay, whose gait was decidedly unsteady.

"I am glad to be back on dry land," he admitted to Mehy. "I've been ill throughout the voyage."

"Is His Majesty not with you?"

"The king has entrusted me with two missions. The first is to find out whether Prince Amenmessu has indeed died, and whether calm reigns in the good city of Thebes."

"It has finally been delivered from a yoke it bore with ever-greater difficulty, and I am proud to have been able to avert the disturbances I feared."

"Has security really been assured?"

"Amenmessu's last supporters are few," said Mehy, "and all they think of is hiding. Nevertheless, I think it would be wise to wait a while before answering yes without hesitation."

"Thank you for your frankness, General; it will be appreciated in high places."

"And your second mission, Tjaty?"

"I must go to the Place of Truth immediately."

"Commander Sobek's guards are not easy to handle. If you wish, I will accompany you, together with a few soldiers."

"I should be glad of it, General."

Mehy was delighted. His actions would have an official veneer, and the tjaty would confirm that the commander in chief of the Theban troops had been the first to wipe out all memory of Amenmessu.

Bay examined the chariot suspiciously. "I must ask you not to go too fast: I suffer from travel sickness."

"I'll take good care of you, Tjaty," promised Mehy.

The two men climbed into the chariot, and the charioteer whipped up his horses.

"This must have been a terribly painful time for you, General," said Bay.

"I had one overriding obsession, Tjaty: persuading Prince Amenmessu not to attack the North."

"For my part, I'm afraid I didn't manage to persuade Seti to put our plan into action, because he always hoped peace would return, despite my gloomy predictions."

"In his wisdom, Pharaoh saw further than we did."

"Indeed, General, but we must close this painful chapter of our history."

"The Master of the Place of Truth is not very diplomatic, and tends to see the world only through the eyes of his Brotherhood. I wouldn't like him to cause himself serious problems."

"I have full powers, General, and Seti's demands will be met."

Mehy reined in his joy: this time, Nefer's fate was sealed. By opposing the king, he would attract his fury and leave the Brotherhood with no defense except Paneb. Paneb terrified many people, but Serketa had a plan to get rid of him, and the future looked to be set fair at last.

Sobek was standing in the middle of the roadway, in front of the Fifth Fort. Mehy's chariot halted less than a pace from him.

"Go and fetch the Scribe of the Tomb and the Master," ordered the general. "Tjaty Bay, emissary of Pharaoh Seti II, wants to see them immediately."

Sobek realized from Mehy's tone that the matter was serious, and he set off at once; but he came back with only the Wise Woman.

"Am I to understand," asked Bay, "that your husband is working on the tomb of Amenmessu, in the Valley of the Kings?"

"Yes, he is," replied Ubekhet.

The chariot turned round and headed toward the valley. The road that led to it was so forbidding that the troops fell silent. Afraid of being attacked by the spirits roaming the mountains, they remained tightly packed together, constantly glancing up at the crests of the hills.

They arrived at the entrance to the valley unharmed but with their nerves on edge. Faced with such a show of force, the Nubian guards on duty lowered their weapons.

"Are we permitted to pass through this stone gateway?" asked Bay anxiously.

"You have full powers, Tjaty, have you not?" said Mehy.

The two men ventured into the sacred domain, which left Bay speechless. Mehy was impatient to catch the Master red-handed, working in the tomb of Amenmessu and thus proving his treason.

Penbu was guarding the storeroom where the craftsmen kept their equipment, and he confronted them, brandishing his short sword.

"I am accompanying Tjaty Bay, who is acting in the name of Pharaoh," said Mehy. "Is the Master here?"

Penbu nodded.

"Take us to him."

"I'm not allowed to go any farther."

"Then call him!"

Penbu imitated the sound of an owl hooting, and the cry echoed strangely in the rocky silence of the Valley of the Kings.

A few minutes later Paneb appeared, carrying a large pickax; his hair was tousled, his body covered with stone dust.

"Leave this place instantly," he commanded, his eyes filled with anger.

"I am Tjaty Bay. King Seti has entrusted me with an urgent mission, and I have full powers to carry it out."

"We are accompanied by a large company of soldiers," added Mehy.

"What do you want?"

"To see the Master," replied Bay.

"He is overseeing work. You can see him this evening, in the village."

"I'm sorry, but it's extremely urgent."

"What work?" cut in Mehy.

"I don't have to answer you."

"Go and find him, Paneb."

Paneb gripped the handle of his pickax more tightly. He'd

gladly have used it to kill these intruders, but it would probably be better to consult the Master first.

▲

Nefer's calm fascinated the general. Bay's presence showed that Seti had once again taken up the reins of power and that the Place of Truth must submit by taking responsibility for its errors; but the leader of the Brotherhood retained a royal bearing, as though he were still the master of the game.

"Did you have a good journey, Tjaty?" asked Nefer.

"To be frank, I don't always enjoy the motion so characteristic of a boat, and I prefer our old Egyptian earth. But as soon as the pharaoh learned of his son's death, he ordered me to come to Thebes to put an end to the difficult period that has placed our land in peril. I assume that you have reopened Seti's House of Eternity, to continue its construction?"

"Not yet, Tjaty."

"Then what work are your craftsmen doing?"

"We are completing Amenmessu's burial chamber."

"Is he depicted . . . as a pharaoh?"

"Tradition has been respected."

Mehy rejoiced inwardly. As always, the Master was incapable of lying.

"After his death," said the tjaty, "you should have destroyed his tomb in order to wipe out the traces of his usurpation."

"You don't know the Place of Truth very well, Tjaty. The villagers unanimously rejected that solution, and you won't find a single craftsman willing to raise his hand against the work that has been carried out."

Mehy had not been expecting so much. Nefer was condemning not only himself but his entire community. Nothing could be more stupid than this righteousness, which was incapable of adapting to circumstances and drawing profit from a situation. He could already picture Nefer and his brothers, arrested, sentenced, and deported to a copper mine where they would end their days; and the village open and deserted, with the Stone of Light and the other secrets of the Place of Truth in his hands. All that remained was for him to honor his promises to the traitor, who had been wholly ineffective. Mehy would entrust that little problem to Serketa.

"You should have realized," the tjaty continued, "that Seti would not leave matters as they stood."

"I have told you the Brotherhood's position, and it will not alter. Since Pharaoh is our supreme master, he must do with us as he wishes."

"Seti knew you as little as I must admit I did. He was afraid that, to please him and to save your own life, you would have destroyed his son's House of Eternity. It is time to restore harmony and unity to the Two Lands, and to forget the reign of Amenmessu, but Pharaoh is anxious for you to finish his son's tomb as quickly as possible. Thanks to General Mehy's respect for a dead prince of the royal blood, the mummification is taking place, and the rites will be celebrated on his Osiran body. Afterward, Master, you shall continue work on Seti's House of Eternity."

—— 58 ——

Before collapsing onto his bed, Mehy had wrecked his bedchamber. Furniture overturned, fabrics torn, mirrors broken: it was a distressing sight. But Serketa's main concern was to calm her husband by applying cool towels to his forehead.

"That damned Bay!" he raged. "He let me believe Seti was at last going to act like a king. And what does Seti do? He practices forgiveness and tolerance!"

"When the tjaty spoke with the leading scribes and officials in Thebes, he didn't criticize you in any way."

"No, but he didn't confirm me in my offices, either! He's going to report to the king, and no one can tell what Seti will decide to do." Mehi flung the towel away from him and sat up. "But you're right, the situation could be worse. The tjaty will never be an ally, though. He's deeply attached to the royal couple and will serve only them."

"You're still the strongest man of Thebes," said Serketa, "and that's what matters."

"Yes, but for how long? If Bay separates me from my army, I'll have no strength left."

"We wouldn't accept that decision, and neither would your men."

The general stood up and walked into the bathing room, where he splashed himself with scented water, as if it would wash away his failures.

"The real obstacle still in my way is the Place of Truth. It's humiliated me and is stopping me from reaching my goal. I must have the Stone of Light, Serketa, I must have that supreme weapon!"

"Now that Egypt is reunited, the village's life will soon return to normal, and then our informant will be able to move about much more freely."

"So far he's found out absolutely nothing about where the stone is hidden!"

"We mustn't be pessimistic, my sweet love," said Serketa. "But we may need to be a bit more active."

"What do you mean?"

"The soul of the Brotherhood is its leader. So long as Nefer leads the Place of Truth, it will seem indestructible. He derives strength from the trials he undergoes, and the more fearsome they are, the stronger he becomes. The whole structure grows more solid, day after day, because of his presence."

Mehy grew calmer and considered his wife's words for a long time.

Then he said, "I hadn't seen the truth so clearly before—it's as if I was blinded by its sheer simplicity. How should we fight Nefer?"

"By depriving him of his closest, most effective supporters," said Serketa. "But even that won't be enough, because the Brotherhood's spirit lives in the Master's heart."

"What do you suggest?"

"Can't you guess, my tender darling?"

Mehy had killed many men without hesitation, but at the thought of killing the Master, even though the man was his worst enemy, he hesitated.

"Surely you aren't afraid of him?" said Serketa sweetly.

"Killing him won't be that easy."

"But it is essential, sweet love," she purred, "though it's true that it will be particularly difficult, because the network of magical protection that surrounds him seems to make him invulnerable. Fortunately, I find the idea exciting, and I shall find the chink in his armor."

"Have you something in mind?"

"An idea, just an idea—but something much more effective than thousands of soldiers."

"What is it?"

She pressed her luscious lips against his. "Inside . . . I shall kill him from inside."

▲

A ray of sunlight lit up the naked bodies of Turquoise and Paneb, who had made love with the abandon of adolescents. His subtle caresses still drove her mad with desire, and he remained enchanted by the splendor of a woman whose supple, sensual body was the complete expression of beauty. All Turquoise had to do was lay her hand gently on her lover's skin, and it unleashed a torrent that she had no desire to resist. Each intimate embrace brought new happiness, and they never tired of each other. Stretched out on top of him, she looked into his eyes and saw, already burning there, the next flame that would engulf them both.

"I must go," she said. "The Wise Woman is waiting for me in the temple, so that we can draw up a list of the objects belonging to the worship of Hathor. Uabet should really be doing it, but she's been excused because of her pregnancy."

Although he yearned to hold her back, Paneb did not try. At least she did not forbid him to gaze at her admiringly as she did her hair.

"When will you begin work again in Seti's tomb?" she asked.

"Next week."

Amenmessu's funeral ceremonies had been conducted by the high priest of Amon and the Master of the Place of Truth; and they had taken place according to the pharaonic ritual, with all the desired solemnity. After the ceremony, Nefer had placed the Brotherhood's seal upon the closed door of the tomb. So ended the brief adventure of the son of Seti II, whose reign was continuing as if nothing serious had happened. Once again, the office of pharaoh had overcome individual conflicts.

"You seem worried, Paneb."

"I used a particular style and I'm wondering if the king will ask me to change it. I may have to begin all over again."

"Are you worried you may have too much work?"

"Far from it, but I wouldn't like to have to give up those paintings, especially the ones of the ritual objects being carried during the funeral ceremony, because they taught me the simplicity of the Line."

"The whole village is talking about that innovation."

"But Seti hasn't approved it yet."

Turquoise put on a long red dress, which outlined the contours of her body. "Have confidence in your talent," she said. "It has never let you down."

He reached out for her, but as usual she escaped his grasp.

▲

North Wind trotted briskly toward Nefer's little estate, where the five peasants provided by the state were working. Paneb followed the donkey, which knew the way better than he did and had no doubts about the right direction to take.

Uabet had suddenly had a yearning for fresh zucchini and she could not wait; so her husband had taken it on himself to satisfy it, with the agreement of the Scribe of the Tomb.

When the donkey stopped, Paneb thought it was mistaken, for there was nobody in the field. Then he spotted some men stretched out, sound asleep, in the shade of a large tamarisk tree. One of them was even snoring loudly. A kick in the plumpest backside awoke a short, fat man who let out a squawk worthy of Bad Girl. His comrades opened their eyes.

"Is this how you take care of Nefer's fields?" said Paneb.

"Who on earth are you?" asked the fat man.

"Someone who's going to give you back your taste for work."

A badly shaven beanpole got to his feet. "There are five of us. Do you think you're impressing us?"

"Well he's impressing me," admitted the fat man.

"Yes, well, you're a reasonable man," said Paneb. "I'll break your head last—unless, of course, you all get on and do the work you're paid to do."

Realizing that the others would not support him, the beanpole tried to run away. But North Wind butted him hard and sent him flying into the thistles. The donkey could not understand why these delicacies made the human being roar so loudly.

"I'm Paneb the Ardent and I need zucchini. Judging from the neglected state of this field and the kitchen garden, I may have to leave empty-handed. This kind of disappointment puts me into a terrible mood—and I do mean terrible."

"I know where there are some," quavered the fat man, "and I'll go and fetch you some straightaway."

"When you've done that, get to work. If this field isn't properly cultivated, we'll sort the matter out among ourselves, before Nefer submits a complaint."

"You will both be satisfied," promised the fat man.

"I'm sure you will; but I shall check. Each day, at a different time, North Wind will make a tour of inspection."

"Is he as rigorous as you?"

"Well, he's like me, it's true. He'll tell me what he's seen, and don't expect any lenience from him."

The fat man gaped at the big donkey, who was grazing in a patch of thistles. "You mean . . . he can talk?"

"In my village, extraordinary things happen. Don't you know that the Wise Woman's magical powers are comparable to those of the queen of Egypt?"

The five peasants huddled together. Even the beanpole no longer played the braggart.

"She hasn't put a curse on us, has she?" asked the fat man anxiously.

"Not yet. But be careful not to make her angry."

▲

For North Wind, the weight of two baskets of zucchini was nothing. He led the way back to the village while Paneb walked behind, whistling a folk tune.

"That's pretty," smiled an attractive young brunette, who was walking close to him.

"What's your name, pretty one?"

"Yema. Round here, everyone knows I've got a green thumb. If you want, I'll provide you with good vegetables."

"Why not?"

"Where are you from?" she asked.

"The craftsmen's village."

"Oh, so you know lots of secrets! When will you come back?"

"In a few days."

"You'll see," she said. "I'll show you wonderful things."

59

Imuni loved tracing people's ancestry, and while poring over the village archives he had made a fascinating discovery: through complex family connections, he could claim to be related to Nefer the Silent, that meant he could demand an adoption that would be much more legitimate than Paneb's. Unfortunately, there were still a few links missing, but he had high hopes of constructing a credible chain if he could only gain access to the most ancient documents, which the Scribe of the Tomb kept in his office.

However did Kenhir manage, at his age, to work at the same rate and still deal with the smallest detail as rigorously as ever? Some whispered that Niut's liveliness was no stranger to this tireless dynamism, but the young woman remained indifferent to unpleasant comments, and everyone recognized that she had an exceptional quality: the ability to put up with the old scribe's impossible character.

Each day, the strange couple's home became more attractive, thanks to Niut's hard work and her taste for well-made furniture, precious fabrics, and bright colors. Although this unbridled luxury cost Kenhir a great deal, he had given up fighting.

"Kenhir, I've finished the inventory of copper chisels and lamp wicks," said Imuni.

"Have you checked the accounts?"

"Everything's correct."

"No accusations against Paneb this time?"

"Thanks to you, the village is run perfectly."

"I detest compliments," said Kenhir, "because they always hide devious aims. I know yours: you dream of taking my place and you lament the fact that my old frame is still holding up well. Think a little less about your future and concern yourself

more with the present, for you have a great deal still to learn before you're fit to become Scribe of the Tomb."

"I assure you that—"

"It's no use lying."

"When I've finished my work, I'd like to read the history of
the village, to get to know it better."

Kenhir was astonished. "That's not a bad idea."

"I've already looked at a few documents, but the most precious ones are kept in your office. Will you grant me access to
them?"

"I see no reason why not." At last, thought Kenhir, the
pedant was changing his attitude. Instead of persecuting Paneb
and attacking the craftsmen's behavior, he was taking an interest
in the Place of Truth itself.

▲

Uabet's pregnancy was progressing well, and she had not put
on much weight, but her desire for fresh vegetables continued
to grow. So Paneb had gone several times to Nefer's estate.
This had been put to rights by the five peasants, who had rediscovered their will to work, aided by substantial payments in
kind.

One day, he was filling the panniers North Wind carried
when a very gentle hand was laid on his arm.

"I have some splendid asparagus to offer you," said pretty
Yema, her dark eyes shining.

"Are your prices reasonable?"

"We'll haggle, no doubt you'll persuade me to lower
them."

"All right, but I'm in a hurry."

The young woman wore only a short tunic, which hid little
of the delicate body she displayed with consummate artistry.
She danced rather than walked as she led him to a little hut in
the reeds.

"Take care, the door is low."

Hardly had he entered the modest dwelling when Yema

took off her tunic. Naked, she rubbed herself against him. "You're so strong! Make love to me."

Paneb lifted her off her feet and held her away from him. "I am the one who takes the initiative, little girl, and I'm fortunate enough to have everything I want. You are very pretty, but I don't want you. Get dressed and go and look after your asparagus."

He set the sulky girl back on the ground and left the hut. Yema followed him. Naked, she climbed up onto the top of a bank of earth.

"Help!" she screamed. "I've been raped!"

The five peasants turned to look.

Paneb spun round and slapped her. "That's quite enough of that!"

Yema collapsed in tears.

Paneb threw her tunic at her. "Hurry up and get dressed— and don't ever come near me again."

With Serketa's support, General Mehy was once again the most powerful and respected man in the Theban province. Until Seti arrived, the royal palace remained forbidden to all, and soldiers guarded the doors. Although the atmosphere was calm on the surface, the people were still tense. Tjaty Bay had left for the North without revealing his plans, and no one knew the pharaoh's real intentions, for he remained strangely silent. Perhaps this wait meant he was thinking about how to punish the city that had bowed its guilty head before Amenmessu?

"A letter from Bay," said Serketa nervously.

Mehy's fingers trembled as he touched the wooden tablet. If he had been dismissed, how would he recover from such a defeat?

His eyes rested on the text, which had been written in cursive hieroglyphs. He let out a deep sigh of relief.

"I've been confirmed in my offices, and in addition the king congratulates me on having preserved peace in difficult circumstances. The tjaty asks me to ensure the region's prosperity and protect the Place of Truth unstintingly."

"Does Seti say when he will be arriving?"

"Complete silence on that point."

"Why doesn't he say?" wondered Serketa.

"The king has been greatly affected by the death of his son. Perhaps he's facing difficulties in Pi-Ramses and is reluctant to leave the capital."

"Fortune continues to favor us," purred Serketa.

▲

The starboard crew were back from the Valley of the Kings and were glad to have a rest. Because of the uncertainty about Thebes's future, some of the craftsmen, such as Karo or Thuty, were openly pessimistic. A fault in the rock had delayed the work, and the Master had had to take precautions to prevent the paintings from being damaged.

"Kenhir has had a bad dream," said Karo. "With a king who dared take the name Seti, we can expect the worst."

"You've seen that he is no war monger," objected Fened.

"He didn't start a civil war," said Casa, "but he won't forgive Thebes for submitting to Amenmessu."

"There was nothing else it could have done," said Gau, "and Seti will understand that."

The temperature had suddenly fallen. A chill wind announced the coming of a winter that promised to be harsher than those that had gone before.

"Tomorrow," decreed the Scribe of the Tomb, "we must cleanse the whole village. The hot weather is over, and the houses and public places must be purified. Who will undertake the cleansing of our meeting place?"

The traitor jumped at the chance. As no one enjoyed the task, his colleagues would see how dedicated he was.

▲

The entire village was smoking, drowned in the strong disease- and insect-killing fog. Ebony, Bad Girl, and the other domestic animals had taken refuge with the lay workers and were playing with the children, who were being looked after by Obed the blacksmith.

Alone in the Brotherhood's meeting place, which he had cleansed thoroughly, the traitor examined the stone benches on which the craftsmen sat. He saw nothing unusual about any of them.

As he was about to go into the shrine, which he was not permitted to enter, the traitor hesitated. Up to now, he had been guilty of only a few minor sins, and had not yet done anything irredeemable. By violating the sacred space, doing things only the Master was allowed to do, he would be trampling on his oath and would cut himself off from the spirit of the Brotherhood.

Should he renounce the lure of profit, which had guided him for so many years, open his heart to Nefer, and beg for forgiveness?

But the traitor found that the voice of his heart no longer spoke to him. Fundamentally, he had never loved the Place of Truth. The thread of life had led him there, because he sought knowledge and a skill that would allow him to outshine others. Henceforth, he needed a fortune, too, and only treason could offer him that.

He slid back the gilded wooden bolt and opened the doors of the innermost shrine, where stood a cubit-high gold statuette of Ma'at: she whom he should have served all his life, never leaving the path of righteousness.

Feverishly, he removed the statue and felt the plinth, hoping to detect a crack or unevenness that might indicate the presence of a lock. But there was nothing but granite, polished to perfection.

Angrily, the traitor examined each nook and cranny of the little shrine, in the hope of finally discovering the hiding place of the Stone of Light.

In vain.

"Is there someone in the meeting place?" called a low voice; the traitor recognized it as Hay's.

In panic, he replaced the statuette of Ma'at, closed the doors of the innermost shrine, bolted them, and went back into the smoke-filled meeting hall.

"Yes, I am."

"I was afraid you'd been taken ill."

"No, no, all's well."

"Then leave the smoke to work," advised Hay, "and come and join us to celebrate a happy event: Uabet the Pure has just given birth to a daughter."

—— 60 ——

Ignoring his infirmity, young Saptah continued to study hard in the library of the Temple of Amon at Pi-Ramses, where the priests watched benevolently over him.

Whenever he could find a little time for himself, Bay liked to talk to the boy about his progress in mathematics and literature. Indifferent to the outside world, the lad had no taste for anything but his research, and he often had to be reminded that eating, even at the most basic level, was essential.

Saptah talked only to the tjaty, who, by small degrees, was initiating him into the workings of central government and the running of the Two Lands. His attentive pupil had a remarkable memory and always asked pertinent questions.

These encounters were the only moments of joy for the tjaty in an extremely somber atmosphere. Amenmessu's death had affected Seti deeply, and Queen Tausert despaired of seeing him regain his taste for life. She carried out her duties as Great Royal Wife diligently and well, and Bay assisted her unstintingly; but it was the pharaoh who continued to place his seal on major decrees, whenever he could be roused from his torpor.

As he entered the king's office, where for once the king was waiting for him, the tjaty was thinking of the inhabitants of Thebes, who must be wondering anxiously what fate Seti had in store for them. True, Bay had written to General Mehy, confirming him in all his offices, and it was reassuring to have a strong man in the region, the faithful servant of the king and a guarantor of peace; but not even Bay himself knew the king's real intentions.

"Did you work with young Saptah today?" inquired Seti.

"Unfortunately not, Majesty. I had to resolve some problems over the development of the western part of the capital."

"Spend more time with this boy; the priests of Amon speak very highly of him. There are too many courtiers prowling round the throne and not enough upright people who think only of their duty. Saptah is one of them, and you're the only person who can teach him."

"No command could make me happier, Majesty."

"I also want you to take charge of the preparations for my journey."

Bay was taken aback. "Where do you wish to go, Majesty?"

"To Khnum. In the city of Thoth I shall acquire the wisdom I need to continue my reign. I shall go there with Queen Tausert, and we shall ask the Master of Knowledge for that serenity that we have lacked ever since the weight of supreme power fell upon my shoulders."

The decision delighted the tjaty, for it showed that Seti's political intelligence was still intact. A large army was still stationed at Khnum, and the soldiers would welcome the king enthusiastically. By spending some time in that fortified city, the southernmost limit of his kingdom during Amenmessu's domination of Upper Egypt, the pharaoh would send a clear message to the Thebans and all the southern provincial leaders: at the least sign of insubordination, he would take immediate action.

"May I know your longer-term plans, Majesty?"

"I hope that Thoth will dictate my conduct, Tjaty. Without

the precision of the ibis's beak and the span of its wings, the exercise of power is, after all, doomed to mediocrity."

▲

The baby seemed so fragile in his arms that Paneb hardly dared breathe.

"Our daughter is beautiful," he said to Uabet, who was filled with happiness at having pleased her husband. "She'll be as slender and delicate as you."

"But she'll have your strength, too, I'm sure of that."

"Have you chosen her name?"

"As she was born when the moon was full, we shall call her Iuwen."

With her delicate auburn hair, green eyes, and finely shaped ears and lips, Iuwen was an unusually pretty baby.

Aapehti peered at her. "I think she's ugly. And she's a girl—she won't be any good at fighting."

"No," said Uabet, "so you'll have to protect her."

"Not me! Let her get by on her own," and the boy ran out of the house.

"He's becoming unbearable," said Paneb.

"Don't be angry with him," begged Uabet. "Until today, he was an only child; his sister's birth has made him very jealous, and we must understand and forgive him. He'll soon be devoted to her."

"Let's hope you're right."

▲

Two priestesses of Hathor were sent by the Wise Woman to help Uabet, who was exhausted by her daughter's birth. The women of the village had a rule of helping one another, and no woman was left to herself when she was going through a difficult time. The young mother would rest for about ten days before resuming her domestic activities. Because of her frail constitution, Uabet would only breast-feed her daughter for a week, after which she would entrust her to a wet nurse paid for by the state.

"Paneb, come quickly!" It was Pai's voice, and he sounded agitated.

"Has Aapehti done something stupid again?"

"No, the Scribe of the Tomb must see you urgently."

To judge from his expression, Kenhir was having a bad day. "Is there anything you wish to tell me about, Paneb?"

"Apart from becoming the father of a wonderful little girl, I can't think of anything."

"This is no time for jokes, believe me. Do you know a certain Yema?"

"No, I don't think so."

"Think carefully. She's a vegetable seller who works near Nefer's fields. Didn't you go there several times recently?"

"Yes, I did. Oh, this must be about that little brunette who tries to seduce every man who comes within reach."

"She accuses you of raping her."

"What's the little pest playing at? She threw herself at me, it's true, but I pushed her away rather roughly, and I even slapped her."

"Yema has witnesses."

"Who?"

"The five peasants who work for Nefer."

"They're lying! I'm going to break their heads!"

"I forbid you to do any such thing," snapped Kenhir. "You'd only make matters worse."

"Nothing happened, Kenhir. I swear it on my daughter's head!"

"Yema has brought a charge of rape, and it has been declared valid by a judge on the west bank."

"This is completely insane. I'm innocent!"

"I know you well, and don't doubt it for a moment; but the complaint has been brought, and the punishment for rape is death."

"Let me take care of the girl Yema and those five peasants. I'll make them tell the truth, believe me!"

"If you lay a finger on your accusers, your guilt will be confirmed."

"Surely we aren't going to let lies win the day?"

"The process of law must be observed, and that begins by convening the village court, which will decide whether or not to expel you."

"Expel me! But I haven't done anything wrong!"

"Are there witnesses who could clear you?" asked Kenhir.

"Why do I need any?"

"I'm deeply worried about you, Paneb."

▲

Serketa was having her back rubbed by a serving woman, but she found the woman's hands too rough.

"Use more oil," she ordered, "and be gentler. Can't you see I have delicate skin?"

Mehy burst into the room, which was filled with the scent of lilies.

"Seti has just arrived in Khnum," he said. "Officially, he's inspecting the troops responsible for preventing the Thebans from pushing northward."

"I thought peace had been reestablished," said Serketa, dismissing the servant with a disdainful gesture.

"The king's making a show of force, to prove that he's in control and that anyone who tried to rebel would instantly be crushed. In my opinion, it's an excellent move: no one will ever again doubt Seti's determination and abilities."

"Has he made any threats against Thebes?"

"According to my spies, the king has given no clues at all of his intentions."

"Well, I have excellent news," purred Serketa. "One of the obstacles in our way will soon be removed."

The general gripped his wife by the shoulders. "What scheme have you hatched, my tender quail?"

"Thanks to our friend Tran-Bel, a delicious little overpaid trollop has trapped Paneb. Tran-bel also paid a few witnesses to confirm a serious accusation that will destroy the man. One less ally for the Master!"

▲

The court of the Place of Truth was made up of the Scribe of the Tomb, the Master, the Wise Woman, Hay, and two priestesses of Hathor. They had listened to Paneb's explanations, and he, albeit with an enormous effort, had managed to maintain some semblance of calm.

Swearing an oath on a likeness of Ma'at, handed to him by the Wise Woman, he had eventually convinced his judges that he was concealing nothing.

"Does anyone demand the expulsion of Paneb the Ardent?" asked Kenhir.

"We all know he's innocent and the victim of defamation," declared Nefer. "Consequently our role, and mine in particular, is to defend him."

"In view of the seriousness of the accusation and the fact that a charge has been brought," said the Scribe of the Tomb, "it will be difficult to keep Paneb beyond the reach of outside justice."

"As long as he remains within these walls," Hay reminded him, "he'll be safe."

"Then let the outside world judge me!" demanded Paneb. "I want my innocence recognized, not just here but everywhere else, too."

—— 61 ——

The Scribe of the Tomb had demanded that the court trying Paneb must convene before the Temple of Ma'at, inside one of the enclosures at Karnak. The jury was made up of priests, craftsmen, and scribes, and presided over by the Second Prophet of Amon, whom Kenhir considered stern but just. With his shaven head, square shoulders, and stiff gait, the judge did not seem a man given to lenience.

Accuser and accused stood facing him. Pretty Yema did not even glance at Paneb, who had promised to keep calm no matter what the provocation.

"Yema," began the judge, "do you still say that Paneb the Ardent, a craftsman from the Place of Truth, raped you?"

"I do."

"Do you swear it by Ma'at and on the name of Pharaoh?"

"I swear it."

"And you, Paneb, do you swear that you are innocent of the crime of which you are accused?"

"I swear it."

"One of you is therefore a liar and a perjuror," concluded the judge. "Remember that that is a very serious offense that carries a severe penalty, in both this world and the next. Do you wish to retract your oaths?"

Neither Yema nor Paneb did so.

"Tell the court what happened, Yema."

"I was in the hut where I keep my baskets, when Paneb rushed at me like a mad bull. He ripped off my clothes and raped me. As soon as I could escape, I called for help. The five peasants in the next field were witnesses to this horrible attack."

"Come forward," the judge told the peasants. "Do you confirm what Yema has said?"

Unnerved by the solemnity of the place and the judge's stern manner, three of the peasants took a step back, to indicate that they had nothing to say.

"I saw everything," said the beanpole, and the fat man nodded his agreement.

"Are you absolutely sure?" asked the Wise Woman; she wore a formal red dress and earrings of red jasper decorated with gold wires. She gazed steadily at the two peasants; there was no animosity in her eyes, but such perception that the fat man could not hold out for long.

"I saw the man and the girl," he admitted, "but that's all."

"What about your friend?"

"I can't speak for him."

"Well, I still say I saw everything," began the beanpole, but his voice started to shake: he felt his throat tightening, as though a powerful hand were choking him.

"I wish you no harm," said the Wise Woman, "but I warn you that you will not be able to breathe if you continue to lie."

"I . . . I confirm . . ."

The Wise Woman did not lift a finger but continued to gaze at him as his breathing became more and more labored. When an unbearable burning sensation threatened to suffocate him, he gave in.

"I saw no more than the others did," he admitted.

"Did you or did you not witness a rape?" demanded the judge.

"No—no, I didn't!"

Yema was disappointed but not perturbed. "I say that I was raped by Paneb."

"It's your word against mine, you little slut!" exclaimed Paneb.

The interruption annoyed the judge. "Can you produce a witness who can clear you?" he asked.

"I swear to you that I'm innocent!"

"And Yema swears that you are guilty. Look at her, so frail and defenseless. How could she have resisted you?"

The Scribe of the Tomb cut in. "You are behaving like an accuser, and you are exceeding your role as judge. The members of the court should take no account of your words. And if you take sides again in such a flagrant manner, I shall demand that you be replaced."

"Very well, very well . . . But has Paneb any defense apart from invective?"

"He has," confirmed the Wise Woman.

"Please explain."

Paneb looked attentively at Ubekhet, and a strange energy entered him. It communicated with him without speaking, directly from thought to thought, and he saw a face in his mind's eye.

"Bring North Wind before the court," he said.

"Is he a friend of yours?" asked the judge.

"He's my donkey. Bring him: he'll show everyone who's lying."

The judge hesitated. "This is most irregular."

"An animal never hides the truth," said the Wise Woman. "It embodies a divine power that cannot lie."

"Does the accuser agree?" asked the judge.

Yema thought, "The donkey will go toward its master." Naively, he thought he could impress the court by using this trick, but in fact it would work against him. So she agreed.

▲

The donkey trotted beside the Wise Woman along the path to the Temple of Ma'at, and halted in front of the judge.

"North Wind, you are here to bear witness in a case of rape. Do you understand the gravity of the situation, and can you indicate the person who has lied during this trial?"

The donkey pawed a flagstone with his front left hoof. A murmur ran round the jurors, who acknowledged the validity of the animal's testimony.

"North Wind, point out the liar."

The animal turned his head toward Paneb. Yema gave a satisfied smile.

But then the donkey swung round, went to the young woman, and touched her shoulder with his muzzle.

As though bitten by a snake, she leapt backward. "Surely you aren't going to believe this animal!"

"Why did you lie, Yema?" demanded the judge, his anger plain in his eyes.

"I've told the truth!"

North Wind charged at the liar, knocked her over with his head, and planted his forefeet on her chest.

"He's going to kill me!" she whimpered in fear.

No one helped her.

Although half-suffocating, Yema found her voice. "I lied, I admit it. I made advances to Paneb, and he rejected me. I was so angry that I decided to take my revenge. I was sure he'd be convicted, and I'd have sneered at him while he languished in prison. It was bad, but you have to understand and forgive me—Paneb shouldn't have treated me with such contempt."

"Your lies could have had terrible consequences," said the judge. "The members of the jury should not forget that as they pronounce their sentence."

"I ask them to be lenient," said Paneb. "Yema is very young, and the fright she's just had will be a lesson to her."

▲

Yema had been sentenced to grow vegetables and bring them to the Place of Truth for a year, in exchange for a tiny wage. She thought she had got off lightly. The jurors had believed her passionate claims to be a spurned young seductress, and the judge had taken his investigation no further.

She had not yet had a chance to speak to Tran-Bel about the promised reward which, in spite of her unexpected failure, was still owed to her. So, as soon as the trial was over, she headed for the Libyan's warehouse.

As soon as he spotted her, Tran-Bel led her into the little room where he kept his records. "What are you doing here, you little fool?" he demanded.

"Paneb was acquitted."

Tran-Bel ran his hand through his black hair. "Acquitted? What on earth are you saying?"

"It was because of his donkey, North Wind. The Wise Woman bewitched the jury, the false witnesses retracted their evidence, and the donkey pointed me out as the one who'd lied."

"You're completely mad, Yema!"

"That's exactly what happened, I assure you, and Paneb left the court a free man."

"Did you mention me at all?"

"No, of course not."

"That's as well for you, my girl. You're not lying, I hope?"

"I was sentenced to serve the Place of Truth for a year—that is all I came away with. Now I want my reward."

"You are to take the first cargo boat leaving for the North and will leave Egypt for Canaan, where you'll work as a servant for one of my friends who is a farmer. Once there, you'll change your name and thus escape from Egyptian justice."

"But I want to stay here."

"You failed, you idiot, and you have no choice. Above me, there are people who won't accept your mistake."

"That means—"

"That means you must leave as soon as possible—and forever—if you want to go on living. You must leave the country tomorrow. And pray that the demons will spare you."

Terrified, the young girl agreed.

Tran-Bel omitted to mention that his farmer friend would use Yema as a slave, subject to all the whims of his peasants, but he was preoccupied with thinking how he was to explain matters to his employers so as to emerge from the episode as white as a piece of first-grade linen.

----- 62 -----

The winter was really harsh in this fourth year of Seti II's reign. An icy wind swept the west bank of Thebes, which was accustomed to milder temperatures, even in the bad season. Some spoke of a punishment inflicted on the land by emissaries of the formidable goddess Sekhmet, angered by the weakness of a king whose plans were still unclear.

When the caravan of donkeys arrived at the Place of Truth, the Scribe of the Tomb was already up and about, wrapped in a thick coat.

He hailed the head donkey driver. "Have you brought the firewood?"

"Not a single bag."

"But I stressed that it was urgent!"

"The government didn't give me any. Frankly, nobody's got any firewood at the moment."

Kenhir went to tell the Master.

"We must find some at once," said Nefer. "The houses are icy cold, and several people are suffering from breathing problems. Without warmth, they'll get worse, especially Paneb's daughter."

"Our stocks seemed more than enough. Who'd have expected the weather to be so bad for so long?"

Paneb broke in angrily, "I accept that I must burn my bed and my furniture, but what will I have left then? I want to know who's responsible for this shortage."

"I am," said Nefer.

"No, you're taking responsibility for other people's mistakes—but that still doesn't get us any firewood."

"You're right," said Nefer, "taking responsibility isn't enough. So I'm going to go and find some."

"You can't take that risk. It's out of the question. I shall see to it myself. Will the Scribe of the Tomb give me official permission?"

"I can't do that," said Kenhir, "so you'll have to watch out for patrols."

"Why don't you go and pester the government?"

"Because I hoped there'd be some firewood in this morning's delivery," said Kenhir, swaying as a gust of wind almost knocked him over. He was much put out by Paneb's insolence, but before he could tell him off Paneb went rushing to Imuni's house.

"Open the storeroom, and give me the best ax," he ordered the assistant scribe.

"Why?"

"Hurry up, Imuni—I'm in no mood to listen to your stupid questions."

"Cutting wood without permission is forbidden, and—"

Paneb seized Imuni under the arms and lifted him off the ground. "If you don't give me that ax in the next few seconds, I shall take all your wood—including the tablets you write on."

▲

The three guards watched the giant for a long time as he chopped down an old, bleached-looking sycamore tree, most of whose branches were dead. Despite the cold wind, he worked bare-chested and swung his heavy ax rhythmically.

"He's breaking the law," said the eldest guard, "but he's also very big."

"If rumor can be believed," observed a bearded colleague, "this might be a craftsman from the Place of Truth, Paneb the Ardent, who can beat nine men single-handedly."

"How can we be sure?"

"Look at his donkey—it's a giant like its master. And everyone knows Paneb has a monster of a donkey."

"Nine men? Really?"

"There are only three of us . . . And have you seen the size of his ax? If we attack him, he'll defend himself. Shouldn't we wait a while before trying to arrest him?"

"You're right, we should weigh up the risks."

Paneb had long since spotted the guards, but he wasn't worried. After filling North Wind's panniers with dry wood and collecting a sizeable load himself, he set off back to the village and walked past the three men.

"Good day, friends," he said. "You were right not to interrupt me."

▲

"This shortage of firewood is unacceptable," said Kenhir angrily. "You know as well as I do that the Place of Truth is a top priority."

Mehy was having difficulty in being as pleasant as usual. On the one hand, the failure of Tran-Bel's plan to destroy Paneb had depressed him; on the other, the soldiers from the barracks on both the west and east banks were all complaining of the cold, but no one dared cut down trees, for fear of infringing a royal privilege and angering Seti.

"I haven't forgotten that," he said, "but my powers are limited. I've written to the king, asking him to allow me to cut down the old trees and to send us wood from Canaan, but I haven't had an answer yet. I don't even know if Seti's still in Khnum."

"Haven't you got a few sacks of charcoal left?"

"Not one, or I'd already have had it delivered to you."

Kenhir was persuaded of the general's good faith. "In that case, we must sort out the matter ourselves, and I require immunity for the craftsman who will bring us back wood."

"That will be Paneb, I assume?"

The Scribe of the Tomb did not reply.

"I'm willing to ignore any guards' reports I receive about him, but he must be discreet."

"Thank you, General. You are indeed the protector of the Place of Truth."

▲

Thanks to Paneb, the villagers were warmer and the sick were no longer in danger. On his return, he cradled his daughter in his arms, watched lovingly by Uabet.

"It'll be time for dinner soon," he said. "Where's Aapehti?"

"At school, being punished. Yesterday, he was rude to the assistant scribe, who was correcting his mathematics homework."

"That man Imuni will never leave us in peace!"

Paneb kissed the child lovingly and handed her back to her mother. Then he went to Imuni's office, where the assistant scribe was speaking crossly to the Master and the Scribe of the Tomb.

"I have grave irregularities to report, and I ask that the court be convened, so that it may pronounce exemplary sentences."

"Are you trying to attack me through my son?" asked Paneb.

Imuni looked surprised. "You? No, not at all."

"What are these irregularities?" asked Nefer.

"First, Userhat has used much more alabaster than he was allowed, so he must be working on his own account and not telling me who the statues are for."

"They aren't for anyone," said the Master. "On my orders, he's making alabaster offertory tables for Seti."

Imuni turned red. "No one told me about it."

"Before making accusations, be sure you know the facts. Next?"

"Gau's wasting far too much papyrus."

"No, he isn't," cut in Paneb. "He's drawing the sketches I shall use for the paintings, and we must have as much papyrus as we need."

Kenhir nodded. "Imuni, you must stop making accusations like these. You're so seldom right."

Imuni swallowed his resentment. Fortunately, his research into his ancestry was going well, and he'd soon have his revenge.

▲

As the postal service had returned to normal after Amenmessu's funeral, the traitor was once more writing to his coconspirators, and he had received a coded message telling him to go to the mound of the ancestors, not far from the village. On their rest days, the craftsmen often went there to pay homage to the primordial gods who, before allowing creation to develop, had chosen to establish their earthly home there.

Since the specter of civil war had faded, it was again possible to leave the village. But the traitor knew Sobek would be as vigilant as ever, so he had not been among the first to cross the Nile to visit members of their families or deal with private business matters.

He took advantage of a morning's rest to walk to the mound of the ancestors. At first he was followed by one of Sobek's men, but the guard, once reassured, returned to the Fifth Fort.

In the middle of a thicket of acacias, a small shrine sheltered the tomb of the gods. The peace that reigned here was that of another world, to which the traitor had long since ceased to be sensitive.

"No one is watching us," confirmed Serketa. She was wearing the white robes of a priestess who had come to lay an offering on the altar of the ancestors. "Have you at last found the Stone of Light's hiding place?"

"Unfortunately not, but I haven't given up hope."

"You'll have a much better chance of succeeding once you remove the main obstacle."

"What is it?"

"The Master himself."

"What do you mean?" asked the traitor, his voice shaking.

"Nefer must be killed. Once he's dead, the village will lose its power and the way to the Stone will be revealed."

"You're ordering me to commit a crime!"

"Think: there's no better solution. Of course, you must arrange matters so that suspicion falls on the craftsman you hate most."

"I can't do it."

"Nefer's death will bring about the death of the Brotherhood, and your reward will be enormous, believe me."

"It's too dangerous."

"Tell me when you've made your plans," said Serketa. "We'll give you ten times the fortune you've already earned."

—— 63 ——

It was the dead of night, and Aapehti tiptoed over to the little wooden bed where his sister lay sleeping. She was always smiling, and his parents adored her, but he hated her more every day. His teachers were always punishing him harshly, and he spent more time carrying out chores for the village than he did enjoying himself with his friends. All he wanted to do was wrestle and prove his strength, and he was bored in this world of craftsmen and priestesses.

Iuwen, by contrast, would no doubt be everything that was perfect. She'd always be obedient, which would delight her parents, and he'd be completely ignored. So the boy had decided to act before it was too late. By suffocating her with her own swaddling clothes, he'd rid himself of this dangerous rival.

At the very instant he laid a hand on the bed, Paneb's powerful fist seized him by the hair.

"What are you doing, Aapehti?"

The boy didn't cry, in spite of the pain; but his efforts to escape were futile.

"I wanted to see if she was asleep."

"Liar! You were planning to harm her, weren't you?" Paneb flung his son to the ground like a bundle of dirty laundry. "If you'd succeeded, I'd have broken every bone in your body. From now on, you are responsible for Iuwen's safety. And you'd better not make a single mistake."

▲

"Has he agreed?" Mehy asked his wife.

"Not yet."

"If there's any sense left in his head, he won't do anything so insane."

"Well, I think he will. I promised him a glittering fortune, and he won't be able to resist the temptation."

"A craftsman from the Place of Truth killing his Master— it's unthinkable."

"Our ally isn't like the others. All his life he's betrayed people, and he's done it so cleverly that no one's realized the truth. There's only one step left for him to climb, and he'll climb it."

"Because of that damned Brotherhood, we failed time and again. Your plan's too crazy to work."

"I know the traitor well by now. Ambition and greed have

eaten away at his heart so much that they've turned him into a demon of darkness, and nothing will make him draw back."

"You seem very sure of yourself," said Mehy.

"The Master isn't the only one to draw strength from the trials he undergoes. The Brotherhood has resisted us for too long, and I hate failing."

"Killing a man isn't easy, and our man's a coward, isn't he?"

"Of course he is, and he'll kill like a coward, by having an innocent man accused. He doesn't realize that he's already decided to act, because he still has to find a way of killing Nefer without getting caught. But don't worry, he'll find a way."

▲

The pharaoh had spent the whole day, alone, in the Temple of Thoth, begun by Ramses the Great and completed by his son Meneptah. Seti himself had commissioned sculptors from the royal workshop to produce a series of offertory scenes, and he had waited for them to be finished before speaking with the god of knowledge.

During their stay in Khnum, Queen Tausert had not once reproached the king for his silence, as if she recognized the need for this long meditation. Perhaps it would enable him to emerge from the interminable period of suffering that had drained him of energy.

While Seti was consulting the priests of Thoth, who had inherited the knowledge of thousands of years, the queen was dealing with matters of state. In constant contact with Bay, who had stayed in the capital, she gave instructions and answered the many questions that inevitably arose.

At once firm and gentle, the Great Royal Wife had managed to charm the dignitaries of the great city of Middle Egypt, and the high priest of Thoth himself spoke in glowing terms of her; he saw her as the plinth of the goddess Ma'at, on whom the entire country rested.

Tausert was writing to Bay to resolve a problem over the taxation of imported foodstuffs when Seti entered the huge office, whose windows looked out over the Temple of Thoth. The king wore the serene expression of a man whose burden had been lightened.

"Is there still a shortage of firewood?" he asked.

"No, Majesty. I've had enough brought from Canaan for all our provinces to be supplied."

"I admire you, Tausert—seldom has a Great Royal Wife carried out her office with such efficiency. Without you, Egypt would have crumbled."

"You have never ceased to be Pharaoh, and Pharaoh has never ceased to watch over his people's well-being."

Seti gazed out at the gentle rays of the setting sun as they turned the temple walls to gold.

"This city is wonderful, isn't it?" he said. "It exudes peace, and its priests follow the path of Thoth. No one ought to disturb its peace, but what have I done? I've filled it with soldiers, and the burning breath of war almost engulfed the valley of tamarisks where the great temple stands."

"Your sculptors have built upon the work of your predecessors," said Tausert.

"That's small compensation. The time has come to leave Khnum and free it from my troops."

"Where are we going, Majesty?"

"To Thebes."

▲

"A little shorter at the back," Ched told Renupe, who was exercising his talents as village barber.

"Kenhir says Seti is approaching Thebes with his army."

"Then he must eventually arrive."

"People are whispering that the king is filled with the anger of Set, and that he'll take savage revenge on the city because it defied him."

"Don't agonize," said Ched. "Just accept what fate brings."

"What if Seti's soldiers don't spare the village?"

"The Master might order us to take up the weapons we have

made and defend ourselves to the death. What more could we hope for?"

"But I want to live!"

"There are many ways of living, friend, but none of them could ever replace freedom. Whatever you do, don't make a mess of cutting my hair. In moments of crisis, one must be supremely elegant."

▲

It was no longer a rumor: Seti was on his way. General Mehy had taken up residence in his headquarters on the east bank, and no information was filtering out. Birds of ill omen were everywhere, a sign that Set's fury would destroy the city of Amon, and the people were becoming more and more frightened.

In the village, Userhat, Ipuy, and Renupe had sculpted several stelae, on which were engraved different numbers of protective snakes: seven, ten, twelve, or eighteen. They would be placed close to the village's two gates and bar the way to evil forces.

Hour after hour, the atmosphere grew heavier and heavier. The craftsmen no longer went to the Valley of the Kings or tended their homes and their Houses of Eternity, as their existence was unthreatened. Led by the Wise Woman, the priestesses called upon Hathor, in the hope that love would triumph over hatred.

"Our ancestors were more fortunate than we are," Paneb said to Nefer. "The times weren't so troubled, and the Brotherhood's unity wasn't compromised."

"They faced other dangers, and we must face ours with one single desire: to safeguard the work of the Stone of Light. Come with me, my son."

The Master's tone impressed Paneb, who followed him to the temple. They crossed the courtyard and entered the first chamber, from which a narrow staircase led up to the roof. The sun was setting, and there was not a cloud in the sky.

Nefer presented Paneb with a small ebony object, about half

a cubit square, with a hole at one corner. Opposite the center of the hole was an engraved line, indicating the position of the plumb line.

"If you look through the hole," said Nefer, "you'll see the highest point of the stars; and I'm going to teach you how to use what we call 'the Instrument of Knowledge,' an instrument made from the central rib of a palm leaf. It will enable you to align the corners of any structure with the cardinal points."

Paneb proved particularly gifted; working with the skies gave him great pleasure.

"You have been initiated into the mysteries of the twelve hours of night," Nefer said, "but you must also know the message of the groups of stars that give the year its rhythm, give you the secret of time, and mark the hours of the rituals."

"Why are you revealing these things to me?"

"So you'll understand that the life of the Place of Truth reflects the life of the stars, and because at some time in the future you may be charged with building a temple. The things I shall teach you tonight will be essential to you."

"But you're the Master!"

"Generations pass, and all that endures is the word of the gods, which is embodied in light or in stone."

The Wise Woman appeared at the top of the staircase. In her left hand, she held the scepter that symbolized the power of Set, whose celestial fire was capable of piercing the most solid materials.

"With this," she told Paneb, "you will measure shadows and obtain a precise orientation based on the movements of the sun. Keep this light in your hand and use it only to build."

The scepter was burning hot, but Paneb's hand was unharmed. He had the feeling that he was holding something almost heavier than he could lift, yet the Wise Woman had handled it with disconcerting ease.

"Let us continue to watch the sky," said Nefer. "You still have much to learn, Paneb."

The anxious village slept. Nefer, Ubekhet, and Paneb spent the night on the roof of the temple, as if the future belonged to them.

———— 64 ————

"What's the latest news from our spies?" Mehy asked his assistant, a young officer.

"Pharaoh has halted at Dendera to pay homage to Hathor. He's moving toward Thebes very slowly, because on the way he's visiting every shrine, large or small, so as to be recognized by the gods, as tradition dictates."

"Has he at last made his intentions known?"

"No, General."

"How is our troops' morale?"

"Not very good. They're waiting for clear orders."

"Here's one: all weapons are to be placed in the barracks, and all Theban soldiers are to prepare to celebrate Seti's arrival."

The officer was relieved. Like many, he had feared Mehy might take inspiration from Amenmessu and stand against the rightful pharaoh, thus causing a bloody war. But the general was proving reasonable and accepting the sovereignty of the Lord of the Two Lands. If Mehy had been less reasonable, the officer would have held his tongue; but since he was putting the interests of Thebes and its people before his own, he spoke.

"General, one of your officers is saying things that may cause you serious problems."

"What things?"

"That you were Amenmessu's right-hand man and that you

lied to Seti, so that, whatever the outcome, your own position would be safeguarded."

Mehy kept his composure. "Who is the man making this contemptible accusation?"

'The captain of archers."

The general was devastated. "I promoted that man from the ranks, I made his career. How can he be so ungrateful?"

"He's hoping that by accusing you he'll be able to save his own head—perhaps even get promoted."

"Whom has he confided in?"

"Only me—he was hoping to win my support. Because I listened to him, he thinks I do support him and that I'll persuade other officers to join us."

"Why are you still loyal to me?"

"Because you're a loyal servant of the state, General, and you think only of Egypt's happiness."

Mehy thought for a moment, then said, "Are you willing to go on letting him think that you're his all, and that you're organizing a plot against me? I want to know whether he'll try to do me harm or give up his sordid plan."

"Wouldn't it be better to arrest him **and** bring him before a military court?"

"First, we must know if he has any accomplices."

"I don't much like this mission, General, but I'll carry it out."

"I shan't forget your dedication," promised Mehy.

▲

"The latest news is alarming," the Master told the craftsmen. "Sobek can't tell what's true and what isn't, but it seems that Seti wants his revenge on Thebes and that General Mehy won't take up arms against him."

"What's to become of us?" wailed Pai.

"The daily deliveries are continuing. Even if they're interrupted, we have enough supplies to last us for several weeks, because the Scribe of the Tomb has been patiently building up our stocks."

"What about water?" asked Gau.

"We had better ration it. If there's a shortage, Kenhir will approach the government and Hay will organize a group of men to go out and find more."

"When will we be able to go back to work in the Valley of the Kings?" asked Fened.

"Everything depends on what the king does. For the moment, we have an urgent task: making the Place of Truth impossible to attack."

"How?"

"By doing our work, which will be useful to the temple at Karnak when it celebrates the next festival in honor of Amon. Sobek, Paneb, and I will go to the boatyard on the west bank to obtain the wood needed to build a new ceremonial ship for the Master of Knowledge."

"In these troubled times, that may be dangerous," said Thuty. "Wouldn't it be better to wait?"

"The Wise Woman believes we have little time left. As soon as we have fetched the wood, the crew will work day and night."

▲

The boatyard was usually buzzing like a hive, but today it was empty. Having no specific orders, the boatbuilders and carpenters had laid down their tools and piled up the long planks of acacia and sycamore inside a wood-shed.

When the trio arrived at the entrance, a guard barred their way, and asked, "Who are you?"

"The Master of the Place of Truth, accompanied by the commander of the guards and a craftsman."

"You're Nefer the Silent himself?"

"The very same," confirmed Paneb.

"I'll tell the foreman."

The foreman was aged around fifty, with broad shoulders and a barrel chest. He did not look very accommodating.

"I wasn't expecting you," he said. "What do you want?"

"Enough wood to build a ritual ship," replied Nefer.

"Have you the necessary written order?"

"Only Pharaoh could give me one."

"Then I'm not obliged to give you what you want."

"Will you help us anyway?"

Many of the craftsmen who worked in the yard were jealous of those of the Place of Truth, who had secrets the shipbuilders could never learn. For the foreman, this was a good chance to even things up a little.

"What if I refuse?"

"You'll put us in a very difficult position, because only you have the high-quality planks needed to make something worthy of Amon."

"At least you're frank," said the foreman.

"I know you think our Brotherhood is arrogant, but we work with wood just as you do, and we just try to make it beautiful— we don't want to offend anyone."

"That big man and the officer with you, are they prepared to take the wood by force?"

"On no account," replied the Master with a smile. "They simply intend to help the donkeys carry it. The decision is yours, and yours alone."

"In exchange for the planks, will you give me the key to your woodworking methods?"

"You already know the methods; the secret is another matter."

"So I won't get any reward for being generous?"

"None, except for the generosity itself."

In Nefer's place, Paneb would have knocked out this obstreperous fellow and seized all the wood he needed—such a second-rate man deserved no better.

"Take what you need," said the foreman, "but give me a written note of how much. I don't want any problems with the government."

"The Scribe of the Tomb will vouch for you."

▲

As soon as Nefer had checked that none of the donkeys was overloaded, the caravan set off, North Wind in the lead. Nefer, Sobek, and Paneb carried the wood the donkeys could not manage.

When they reached the village, the craftsmen began work at once. With short-handled adzes, they removed the roughness from the hull, shaped the ship's rail, and made the stem and sternpost, the piece that supported the rudder; they used long-handled adzes to smooth the keel. Following plans drawn up by the Master and Ched, Didia directed the work, assisted by Paneb.

The sculptors had created a hull composed of a mosaic of small planks, cut with extreme care. The stonecutters had enjoyed fixing the little planks one on top of another, using a two-handled sledgehammer to bang the tenons into the mortices. Although each craftsman had his own particular area of skill, they could all work any material, under the critical eye of Ched, who was quick to point out any small imperfection.

And the ship was born, its prow and poop shaped like lotus blossoms, and its shrine made of gold. The acacia wood was smoothed to perfection, and the whole vessel was breathtakingly beautiful.

"If you hadn't already created your masterwork, this would be it," the Master told Thuty.

"I hate rushing like this," grumbled Thuty. "Without Paneb and Gau's help, I wouldn't have been able to make something good."

"Don't think the work's finished," said Ched. "We must add rams' heads to invoke the presence of Amon, and decorate the perimeter of the shrine roof with royal cobras, whose fiery breath will drive away harm."

"And we mustn't forget the veil that will cover the sides of the shrine," added Nefer. "That will allow us to present the pharaoh with Amon's ship, the natural keeper of secrets."

▲

For the traitor, everything had become clear. The Master had recently had news that he had not passed on to the Brotherhood and which, without any doubt, concerned the Place of Truth. The village's fate must have been sealed dramatically, and Nefer had found the best way to remove its most precious treasure, the Stone of Light: hiding it under a ritual veil, in the shrine of the ship of Amon.

Nefer had no doubt negotiated his own safety with the high priest of Karnak, by offering him this priceless gift. He, the leader of the Brotherhood, was behaving like the lowest coward. Killing him might not be such a great crime after all.

In any case, the traitor had been offered a singular opportunity: Nefer would place the Stone in the golden cabin, certain that no craftsman would dare violate the divine dwelling.

Nefer was wrong.

65

General Mehy's assistant had arranged to meet the captain of archers close to the winepress used to provide the soldiers with wine on festival days.

When the captain got there, the place was deserted, and he waited impatiently, delighted at the prospect of such an influential ally. For a long time, the captain had suspected Mehy of playing a double game and thinking only of his own career; he considered him a cynical, cruel predator, capable of doing absolutely anything to strengthen his power. And the inquiries he had carried out himself, secretly and with great caution, had led him to conclude that the general was a criminal. With the support of Mehy's assistant and other senior officers, he would obtain proof.

Perhaps Mehy had even killed Amenmessu? If so, he would

not hesitate to attack Seti. The captain knew he must warn the king, so that Seti could have the general arrested and sentenced. A few brave soldiers would be enough to strike Mehy down before he could seize power, and he would at last be unmasked. Mehy's assistant could recruit them, though he must be careful not to make the general suspicious.

He heard distant footsteps, then silence fell again.

Why had Mehy's assistant stopped? The captain peered into the darkness, and his muscles tensed as he made out several silhouettes, encircling him.

"Who's there?" he said.

They appeared: thirty or more archers, drawing back their bows and aiming at him.

"Surrender," ordered Mehy.

The captain saw that he could not escape, so he reached for the dagger he wore at his belt.

"Fire!" roared Mehy. "He's going to attack!"

Three archers fired at the same time. The first arrow sank into the captain's left eye, the second into his throat, and the third into his chest. He fell to the ground, dead, and the back of his head struck the rim of the winepress.

Mehy went quickly over to the body and stooped over it. Unseen, he slipped a small piece of papyrus into the man's kilt.

"Well done, archers,' he said. "Without your prompt action, one or more of us would have been wounded. Search the body."

The archers' leader did so. "A piece of papyrus, General,"

"Read it."

"Names—names of senior officers!"

"Read them aloud."

The archers were rooted to the spot. So, just as Mehy had explained to them, Amenmessu's former supporters really had been plotting to kill Seti!

"Arrest the conspirators immediately," ordered Mehy. He was glad to have rid himself of some rather lukewarm supporters; they would soon be replaced by more committed men.

▲

Mehy's assistant waited in the antechamber of the general's luxurious house. It was Serketa who came to meet him, accompanied by her steward.

"How tired you look," she remarked. "Aren't you well?"

"I am quite well, my lady."

She told the steward, "This officer works far too hard. Bring him some date liqueur to restore his strength."

The steward obeyed promptly, and the officer did not have to be asked twice to sample the delicious, aromatic brew.

"Follow me," said Serketa, and she showed her guest into the main hall, with its porphyry pillars.

"Your house is truly wonderful," said the officer.

"I'm quite pleased with it, I must confess. Have you noticed the fine red and black tracery on the ceiling?"

The officer put his wine cup down on a low inlaid table, and looked up at the ceiling.

"My husband won't be long," Serketa said. "He thanks you for having arranged this meeting with the captain of archers. The captain will be surprised to see the general, not yourself, but Mehy will make him see sense."

"The general's lenience surprises me, I must admit. If the captain had been taken before a court, he'd have been sentenced to a severe punishment."

"My husband's often lenient toward his subordinates. That's a good quality, isn't it?"

"Yes, of course, my lady. But he's respected most of all for his authority, which is why I'm so surprised that he's showing mercy."

"So, as far as you know, the captain had no accomplices?"

"None—he assured me so. He was relying on me to form a small group of senior officers hostile to the general."

"Now that that contemptible man is dead, there's only one officer left who wants to harm my husband."

"No, my lady, there's no—"

"You yourself, dear friend. You nearly betrayed him."

Beads of sweat stood out on the officer's brow, and he felt a strange fatigue overwhelming him. "Me? No, I didn't do anything like that."

"I know you were swayed by that archer's lies, and that you doubted my husband's honesty."

"No, I swear I didn't!"

"You're a very bad liar, but it doesn't matter. You have been the general's assistant for far too long."

"I . . . I don't understand." The officer tried to stand straight, but he could not. An icy mist was clouding his sight.

"My husband no longer trusts you, so it's become necessary to kill you, as well as the captain."

"What's . . . wrong with me?"

"Overtiredness and too much alcohol, I expect. When one is as tired as you are, one should drink only water."

A searing pain prevented the officer from breathing. Mouth open, unable to move, he sank into nothingness.

Serketa checked that he was indeed dead, then called to her steward. "Come quickly! Our guest has been taken ill!"

The steward bent over the officer. "It's serious, my lady."

"Send for an army doctor."

"I fear it may be too late."

"What a tragedy! The poor boy was so tired that his heart gave out."

To close the incident, the corpse would be entrusted to Daktair, chief doctor at the palace, who would examine the body and diagnose a heart attack.

Serketa was delighted that her poison was so effective, but she shivered slightly as she thought that, without the officer's naïveté, Mehy's rise to power might have been blocked. But good fortune had served her yet again, and once again her husband was marching forward.

Skillful, slightly built, and swift on his feet, Ipuy was well fitted for climbing onto the roof of the ship's tall cabin and sculpting a frieze of gilded royal cobras round its edge, thus completing the Brotherhood's new masterpiece.

"Let me do it," offered Userhat.

"I'm the head sculptor."

"That doesn't mean you're supple enough for this work."

Ipuy proved as agile as a monkey as he climbed up to his goal, without the aid of scaffolding or a safety rope.

"Come down," said Userhat. "It's dangerous."

"That's what you think."

Ipuy affixed the cobras finely chiseled by his colleagues, refined two of their faces, and then found himself at a corner of the shrine, with nothing to hold on to. For a moment, he hung very still in the void, like a bird about to take flight. But he was only a servant of the Place of Truth, and he fell hard onto the boat's rail.

Everyone knew, from his cries of pain, that he was badly hurt.

"Don't touch him," ordered Nefer. "Paneb, go and fetch the Wise Woman."

Ubekhet hurried up, calmly examined the wounded man, and said, "A fractured collarbone. Nakht and Paneb, lay Ipuy on his back and place a folded cloth between his shoulder blades."

Trusting the Wise Woman's skill, the sculptor made no complaint as it was done.

"Now drag him by the shoulders so that the collarbone is pulled out, reducing the fracture."

They succeeded in doing so without hurting Ipuy too much.

The Wise Woman used two splints covered with linen, placing the first on the inside of the arm and the second underneath.

"Will I be permanently handicapped?" asked Ipuy anxiously.

"Of course not," Ubekhet reassured him. "I shall change the bandages for several days and apply the excellent medicinal honey we possess. The wound is a good, clean one, and there will be no complications."

Ipuy looked up anxiously at the golden shrine. "Did I at least succeed?"

"The work has been completed," replied Nefer.

While Nakht and Paneb carried Ipuy away on a stretcher, Turquoise and two other priestesses of Hathor brought a large golden veil, which would be used to mask the contents of the shrine.

Contents that the traitor was certain he had identified.

—— 66 ——

The ritual of bringing the ship to life took place during the night. The Master and the leader of the port crew came out of the sculptors' workshop carrying something that was hidden under a thick cloth, and laid their precious burden inside the shrine. When the ship was carried in procession around the Temple of Amon, the shrine brought to life the ten entities that made up the visible world: the sun, the moon, air, fire, human beings, other beings that walked on the earth, celestial beings, beings of the water and beings that lived underground. Linking all the forms of life, the ship represented the most complete symbol of the constantly changing energy that maintained the unity of the universe.

After the ceremony, the craftsmen went back to their homes. Ipuy's pain had been calmed by drugs, and he was sleeping peacefully beside his relieved wife.

The ship had been set on a plinth, between the main temple and a little shrine built by Ramses the Great and dedicated to Amon. Because of its sacred nature and the magic power emanating from it, the Master had felt it unnecessary to set a guard on it.

Nevertheless, when he emerged from his house, the traitor took stringent precautions. He began by checking that the domestic animals, Bad Girl and Ebony in particular, were not roaming around the village. Fortunately for him it was a cold night and they preferred to sleep in their houses. Next, he searched around to make sure that there were no traps.

The area seemed deserted, but the traitor stayed very still for a long time, a good distance from the ship. An owl hooted, and jackals called to one another in the mountains, then silence descended once more.

He went a little closer, took up a new position, and waited again. If there had been a craftsman hidden there, to watch him, he would have spotted him. The coast was clear.

He gripped the rail to climb into the ship and slipped under the veil covering the doors of the shrine. They were locked only with a small bolt, which he slid back.

His hands trembled. It occurred to him that he should stand to one side and close his eyes, for the light from the Stone might blind him. The doors opened a little way, giving him access to the treasure he had coveted for so many years. In a few hours, he would be one of the richest men in Thebes, and he would finally have his revenge on the Brotherhood that had not had the sense to recognize his merits.

When he opened his eyes, the only light was the bluish glow from the moon. Astonished, he looked inside the shrine.

It contained not the Stone of Light but a little statue of Amon in the form of Min, standing with his right arm raised and his penis erect. This image of the primordial god, who ceaselessly re-created himself with his own semen, also contained most of the secrets of the sacred geometry the Brotherhood used. During processions, which took place every ten days, only the head of Amon-Min was visible, the rest of the body remaining veiled.

Perhaps the Stone of Light was hidden under the statue, or behind it? No, there was not enough room. He ought to check all the same, but he would have to touch the statue to move it and that would be sacrilege. The traitor hesitated.

After such an act, what would he have left in common with the Servants of the Place of Truth? His last links with the Brotherhood would be cut, and he would be renouncing the way of Ma'at forever. But had he ever followed it, even for a second? He had sought not wisdom or the accomplishment of the work, but only his own interest, which was incompatible with the craftsmen's rule.

The traitor was fully aware of what he was doing, but he did not draw back. With a firm hand, he seized the statue by the two tall gold feathers fixed into the crown, and moved it.

The Stone of Light was not hidden in the shrine.

As he was replacing the statue, he felt a sharp pain in the palm of his hand. A deep wound ran across the skin, but not one drop of blood was emerging from it.

Hastily he closed the shrine doors, slid back the bolt, and pulled down the veil. He hoped that an ointment would ease the pain.

▲

As he did every morning, Kenhir was rubbing his hair with castor oil. Apart from its regenerative powers, it removed the traces of any nightmares, which were not always removed by fresh herbs soaked in beer mixed with myrrh. And that night had been particularly trying, since the Scribe of the Tomb had had three dreams: he had seen himself eating cucumbers, drinking hot beer, and devouring a crocodile! The first meant "encountering difficulties," the second "losing possessions," and the third "to be right about an official." But he could not remember the order in which the dreams had come; and the last one would take precedence over the other two.

"Breakfast," announced Niut. "Let me wipe your head, or you'll catch cold."

The old scribe gave in, as he did in all other domestic matters. The young woman was a perfect housewife, and succeeded in everything she undertook. Kenhir's home had become delightful, and the other village women, although a little jealous of Niut's talents, were inspired by her methods.

"You don't have enough time off," the old man scolded her.

"I have lots to do here, and doing things properly takes time."

"You're remarkable, Niut, but I was talking about your romantic life. People tell me Fened thinks you're very beautiful."

"Are you forgetting that I'm a married woman?"

"Our contract was clear, Niut. You will be my heir, but you're free to do as you wish. And if you don't like Fened, choose someone else. At your age, you shouldn't spend all your time with an old graybeard like me."

"And what if that's precisely what gives me my freedom?"

"Aren't you interested in boys?"

"Not at all, at the moment. Running the house and performing the rites with the priestesses of Hathor are inspiring, and they're quite enough for me. You're behaving to me exactly as you promised, so why should I go and look for elusive happiness somewhere else?"

Kenhir did not know what to say. Clearly she was not the cause of the "grave difficulties" he was going to encounter. In fact, the opposite was true: this incongruous marriage was eminently satisfactory to both of them.

So he enthusiastically munched his hotcakes stuffed with beans until Paneb disturbed his peace by informing him, "There's yet another delivery problem."

"Is it the water?"

"No, the meat."

"It's impossible."

"That's not what Bes the butcher says."

▲

Bes had very short hair and wore a leather apron. In his right hand he carried a knife, and in his left a sharpening stone. He had gathered all the lay workers together.

"No beef, no mutton, no pork, not even any poultry. What are they playing at? If I don't work, I don't get paid."

"Calm down," said Kenhir, annoyed at having had his good breakfast interrupted.

"Why should I? It's a week since I had a delivery."

"Why didn't you tell me sooner?"

"Because the porters made all sorts of fine promises. And now what are we going to do?"

The first dream had been correct: grave difficulties to confront.

"I'll deal with it," said Kenhir. He felt tired already, before the day had even started.

▲

Accompanied by the Master, Kenhir went to Ramses' Temple of a Million Years, where they were received by the Scribe of the Flocks, a small man with a mustache and little talent for conversation. He was comfortably settled at the entrance to the vaulted brick buildings where substantial stocks of food were kept.

"The Place of Truth has received no meat for a week," said Kenhir accusingly.

"That's not surprising, given what's happening on the east bank. The government can do nothing."

"May I remind you that, whatever the circumstances, the Temple of a Million Years must attend to our needs—many head of the livestock and a poultry yard on its lands belong to us."

"Lost."

"What do you mean, 'lost'?"

"I mean the documents that set out your rights have been lost. Sorry, but I was obliged to suspend deliveries."

"You lost the documents yourself, didn't you?" said Nefer.

"Perhaps, but they're still lost."

"You're ignoring another, and much more important, fact: so long as Ma'at rules over this land, the government must act responsibly and must put right its mistakes without prejudice to those it governs."

The scribe stiffened. "The government decides, and—"

"Arrange for a delivery this very afternoon," said Nefer. "And don't ever transgress against the law of the Place of Truth again, or Pharaoh himself will intervene."

The Master's regal bearing and imperious tone deterred the scribe from putting a lot more false arguments that would have allowed him to take more of the meat for himself.

"The village will have its delivery," he promised.

Kenhir was relieved. Fortunately, devouring the crocodile had been the third and last dream.

▲

Mehy loathed the summer heat and strong sunshine. He was enjoying this unusually long period of cold weather, and relishing the fact that his popularity was still intact. The Theban army had congratulated itself on the purge that had killed Amenmessu's last supporters, and everyone had rejoiced at the death of a captain of archers base enough to plot against Seti.

The general had attended the funeral ceremonies for his assistant, who had been untimely carried off by a heart attack, and presented his most sincere condolences to that man's nearest and dearest—not forgetting to give them a plot of land out of gratitude for the services the dear departed had rendered him.

"Have you heard anything from our ally in the Place of Truth?" he asked Serketa.

"Not yet, but he'll accept our suggestion."

"I'm getting less and less sure of that."

Mehy's new assistant came in saluted. "General, a report from the river guards. The royal flotilla is within sight of Thebes."

—— 67 ——

The air was mild again, and filled with the scent of a thousand flowers. Winter was ending at last, and the caressing warmth of springtime heralded the arrival of the royal barge, which was cheered from the riverbanks by thousands of Thebans. Instead of their usual weapons, Mehy's soldiers brandished palm leaves, and dozens of musicians were playing cheerful tunes, as if no one doubted that Seti would look kindly on the greatest city of the South.

Only the general was deeply anxious, for he knew nothing of the king's real intentions. And when Seti and Queen Tausert came down the gangplank, Mehy wondered if he would be sent to Canaan or Nubia, to take charge of an isolated fortress until the end of his days. Seti was strange, at once a strong man and a dreamer; even when very close to him, the general could not read his thoughts.

Mehy bowed low and said, "Your Majesties, what joy to welcome you!"

"We are happy that we are at last able to visit the city of Amon in peace," said the Great Royal Wife, with a charming smile. "I dare to hope, General, that nothing and no one will threaten our safety."

"Thebes is yours, Majesty, and you may count on its total fidelity."

"We shall go to Karnak," said Tausert. "The king wishes to speak with the high priest."

"Does Pharaoh not wish to receive the homage of his Theban troops?"

"When we have decided, you will be informed, General."

Mehy bowed, still racked by uncertainty. He noticed that the king looked tired, and that he moved with difficulty, like an old man.

▲

Kenhir had made sure that the entire village, including the lay workers' houses, was spotlessly clean for the king's visit.

"Is Seti still staying in the Temple of Amon?" he asked Sobek.

"He left yesterday, to preside over a council of dignitaries. No one was punished, so Thebes is breathing more easily."

"So it won't be long before he pays us a visit."

"For several days," confided Sobek, "I've had a bad feeling about the king's visit."

"But he's obviously forgiven Thebes—the city of Amon has nothing to fear from him."

"Perhaps. But something's on the prowl, perhaps an evildoer who wants to harm us."

"If that were so, I'd have had a nightmare."

"Be on your guard," advised Sobek. "My instinct is never wrong."

"Surely you aren't thinking of the traitor who was supposed to be hidden among us? If he really existed, we'd have identified him long ago. The bad days are past, the Two Lands are re-united, and the Place of Truth will again work in perfect peace."

"May the gods protect us," said the big Nubian, but there was anxiety in his voice.

From the top of the nearest hill, one of his men was signaling.

"The royal procession is approaching," he said.

▲

Seti no longer drove his own chariot, and his groom kept to a moderate pace to avoid jolting the king and causing him discomfort. Though in his mid-fifties, he seemed twenty years older, as though his *ka* had fled from his body.

Mehy was in charge of the procession's safety. He felt very relieved: the king still trusted him and had confirmed him in all his offices, including that of protector of the Place of Truth. Congratulating the general on preserving peace, Seti had decorated him with a golden collar before all the city worthies, thus raising him to the ranks of the great men of Egypt.

The king's chariot halted and the main gate of the village opened.

"May awe inhabit your hearts," the Master told the craftsmen. "Don't hurry. Arrange yourselves carefully in the correct positions to move the ship, for the master of life has chosen it to sail in."

The procession set off. At its head were the Master and the

Wise Woman; then the two crews, carrying the ship of Amon on two long cedar poles. The Scribe of the Tomb brought up the rear.

Under the late-morning sun, the golden shrine shone like fire. Even Mehy was dazzled by the Brotherhood's masterpiece. His longing to possess their secrets grew even more intense.

"The ship's shrine is engraved with your name, Majesty," said Nefer. "May Amon continue to heap his bounty upon you."

"Lead me to the temple where Ramses the Great stayed during his visit to the village," said Seti. "I shall pay homage to him, then we shall go to my House of Eternity."

▲

The Master broke the mud seal bearing the mark of the Place of Truth, drew back the bolt, and pushed open the double doors of gilded wood. Holding a torch with three wicks, he showed the king the pictures of Ma'at, the sculptures showing the pharaoh as Osiris, and the *Invocation to Ra,* which revealed the many names of the Divine Light.

Seti read the hieroglyphs and moved very slowly toward the small chamber where Paneb had painted the ritual objects destined for the tomb, in a beautiful shade of ocher yellow. He lingered before each one, as though he were experiencing the ceremony during which these symbols would help to turn his mummified body into Light.

"Is it true that no royal tomb has been decorated like this before?"

"Yes, Majesty."

"Who did the paintings?"

"The painter Paneb the Ardent. Are you shocked by his style?"

"On the contrary, Master, on the contrary. He has depicted exactly what I wanted, and with incredible precision, even though I could not have put it into words myself. Not a single detail must be changed."

The king went down into the four-pillared chamber and communed with each of the gods Paneb had painted. Then he set off into the last area to have been excavated, which was reached by a door crowned with a representation of the pharaoh making offerings to Ma'at.

On the walls, Ched and Paneb had depicted the triple birth, in the sky, on the deified earth, and in the underground kingdom of Osiris. Inside shrines, several mummies invoked the creative forces that awoke the new sun each day.

"We plan to dig deeper into the rock, Majesty, and create a vast chamber for your sarcophagus."

"There's no need. I consider my House of Eternity finished. You shall place a red granite sarcophagus in here, and on the ceiling you will paint a sky-goddess, whose beating wings will make me breathe the air of life forever."

▲

Paneb's fury shook the very walls of the artists' workshop. "Stop work? But that's absurd! I've planned wonderful decorations for the next passageways and the chamber of resurrection!"

"We must respect the will of Pharaoh," said Nefer firmly.

"Even when it stops us completing our work properly?"

"It's his work we're doing, not our own."

"Ask Ched, he'll tell you what we've prepared—and it's taken hundreds of drawings! We're past the stage of sketches. Now we must do the work." He was shaking was anger. "Master, you must use your authority to convince the king he's wrong!"

"He has given me his reasons, and I agree with them," said Nefer calmly.

"In other words, months of hard work are to go for nothing."

"You don't paint for pleasure, Paneb, because you're a Servant of the Place of Truth. If you can't see how important that office is, your hand is in danger of losing its creativity."

Paneb stormed out of the workshop.

"When I faced a similar crisis," recalled Ched, "I reacted just like that. Can there be any better proof of his love of his craft?"

Nefer left without replying.

"This is the first serious argument between the Master and

his adopted son," remarked Unesh. "Let's hope it doesn't herald discord, which would be damaging to the Brotherhood."

▲

Before entering the meeting hall, to which Nefer had summoned the starboard crew, Paneb spoke to the Master, who was meditating beside the lake of purification.

"Please accept my apologies. I behaved like a pretentious fool. It won't happen again."

"Have you really detached yourself from your own creation?"

"Certainly not, Master, because it's my life, and I don't feel old enough to give it up. But I've realized that serving the work is more important than any individual success. Will you forgive me?"

Nefer gave a serene smile. "You still have many battles to fight, Paneb, but I have confidence in you."

"Without you, Master, I wouldn't even exist."

"Of course you would, because you're guided by a true flame. Whatever else you do, never let it go out."

The better Paneb knew Nefer, the more he had the feeling that the Master's thoughts drifted in a universe beyond the hours of night and day, beyond the space in which humans dwelt. Nefer was like the stone in the Valley of the Kings: he fed on the Invisible.

After Nefer's long conversation with Seti, all the craftsmen waited impatiently to hear what he had to say.

"Pharaoh has set us three goals. First, we must finish his House of Eternity as quickly as possible and lower the sarcophagus into it. Next, we must build a tomb for the Great Royal Wife, Tausert, in the Valley of the Queens. Lastly, we must build a shrine at Karnak in honor of the Theban trinity."

"Karnak has its own builders," objected Gau. "Why should we work on the east bank?"

"The shrine will be built outside the enclosure of the Great Temple of Amon, and Seti wants the work done by our sculptors."

"Is this a first step toward making us work in the outside world, and closing down the village?" asked Casa anxiously.

"Not at all," replied Nefer. "Our predecessors often had to carry out isolated tasks such as this."

Administrative and timing problems were discussed, then the craftsmen went their separate ways.

"You don't look very happy," commented Renupe to Paneb.

"I'll obey the Master, but I think he's not being firm enough with the king."

── 68 ──

Although handicapped by his club foot, young Saptah walked calmly into the great audience chamber of the palace at Pi-Ramses, where Bay was waiting for him. Also present were some senior members of the government; they were curious to test the young prodigy, whose reputation was growing by the day.

Saptah had just been appointed a royal scribe, and had therefore reached the highest level of learning. His particular talent in the field of discoveries and new learning made most of the old officials look down on him, for few scribes interested in newfangled things had the skills to run affairs of state correctly. Besides, despite the tjaty's warm recommendation, many were hesitant to entrust a position of responsibility to such a young man.

The eldest man attacked first. "What do you know of the law concerning the hiring of boats?"

"It concerns only light boats, and was reformed by King Horemheb because of many abuses. But it did not abolish the precept according to which a wealthy man must allow a man to cross the river without charge if he hasn't the means to pay for the ferry. Shall I list the prices, according to the size of the boats?"

"That won't be necessary."

Legal questions came from all sides. Saptah replied calmly and accurately, to the surprise of Bay, who had not realized his knowledge of this complex area was so extensive. When the official in charge of canals confronted the young man with difficult financial problems, Bay feared that Saprah might fail; but the lad took the time to make calculations on a wooden tablet, and produced an analysis worthy of a specialist.

Admiration took the place of skepticism, and the entire assembly was won over, even the oldest official losing his hostility; Bay was as happy as a father watching his son triumph. Perhaps the most interested participant was the high priest of Ptah, an eminent member of the Council of Wise Men, without whose assent a claimant to the throne could not be crowned.

▲

The traitor was pretending to be asleep in the shade of a tamarisk tree not far from the House of Ramses. Any guards watching him would see only a tired craftsman taking advantage of his day's holiday to enjoy the greenery, which could not be found in the village. On the other side of the tree was a woman selling baskets made from plaited reeds. As always for meetings like this, Serketa had made herself unrecognizable.

"You wanted to see me," she said, "and here I am."

"I've been thinking about your proposition, and I know you aren't serious."

"You're wrong."

"Ten times the fortune I've built up outside the village? You're lying to me."

Serketa knew she had to find a powerful argument in order to convince him. "I am the wife of General Mehy, and my husband is one of the most powerful men in Egypt. He'll have no difficulty whatsoever in keeping his promises. If you want more, say so."

The traitor felt dizzy. So the fortune he was being offered was real!

"The news is bad," continued Serketa. "Nefer has become

the king's confidant, and the Place of Truth is more untouchable than ever, all the more so since my husband is its official protector and cannot do anything to jeopardize that role."

"Why does he want the Stone of Light so much?"

"Who wouldn't want such a treasure?"

"He wants supreme power, doesn't he?"

"He has the qualities necessary to exercise it."

The traitor sensed that he could trust the general's wife. She had told him the truth, and in doing so had put her husband in danger. The enormous risk she was taking proved she was sincere.

She said, "If you really want to be rich, kill the Master and give us the Stone of Light. You're the only one who can do it."

The traitor put his hands over his eyes. "I don't have many needs," he admitted, "and this fortune will please my wife more than myself. I set myself this goal in order to forget the daily humiliations I've suffered for so many years. It is I, not Nefer, who should be Master of the Place of Truth."

The craftsman's icy rage pleased Serketa. He had not only a remarkable talent for deception but a killer's temperament—though he did not realize it yet.

She used a fragile, almost touching voice. "So, what have you decided?"

"You're lucky. Something happened recently that has inspired me."

Serketa shivered with pleasure. "You mean you accept?"

"It's the only answer. I'll kill Nefer the Silent."

▲

The master builder in charge of the upkeep of the temples in Karnak and their associated buildings was a tall, stern man with a closed expression.

"The king has ordered me to place myself at your disposition," he told the Master. His tone was extremely dry, mingled with a note of reproach.

"That won't be necessary," said Nefer gently.

"Not necessary? But you haven't the right to build on the sacred domain of Karnak without the authorization of the high priest and myself."

"Pharaoh's authorization ought to be sufficient, don't you think?"

"Well yes, of course," mumbled the man, ashamed to have lost his temper and been wrongheaded.

"The king wishes us to build a threefold shrine outside the enclosure of the Temple of Amon, on a platform some distance from the landing stage. So we shan't cause you or the ritualists any inconvenience. I ask you simply to have the necessary blocks of sandstone delivered to the place I shall show you."

"Is the plan of this building a state secret, like everything else to do with the Place of Truth?"

"It will have doorways of quartzite," replied Nefer, "and three shrines dedicated to Amon, his wife Mut, and their son Khonsu. Statues of the royal *ka* will be placed in the alcoves, and hieroglyphic texts engraved on the walls will bring them to eternal life. My colleague Hay will direct the work, and he will gladly listen to your advice so that the style and soul of this altar of repose are in harmony with those of Karnak."

The master builder seemed disappointed. "I thought you'd be quite different," he said. "Anyone would think you were ready to handle mallet and chisel yourself, and do an apprentice's work."

"But I am," replied Nefer with a smile. "So long as I know the plan of the work, of course, for that is the inherent duty of my office."

▲

Whereas the Valley of the Kings was a closed world, hostile in appearance, locked away in secrecy and silence, the Valley of the Queens was open, easy to reach, and opened out onto a broad and verdant plain, at the southernmost end of the Theban burial grounds. Since Ramses I's decision that his wife should have her own House of Eternity, instead of sharing his, "the Place of

Perfect Beauty," to give it its ritual name, had welcomed the mothers and wives of pharaohs, together with important people bearing the title of Royal Son. A temple to Ptah, god of builders, had been built to the east of the site, and the craftsmen had built a modest settlement of simple houses, where they lived when working on lengthy projects.

Tausert was escorted to the valley by the Master, accompanied by the Wise Woman, and Fened the Nose. The queen gazed for a long time at the place, which was in no way funereal. The sun was gentle, the wind mild, as if spring had decided to hail the beautiful queen's visit in its own way.

"This is where Queen Nefertari lies, is it not?"

"Yes Majesty," replied the Master. "It's said that the beauty of the paintings in her House of Eternity has never been equaled."

Nefer sensed that the queen was dreaming of a greatness that Seti had failed to attain.

"The king is satisfied with the work that has been done," she said, "and he wishes me to rest in this valley, together with other queens of the Two Lands. How will you choose the site of my House of Eternity?"

"In two ways, Majesty. Permit me to show you."

Nefer asked Tausert to enter the workshop, where a stone table had been set up. On it he unrolled a papyrus scroll.

"Majesty, this is the map of the Valley of the Queens, showing where tombs have been excavated and decorated since the site was consecrated. As you can see, there are many possibilities."

Tausert read the names of the queens who had gone before her, and had the feeling that she was reliving inspiring moments from Egyptian history.

"What is the second way?" she asked.

"In this valley, many of the veins of limestone are of poor quality, so even if skillfully worked the walls and ceilings could collapse. That is why Fened is so important: he won't be deceived by rock that looks attractive but contains serious flaws."

"Let us look for a site as close as possible to the tomb of Nefertari," said Tausert.

Nefer and Fened tried to meet her wishes, but neither of them found the site satisfactory. Disappointed, the queen agreed that they might search farther afield, and at last Fened detected a good rock in the western part of the valley.

"No, the tomb cannot be there," said the Wise Woman.

"Why not?" asked Tausert.

"Because I cannot feel the protecting presence of Hathor. This house would not be a happy one."

Another attempt also ended in disappointment.

"We'll never succeed," concluded Ubekhet.

"Why is it so difficult?" asked Tausert in astonishment.

"Because the time is not right, Majesty," said Nefer. "We shall return later."

Ubekhet knew he understood the real reason for their failure: the Valley of the Queens was refusing to admit Tausert.

69

A strange ship was sailing down the Nile toward Abydos, the holy city of Osiris, which lay far to the north of Thebes. Instead of a cabin there was a funerary shrine, guarded by the Wise Woman, who was playing the part of Isis, and Turquoise, who was acting as her sister Nephthys; silent priests acted as sailors.

Nefer and Paneb were standing in the bow.

"Are you ever going to tell me where we're going?" asked Paneb.

"To the House of Gold," replied the Master.

Paneb was thunderstruck. "But isn't that inside the Place of Truth?"

"It is re-created wherever it's needed, but, to be worthy and capable of entering it, one must have encountered one's own death. That's why this voyage is essential."

"I wasn't expecting . . ."

"Expecting is futile," said Nefer. "You must simply be ready."

The two men did not exchange another word on their journey. Paneb felt that he was entering a fathomless silence that no sound could reach—neither birdsong, nor the sound of the ship's prow parting the river water. Time stopped; all that existed was the inscrutable presence of the shrine and the solemn travelers, who seemed about to undergo a formidable ordeal.

By the time they reached the landing stage, night was falling.

Shaven-headed priests were standing on the quayside.

One of them came to meet Nefer, and asked, "Is the Lord of the West among you?"

"His sisters have protected him throughout the voyage."

"Does Paneb the Ardent wish to follow the path of Osiris, which leads to the House of Gold?"

"I do," replied Paneb.

Striking the ground with a long staff of gilded wood, the priest led a procession containing the Master, the Wise Woman, and Turquoise. Flanked by two ugly priests, Paneb was led to a mound surrounded by trees.

To the west was a well some twenty cubits deep, feebly illuminated by a light rising from the depths.

"Enter the world of Osiris," said the Master, "and go beyond your first birth."

Paneb did not hesitate. He climbed down into the well and came to the entrance to a corridor more than a hundred paces long. As he walked along it, the light receded; but there was enough to make out columns of hieroglyphs, which told of the journey of the night sun, through caverns where mummified forms waited for its radiance in order to come back to life.

Suddenly, Paneb was blinded by a brilliant light from the end of the passageway.

"I must bandage your eyes," said the voice of a ritualist behind him. "Thanks to his fabric, you will not fear the darkness. But first you must be equipped with sandals that will prevent you from stumbling. Sit down and stretch out your legs."

Another ritualist painted red sandals onto the soles of Paneb's feet. then he was lifted up and blindfolded with a red scarf.

"We are taking you to the entrance to the House of Gold," announced the Master. "It is there that statues containing the *ka,* the imperishable energy, are brought to life. None may enter except initiates who work according to Ma'at and perceive gold as the flesh of the gods."

Paneb was pushed forward.

"I am the door," declared a solemn voice, "and I shall not allow you to pass through me unless you tell me my name."

Paneb tried to remember everything he had learned since entering the Place of Truth. The answer came to him: "Your name is righteousness."

"Pass through me, since you know me."

The blindfold was removed, and the ritualist took Paneb by the hand to guide him into a second passageway, at right angles to the first. He took off Paneb's clothes and dressed him in the skin of a wild animal.

"You are now wrapped in the shroud of Set," said the Master. "Allow yourself to be led into the workshop of regeneration."

Four disciples of Osiris placed the craftsman on a sled and hauled him to an immense chamber, whose roof was supported by ten enormous, monolithic pillars of pink granite.

You have reached the island of the first morning," said Nefer. "When Light created, this island emerged from the primordial ocean."

Paneb was raised up, and he gazed at a fine statue of Osiris stretched out on a black bed that the Master was polishing with the Stone of Light.

"The body of the reborn soul is transformed into gold, matter is illuminated, statues are brought into the world and shine like the sun's rays. You see what is invisible and you gain access to what is inaccessible."

The Wise Woman took water and milk, and sprayed an acacia planted in a mound decorated with an eye. "As Isis, I am tending my brother Osiris. I, the woman who acts like a man, will rejuvenate him in this House of Gold, so that he may live on light."

"Since you have been wrapped in the skin of Set and it has not destroyed you," said a priest, "be delivered from it, Paneb, and kiss Osiris."

The shroud was removed, and Paneb approached the statue and kissed the god's forehead.

"It is Set who possesses the secret of gold," said the Wise Woman, "and it is his sister Isis who brings Osiris from the state of inert matter to that of living gold."

As they were lit up by the Stone, which was held by the Wise Woman, the bed and the statue were transformed into gold. Paneb looked on in amazement.

Acting as Nephthys, "the Sovereign of the Temple," Turquoise placed a necklace of willow and persea leaves round his neck, and placed disks of gold upon his eyes, his forehead, his lips, his neck, and his big toes. Then, while the Wise Woman touched his heart with a knot of Isis made from red jasper, Turquoise handed him a cup.

"The rite identifies you as Osiris. Drink this poison, which you will transform into the water of life."

Paneb emptied the cup in a single draught. A disagreeably bitter taste was followed almost immediately by a taste of honey, the vegetable gold.

"May you take hold of the Light and seize the stone of Ma'at," Turquoise told him, slipping gold sheaths onto his fingers, "for henceforth your hands shall be linked to the stars."

For the first time, Paneb could touch the Stone of Light.

"Be regenerated by the gold," chanted the Wise Woman. "It lights up your face and gives you breath."

Paneb handed the Stone back to the Master, and a priest led him into the final room of the shrine, a huge chamber containing a gold sarcophagus. The vaulted ceiling, in the shape of an upside-down V, was decorated with an immense figure of the sky goddess, raised up by the Divine Light.

"Osiris Paneb," ordered the Master, "take your place in the House of Life."

Paneb lay down on his back in the sarcophagus.

"You have gone, but you will return," declared the Wise Woman. "You have slept, but you will awaken. You have reached the shores of the afterlife, but you will live again. May your bones be knit again and your limbs made whole."

In the long silence that followed, Paneb had the impression that he was traveling inside the body of his mother the sky, accompanied by the stars and the ship of the sun. Then the Wise Woman and the Master set up a pillar of gold near the head of the sarcophagus.

"Rise up, Osiris!" commanded Nefer. "The corpse has disappeared, you are made of gold, forever living, for your being is as stable as the Stone of Light."

"You are reborn from the creative power that was born of itself," continued the Wise Woman. "It conceived you in its heart, and you are not of mortal birth."

Two priests helped Paneb out of the sarcophagus and dressed him in a white tunic. Turquoise circled his brow with the crown of the just, a golden ribbon decorated with two complete eyes, confirming that the new Osiris was "of just voice."

"I entrust the life of the work to you," said the Master, handing Paneb a small block of granite shaped and smoothed to perfection. The block's name, *ankh*, was synonymous with the word *life*.

"You have seen the mysteries of Osiris in the secrecy of the House of Gold," the Wise Woman said. "When this world disappears, only the master of the great mysteries will remain, he who has vanquished death to give life. May he guide your eyes and your actions. Like him, be fire, air, water, and earth, be the permanent transformation that is never fixed, reconcile the One and the many. When Osiris is reborn, the fields become fertile; he is the black of the silt and the green of the vegetation, but his being is made up of celestial gold, and he shines like a star. Remember that each province of Egypt keeps a part of his body as its most important relic, and that the duty of a craftsman of the Place of Truth is to bring together that which is scattered."

The Master approached Paneb, placed his right hand on the nape of Paneb's neck and his left hand on his right shoulder, and embraced him as a brother.

Then the Wise Woman, Nefer, Turquoise, Paneb, and the ritualists formed an oval around the golden coffin, their arms stretched out, hand in hand. The painter felt an incredibly powerful energy passing through him.

"May the new initiate of the House of Gold prove worthy of the tasks entrusted to him," declared the Master.

—— 70 ——

Pai had a headache and was feeling terribly bloated after a lavish lunch, so he decided to aid his digestion by going for a walk down the main street of the village. As he passed Nefer and Ubekhet's house, something unusual struck him and he retraced his steps.

"What on earth . . . ?" Pai went up to the front door and peered at it. "This is terrible!"

His exclamation attracted the attention of Unesh the Jackal, who was drawing water from a terra cotta jar a little farther

along the street. He came and joined Pai, and he, too, was horrified by the macabre red hand painted on the wood.

"What an abomination! Who could have—"

"And look at the size of it!" said Pai. "It's a giant's hand."

"The Master mustn't see this. We must rub it off and keep
quiet."

"What if it happens again?"

"We shall see."

It was the fifth year of Seti II's reign, and the freezing cold winter was followed by an unusually hot spring. The heat overwhelmed Thebes suddenly, and the donkey drivers had to
deliver twice the normal amount of water to the Place of Truth.
In the village itself, the narrow streets were roofed over with the
branches of palm trees, to keep them as cool as possible.

The person least affected by the heat was Paneb, who
seemed even more energetic than usual. He was pleased to see
that even his demon of a son had yielded to the delights of the
afternoon nap, and that his much-loved daughter, Iuwen, was
becoming more beautiful by the day, under Uabet's watchful eye.

Paneb accompanied the Master to the east bank, to help the
port crew complete the altar of repose dedicated to the Theban
trinity.

Hay welcomed him with a new warmth. "I congratulate you
on your initiation into the House of Gold, Osiris Paneb.
Unfortunately, my duties kept me here, leading the Brotherhood
in the absence of the Master and the Wise Woman, but my
spirit was present at the ceremony."

"Those few hours were so intense!"

Hay smiled. "The ritual lasted nine days."

Paneb turned to Nefer. "That's impossible!"

"Who but Osiris, the master of time, could abolish it?"

The altar of repose was almost finished, and Paneb had only
to add color to some fine relief carvings in the classical style,
comparable to sculptures from the reign of Seti I or Ramses the

Great. His hand was driven by a new energy, and his work was swifter and more precise. Imbued with a sense that profound peace surrounded him, Paneb brought offertory scenes to life with warm, radiant hues.

▲

Seti was finding it more and more difficult to walk, but he was determined to celebrate the dedication ritual at the altar of repose in Karnak. And so he glorified the presence of Amon the Hidden One, Mut the cosmic mother, and Khonsu the infant god. The Great Royal Wife assisted him, surrounding him with protective magic so that he had the strength to complete the ceremony.

"This building is magnificent," the king told the Master. "One day, when Karnak has been developed according to the gods' plan, it will become one of the shrines of the Great Temple, and the creative trinity will continue to be worshipped here. Is my burial furniture ready, Nefer?"

"I myself shall complete the lid of the sarcophagus, while the goldsmith puts the finishing touches to the scepters."

"Hurry. My days are numbered."

▲

As the king left for the palace, carried in a chair by bearers, Tausert beckoned Nefer over and asked,

"Have you found a suitable location in the Valley of the Queens?"

"Not yet, Majesty."

"Why is it taking so long?"

"The Wise Woman feels we must wait for a favorable time, and not hurry matters along."

"What if I were to tell you to excavate my House of Eternity next to Nefertari's?"

"I would obey you, of course, but so many things would go wrong with our work that we would have to abandon it."

"Tell me honestly, Master: am I under a curse?"

"The Wise Woman doesn't think so, Majesty. She believes

we must simply have patience and wait until the veil is torn from our sight."

▲

Tjaty Bay tore into tiny shreds the long letter Queen Tausert had sent him, for it contained a state secret that no courtier must know: King Seti was dying. Only one person could succeed him, only one person could avert a crisis: the Great Royal Wife herself.

But Tausert was staying in Thebes; she refused to leave her husband to return to the capital. Bay therefore found himself in the front line. His objective was clear: he must prevent fresh disturbances breaking out, and bar the way to any ambitious man who might attempt to seize the North and then extend his domination over the entire country.

Tausert must return as a matter of urgency, and be crowned pharaoh, as several other women had been before her. But the tjaty had no illusions: the queen would never leave her husband at the moment of the supreme test, and she would be present to ensure that the funerary rites were carried out correctly. Despite Bay's insistence, she would remain in Thebes for as long as necessary, and would not be able to mount direct opposition to the plots that were bound to surface.

There was only one thing to do. They must select and crown a pharaoh who could not carry out all his duties, so that Egypt could be governed by a queen-regent, the Great Royal Wife Tausert. And the tjaty had an ideal candidate in mind: young Saptah.

Saptah did not belong to any tribe, and so would not be unacceptable to anyone. And who would fear a sickly adolescent, so far removed from cruel power struggles?

One matter demanded urgent attention: Bay must speed up Saptah's training so that he would be able to stand up for himself. Using code, the tjaty wrote to the queen, in an attempt to reassure her.

▲

The royal couple had invited the Master and the Wise Woman to eat their midday meal with them at the palace in Karnak. Seti made only a brief appearance at the start of the meal, to apologize for being unable to visit the village to celebrate, in the presence of all the villagers, the completion of his House of Eternity; he no longer felt strong enough to cross the Nile. Leaving his bedchamber demanded considerable effort; but, against his doctors' advice, he had risen to greet Nefer and Ubekhet, who had given his last days an unhoped-for serenity.

The Wise Woman was certain she was seeing Seti for the last time, and Tausert noticed her distress.

"The king has no fear of death," said the queen. "At Thebes, he has lived peacefully and happily, to a large extent because of you and the Master. I shall not forget that."

"If my remedies can be of any use to you . . ."

"It's too late, Ubekhet. The king receives no remedies anymore, only potions that reduce his pain. His body is worn out: nothing can save him."

"The Brotherhood has prepared all the symbols necessary for Pharaoh's journey to the paradise of the afterlife," said the Master.

"The king knows that, and nothing makes him more content. But there is one question you dare not ask me: what is to become of the monarchy and, consequently, the Place of Truth? The situation will be complex, but I shall gain control of it. Have no fear. The Brotherhood will remain a vital institution and it will continue to work as it has always done."

▲

Nefer and Ubekhet lingered in the palace garden, walking its flower-lined pathways before sitting down in the shade of a pomegranate tree with smooth, shiny leaves. Hand in hand, their faces caressed by the northerly breeze, they gazed into a pool filled with lotuses in full bloom.

A pair of wild ducks flew overhead. They were the embodiment of conjugal fidelity and flew with broad-spanned wings as though the sky belonged to them.

At that same moment, Nefer and Ubekhet thought back to their first meeting, when they had been both far from and close to the Place of Truth. Life could have offered them no finer destiny than to devote themselves wholeheartedly to the Brotherhood, whose vocation was to turn matter into Light.

Nefer smiled. "Do you remember how shy I was? I was so timid that I could hardly bring myself to speak to you."

"I've always disliked forward men, and you didn't win my heart at first sight—well, not completely."

"I am a rather severe man, with little talent for sweet words, and I'd have liked to pamper you more. Forgive me for not knowing how to do it."

Her radiant blue eyes gazed at him with passion and tenderness, and Nefer fell deeply in love all over again.

She said, "Nothing and no one has separated us, and not even a blade of grass could slide between us. Knowing such happiness, we should thank the gods and the ancestors every morning for their generosity."

The sunlight dappled the leaves of the pomegranate tree.

"My office forbids it," murmured Nefer, "but I would dearly love to stay here with you for all eternity."

"A spring evening like this is just like eternity."

—— 71 ——

"I have one more secret left to reveal to you," the Master told Paneb, "and that is the location of the Stone of Light."

Paneb's heart beat faster. "How can I thank you for everything you've given me?"

"I'm only doing my duty," said Nefer. "Now that you've been

initiated into the mysteries of the House of Gold, you must be linked to the greatest of them all."

The two men walked slowly down the main street of the village, as if they were discussing some work in progress.

"Have you ever wondered where the Stone is hidden?" asked Nefer.

"Never," replied Paneb. "Knowledge like that is one of your responsibilities, and I had no wish to share them."

The route the Master took surprised his adopted son. When they halted, and Nefer showed Paneb the Stone's hiding place, Paneb realized that Nefer had, in fact, given him precious clues in the past.

"Surely it isn't hidden here?"

"Do you think it should be somewhere else?"

"No, of course not."

"You have a rare quality," said Nefer. "You want to learn, but you aren't inquisitive. Thanks to the Stone, you will understand that time and space are aspects of the same thing, that the radiant void is alive and constantly creating building materials, which the universe breathes in and out, and that it is contained in its entirety within the Light of the Stone. But gaining such knowledge, in the Place of Truth, is not without its consequences."

They turned back toward the center of the village.

"What are they?" asked Paneb.

"I'm fifty years old, and no longer as strong as when I was a young man. Unless my instinct deceives me, our Brotherhood has a great deal of work before it. My responsibilities must therefore be shared."

"I don't understand."

"Hay is an excellent leader of the port crew, and I need someone like him equivalent to lead the starboard crew. That person, Paneb, will be you."

The giant loved thunderbolts, but this one left him almost speechless. "You . . . can't really mean it," he stammered.

"You'll soon be forty, you're well versed in all aspects of the

art of building, you excel in your own craft and you've been initiated into the House of Gold. Frankly, I have no choice. Any
Master of the Place of Truth would take the same decision."

"It's impossible, I—"

"It's not like you to refuse a challenge," said Nefer.

Cut to the quick, the giant clenched his fists. "You know me
better than anyone, Master. Can you really imagine me as a crew
leader?"

"I'm not given to making flippant remarks, am I?"

▲

Even Bad Girl listened attentively to Paneb. As for Uabet, who
was cradling her daughter, she thought she was hearing things.

"Crew leader! That is really what the Master has decided?"

"Don't you think I can do it?"

"Of course I do! But will you still have time for your children
and your wife? With your energy, you'll double the work rate."

"Don't worry, there are strict rules about that sort of thing."

"Nefer has made the right decision," she said, her voice filled
with pride and emotion.

"The court still has to agree."

"If the Place of Truth can't recognize the men who are fit to
lead, it won't survive much longer."

Paneb kissed his daughter's forehead and left, to wander
around the western burial ground. True, the Master's authority
was undeniable, but how many craftsmen would oppose the appointment of his adopted son? Paneb clung to that hope to
avoid thinking that, soon, he would have to give orders to the
work mates who had trained him.

As he neared Nefer's House of Eternity, which was almost
finished, he saw Turquoise, sitting on a flight of sun-bathed
stone steps. Her long red hair had never looked so beautiful.

"I've been waiting for you," she said.

"How did you know I'd come here?"

"You seem to have forgotten that Hathor gives her priestesses the gift of divination."

"Then you know what's happened to me."

"Looking at you," she said with a smile, "it would seem that you've found a worthy opponent—yourself, no doubt. Don't give up, Paneb, and above all don't hope to escape your destiny by running away. You must repay the strength that Set has given you by using it in the service of others. If not, it will destroy you."

▲

"Seti's soul has taken flight," announced the Scribe of the Tomb to the villagers, "and it has entered the land of Light; it has united with the sun's disk and so rejoined its creator. May it continue to shine, and may the sky remain dazzlingly bright as we await the new Horus."

The news arrived on the very day when Kenhir had convened the court of the Place of Truth to endorse or reject Paneb's appointment as leader of the starboard crew.

"Queen Tausert has given me assurances about the future," said Nefer. "Like the late king, she considers the Brotherhood's role a fundamental one."

"Perhaps we should delay the judgment," suggested Kenhir.

"Certainly not," said Nefer. "I hope the new crew leader will take an active part in the preparations for the royal funeral."

The governing assembly of the village therefore met in the open-air courtyard of the Temple of Hathor and Ma'at, presided over by the Scribe of the Tomb.

"I approve of the Master's choice," declared Kenhir. "Does anyone oppose it?"

Hay asked permission to speak. "I've watched Paneb ever since he entered the Brotherhood. Like all of us, I know his faults, but I believe he is capable of fulfilling the office the Master wishes to confer upon him."

The Wise Woman gave her assent with a simple nod.

"Hay, have you consulted the members of your crew?" the Master asked.

"They are unanimously in favor of Paneb."

"As are the priestesses of Hathor," added the Wise Woman.

"Uabet, have you any objections?" asked Kenhir.

"No," she replied.

"Then all that remains is for me to consult the starboard crew, so that the Brotherhood may speak with one voice. Craftsmen of the starboard crew, have you considered your decision?"

"Is that really necessary?" wondered Ched. "When we recognized Nefer as Master, it was so that he might guide the Brotherhood onto the correct path, regardless of personal preferences. Since he has chosen Paneb the Ardent as the new crew leader, we should obey him."

Casa's large, dark brown eyes glittered with anger, and his square face turned red. "Anyone who knows Paneb well knows he's likely to ignore the rules and pay no heed to official working hours. Unlike us, he never gets tired, and he takes no account of other people's weaknesses. Such behavior is inappropriate for a crew leader."

"You're right to mention such things," said Pai. "Paneb has listened to you, and he'll take note of your warning. But is that sufficient reason to reject his appointment?"

Casa gave a disgruntled shrug.

"If I'd beaten Paneb in a wrestling bout," said Nakht, "I'd have opposed his appointment. It's good that our new crew leader should be the strongest man among us and that he should fight on our behalf, whatever the circumstances."

The crew members agreed.

"We haven't yet heard from Assistant Scribe Imuni," observed the Master.

Kenhir looked embarrassed. "My assistant's opinion should be the same as my own."

"But surely it's desirable for him to speak his mind before Paneb?"

Reluctantly, the Scribe of the Tomb gave in.

The little rat-faced scribe glanced anxiously at Paneb, who was staring at him like a beast of prey.

"It's not for me to disagree with your decisions and—"

"You belong to the Brotherhood, and we're asking for your opinion. Do you approve Paneb's appointment, yes or no?"

Imuni's pallid complexion took on an unpleasant, greenish tinge. Single-handedly, he could throw everything into doubt and spark off lengthy debates, but then he'd have to give serious reasons for his refusal.

"Er . . . yes . . . I approve it."

The little scribe scurried back to join the craftsmen and stop being the focal point of the meeting.

The Scribe of the Tomb said, with some satisfaction, "Paneb the Ardent, you are appointed leader of the starboard crew of the Place of Truth, whose members owe you obedience. You shall bring the Master's plan to life, respecting the Brotherhood's rule and placing the way of Ma'at at the heart of your being. By reason of your new office, you will be allocated a larger house at the southeastern corner of the village, a plot of land outside the walls, and an extra allowance of food and possessions. In exchange for these benefits, your rest time will be reduced, you will take part in all meetings of the court, and you will perform more services to the temple. Do you swear to carry out your duties without fail?"

"On the lives of Pharaoh and my adoptive parents, I swear it."

72

Beken the potter, leader of the lay workers, was drawing water from a small watercourse when he saw it. Horrified, he dropped his waterjar and—despite his ever-increasing portliness—ran full pelt to the village.

"What's happened?" asked Obed the blacksmith, seeing that he was out of breath.

"Go and tell the Wise Woman I must speak with her. Now!"

This was so unlike Beken that Obed realized the matter was serious, so he went and asked the gatekeeper for his help.

Beken had to wait more than an hour, because Ubekhet was busy with her patients. When she emerged from the village, he ran to her.

"The turtle!" he said "I saw the turtle of the Earth god. It was enormous, and its mouth was as wide as a well."

Considered a fish, the turtle announced the arrival of the annual Nile flood; with its phallus, the male rendered the earth fertile. For anyone who could read the signs, the turtle would reveal the extent of the flood. Usually people feared that the creature would be so thirsty that it would drink most of the floodwaters, but this time the fear was of a different kind.

"Aren't you exaggerating a little?" asked Ubekhet.

"Perhaps," conceded the potter, "but I can assure you that its mouth was unusually large and that it was heading quickly toward the fields. And then it just disappeared."

"Did anyone else see it?"

"No, I was alone. But I promise you it's the truth."

"I believe you, Beken, and I'm going to tell the authorities."

▲

General Mehy couldn't believe his ears. "Are you sure?" he asked.

The officer standing before him, who had just returned from Pi-Ramses, nodded. "Yes, sir. Young Saptah has been named as Pharaoh by the Council of Wise Men, with the agreement of Queen Tausert."

"Who is he?"

"A young orphan whose education has been supervised by Tjaty Bay."

"That doesn't make sense! No one knows this boy Saptah, and the tjaty is a realist."

"It seems that the new king has remarkable skills, which impressed the court."

Mehy remained skeptical. Tausert would never give up the power she was made for, but if she had proclaimed herself pharaoh she would have encountered strong opposition. So she had installed a puppet king on the throne and would hide behind him in order to attack the many factions hostile to her.

A soldier came in and saluted. "General, the Wise Woman wants to see you urgently."

Mehy received her straightaway.

"The next flood will be dangerous," she told him. "You must take measures to prevent a disaster."

"What evidence is there to support what you say?"

"The appearance of a giant turtle."

The general was astonished. "Isn't this evidence rather . . . flimsy?"

"The omen has never deceived us. The leader of the lay workers saw it, quite by chance, and informed me immediately."

"Wouldn't it be best to wait for the experts to form an opinion?"

"That would be too late, and Thebes is in serious danger. If you don't take action, I shall request an audience with Queen Tausert."

Mehy saw the danger: he could be accused of negligence. "We'll go and see her together. The experts won't listen to me, and your word will no doubt carry more weight with Her Majesty than mine."

▲

Tausert was preparing to preside over a meeting of the Great Council, to announce to the leading citizens of Thebes that she would be leaving the city of Amon as soon as the funeral ceremonies were over. However, when a steward informed her that General Mehy and the Wise Woman wished to speak with her, she agreed to see them.

The general left it to Ubekhet to describe her fears, hoping that the queen would find them ridiculous; but Tausert's reaction disappointed him.

"We must not ignore the warning. General Mehy, the majority of your men must assist in strengthening the dykes, as a matter of urgency. Moreover, you will send a message to the governor of each province and you will arrange the evacuation of peasants who live on low ground, so that they can take shelter in villages built on the hills."

"It will take a great deal of organization, Majesty, and—"

"That's why I am entrusting it to you."

"May I at least attend the Great Council?"

"No, don't waste a second. However, here is my most important declaration: Saptah will be crowned pharaoh as soon as the Master of the Place of Truth has placed the seal on the entrance to Seti's tomb. I shall ask to be appointed queen-regent until such time as the new king is capable of ruling alone. To work, General—and hurry."

Mehy was annoyed when the queen asked the Wise Woman to stay behind for a moment. What spell would that sorceress cast this time? Fortunately, Nefer's imminent death would destroy his wife and render her incapable of action.

When Mehy had left, the queen said, "You wanted to speak with me alone, didn't you?"

"You read my thoughts, Majesty."

"If this dramatic prediction comes true, it will be thanks to you that misfortune spares Egypt and that I save my throne. I owe you a great deal, Ubekhet."

"Don't leave Thebes, Majesty."

The queen was annoyed. "You ask too much of me! In ten days' time, my husband's mummy will be placed in its sarcophagus, and then I must return to Pi-Ramses as a matter of urgency. If I don't, there'll be chaos."

"Even if you left today, you wouldn't escape the fury of the flood, and you'd be drowned. I have no other argument to keep you here, and I pray to the gods that you will listen to me."

▲

The ferocity of the flood was terrifying. Several dykes were breached, and some cattle drowned, but no human lives were lost, thanks to the precautions that had been taken. Mehy's soldiers rescued those peasants who had delayed too long before leaving their lands and had taken refuge in the tops of palm trees.

When Set stopped attacking the moon, the left eye of his brother Horus, the moon began to grow and soon the silver disk would shine in its entirety, the image of an intact Egypt, made up of the union of all its provinces.

At the quay beside the royal palace, Queen Tausert's barge was engulfed by a huge wave and sank; the queen, who had chosen to remain in Thebes, was unharmed. And she went to the temple in Karnak to offer up two mirrors, one gold and one silver, representing the sun and the moon, so that their reflections might drive away the harmful effects of the flood.

The muddy red tide gradually grew calmer, and the Thebans, like the other inhabitants of Upper Egypt, were eventually able to travel by boat again, so long as they took care to avoid whirlpools.

Queen Tausert contained her anger at Tjaty Bay, who—despite his reassuring letter—had betrayed her by placing an unknown young man on the throne. She went to the village to thank the Wise Woman for saving her life, and the Master for ensuring that Seti's funeral ceremonies had passed smoothly.

The queen would never remarry. Already, rumor was linking her with lovers, and everyone was expecting her to set her cap on some Theban noble, form a new royal couple, get rid of Saptah, and take power again. But Tausert was indifferent to gossip and did not even bother to issue a denial; ambitious people and fools needed such putrefying food. She entrusted no one with her secret: she would remain faithful to Seti, the man whom she loved beyond death.

After paying homage to Ma'at at her shrine in the Place of Truth, Tausert walked along the main street with Ubekhet.

"Tjaty Bay has betrayed me," she confided, "but he has saved

Egypt from a grave crisis. Who could have foreseen that the flood would strand me in Thebes and that a king would be needed to stifle tribal ambitions? I thought the reason why you could find no place for me in the Valley of the Queens was because I was going to become pharaoh. But I was wrong. Saptah reigns now, and I am only a regent. Will Hathor at last agree to welcome me among the queens?"

"No, Majesty. I have been back there, and the answer is still the same."

▲

Bay was at last allowing himself an evening's rest. He was alone in his office at the palace, surrounded by official documents. Egypt had a pharaoh and, contrary to what the tjaty had feared, no one had opposed the coming of King Saptah, though the young man had suffered great physical discomfort during the long coronation ritual. But the high priest of Ptah's nominee had overcome the trial and been acclaimed Pharaoh. No one was suspicious of him, and everyone thought that the tjaty would be the real master of the country—after throttling Tausert's ambition and reducing her to a secondary role.

They were all wrong.

Bay felt boundless admiration for the queen and a great deal of affection for young Saptah. Tausert would rule, and Saptah would be a good administrator, thorough and honest. He would serve as a screen for Seti's widow, whose enemies were numerous and influential. And after proving her worth, Tausert, like the famous Hatshepsut, would be raised to the supreme office.

The tjaty had only one desire: to explain everything to Tausert, and prove to her that he had not betrayed her—in fact, quite the reverse.

—— 73 ——

When Serketa met the traitor again, the future seemed much brighter. Queen Tausert had left for Pi-Ramses, and everyone was sure that, as soon as she arrived in the capital, she would take steps to deal with Bay and rid herself of Saptah, the puppet king. And Mehy would appear as the only stabilizing factor around whom reasonable leaders could group, in the North and the South alike.

"I've brought you what you asked for," she told the traitor, handing him a phial.

"Are you sure it works?"

"Very sure."

"How long will it take?"

"About an hour. Does this mean that at last you're finally ready to act?"

"An excellent opportunity has arisen."

"Succeed, and you will be rich."

▲

The mourning for Seti was at an end, and the Brotherhood could at last celebrate Paneb's appointment as leader of the starboard crew. The banquet would be a particularly joyful one because since taking office Paneb had reassured even the most anxious of his colleagues by behaving strictly in accordance with the rules, by which the Scribe of the Tomb set great store.

Paneb had taken charge as Seti's sarcophagus was expertly lowered into his tomb, and had examined one by one the items that made up the treasure destined to accompany the royal soul into the afterlife. His authority was sometimes a bit abrupt, but, as he always asked more of himself than of other people, no one could find fault with him.

At the feast, Nefer and Ubekhet delighted in the villagers'

simple, profound joy. The appointment of a new crew leader being a very rare event, the food was truly memorable, with sides of beef, several sorts of fish, vegetable purées, cream cheese, honey cakes, strong beer, and excellent wines. Even the green monkey, Charmer, Bad Girl, and Ebony enjoyed themselves and ate as much as they liked; Ebony was stuffed so full of meat that he was almost asleep at his master's feet. Jokes—some of them in extremely bad taste—came from all sides, and even Paneb's fiercest opponents, like Casa and Nakht, had called a truce to congratulate the giant warmly.

"Face it," said Nahkt, "you're trapped. We can enjoy your promotion, but it's different for you. As soon as a crew member has a problem or a grievance, one name will be spoken: Paneb. And the leader is responsible for his crew's mistakes, isn't he?"

"That doesn't particularly amuse me," said Paneb, "but you're right."

Aapehti, who had been drinking beer while his parents were not looking, had collapsed onto a stool and fallen asleep; after running around and around the huge communal table countless times, the other children were drunk with fatigue and were also nearly asleep.

Prouder of her husband than she would have dared admit to the other priestesses of Hathor, Uabet took her daughter in her arms and signaled that it was time to leave. Soon, the other women followed suit.

Before going home, the Master embraced his adopted son. "We have much work to do, Paneb. As soon as the celebration is over, we must discuss it with Hay and Kenhir."

As Nefer was leaving with the Wise Woman, Renupe presented the giant with a huge jar of wine.

"An exceptional vintage from Kenhir's cellar—I opened it myself an hour ago. Just smell that!"

Paneb agreed that the wine, which dated from the last year of Ramses II's reign, smelled wonderful.

"Crew leader," said Nakht, "do us the honor of sampling it and drinking our health."

Paneb did not balk at the test, and emptied the jar in record time.

"Long life to Paneb!" shouted Pai, with infectious enthusiasm.

▲

The village was asleep, but Paneb did not feel like going home. Although not drunk, he was starting to feel very strange, and he hoped that the night air would clear his head. But his heart was beating irregularly, his back was covered in sweat, and he could see stripes of red, blue, and green across the sky.

Then a burning fury took possession of his hands and he punched a low wall into fragments, which increased his strength tenfold. He had the mad idea of destroying a house, and realized that a demon had possessed him.

Alone, he could not rid himself of it. Walking jerkily, he headed for the Master's house: Ubekhet must know a remedy. But the street was dancing before his eyes. He saw ten of everything, and gaping holes were opening up at his feet.

Rigid with terror for a moment, he kept on walking. Yes, this was the right door. With an enormous effort, he tried to break it down with a stone.

"Open up, Nefer," he shouted, "or there'll be a death, this very night!"

He didn't recognize his own voice. He no longer knew what he was saying or doing.

The door opened.

"Paneb!" exclaimed Nefer. "What's happened to you?"

"I can't see you . . . I can't hear properly."

The Master put an arm round his adopted son, led him inside, and helped him to sit down. Neither of them had noticed Imuni, who had witnessed the scene from a distance.

Roused from sleep, Ubekhet bent over Paneb. She examined his eyes, took his pulses, listened to the voice of his heart and that of his stomach.

"Paneb has been drugged," she concluded. "Probably a mixture of mandragora, stinking thorn-apple, and lotus."

"Is his life in danger?"

"I don't think so, but I'm going to make him vomit. If not, any further hallucinations would make him dangerous."

Gradually, she succeeded in removing the poisons from Paneb's system with infinitesimal doses of those substances.

Paneb regained consciousness as dawn was breaking. He remembered nothing.

▲

Tjaty Bay bowed low himself before Queen Tausert, who had just disembarked at Pi-Ramses.

"Majesty, how happy I am—"

"Take me to the palace, so that I may pay homage to Pharaoh and lock myself away forever in my private quarters."

"No, Majesty, that is not what Saptah wishes; nor is it what Egypt desires. I did what I did for Egypt, and also for you."

Tausert listened to his emotional explanations and had no doubt of his sincerity. But as they entered the palace, she criticized his strategy.

"Saptah's coronation undoubtedly prevented a serious crisis," she acknowledged, "but if he wishes to reign, I shall be regent in name only."

"I am sure he won't behave like that."

"Despite your experience, Tjaty, I fear you are surprisingly naïve."

▲

The queen did not have to request an audience, for Saptah himself came limping toward her, dressed as a simple scribe, and bowed before her.

"The tjaty and I have been waiting impatiently for you, Majesty. I feel I am the plaything of unknown forces and that you alone can control them. The double crown is much too heavy for my head, and my only ambition is to obey the sovereign who has the skill to govern this land."

Astonished, Tausert wondered if the youth was as sincere as the tjaty, or if he had already attained the summit of hypocrisy. In order to find out, all she would need to do was work with him for a few days.

"A pharaoh must draw up decrees that fight injustice and bring to life the Rule of Ma'at, for both great and small. What decrees have you issued so far?"

"None, Majesty, for I don't consider myself capable of making such important decisions. But I have prepared some documents that may perhaps clarify matters for you."

To the disappointment of many courtiers, who had hoped for an angry confrontation between Saptah and Tausert, the two shut themselves away in an office and emerged only to issue a series of financial and social measures, which were announced by the tjaty. The ministers and the population welcomed them, and people started to think that the strange pairing of a widow and a cripple might not be such an unwise one after all.

▲

While Tausert was taking the air in the palace garden, and stroking a tabby cat that she had taught not to attack birds, she agreed to grant Bay a private audience for the first time since her return to the capital.

To hide his emotion, Bay assumed the mask of the perfect senior scribe. He refused to admit his feelings for her: she was far beyond his reach.

"I thought you had betrayed me," she said, "but I was wrong. Egypt owes you a great deal."

"Majesty, all I did was my duty."

"You have trained young Saptah remarkably well. I regard him as a son, and we shall work together to ensure the well-being of the Two Lands."

"I acted only in your interest, Majesty, and I—"

"Tell the Master of the Place of Truth to prepare King Saptah's House of Eternity and Temple of a Million Years; the monuments are essential to the success of his reign."

"I shall write to him immediately."

Tausert allowed the tjaty to leave without revealing to him that she had a fabulous reward in store for him, a reward beyond his wildest dreams.

— 74 —

The Master, the Wise Woman, and Fened the Nose were in complete agreement about the location of Saptah's House of Eternity in the Valley of the Kings. It was to be close to the tomb of Seti II, and slightly to the northwest.

Dressed in his ritual golden apron, Nefer the Silent struck the virgin rock for the first time with a mallet and a golden chisel; then Paneb swung up his great pickax, which contained the fire of the heavens.

It fell to Paneb to direct the construction and decoration of the tomb according to an ambitious scheme devised by Nefer.

"The quality of the limestone is good," said Paneb, "so we needn't worry about unpleasant surprises."

"Be cautious, all the same," advised Nefer. "The rock can be capricious sometimes. Being too sure of oneself can lead to bad mistakes."

"I trust this cliff face—it won't lie. Besides, you will be here to put me right if I stray from the right path."

"A crew leader who makes mistakes no longer deserves to hold that office."

A violent punch would have hurt Paneb less. "Do you think I could ever be so undeserving?"

"Our craft is an adventure, filled with traps. Be vigilant and persevere; and don't forget that matter, like men, tends perpetually toward idleness and chaos. Because you lead, you no longer have the right to rest on your laurels; even while you're asleep, you should dream of the previous day's work and the next."

The sun was setting over the Valley of the Kings. The craftsmen were arranging their tools and preparing to leave for the camp on the pass, where they would spend the night before beginning work. The two men were alone before Saptah's future House of Eternity.

Nefer said thoughtfully, "What an extraordinary life the heavens offer us. Are you aware of the good fortune the gods dispense to us so freely?"

"Each day, I make my dream reality; what more could I ask? And yet I know I must explore the power of this place, and the wisdom of the Brotherhood, still further. And I must pass on what has been given to me."

Slowly they followed the rest of the crew. Nefer knew Paneb was at the start of a new path; Paneb admired Nefer more than words could express. In the peace of the evening, brotherhood united them with the warm colors of the setting sun.

▲

After the dawn rites, Nefer was slow to give the signal to leave the camp and descend to the village. The craftsmen were eager to see their families again, and he longed to see Ubekhet, but he was reluctant to leave the mountain, as if it gave the Brotherhood a protection it needed.

"I'm ready for a rest," said Casa. "We may have chosen the right place to excavate, but the rock is putting up stiff resistance, and my arms have had enough!"

The Master set off down the pathway, thinking of the troubles that had beset Egypt since the death of Ramses the Great. A pharaoh of that stature had so profoundly set his mark on the land that his successors suffered in comparison and struggled to fill the void caused by his death. How much longer would it be before another sovereign emerged equal in stature to Ramses?

Despite the turmoil, the Place of Truth had continued to carry out its work and imbue stone with Light. With two crew leaders as different in temperament as Paneb and Hay, the Brotherhood would retain the dynamism essential to achieving its ends, while the Master would ensure its unity and the Wise Woman's magic would mark out new paths to be followed.

Paneb had filled a bag with pointed flints, and was carrying it on his shoulders as though it weighed nothing at all.

"What are you going to do with those stones?" asked Ipuy, who was now fully recovered.

"I've seldom seen them this shape. I shall carve them into chisels and give them to the sculptors."

"More work," complained Renupe.

"Don't pretend you're surprised," smiled Ched. "A new crew leader must show what he can do, and we must show that we can satisfy his demands."

"We're only men!" protested Casa.

"I shan't forget that," said Paneb. "It's why too much rest would do you harm. When the hand lies idle, it loses its skill."

Several craftsmen wondered if Paneb would disregard the rules in an emergency—the preparation of Saptah's funerary goods might well be considered one.

▲

Mehy's horse was utterly exhausted. Soaked in sweat, panting, its heart pounding, it could go no farther.

"A worthless animal," said the general, handing the reins to his groom.

It was the third horse Mehy had worn out that morning. He had used them to calm his own nerves and showed not the slightest concern for them.

The archers had also borne the brunt of his anger: too soft, too slow, and not accurate enough! The general had demonstrated that he could still shoot better than any of them, before defeating a solidly built infantryman in a wrestling bout.

He entered his house, waving away his steward's offer of a cool drink and scented cloths, and threw himself on his wife. Tearing her new dress, he made love to her with such savagery that—for a few seconds—Serketa thought she might even reach orgasm.

"You hurt me, my sweet jackal!" she cooed.

"This endless waiting is infuriating. Rub my stomach—I ate too much this morning." His muscles were in spasm. "Our ally won't succeed," he predicted.

"He is usually very cautious, but this time he seemed optimistic," said Serketa.

"That village has already inflicted so many defeats on us!"

"That's because we didn't attack it the right way, my tender lion. This time we strike at its head."

"Some invisible force will protect him. Nefer seems indestructible."

"Once he's dead," promised Serketa, "the Brotherhood will fall apart."

"Let's hope the same thing will happen to the three people who are ruling the country. I cannot fathom Bay's strategy."

"But it's simple: the tjaty loves the queen. He knows he can never have her, but he's doing everything in his power to make her Pharaoh. Poor little Saptah, a cripple with no personality, is simply a decoy designed to fool the courtiers while Tausert establishes a basis for her future power."

"Bay's a more formidable opponent than I thought."

"He lives only for Tausert. When we've killed the Master, we'll deal with her. She'll be a fine adversary, almost as dangerous as I am."

Mehy rolled onto his stomach. "Rub my back. Those stupid horses have strained it."

"Tausert trusts you, and that mistake will be fatal for her."

Reaching behind him, the general seized his wife by the hair. "The queen is nothing. The only thing that matters is the Stone of Light. While the Master is alive, it's out of reach."

"Then it won't be so for much longer."

▲

"All the tools are here," said Imuni, after a thorough check.

"Good," said Kenhir, in a tired voice. "Anything to report?"

"For the moment, no."

"Are you absolutely sure?"

"You can rely on me."

Kenhir was only partially reassured. Admittedly Imuni was obsessively nosy and would have noticed the slightest anomaly; but the old scribe felt great anxiety, as if imminent disaster threatened the village. He had spent all day scouring the village streets, inquiring after people, but had found nothing alarming.

His young wife, Niut, saw how anxious he was. "What is it that you're so worried about?"

"Just a bad dream, but a waking one! Ever since this morning, I've had forebodings."

"Have you been overeating behind my back?"

"Of course not! I'm going to read one of my favorite authors; that will calm me down."

Normally serene in the face of adversity, Niut suddenly felt great anguish. Kenhir had transmitted his worries to her. However, a few energetic sweeps of her broom soon drove the bad feelings away.

▲

Ebony was usually calm whenever he was in the Master's house, but he kept pacing back and forth, demanding to be stroked, lying down and then getting up again.

Nefer tried in vain to calm him; there was a questioning look in the dog's eyes that he could not decipher.

"You haven't lost your amulet, have you?" asked Ubekhet worriedly.

Nefer put his hand to his throat. His knot of Isis had disappeared. "The cord must have snapped. I didn't realize."

"I'll give you another, first thing tomorrow."

The Wise Woman noticed a small piece of papyrus that had been slipped under the front door. She picked it up, read it, and placed it on a low table.

"The lay workers are asking for me; there's been an accident. I'll take Ebony with me—he needs the exercise."

▲

Obed the blacksmith was very surprised. "An accident? No, I don't think so. The other workers left a while ago."

"All the same, we must check," said Ubekhet.

They went and inspected the workshops. All were empty.

When she got back home, the Wise Woman saw immediately that the fragment of papyrus was no longer on the table.

Ebony bounded toward the bedchamber and let out a heart rending howl.

"Nefer, what's happened? Nefer? Answer me!"

The Master was sitting in his chair, his hands clenched on the arms, a flint embedded in his heart. There was a barely perceptible glimmer of light in his eyes. Nefer had fought with every ounce of his strength to see the woman he loved one more time, the woman whom he had loved so much during his earthly life and whom he would go on loving for all eternity.

No sound could emerge from his mouth, which was already frozen in death, but as Ubekhet laid her hands upon his, her entire soul joined with his in the final moment of communion and happiness which Nefer the Silent had managed to snatch from the jaws of destiny.

—— 75 ——

Since Nefer's death, a fierce sandstorm had been blowing around the village, whose streets were filled with plaintive cries that seemed to come from the Peak of the West. The sacred mountain was growling, as though it might come crashing down upon the Place of Truth. The sun could not force its way through the gray and yellow clouds, and day seemed like night.

Men, women, and children were all devastated, unable even to eat. No one dared say a word. Bad Girl hid her head under her wing, Charmer had gone to ground under a rush-seated chair, and Ebony under Ubekhet's bed.

No priestess had the courage to lay offerings on the altars of the ancestors, as if the ancestors had abandoned the Brotherhood. The entire village was transfixed by the death of its Master, without whom ordinary daily tasks had no meaning.

Little by little, sand was covering the terraces, and no one could be bothered to preserve their houses from its inroads. It would be only justice if the gods' anger, provoked by a crime that surpassed the bounds of horror, should wipe out the little community. Now that Nefer was dead, who could have any taste for wielding tools, or the impudence to dream of happiness? He had left behind him orphans, incapable of survival.

"We have no right to behave like this," said Paneb to Ubekhet. "It's an insult to Nefer, and ruins his life's work. We must celebrate our Master's funeral ceremonies according to the sacred rites. If we don't, he'll be truly dead. Our Brotherhood's duty is to ensure his eternal presence among us."

The Wise Woman got to her feet with difficulty. He gave her his arm.

When she appeared in the main street of the village, the storm died down. One by one, with heavy steps, the Servants of the Place of Truth followed Ubekhet as she made her way to the temple.

▲

Nefer the Silent's burial goods included hammers, chisels, adzes, a set square, a level, a plumb line, offertory tables, a bed, mirrors, sandals, chests, and many other things, all made with love by the craftsmen of the Place of Truth, and placed in his tomb. Among the statues, the most moving was one showing the Master and his wife sitting side by side; Ubekhet's left arm was round her husband's shoulders, as a sign of protection, and they gazed out with extraordinary intensity.

On the threshold of the House of Eternity stood a chair whose legs ended in bull's hooves, surmounted by statuettes symbolizing the Master's *ka,* his creative power, which would live forever in the world beyond.

The ritual was coming to an end, and the Wise Woman planted a persea tree before the door of the tomb. Osiris had created the persea for both gods and human beings, and its leaves were shaped like hearts.

No one could suppress their tears, and everyone marveled at the dignity of Nefer's widow, though she seemed grief-stricken to the point of illness; by her side, Ebony whined piteously. It was only with a superhuman effort, and the aid of Paneb, that she managed to get back home and collapse onto her bed.

The village was in shock, plunged into an atmosphere of oppressive grief that was empty of children's laughter. The Brotherhood had lost its leader; surely it was now condemned to die.

▲

Three days had passed.

The door opened, and the Wise Woman appeared. She was worn out by pain, but had had the courage to put on her makeup and wear the robes of the high priestess of Hathor. Supremely beautiful, she seemed to belong to another world where neither joy nor pain existed.

"If anyone needs me," she told Kenhir, "I am ready to treat them."

"There is a more urgent matter," he said. "I've managed to calm the most impulsive people, but we must convene the village court immediately. Too many complaints have accumulated."

"Complaints? Against whom?"

"Against Paneb. They're serious, and I cannot ignore them."

▲

All the villagers had assembled in the courtyard of the Temple of Ma'at and Hathor. It fell to the president of the court, the Scribe of the Tomb, to hear the accusations and the defense before carrying out a detailed investigation. Beside him were the Wise Woman, Hay, and two priestesses of Hathor, the wives of Pai the Good Bread and Karo the Impatient.

"We are faced with the worst tragedy that the village has ever experienced," declared Kenhir, his voice breaking with emotion. "Our Master, Nefer the Silent, has been murdered in his own home, and one of us committed this abominable crime. If any righteousness still dwells within the murderer, let him confess and try to explain his actions."

No voice broke the heavy silence.

"Can the Wise Woman state the precise circumstances of the Master's death?" asked Kenhir.

"I received a message, asking me to go and treat a wounded lay worker. It was a forgery, designed to get me away from the house. When I came back, the message had disappeared and my husband was dead."

"How was he killed?"

"He was stabbed through the heart with a very sharp-pointed flint, which had been shaped with great care."

"So the guilty party must be very strong," said Ipuy, "and I saw Paneb bring back several flints he'd collected at the camp on the pass. Ched will confirm what I say."

Ched was obliged to do so.

Paneb reacted fiercely. "You dare accuse me of having killed my adoptive father, the man I worshipped, simply because I brought some stones back from the mountain?"

"Paneb did indeed bring those stones back," said Ched, "and several of the starboard crew noticed it—starting with the murderer! That's precisely why he used a flint: so that our new crew leader would be accused."

"I was present at a violent quarrel between Nefer and

Paneb," said Unesh. "They disagreed about how to finish Seti's tomb."

"That is true," agreed Paneb, "but we made up our differences."

"You told me you didn't approve of the Master's conduct toward the king," said Renupe.

"And there's something else, something much worse," Unesh went on. "Pai and I rubbed out a red hand painted on the Master's door—we hoped rubbing it out would make the bad omen ineffective. That hand was as big as Paneb's."

Pai nodded.

"I cannot accept evidence you have destroyed," said Kenhir testily.

"Surely you cannot doubt the word of these two craftsmen," said Imuni, "particularly since I saw Paneb try to break down the Master's door and distinctly heard his terrible threat: "Open up, Nefer, or there'll be a death this very night!'"

"Paneb had been drugged by the murderer," disclosed the Wise Woman. "It was his own death he was talking about."

"Paneb is guilty," insisted Imuni. "All he wanted was for Nefer to adopt him, so that he would choose him as crew leader. Once Paneb had attained his goal, he got rid of his protector because Nefer had at last unmasked the impostor. I have studied the Brotherhood's records, and I can prove that I have family ties, albeit distant ones, with Nefer. And he should have chosen me as his an adopted son, not Paneb!"

Imuni produced a sheet of papyrus, on which he had made notes justifying his claims. Paneb wanted to rush at the rat-faced scribe, but Ched held him back.

"Imuni's allegations are unfounded," declared the Wise Woman serenely. "Whatever ties he is referring to, there were no differences between Nefer and Paneb, the son he chose freely, and they were united by a never-failing brotherhood."

Despite her words, Imuni did not give up. "Everything points to Paneb! I demand that the court declare him guilty."

"Imuni's jealousy must not lead us astray," objected Ched.

"There is no formal proof," added Kenhir.

"There is one way of finding out the truth," said the Wise Woman gravely. "We can submit Paneb to the ordeal of the House of the Acacia. If he emerges alive, he is definitely innocent."

▲

In the House of the Acacia, the few priestesses of Hathor who had been initiated into the mysteries of Osiris held their meetings. On the tomb of the god murdered by his brother Set grew an acacia tree, whose formidable thorns would pierce a liar's flesh.

Standing before them, Paneb declared that he was innocent of Nefer's murder.

"Life and death unite in the acacia," said the Wise Woman. "When it wastes away, life leaves the living until Isis cures the wounds inflicted by Set; then the tree covers itself in leaves, and the just man has nothing to fear from it. Step forward, Paneb, and unite with the acacia."

The enormous thorns were so sharp that they seemed more dangerous than daggers, and could pierce flesh with ease. But Paneb could not shirk the ordeal, or he would be considered guilty and would be sentenced to death.

He embraced the tree of life and death.

▲

When Paneb emerged, unscathed, from the House of the Acacia, even Imuni was obliged to bow to the judgement of Osiris. The tree's thorns had retracted, causing not the slightest wound, for he had spoken the truth. No charge would be made against him, and he was formally cleared of the accusation leveled at him.

"I never thought you were guilty," said Ubekhet, "not for one moment."

"This crime won't go unpunished, I swear it."

The Wise Woman climbed up the hill to the Master's House of Eternity, and Paneb followed.

"Look at the village," she told him. "It's like a ship sailing through a storm. If we don't keep watch, if we don't give it the best of ourselves, it is in danger of sinking, and then Nefer's murderer will have killed the entire Brotherhood. Nefer can never be replaced, and our suffering will never grow less. But we must continue his work and bring life to the Place of Truth."

A falcon soared high above the village, traced several circles above the burial ground, and then flapped its powerful wings, driving itself up toward the sun.

"That is Nefer's soul," whispered Ubekhet. "It is showing us the way toward the Light."

© XO

CHRISTIAN JACQ is the author of the bestselling
five-volume Ramses series, which sold eleven million
copies in twenty-nine countries. He has a doctorate
in Egyptian studies from the Sorbonne in France.
He founded, and now heads, the Ramses Institute,
which is dedicated to preserving the endangered
archaeological sites of Egypt.